CRY
MURDER

Miss Edith C. Howie

CRY
MURDER

Edith Howie

COACHWHIP PUBLICATIONS
Greenville, Ohio

Cry Murder, by Edith Howie
© 2022 Coachwhip Publications edition
Introduction © Curtis Evans
Front cover: Tivoli Theater (Historic American Buildings
Survey, Library of Congress)

First published 1944
Edith Howie, 1900-1979
CoachwhipBooks.com (print) / Coachwhip.com (epub)

ISBN 1-61646-527-1
ISBN-13 978-1-61646-527-8

Murders End in Lovers Meeting: The Mysteries of Edith Howie

Curtis Evans

Dear miss Howie

I saw a picture in the family circle and liked the looks of you. Thought I would like for you to correspond with me. I am single not been married but would like to if I could find the rite girl ha ha. Maybe that you. I hope it is. Please write to me. Send picture of your self and I will do the same. I would like to come up and see you if that all rite with you. I have been in Dakota a few years now and liked it all rite. How is crops. They look good here. I am 43 years old and have brown eyes and dark haire and weigh 175 and 6 feet tall. Write. Tell me all a bought your self. I will cease now.

A friend

When an August 1941 profile in the Sioux Falls *Argus-Leader*, the leading newspaper of the Great Plains state of South Dakota, described Edith Howie as an "unpretentious person, quiet, small-featured and trim," with auburn hair, "deep blue eyes and . . . small, tapered . . . unusually beautiful hands," Edith, an unmarried woman of forty-one years who lived quietly in Sioux Falls with her parents,

5

had just published her maiden mystery novel, *Murder for Tea*, about the fatal poisoning of the town vamp at a literary luncheon. The novel had appeared in *Three Prize Murders*, a trilogy of tales which had received honorable mentions in publisher Farrar and Rinehart's second annual Mary Roberts Rinehart mystery contest, named for America's preeminent woman crime writer (one of her sons had co-founded the company); and it had been highly praised in the *New York Times Book Review* by Isaac Anderson, who pronounced it "as puzzling and as entertaining a mystery as one could desire." (The previous year Elizabeth Daly had entered her debut novel, *Unexpected Night*, in the first Mary Roberts Rinehart mystery contest, in which she, like Edith Howie the next year, was a runner-up.)

Living up to her "unpretentious" reputation, Edith Howie wryly noted to her *Argus-Leader* interviewer, Lois Thrasher (who the next year would transfer to the *Chicago Daily News*, where she became night editor in 1945), that so far her greatest putative perk of fame as an author consisted of receiving myriad marriage proposals from importunate "mail-order bachelors," like the gentleman quoted at the top of this introduction, who had eagerly espied Edith's picture in *The Family Circle*, a women's household magazine distributed for free at the once omnipresent Piggly Wiggly grocery store chain. Another of Edith's male mystery admirers rang her up at home on the telephone one night, obviously inebriated and gushingly praising her books. When he failed to make any headway with the object of his fervent devotion, he rang off, angrily admonishing her, "I guess your books aren't so good after all!" Edith, resistant to the charms of such men, remained single for the rest of her life. Yet she enjoyed an impressively full creative existence, allowing her to give rewarding expression to her twin true loves: professional writing and amateur acting.

Between 1938 and 1946 Edith wrote eight mystery novels, seven of which were published in the United States and the United Kingdom as well as other countries (there are some particularly nice Spanish-language paperback editions); and during this time as well, and for many years afterward, she was one of the leading lights in Sioux Falls' community theater, both writing plays and performing in them. After her retirement from acting in the 1970s Edith reviewed local productions for the *Argus-Leader*, publishing her final review (*The Fantasticks*) in March 1979, just two months before her death at the age of seventy-eight. Although her career as a mystery writer was a brief one, lasting less than a decade, Edith during this time established herself as an American exponent of regional mystery and became as well a pioneer of the "cozy" detective story, where the tone remains light amid larcenies and criminal mayhem fails utterly to falsify the adage "murders end in lovers meeting."

****

Edith Christy Ann Howie was born on July 12, 1900, the eldest of three children of William Henry Howie and Christy Ann McLean, natives of Ontario, Canada of Scottish derivation. Shortly after the couple's marriage on April 12, 1899, they moved to Bradley, a town of fewer than 350 souls in the northern part of the raw, decade-old state of South Dakota, where Edith entered the world. William Henry Howie was the son of Cyrus Thompson Howie, an Oxford Mills farmer and Wesleyan Methodist, while Christy McLean was the daughter of Hugh McLean, a Maxville furniture store owner, Presbyterian and freemason. For four years prior to his marriage William had been a member of Canada's Northwest Mounted Police and at the time of his nuptials he managed a cheese factory in

Maxville. He carried on this latter occupation in Bradley, also adopting his wife's faith, before moving with his growing family in 1905 to the city of Sioux Falls, South Dakota, the state's largest city, located on the bank of the Sioux River in the far southeastern corner of the state, tucked between Minnesota and Iowa. For many years there he sold farm machinery for International Harvester Company. In this capacity he was often away on the road, plying his vital trade among Great Plains farmers, but his family became staunch members of Sioux Falls' First Presbyterian Church, where Edith in the 1920s served as an organist. "Always an organist and never a bride," self-deprecatingly comments a character in one of Edith's later mystery novels, which was true enough in her case.

Edith's father lived a more outwardly eventful life. For eleven months between June 1924 and April 1925, William Howie served, at the request of his highly-placed friend, Mayor Thomas Mckinnon, as chief of police at Sioux Falls, which then had a population of about 30,000 individuals. In 1925 Chief of Police Howie reported that the police department had made 1135 arrests during the previous year, about 4% of the population. The great majority of these arrests were for minor violations of liquor laws and traffic ordinances, although there were also eight cases of burglary, seven of bootlegging, five of bank robbery, five of prostitution, four of grand larceny and four of forgery, as well as two rapes and an assault. Happily not a single murder was reported that year. "Nashiona (aka Sioux Falls) is small town Middle West and doesn't go in for murders," asserts the narrator of _Murder for Tea_ with unintended irony. "It isn't that sort of town." Most of the other offenses with which Chief Howie and his men had to deal, like discharging firecrackers within city limits and bathing outdoors in the nude (i.e., skinny-dipping), admittedly strike one as disarmingly minor.

Hanson & Leigh Photo
Chief W. H. Howie

As Halloween approached in October 1924, Chief Howie issued a stern reminder to the city's boisterous youth that pranks were only tolerated on All Hallows' Eve itself, while the commission of acts of actual damage to people's property would most definitely be prosecuted. Rather more seriously, Chief Howie the previous month warned local representatives of the Ku Klux Klan that his department was prepared to make "wholesale arrests" of any masked persons parading through city streets. During the Twenties, which saw a national resurgence of the Klan, South Dakota, like other Midwestern states, was, as one authority puts it, "plagued by cross- and circle-burnings, tar-and-featherings, and mass rallies and parades, including one attended by nearly 8000 people," mostly with the goal of intimidating the state's Catholic population. Perhaps it was this sort of thing which prompted Chief Howie to resign from office after having served for less than a year. He had been long retired from policing in 1934, when John Dillinger and his gang dramatically robbed Sioux Falls' Security National Bank, in the process pumping eight bullets into a local motorcycle cop.

During his short tenure the Chief had done his part to make Sioux Falls safe for law-abiding people like his daughter Edith, who lived a virtuous and placid life in the city, presumably eschewing even illicit firecracker lighting and skinny-dipping, not to mention acts of grand larceny. In addition to her performances at the organ and piano at public programs (she confided that she had relinquished any hope of becoming a concert pianist on account of the "smallness of her hands"), Edith in the 1920s was active, along with her slightly younger sister Bessie, in the local chapter of the Delphian Society, an international organization which promoted women's cultural education. For a time Edith, who attended writing classes at the University of South Dakota in Vermillion but never took a degree,

succumbed to the vogue for archaic Old English names
and self-consciously styled herself "Edythe," but happily
she abandoned this affectation.

During the Thirties just plain Edith Howie became
active in Sioux Falls' community theater and began publishing short stories in magazines, including *Good House-
keeping, Ladies' Home Journal, Liberty* and the Canadian
Chatelaine. In 1938 she completed her first mystery novel,
Treeholme House. The novice mystery writer submitted the
manuscript to Doubleday, Doran's Crime Club imprint,
who snobbishly turned it down, sadly, on the grounds,
Edith later wryly confided to *Argus-Leader* reporter Rob-
ert Gunsolly, that "four of the five persons murdered in
the book were servants." Instead the tale appeared later
that year, spiffily illustrated, in the Canadian magazine
Maclean's.

Undaunted by her limited success at mystery writing,
Edith in 1939 began simultaneously writing two new mysteries, which she entitled *Murder for Tea* and *Santa Claus
Died*. She submitted the two manuscripts to Farrar and
Rinehart, who accepted both works and published them
within a few months of each other in 1941, *Tea* in August
in its *Three Prize Murders* volume and *Santa* in December
(appropriately enough), with its title altered to the rather
more anodyne *Murder for Christmas*. Presumably the publisher was leery of traumatizing, with Edith's original
blunt title, dewy-eyed innocents desirous of raking in their
annual seasonal haul from Saint Nick.

Both *Murder for Tea* and *Murder for Christmas* are light
"couples mysteries," in which a husband and wife are confronted with murder, respectively during a tea party at a
literary luncheon and at a country house Christmas gath-
ering, where, reminiscent of Ngaio Marsh's popular Seven-
ties mystery *Tied up in Tinsel*, a man dressed up as Santa
Claus is violently done to death. *Tea* takes place in Edith

Howie's fictional Great Plains city of Nashiona, an imaginative rendering of Sioux Falls, which also appears under the same name in one of Edith's later mysteries, *Cry Murder*. Conversely *Christmas* is set in rural New York State, perhaps as a sop to Plains wary editors, who once queried her having some of her characters travel twenty miles without encountering a single house. Edith worked on her first two published mystery novels in tandem, taking up one as she became stuck with the other, a process which she again employed with *Murder at Stone House* and *Murder's So Permanent*, both of which were published in 1942, and *No Face to Murder* and *The Band Played Murder*, both of which were published in 1946. *Cry Murder* appeared singly in 1944.

Once she had her characters and their milieu set firmly in her mind, Edith would begin writing, even though she claimed that typically she had no notion when she started of who her actual murderer would be. She might change her mind on that matter more than once as she wrote. All of her mysteries are brightly narrated by chatty young women, either married or well on their way to wedding their crime-busting beaux by the end of the story. While arguably not the most rigorously plotted of Golden Age mysteries, Edith's detective stories deliver the entertainment goods to likeminded readers, in the ingratiating manner of the modern "cozy" mystery.

In his reviews of Howie's mysteries in the *San Francisco Chronicle*, prominent American reviewer Anthony Boucher emphasized their amorous underpinnings: "Ross Langdon doubles as love interest and detective. . . . Good reading for the romance public. . . . (*Cry Murder*); "Randolph Garrison is more efficient as a lover than as head of homicide, but the telling and the church background . . . are pleasing." (*No Face to Murder*); "Jewel thefts, love and marihuana tie into the murders of two girl vocalists with

a big-time band. . . . Colorful, unassuming and pleasant"
(*The Band Played Murder*).

Five of Edith Howie's seven published mystery novels
are set in cities on the Great Plains, including the three
reprinted by Coachwhip (and reviewed by Boucher above):
Cry Murder, No Face to Murder, and *The Band Played Murder. Cry Murder* concerns killings and attempted killings
which take place in Nashiona among a little theater group
putting on a trial run of a play by a famed New York playwright (and former Nashiona native). The first murder, of
hateful diva actress Nola Powers, takes place at the Olympia Theater, for which the author likely had been inspired
by Sioux Falls' own Orpheum Theater, a beloved institution still standing today.

The Orpheum opened in 1913 and staged vaudeville
acts until 1927, when it was sold and converted into a
second-run and B-movie theater. By the time Edith wrote
Cry Murder sixteen years later, the theater had fallen into
disuse and been abandoned, but in 1954 the building was
purchased and renovated as a stage theater by the Sioux
Falls Community Playhouse, of which Edith was an important member. Mary Thorpe, the narrator and heroine
of *Cry Murder*, memorably describes the Olympia Theater
with WASPish middle-class distaste as follows:

> The Olympia was an eight hundred-seat theater that, once in use almost exclusively for
> vaudeville and stock, had, with their passing,
> degenerated into a third-run movie house.
> . . . Cheap hotels and cheaper restaurants surrounded it and its audiences were drawn quite
> frankly from that class of people who scorned
> to pay the 'forty cents and tax' price of firstrun theaters and were willing to wait for their
> pictures. One visit there, during my noviciate

in town, had been enough for me. The place
had been poorly lighted and smelly, the screen
a flickering disgrace. The seat to which I'd
been ushered had been broken and sagging; I
was suspicious of the probability of mice, or
their big brothers, rats; while overhead the
tireless dance of two creatures, which could
have been none other than those anomalies of
the animal kingdom, bats, had appalled me.
My first visit had been my last.

Appropriately Edith stages the most atmospheric sec-
tion of her novel here, when Mary goes there to meet Nola
and encounters . . . well, read it for yourself and see! The
case ultimately is solved by Mary's love interest, handsome
private detective Ross Langdon, although not without
Mary's help. Also contributing to the case is folksy Chief
Hanover of the Nashiona police, whom Mary explains had
"been a small groceryman before he picked off the plumiest of Nashiona's appointive jobs." Somewhat defensively
Chief Hanover tells Mary and Ross: "[W]hile maybe you're
thinking I'm only a dumb old fogy who got the job of
police chief in Nashiona by reason of being a good friend
of the mayor's, you want to remember I've held onto that
job mainly by getting results. And results are just what I
aim to keep getting." Mary describes the Chief as a "short,
stout, ordinary-looking man in a wrinkled gray suit whose
waistcoat was crossed by an old-fashioned watch chain. He
had thinning gray hair, a somewhat straggly gray mustache
and eyes that were shrewd and sensible behind gold-rimmed
spectacles." The description matches that of Edith's father
when, at age fifty-two, he headed Sioux Falls' police force.

The *Fort Worth Star-Telegram* delightedly described *Cry
Murder* as "a typical murder mystery, the sort everybody
enjoys," with "appealing characters and situations and an

atmosphere of eerie danger and suspense that marks the most satisfying type of mystery thrillers." In its review the *Argus-Leader* spotted similarities between Nashiona and Sioux Falls, including the fact that with the advent of the Second World War, Nashiona's population, like that of Sioux Falls, had virtually exploded. Observes Mary in the novel:

> Nashionites consider that they dwell in a metropolis, which I suppose they do—it being the largest city within the border of two sister states—but nowhere has there been normality since Pearl Harbor, and Nashiona was no exception to the rule. Close against the boundaries now sprawled the mushroom growth of the huge army school. . . . No one knew just how many soldiers were stationed there in the rows of wooden, tar-paper covered barracks but the number hovered somewhere between the twenty and thirty thousand marks. . . . the soldiers formed a little city in themselves. . . . sweethearts and wives . . . simply picked up their belongings and moved to Nashiona on the chance of finding accommodations that would enable them to spend a few more precious months with their loves ones. . . . Every apartment, every hotel, every rooming house was jammed to its roof top. Rents had risen—temporarily, for a freezing order was imminent—to unprecedented levels. Tourist homes and cabin camps . . . were being rented upon a monthly basis. At the edge of town a flourishing trailer city had sprung up overnight.
>
> It was all pretty breath-taking. . . .

In real life, Sioux Falls in 1942 became the site of the Army Air Forces Technical School, which over the course of the war trained nearly 50,000 hostilities-bound men in radio communication, Morse code, and aircraft identification. The school enabled Sioux Falls finally to recover from the lingering effects of the Great Depression, lessened the city's Plains parochialism and launched a building boom which lasted well into the 1950s, as many recruits remained there after the war, married and started families. Much of this phenomenon is captured, albeit fleetingly, in *Cry Murder*—not the least of the novel's felicities.

No Edith Howie novel appeared in 1945, but in January 1946 the author published *No Face to Murder*, which, like *Cry Murder*, is set during the war, in 1944, with wartime scarcity rather more advanced. (In *Cry Murder*, characters are still able regularly to consume waffles and grapefruit for breakfast and chocolate cakes with chocolate icing for dessert.) *Face* takes place in the Great Plains city of Dorchester rather than at Nashiona, but Dorchester, like Nashiona, sounds a lot like Sioux Falls, or possibly Sioux City, Iowa, about ninety miles south of Sioux Falls, where Edith's sister, Bessie, a bank cashier, had moved and Edith frequently visited. The novel's St. Thomas' Episcopal Cathedral seems quite a lot like Sioux City's St. Thomas' Episcopal Church, imposingly constructed in the Richardsonian Romanesque style and completed in 1892.

In the novel double slashing murders, respectively of the church caretaker and the organist, incongruously take place at St. Thomas' Episcopal Cathedral, in an opening surprisingly reminiscent of P. D. James' lauded 1986 crime novel *A Taste for Death*, where two people, a homeless man and an MP, similarly are found dead at St. Matthews' Catholic Church, their throats cut. Despite its uncharacteristically grim opening circumstances, however, *Face* ultimately bears a much greater resemblance to

Agatha Christie's *The Murder at the Vicarage*, peopled as it is with a charming cast of principal characters, including the young church secretary narrator, Tess King; church dean Alec MacDonald and his wife Ruth; Bishop Walters, who takes an interest in the case; and Randolph "Ran" Garrison, the handsome head of the Dorchester police department's homicide division and Tess' love interest.

Drexel Drake of the *Chicago Tribune* deemed *No Face to Murder*, which in my view is the author's finest mystery, a "well-written yarn" with a "well-planned puzzle," while noted crime writer Dorothy B. Hughes in the *Albuquerque Tribune* praised the "English atmosphere to this Midwestern mystery," tipped off by the name of the city in which it is located, as well as the "authenticity" of its church setting and the "quite nice feeling to the whole . . . along with the bite of small-town nastiness." For her part Avis DeVoto in the *Boston Globe* gave the novel an unqualified rave review, selecting it as her mystery of the week. "An unusually penetrating picture of a small community, with a double murder in a church as the highlight. Practically every member of the choir, around which the story is built, is a suspect," DeVoto wrote. "Inspector Ran Garrison, assisted no little by his girlfriend, who is also the rector's secretary, and a cooking bishop come through with all the answers, just too late."

Ten months later came *The Band Played Murder*, Edith Howie's final published crime novel. While with *Cry Murder* and *No Face to Murder* Edith had been able to draw heavily on her own familiarity with theater and church milieus, with *The Band Played Murder* she had to bone up on swing music, dance bands and "crooning" by reading back issues of *Downbeat* at the Sioux Falls Carnegie Free Public Library. Her protagonist and narrator, Connie Waring, another would-be concert pianist, is persuaded to serve as a last-minute substitute singer in Gale Ullman's

—Harold Photo.

Edith Howie with her nephews Billy and Gary

band. When murder beats the band at the city of Harriston during its annual Harvest Festival, Connie, who discovers the dead body, finds herself a person of interest to both local police and the actual murderer. The devoted Edith Howie reader can be certain there will be ample love interest in the novel as well.

The Band Played Murder is another enjoyable Edith Howie mystery, pleasingly more sympathetic and informed about its subject than Ngaio Marsh's Swing, Brother, Swing, which appeared in print three years later. "Reading Ngaio Marsh's Swing, Bother, Swing," wrote crime writer and composer Edmund Crispin disgustedly in 1966. "Poor, and if she's going to try and write about jazz bands, why can't she find out something about them? 'Tympanist,' indeed." Edith did rather better in this regard than Ngaio, although like Cornell Woolrich in his notorious 1941 crime novella "Marihana," the author propagates the myth that the drug can immediately transform people into murderous maniacs. (One guesses that Edith, like the heroine of her story, had never personally tried it.) The Lexington Herald deemed Edith's "swinging" novel "a bang-up yarn that does not drag a paragraph throughout the whole 243 pages," while the Knoxville Journal avowed: "It's an unusual background and a well written story told in the first person by a girl who is as confused by life in a dance band as most readers would be."

After Band came silence. Edith accepted a position as a librarian at the Carnegie Library and continued working on mystery writing, but she never published another novel, criminous or otherwise. In 1951 Argus-Leader reporter Bob Gunsolley wrote that Edith was simultaneously working on not two, but three, mysteries, the most promising of which concerned an identical twin sister who, after awakening in bed with a choking sensation, later that morning learns that her twin was strangled during the night. Of course she sets out to find her sister's killer. Apparently Edith completed neither this novel, nor the other two which she was writing (one of which took place among a horsey set in Kentucky bluegrass country), although by her own admission she remained a "rabid mystery fan," getting first dibs on all the new mysteries at the public library.

After the deaths of her parents Edith in 1960 retired from the library and moved to Sioux City to live with her sister Bessie in a two-story, foursquare Craftsman-style house, which still stands today. She remained active in Sioux Falls little theater, for decades indulging her own "taste for death" with parts in such mysterious plays as the chiller *Night Must Fall*, the farce *Arsenic and Old Lace*, the ghostly *The Innocents* (the stage adaptation of Henry James "The Turn of the Screw") and a 1969 performance of Agatha Christie's *And Then There Were None*, arguably the most renowned murder mystery of them all, where, at nearly seventy years of age, she played coldly pious spinster Emily Brent, who memorably gets figuratively "stung" to death by a "bee."

In real life Edith Howie passed away, a decade after this performance, at the age of seventy-eight on May 1, 1979. Her younger brother, William Lawrence Howie, a photography enthusiast who four decades earlier had advised her on the properties of potassium cyanide for her first published mystery novel, had predeceased her in 1961, while her sister Bessie expired in 1996, at the age of ninety-three. "Reviewer, Thespian Here Dies," read the headline to Edith's 1979 obituary in the *Sioux City Journal*, omitting mention of her mysteries until the body of the article, in which it was briefly noted that "she had eight books and 40 short stories published. Stories by Miss Howie have been widely published in the United States, England and

Australia, and have been frequently translated for publication in Norway, Denmark and Spain."

Having noticed that copies of Edith Howie's novels were quite scarce and highly collectible, I wrote in 2012 about the author's *Murder for Christmas* at my vintage mystery blog *The Passing Tramp*, while two years later Edith was profiled in a series of articles by *Argus-Leader* features writer Jill Callison. Finally in 2022, over eighty years after the publication of her first mystery, Edith Howie's books are again back in print, as part of the remarkable ongoing reclamation of worthy crime writers from our past. Death for Edith Howie, it seems, came not as the end, but rather an intermission.

CRY
MURDER

1

The whole thing began on one of those ugly dull days in November when sullen skies hint at snows to come and thin mist streaks windshields and pavements. Twin candles flickered upon our breakfast table, sending the corners of the room into dark retreat. It was eight o'clock.

Father didn't like the candles. He quirked an eyebrow at them and said, "Mary, if you ever get out of this nonsensical artistic phase, I shall be thankful."

"I like candles," I said dreamily. "I don't like getting up in the middle of the night, but when I do I certainly am in no mood for electricity. Candles are kind. They soften the ravages of sleeplessness."

Father said, "Humph!" and I steeled myself for a diatribe upon those long ago days when he, as a farm boy, had risen at four o'clock summer and winter. It didn't come. He had other things on his mind.

He approached them in devious fashion. "I am so accustomed to a solitary breakfast and so inexpressibly shocked—and honored, shall I say?—at your presence that I will pass the candles," he said magnanimously. "But—do you mind telling me?—just what is the reason that moves you to grace my table at this unprecedented hour?"

I finished my orange juice and poured coffee.

"A train," I said. "I'm meeting it. At nine. The Milwaukee."

"Indeed!" Father pushed his own cup in my direction. "Arrival or departure?"

"Arrival," I said firmly. "Miss Nola Powers. Chris Latimer asked me—"

"That's enough," Father interrupted. "I am answered. I can guess the rest."

So could I. Or thought I could. The "rest" was by way of being my car, a rather imposing one, a graduation gift from Father's sister, Mrs. Loring, who possessed, in Father's phraseology, "more money than brains." I had an idea that the car was the reason Chris wanted me to meet the train, that he trusted in its glitter impressing the important Miss Powers. I didn't see why it wouldn't myself.

Father had finished his coffee and was standing up. "In that event," he remarked, "you might stop at the Club for Hilda. One of our soldiers is to be married this afternoon and his fiancée comes in on that train. From what he says she's a young thing and not used to traveling so I promised Hilda'd meet her."

Well, there it was—good-by to any tête-à-tête I might have hoped for with Miss Powers. For, of course, if I took Hilda down, I'd have to bring her back.

"All right," I said resignedly. "I suppose the wedding's today. Do I sing or play, or a little of both?"

"You play, I believe," Father admitted. For the first time he let himself smile—or grin, rather; it was more than a smile. "One of his buddies will sing. I'm to give the bride away."

I listened abstractedly to the noises of his departure while I planned, as I'd planned before, to keep track of the weddings I'd played for since we'd moved to Nashiona. Too many, I decided. Goodness knows I was practically turning into one of those slogans: "Always an organist and never a bride." Soldiers came and bridegrooms went but I played on forever. I wondered if the prospective vocalist could sing or if I'd find myself transposing *Because* or *I Love You Truly* at sight into some nifty little key such as five sharps or six flats.

Oh, well, I told myself, it was all in the day's work and no good worrying about it. It was too late. Father's job as USO secretary had somehow included me as assistant extraordinary. I didn't really mind either, although some of these weddings bit seriously into my own plans, but there it was. The boys at the camp had so pitifully little time for weddings and happiness.

We hadn't been in Nashiona long. About three months. Before that we'd lived in New York State where Father'd been director of athletics at one of the big universities. But athletic jobs are as tenuous for holding as water and Father was getting to the ticklish age and knew it, and in spite of that, like everyone else, he was itching for some part in the war effort. The army wouldn't have him as a gift. Neither would the navy nor any of the other armed forces—he has a rather questionable heart. He was getting pretty discouraged when this USO thing came along, so he jumped at it. I can't say that I was pleased at the prospect of pulling up our very comfortable roots in the east and re-planting them in the unknown middlewest but, as Father reminded me, these were war times and every loyal citizen must hold himself ready to make sacrifices. If the sacrifice asked of us entailed no more of hardship than moving from our established home . . .

As it happened, the hardships turned out to be negligible. The uprooting was ridiculously easy. Almost before we were aware of what was going on, we'd sublet our rambling old brick house on University Street to a darling, white-whiskered newcomer in the English Department and were blithely on our way to horizons new, or, as Father put it, to wider fields of endeavor. There are moments when Father's way of expressing himself smacks of the ministerial.

I'll admit that, once the first shock was over, I'd succumbed to wild excitement over the adventure. I remember bouncing on the red plush of the pullman lounge and demanding, as I suppose every easterner in like situation has demanded: "Do you think it'll be awfully wild? Shall we see many Indians?"

Father had laughed indulgently. "You've been reading too many westerns, my dear. Not that you won't see Indians—if Federal Court holds during our stay in Nashiona, you undoubtedly will. But please get it out of your head, once and for all, that you're slipping completely out of civilization. You're not. The wild west simply doesn't exist any more."

It didn't. The Chicago train, rumbling into the Nashiona depot that bright August morning, debarked us upon a wide platform that fronted a glittering curve of water, the Nashiona River. A yellow cab conveyed us over smooth asphalt pavement the half a dozen blocks through the business district to Nashiona's largest hotel where we were to remain, barring Father's inspection of the house the local committee had selected.

I was disappointed. I'd pressed my nose flatly to the glass of the cab window and taken bitter stock of the visible trappings of civilization—the street and traffic lights, blue uniformed policemen, theaters and neon signs and the clean lines of brick and stone buildings. "Oh, bother!" I'd said. "There isn't a single thing different about this. It might be any place in the world for all I can see!"

And Father had chuckled.

"You set your expectations too low, my child. Personally I've no reason to disbelieve exactly what I was told before coming here—that in every sense of the word Nashiona is a most progressive little city."

It was. Or is, rather, for Nashiona is still very much in existence.

At that, knowing them as I do, now, I don't imagine the citizens of Nashiona would have cared for Father's terminology. "Progressive" is all right but "little city"—never! Nashionites consider that they dwell in a metropolis, which I suppose they do—it being the largest city within the borders of two sister states. In normal times it had a population of just under fifty thousand, but nowhere had there been normality since Pearl Harbor, and Nashiona was no exception to the rule. Close against its boundaries now sprawled the mushroom growth of the huge army school responsible for our coming. No one knew just how many soldiers were stationed there in the rows of wooden, tar-paper covered barracks but the number hovered somewhere between the twenty and forty thousand marks. Looked at in the light of cold figures, it was appalling—the soldiers formed a little city in themselves.

Nor was that all that was appalling. The problem of housing the rank and file of soldiers had been simple enough—the government had attended to that—but there were still the families of the officers and the permanent staff for whom Nashiona was responsible—to say nothing of the service men's fathers and mothers, their sweethearts and wives, hundreds of whom simply picked up their belongings and moved to Nashiona on the chance of finding accommodations that would enable them to spend a few more precious months with their loved ones. The result was that Nashiona was filled to overflowing. Every apartment, every hotel, every rooming house was jammed to its roof top. Rents had risen—temporarily, for a freezing order was imminent—to unprecedented levels. Tourist

homes and such cabin camps as were equipped to give
all-season service were being rented upon a monthly
basis. At the edge of the town a flourishing trailer city had
sprung up overnight.

It was all pretty breath-taking. I remember Father's first
afternoon conference with the secretary of the Nashiona
Chamber of Commerce, a quick little man whose black
eyebrows executed a nervous dance over his forehead. "It's
a tremendous thing, Mr. Thorpe—these are wonderful days
for Nashiona. Business here has more than doubled since
the camp opened. Our theaters are filled, our streets are
crowded, our housing problems are almost beyond solving.
Bus and train traffic has practically tripled, while as for
our restaurants and eating places—" Words failed him. He
threw up his hands. "It's the difference between stagnation
and life, Mr. Thorpe. It's like the old boom times come
again!"

"Boom times, eh?" Father'd repeated softly. "And then—
after the boom times are over—what? Have you thought
of that?"

The little secretary hadn't. He'd only shrugged and
looked away.

Father had scolded all the way back to the hotel after
that meeting. It was nearly six o'clock and a Friday night
and the streets of Nashiona's business district were brown
with khaki. Soldiers stood on street corners or wandered
aimlessly up and down, staring into shop windows, quick
with an eye for a pretty girl, smoking, jostling, laughing.
More were in constant descent from taxi and bus lines. I
counted thirty in one group at a crossing before I stopped.
I said, "Whew! Nobody told me it would be like this!"

Father was muttering angrily to himself. "Boom times—
bah! Restaurants full and theaters and bus lines—what
about the bars, I ask you? What about the bars? That secretary fellow didn't mention them!"

"Well, what about them?" I asked placidly. We were directly in front of the Horse's Neck by this time and I tried to peer in at its dimly dark interior. More khaki. "Business seems to be good there too," I remarked.

But Father wasn't listening. He was staring down the street at the milling mobs. "The poor youngsters—the poor youngsters. Thousands of them—strangers in a strange land—and not a single damn thing for them to do!"

It's very unusual to hear Father swear. I raised my brows. "Come on," I said. "What's the good of talking about it now? Besides—isn't that your particular job—giving those poor damn youngsters something to do?"

Father looked at me and laughed a little. "Be very careful on direct quotation, Mary—it invariably trips you up. But you're right—the large part of the responsibility is on my shoulders. Tomorrow—tomorrow we'll see."

We did more than see. We—or rather Father—began to do. He plunged head-first into a melee of committee meetings and long distance telephone calls, of consultations with army officials and Y secretaries and ministers and heads of service clubs and what-not until, almost overnight, order began to emerge out of chaos. The entire lower floor of the YMCA building was turned over to the USO. It included recreation and reading rooms and an auditorium that seated five hundred. The other facilities of the Y—swimming pool, showers, bowling alleys—were also made available. In no time at all, Father had an office, a secretary, a staff of volunteer helpers. The USO was in its full stride of operation.

Meanwhile the domestic side of our enterprise had been placed in my hands. Left to himself, I believe Father would have slept willingly upon an office cot or a davenport in the Y lounge but, with me in the offing, some sort of home was imperative. I found one—not the one the over-optimistic committee had selected, but a comfortable, white-painted, green-shuttered house which belonged to an insurance man now stationed in California. Our boxes of bedding, of linens and books, made their appearance. Suddenly we were settled in. Life took up its ordinary routine.

The first weeks were rather ghastly. Nashiona, widely awake to soldier needs, had little time for or interest in the loneliness of casual civilians. Father was busy from morning to night but, once my household tasks were done, I had nothing to do. True I was at the beck and call of the USO as personified by Father and Hilda Adams, his secretary, but the majority of people I met through them were soldiers and, as a steady diet, the military palled. Tentatively I'd essayed a little Red Cross work but the women who were so glad to greet me at the surgical dressings tables I seldom saw again. I attended church and was subjected to a barrage of names and cordial handshakes but all intimacy ended at the church door. Then, just as I was becoming desperate, September rolled around and the Little Theater of Nashiona began its seventeenth season.

It began, inconspicuously, with a notice in the *Nashiona Journal* stating that tryouts for the first play of the season would be held Wednesday and Thursday nights in the YMCA auditorium. All those interested were cordially invited to attend.

I'd read and re-read it with a spirit of hope. "Interested"—well, that could be me. Hadn't I majored in drama and public speaking at the U and, more useful still, hadn't I spent three summers with the Red Barn Players on Cape Cod? Besides, even if all this hadn't happened to be true, I'd have forced myself to be violently interested in anything that promised relief from the doldrums of boredom in which I was finding myself enmeshed. I'd gone down to the Y that first evening with mixed emotions of anticipation and apprehension. The Y auditorium was directly across from Father's office. If I found myself unwelcome or ignored, I could slip over there and trust no one to be the wiser for my going.

I needn't have worried. Within fifteen minutes after I'd pushed through the swinging doors into the auditorium proper, I was being taken to the collective hearts of one of the gayest, friendliest, most charming groups of human beings it has ever been my good fortune to meet. That was my impression then and it still stands. The fact that for a little while this impression was to be clouded over by suspicion and distrust, distorted by fear and the terror of a death that struck relentlessly and without warning, has nothing to do with it. In all essentials, the original impression remains.

I was never lonely again, not after that first night when I was caught up in that irresistible circle of friendship. There were perhaps a dozen young men and women who comprised the nucleus of the Little Theater movement and they were all equally charming and clever and cordial. Had I really played with the Red Barn Players? I had? Honestly? Then I must sit right down and tell them all about it.

I didn't, of course, but along with a half a dozen others, I'd gone to the Latimers' home after the tryouts. Here, in an immense barren room fitted with a tiny stage, Faye Latimer made coffee and played Tchaikovsky records on the battered old Capehart while the rest of us manufactured sandwiches and Chris Latimer sat cross-legged on the floor and discoursed to all who cared to listen upon theaters past, present and to come.

I'd gone back to Father that night in a daze of happiness. I'd loved them all—and no one less than the other. Chris Latimer with his graying crest of hair and his eyes like a lost archangel's. His wife, Faye, slender and swaying, dove-eyed, daffodil-crowned. Alice Wilson with her dark

red hair drawn in smooth bands about a lovely Benda-
mask face. Molly Dunbar, tiny and dark and piquant. Rita
Carstairs, tall and statuesque, with a haunting irregular-
ity of feature. Pete Dunbar, as long and loose-limbed as
his Molly was small and compact. Mark Kerrigan, with
his ugly bulldog face. The very young and apple-cheeked
Victor Jameson. Johnny Forrester, with his twisted bitter
mouth and the hint of frustration in his eyes.

I'd adored them all that night and I'd yearned to know
them better. Never was wish so swiftly granted. I did. And
do.

But after that first night, I never lacked again for friends
or a place to go. I was caught up in a whirl of activity. We
put on the first play in mid-October and I attended rehearsals in the capacity of prompter, helped paint scenery
and collected properties. The play was given four nights
for the general public of Nashiona and then four more out
in the big theater at the army camp and the whole venture
involved more fun than I've ever experienced before. Best
of all, I knew that it was fun that was only beginning, for
the projected season's schedule was a heavy one.

And then, the last night of the show, Chris had dropped
his bombshell—a bombshell to the rest of them rather than
to me for I was too new to comprehend its significance,
and no one took the trouble to explain. He'd come, strid-
ing into the big bare space that we were using for a green
room, and clapped his hands. "Just a minute, everyone!"
he'd said and the crisp, clearly enunciated tones of his
voice had silenced the rise and fall of separate conversation. "I've a letter to read to you."

I remember that I thought it was queer that the letter
was addressed to the Junior Chamber of Commerce, who
sponsored the Little Theater, rather than to Chris who
was not only its director but its heart and soul, but in
my general excitement over the contents I let that pass.

Because the letter itself was something to make anyone sit up and take notice. It was written from New York and signed by Gordon Kearnes, and everyone in the theatrical world knew who he was. His newest play, it appeared, was one of whose reception by the public both he and his manager were dubious. Therefore, he wrote, they would like to bring the play to Nashiona and have it thoroughly tested before actual audiences by the Little Theater group. Direction, naturally, would be in the hands of the local director, but Kearnes himself would be present for consultation, rewriting and advice and, for the actual date of production, his producers and their director would be present, They, in event of agreement, would assume responsibility for all production costs. He would appreciate a reply at once, by wire, and he remained theirs very truly, Gordon John Kearnes.

Oddly enough, when Chris was finished the reading, there'd been none of the surge of excitement I'd expected. Instead, a little pulsing silence seemed to have settled down over the occupants of the green room. The words of congratulation I'd been framing died, stillborn, upon my lips. I'd felt, rather than seen, furtive glances exchanged, heard the shuffling of feet, the awkward clearing of throats, the slow drag of a match drawn across sandpaper for a cigarette's lighting. My own throat seemed to have dried unaccountably. I'd looked down and observed that, for no reason at all, my hands were tightly clenched. And still the paralysis of silence endured until I'd longed to shout, to scream aloud, to do anything that would break its unreality.

If it had affected me, it had not less affected Chris. With a savage movement, he'd crumpled the letter together and thrust it into his coat pocket. "Well, I've read it!" he'd said in a hard high voice, "You heard me! For God's sake, can't any of you *say* something?"

It had been Mark Kerrigan who had answered. He'd removed his cigarette and stared thoughtfully at its length of curling smoke. "I don't suppose there's anything to say," he'd offered mildly. "If I know my colleagues of the Junior Chamber—?" His voice had lifted in question.

"Oh, it's settled, right enough," Chris had agreed grimly, "Signed, sealed and delivered. They're as happy over the idea as a puppy with a root. They wouldn't listen to me—why should they? What difference does it make to them that the man's a skunk? That no decent man or woman—that no decent man—"

He'd choked over that last, unable to finish. He'd given us one last wild glance and then turned and stalked across the far side of the stage to disappear into the opaque darkness that surrounded the mysteries of the switchboard.

For a second the silence had continued, and then all at once it had broken into a babble of sound, a determined concentration of movement. Whatever this interlude had meant to them, like good troupers they were suffering it to pass over them. The show must go on.

But my own bewilderment and shock had not been so easily set aside. Johnny Forrester had been nearest and I'd turned to him. "What does it all mean?" I'd begged. "The way they acted—the way Chris looked—I don't understand—"

Johnny'd been cautious about answering. His heavy-lidded eyes had moved to take in every element of risk before he'd replied, "Why should you, darling? You're a stranger here. But the rest of them knew—oh, God, yes, *they* understood! Did you see their faces? It was worth the price of admission—"

I'd been ready to cry. "No, I didn't," I told him angrily. "I don't care how they looked—what I want to know is *why!*"

He'd taken pity on me then. "Not much to know, Mary. It's all ancient history—pretty ancient. You see, Brother

Kearnes comes from here. There was a time in the not
so distant past when he was one of us—in this theater
group—till he made the town too hot to hold him. Chris
is right—the fellow's a skunk. We all know it and there
isn't one of us who wouldn't cheer at the privilege of contributing a few pennies toward a wreath for his funeral—
if that lucky day ever comes along. In the meantime—"
He'd shaken his head perplexedly. "Where he dug up nerve
enough to come back here beats me!"

This hadn't been getting me anywhere. All of it I might
have worked out for myself, given a chance, since I possess
a fair imagination. I'd drawn a long breath and clutched at
his arm for he'd been evidencing signs of departure. "But,
wait! I still don't understand. What did he do that made
the town too hot to hold him?"

At that, he'd given me a queer tight-lipped smile.
"You'll find out, my pet. Don't be surprised if there's a
hot time in the old place some of these days and you a
spectator. What did he do? Many things, but the principal
reason for his sudden yearning after the green of distant
pastures was the theft of another man's wife. And that'll
have to hold you for the moment, my girl!" he'd broken off
to remark in tones of some satisfaction. "His Nibs requires
my assistance at the switchboard."

It *had* held me. Try as I might, I'd gained no further
information that night. In tacit agreement, the others
shied from my questions. They'd been evasive or they'd
flatly pretended to misunderstand. After an abortive attempt or two I'd given up. What was the good of trying to
buck a conspiracy of silence? Probably Johnny was right—
in time I'd know everything.

It was lucky I'd committed myself to philosophy for
a sudden heavy cold cut me off entirely from the doings
of the Little Theater group. It—the cold—had lasted for
nearly a week and during that time all I'd been able to

learn about their movements came through the medium of the local papers which were being hysterical over the honor the great Mr. Kearnes, lately their fellow citizen, was about to confer upon his native city. Columnists rhapsodized over the success of his plays and spoke reverently of his assured position as leading American dramatist. But this fulsomeness nauseated when set against the memory of Chris's inarticulate anger and the slow drawl of Johnny's condemnation. Surely, if a man be judged by his peers . . .

My condition of enforced ignorance had ended last night with the unmistakable tones of Chris's voice coming to me via the telephone. He'd heard I'd been sick. How was I? Better, he hoped. (Breathlessly I'd confirmed it, assured him that I was now practically well.) Good. Then what were the chances of me doing him a favor? (Good—excellent. I was still breathless.) I'd been reading the papers? I knew about Kearnes' play and the part the Little Theater would play in its production? He'd been busy—they all had—ironing out details; I'd know the sort of stuff. But they were moving nicely forward now—the script had been received and Kearnes himself would arrive next week. In the meantime—well, there'd been a condition or two attached to Kearnes' request, one of them being that the actress who would create the part of Roselle on Broadway should play the role here. She was arriving next morning. Nola Powers. I'd heard of her?

Of course I had. Anyone who ever read dramatic columns had. She'd skyrocketed to fame in the first of the Gordon Kearnes plays and then had starred in all the others. Her two attempts at moving pictures had been successful. I'd said, "Why, yes. I know about her. Is she really coming here?"

She was really coming. Chris's voice remained clipped and matter of fact. Tomorrow morning—from Chicago. Did I think I could meet her—drive her to the hotel where a room had been engaged? Everyone else was busy—he himself had a committee meeting—but he thought she'd expect some attention at the train.

I'd been flattered. I'd promised to go.

There'd been a little silence at the other end of the wire. Then Chris had said abruptly, "All right. Bless you, Mary," and hung up, leaving me with the odd feeling that not all he'd meant to say upon the subject had been said.

I'd remained there at the telephone for a full moment, wondering, uneasy, half inclined to call him back. But I hadn't. In the end, I'd shrugged my shoulders and left it as it was.

I was remembering all this as I paced the platform waiting for the Flyer to come in. Hilda didn't pace with me, but then, presumably, she had nothing to wonder about. She stood against the brick station, her feet in sensible broad shoes planted flatly and watched me through her horn-rimmed glasses with sympathetic indulgence. She looked just what she was, pleasant, unimaginative, dependable. Father named her a jewel of a secretary. I suppose she was.

I was rather surprised to see that except for a few assorted soldiers and some obvious husbands and parents there were few people meeting the train. Save for myself not one of the Little Theater crowd had showed up. I did catch a glimpse of the *Journal's* photographer, laden with the paraphernalia of his trade, and a couple of reporters. But where were the representatives of the Junior Chamber of Commerce, the autograph hounds or the curiosity seekers whose presence might have been expected? It was queer—darned queer. Unless, of course, I told myself hopefully, her arrival had been kept secret. But in that case, why the reporters?

The Flyer came in just then with a rattle and roar and Hilda and I separated to seek our respective quarries. Just how Hilda expected to discover hers, I couldn't guess, but she'd managed it before and doubtless would this time too.

She did. Almost immediately I saw her pass, trailed by a pallid girl whom I assumed to be the afternoon's bride.

All about us people were meeting and reuniting, but the reporters, the photographer and I still waited. As might have been expected, Nola Powers was the last off the train and if a person could be said to make an entrance exiting she managed it. She posed for an instant on the steps—long enough for the photographer to snap a picture—mink coat open, gardenias trailing along its lapel, small smart hat dripping yards of veiling, long beautiful legs, high-heeled suede shoes. In spite of the fact that I'd dressed carefully I felt the complete frump.

She looked exactly like her pictures. Black, shoulder-length hair, curly bang down to her brilliant topaz eyes, wide mobile mouth. You'd call her beautiful, I expect.

Her manner to the reporters was both languid and gracious. "Later—later," she told them with a wave of a white-gloved hand. "Come to the hotel after lunch. I'll give you a story then."

She was gracious to me, too, in an abstracted, dissatisfied way. She said all the proper things but she continued to gaze around and past me, as though in search of someone or something she'd expected to see.

When she reached the car to which we'd repaired, with the reporters, in lieu of redcaps, staggering under her bags, she found Hilda and her pale charge already established there. Nola Powers, after a single glance in their direction, elected to sit in front with me. The bags were piled in and, after a few preliminary jerks due to my nervousness, we were off.

I dropped Hilda and the bride-to-be first. It was easy to swing up around to the Y and then back to the hotel. There was no conversation among my passengers—Hilda had, as usual, nothing to say and I've no doubt the bride was overawed at her proximity to mink and flowers.

Miss Powers herself was silent; she stared out at the misty streets, her eyes heavy with boredom. Once or twice I thought she meant to speak, but she thought better of it almost at once. Occasionally she shivered a little.

I went with her to the hotel room. Long before—at our moment of meeting—I'd decided we weren't apt to love one another overly much, but I'd contracted to meet her and get her settled and I meant to do it right.

It wasn't easy. She sauntered into the pretty rose and cream room, viewed it without approval and said languidly, "Oh, it'll do, I suppose. The whole place reminds me of a hovel but—"

I proceeded to get mad. It wasn't a hovel. It was a perfectly nice room and someone was going to have to pay ten dollars a day for it. I had difficulty keeping my voice from trembling as I said, "I'm sorry you don't like it. But perhaps you won't have it long. If a big fat major comes along and takes a notion to it they'll move you out fast enough! Nashiona's policy at the moment is to cater to the army first—civilians get whatever's left!"

I suppose it was unpardonably rude but at least it shocked her out of her pose of indifference. She looked at me. She said in a quite different tone, "Have I ever met you before, Miss—what was it?—Miss Thorpe?"

I said no, that she hadn't and added reluctantly that I'd only lived in Nashiona a short while. Less than four months.

That seemed to puzzle her. She said, "But then how'd it happen that you came to meet me today?"

I explained that stiffly. I was a member of the Little Theater group and I'd happened to be free.

She lost interest at once. She'd thrown off her coat. It made a huddle of richness across the bed. Without removing her hat she walked over to the window and stood staring down at the rain-drenched street.

"Lovely day, isn't it?" she asked and her voice, with its rich undertones, was bitter and hard. "And a swell day to welcome home the conquering heroine—or the prodigal daughter—I don't think! Had the band out and everything; didn't they? Where were they all—tell me that? Surely they don't hate me that much, do they? Mark and Rita and—and Chris—"

I couldn't have answered if I'd tried. I was completely out of my depth and in the grip of what I now suspected was going to be a perfectly appalling revelation.

She'd turned from the window and was looking at me. She saw my bewilderment—I don't see how she could have missed it; my mouth must have been wide open—and watching, her tawny eyes seemed to glow, and to grow larger and to darken. "You don't mean that you don't know— that they haven't told you? Oh, my dear!" All of a sudden she was laughing, wild laughter that somehow jarred along my spine. "Of course they haven't! They wouldn't! But how priceless—how perfectly priceless! Why, Nashiona's my home town, darling—didn't you know? I lived here—I was Chris Latimer's wife!"

"You—you ran away," I said accusingly. It was all I could think of to say and it seemed to be about the worst thing I could have thought of, for she stopped laughing and fairly spat at me.

"Of course I ran away—so would you! But now I'm back—and they're all here too! Chris and all! But this time I'm the one who's got the upper hand— My God, *how* I've got the upper hand! And what a time I'm going to have me—what a marvelous time—in Nashiona!"

Abruptly she was laughing again. I turned and went out and that laughter was the last thing I heard before I closed the door. For a moment I leaned against it, getting my breath, and then I began to walk very quickly along the hall.

2

The first thing I did when I reached home was to call Chris. I had no particular reason. It was just that, suddenly, it seemed the thing to do.

Chris, in business life, was a C.P.A. He had his own office and I was put through to him without difficulty. I said, "Chris? This is Mary. I wanted to tell you that I met and took her to the hotel and— Oh, Chris— I *do* think she's perfectly poisonous!"

He didn't say anything for a moment. I stood there, hanging to the receiver and hearing only the humming of the wires and somewhere, back of it, the distant clicking of a typewriter. Then, abruptly, his voice came again. "Did she mention me?"

It wasn't at all what I'd expected him to say and, all at once, I felt rebuffed, deflated. My voice, when I spoke, sounded flat and unnatural. "She asked me why you hadn't come to meet her."

He said "Oh" to that and then nothing more for another minute. The wires continued to hum, the typewriter to click. "We'll have this thing going in a day or so," he said finally when I'd about given up hope. "The script's come. Tryouts will be Monday night. You'll be down? There's a part for you, I think."

"Yes," I said, breathless now. "Why, yes. I'll— I'll be there."

"Good." There was another pause. Then, "Thanks, Mary," he said quietly and instantly I heard the sound of the breaking connection.

Slowly I replaced the receiver and I felt the complete fool he must have thought me. I'd made the call upon impulse but what on earth had I thought I was doing? Offering sympathy to a man who obviously wasn't having any was bad enough but to put myself in a position of openly criticizing his former wife . . .

Stubbornness and pride came to my rescue. I didn't care. I'd meant every word I'd said. She *had* been poisonous.

Nevertheless, feeling slightly shaken, I went into the living room, hunted out cigarettes and tried to think the thing out. If indications meant anything—and I'd an idea they did—the Little Theater of Nashiona was in for a rough time at the hands of their former associate, Miss Nola Powers. Or, to put it the other way round, it was quite possible that Miss Powers was in for an even rougher time at the hands of the Little Theater. In either event, the results ought to be interesting. Just the same, as an interested bystander, I had a hunch that any bets I placed would be on Miss Powers in spite of the odds that the others' weight of numbers would carry.

My first cigarette had gone out. I lit another. Boiled down to understandable facts, the situation stood something like this: Nola Powers, who, in the days before her Broadway event, had been Chris Latimer's wife, had known Gordon Kearnes, an aspiring playwright and a native of Nashiona, and, for love or some other unguessed reason, had run away with him to New York. Presumably, although I was open to conviction on this point, they had married.

Now, acknowledged leaders in their separate worlds of the theater, they had come back to Nashiona to—

Which was where I bogged down. *Why* had they come back to Nashiona? Of course there was a perfectly logical reason but somehow it wasn't one that satisfied me. Was the play-tryout story really on the level or were they motivated by some other more subtle reason? There must be in existence theater groups in plenty of towns closer to New York who would have jumped at the chance to test a new play by a writer of Kearnes' standing. Coming halfway across the continent for that purpose just didn't make sense. Not good sense.

Why, then, had they come? For revenge, the melodramatic side of my brain suggested hopefully. To punish those by whom, during the Kearnes-Powers' less successful days, they had been despised and, possibly, ostracized.

I gave up that idea almost at once. Surely they weren't such fools as to imagine that people forget that easily. Their affair, long ago though it had been, was no secret. All of the members of the Theater group were familiar with it—all, that is, but me and the only reason I wasn't, was because I was a stranger to them. Midwestern morality, even in the face of fame and fortune, wasn't that forgiving. The other night had proved that. The sympathy, then, had been entirely with Chris.

Oh, it was an impossible, a ridiculous situation if you liked, but just the same I was beginning to be aware of an odd feeling of excitement and anticipation, a sort of sensitivity to the overtones of forthcoming conflict. The whole aspect of life in Nashiona had altered practically overnight. From now on, I was certain, anything might happen—and probably would. It was in this mood, restless and anticipatory, that I decided to go over and see Faye. Don't ask me why. It was just another of those inexplicable urges. The house was dark and dreary, Father wouldn't be home for lunch and I had nothing to do. I had to talk to someone and Faye seemed to be the only person I was sure wouldn't be busy. Besides, I liked her.

Out of doors the rain had turned to snow. Great soft mats of white were floating gently down to dissolve soggily upon the pavements and to clog windshield-wipers out of activity. The Latimers' English-type cottage looked forlorn and dreary. Leafless vines rattled against its shutters and the ship's lantern above the door joggled in the damp eastern wind.

Faye's appearance, too, was in line with the general dreariness of the out-of-doors. She had been crying and the edges of her eyelids showed faintly pink. She said, "Oh, hello, Mary—come on in," and led the way to the big bare north room that looked unfurnished at the best of times and doubly so on a day like this. Once inside, she waved me to a chair and curled herself up on the window seat where, head turned away, she stared listlessly at the falling snow.

I sat down with qualms of misgiving which were not alleviated by her opening remark. "I suppose you've seen her, haven't you? What's she like?"

I took my time answering that. Ordinarily Faye looks like the answer to a painter's dream of spring. She's slim and lissome and her coloring is a study in pastels—pale golden hair and sea-gray eyes and a skin that's tinted like a blush rose. She's much, much younger than Chris— only twenty-four—and she has a child's gravity when she speaks, which is seldom, and a child's quaintness of wisdom in what she says. Chris is quite mad about her. He says she has "dove's eyes" and once he told me that every time he looked at her, he thought of the Bible verse "Thou art all fair, my love; there is no spot in thee." I don't know

what nicer thing anyone could expect her husband to say
about her.

She wasn't "all fair" today. She looked tired and desperate and more than half ill. Her coloring, never intrusive,
seemed to be dimmed. Even her hair looked faded and
dull.

I said carefully, "Yes, I saw her. As a matter of fact, I
met her and took her to the hotel. She's—oh, I suppose
you'd say she was beautiful—glamorous. I hated her!"

She turned and looked at me then. Doubtfully. She put
up a hand and wearily brushed at the hair that lay so heavily across her forehead. She said, "Did you really? You're
sure you're not just saying that because of me?"

I was indignant at that and glad I had something to be
indignant about. I said, "Certainly not! I didn't like her—
there are people, you know, whom you dislike on sight.
She—well, I suppose she's one of them. We were not," I
went on desperately striving for a lighter tone, "sympathetic. We never could be. I'm certain of that."

"Are you?" Her gray eyes, heavy-shadowed, were earnest on mine. "But she can't be too horrid, I think. Chris
loved her, you see."

I almost caught my breath at that. Chris! I said, "Oh,
well—he's a man and men—! I told you she's beautiful,
didn't I? Besides Chris isn't in love with her now. He loves
you."

"Does he?" she said slowly. "I don't know. Perhaps."

There was something about her then—her appearance,
the pathetic little catch in her grave childish voice, the
halting mode of her expression—that frightened me. I'd
been sorry, just at first, that I'd come. I wasn't now. I
knew what I was going to do—or try to do—and I did it.

I told her not to be a fool. I told her that Chris wor-
shiped the ground she walked on and that everyone who

knew them both was aware of it. I reminded her of the
very definite tone changes in his voice when he spoke to
her—and that was true enough; bitter and morose as Chris
often was, he was gentleness itself where his wife was concerned. I even told her about the "dove's eyes" and about
the Bible verse until, gradually, pink crept back I into her
cheeks and her eyes began to shine again.

I stopped then, exhausted but satisfied. Because my
work had been good. She believed me.

She was leaning far forward, her whole face alight. She
said, "Oh, I'm so glad you came. I wasn't at first, you
know—I thought perhaps you had come out of curiosity—
to gloat over me—because I'm everything that she isn't,
you see. She's—clever and beautiful and famous—and I'm
nothing. And I don't care. I don't want to be. I just want
to be let alone and—and to have Chris love me—"

"Well, he does," I said in as flatly a convincing tone as
I could muster.

"You make me think he does," she agreed. "But he did
love her once—terribly. I know. He used to talk to me
about it. That was when I first came to Nashiona—just
after she'd left him. You see, I was here going to school,
and Chris and I stayed at the same rooming house and he
used to take me for walks at night—miles—and he'd talk
about her and I'd let him. Sometimes," she half caught
her breath, "it was as though he were out of his mind—
crazed—he wanted her so. You see," she said shyly, "I fell
in love with him then—oh, so dreadfully—but it was a
long time—two whole years—before he—before he—"

"Came to his senses," I finished for her with grimness.
"Then you never knew her? She was gone from here before
you came?"

"It was just after she'd gone. Chris had closed the house
and moved to the boarding house. Everyone knew the

story and was talking about it. I heard it, too, and I was so sorry for him. He seemed to like to talk to me."

From then on our talk degenerated into a panegyric upon Chris's virtues—apparently he had no vices. I didn't care particularly. If it made her feel better, I could stand it. Anything to get away from that "lost soul" expression that had so frightened me.

We had lunch together—one of the kind women enjoy, creaming a half a dozen leftovers together and eating them on toast. We had a salad with Roquefort dressing and plenty of strong coffee. It was when we reached the stage of cigarettes that she told me her bit of news.

"I'm so glad you came, Mary," she said for the second time. "It was so horrible sitting here alone and I felt so awful. I wanted to die—only I knew I mustn't. Because I'm going to have a baby, you see—Chris's baby—and being upset is bad for me."

I don't know what I said then. I trust I was properly congratulatory and consoling, but it seemed the perfect complication to me. The poor kid! Now of all times to be having a baby—just when she'd naturally want to feel and look her best—and with that tiger of a woman prowling about . . .

We were still at coffee and cigarettes when the telephone rang. Faye sprang to her feet with such glad alacrity that it was evident she expected the caller would be Chris. I hoped it would be but it wasn't. It was Father and he was mad.

He wanted to know why I didn't have sense enough to notify him of my whereabouts when I left the house. He said that he'd tried every possible place in town where he thought I could be, only to find me at the one house he considered impossible. Would I mind telling him why I'd forced myself on that poor girl today? He should think I would have had better taste—

From which it may be deduced that Father, having met Faye, approved of her. Most men do, I've noticed.

I got the kernel out of his remarks presently. It seemed that Hilda wanted me. Something about the wedding this afternoon. Would I come right down? I said I would and hung up.

Faye, who looked quite like her old self again, came to the door with me. It had cleared outside as well as in and the sun was struggling through a mass of thin gray clouds.

I said, "It'll be a nice day after all."

"It always is after a storm," Faye said quaintly. "Thanks again for coming, Mary. You've helped me—oh, so much. I felt so blue and awful this morning. And so afraid."

I humored her. "Afraid of what?"

"Of her—Nola. Afraid she wanted Chris again. Because—why else would she come?" Her eyes were wide and grave on mine.

I shrugged. It was a problem that was puzzling me too.

"Well, she can't have him," Faye said darkly. "Not if that's the reason she came. She left him once and he's mine. I'm not going to give him up! I'll kill her first! And him too!"

I laughed. It sounded so comical, coming from Faye—as though a white kitten had threatened mayhem upon a mastiff.

Faye laughed too. "It *is* funny," she said grudgingly. "But I do feel better. Tonight I'm going to cook Chris a perfectly marvelous dinner—everything he likes—and surprise him. Afterwards I'll tell him how silly I was and we'll both laugh. . . ."

It was on that note that, I left her and drove down to the USO headquarters where I collected Hilda. She was in a dither about the wedding, and it was such a pronounced dither that I didn't even try to drive the car—I just sat in it out in front, double-parked, while she told me about it.

Somehow you don't suspect Hilda with her efficiency and her eyeglasses and her flat sensible shoes of being sentimental, but she is. I suppose all old maids are. Hilda must be close to fifty; her hair is gray and permanently waved—but neither successfully nor becomingly—and she wastes neither time nor money upon her skin, and her dresses are chosen for utility rather than style. She's definitely a business woman not a career girl, which was the reason she so shocked me this afternoon. For Hilda had been crying. The tip of her nose was red and so were her eyes. I began to wonder just what was the matter with this day anyway, and if my role for the second time was to be Mary Sunshine.

It developed that it was the bride-to-be who'd gotten Hilda down. She—the bride—was at Hilda's apartment. Hilda had taken her there when she discovered that the girl had no money. "She's got a white satin dress and white slippers and a veil, and that's all she's got in the world except her clothes and the money for her ticket home."

"Good heavens!" I said, startled in spite of myself. "Is she crazy? Or what?"

Not crazy, Hilda insisted. Only poor and very much in love. They'd been engaged for a long time and the boy had a good job until he was drafted. He'd wanted to be married when he knew he had to go but she'd refused. She was a stenographer in a mill and she had an invalid mother to support.

"What made her change her mind?" I asked. "Because I suppose she *has* changed it—"

The boy's course here was nearly over, Hilda told me. He'd graduate in a week or two and from then on where he'd be was doubtful. He was near the top of his class and the probability was he'd be shipped right out of the country. Hilda supposed that was what had frightened them, made them desperate. "They're reaching out for the little happiness they can still have," she said soberly. "You can't blame them. She's got a ten-day vacation from the mills and her aunt's staying with her mother."

I said, "Oh, heavenly days! Well, where do I come in on this tragedy of errors?"

It was the church, Hilda said. They were to be married at—she named it. The girl insisted on a church wedding but it was a bare ugly place at best—did I remember? I did. I said, "But what can *we* do?"

Hilda'd thought of that. She had saved twenty-five dollars—she'd meant to use it toward a new winter coat but she didn't need a coat. (I threw a catch glance at hers and didn't agree.) She was going to take the twenty-five dollars and buy flowers—plenty of flowers. Then we—she and I—could decorate the chapel.

Absolutely, I told myself as I engaged the gears, this was the screwiest day I'd ever been mixed up with. It kept right on being. We drove out to the Horstill Greenhouse where Hilda demanded, and got, the proprietor herself. Mrs. Horstill, a fellow Altrusan and thus a "Sister" in Hilda's lodge, became almost as excited as Hilda over the circumstances of the wedding and gave us carte blanche in her rooms of cut flowers. She laughed off all talk of payment. We were not to be silly—flowers didn't last forever, we knew that, and we were more than welcome to whatever we wanted.

We chose flowers until we were ashamed to take any more and then Mrs. Horstill loaded the car down with vases and containers and a couple of bolts of pale pink tulle. She added gorgeous corsages for Hilda and myself, a more gorgeous one for the bride and would have sent a boutonniere for the groom if we hadn't convinced her that military dress had its restrictions.

Hilda was delighted over the way the flower contingency had smoothed itself out. "Mae Horstill was glad to do it," she said gleefully, "and I've still got the twenty-five dollars. So I think we'll have a nice little supper after-wards for the wedding party."

"You're completely insane!" I said in acute horror. "You can't afford it—"

"Nonsense!" Hilda said roundly. "There won't be so many—you and your father and me and the bride and groom and the soloist, of course. . . ."

I groaned. In the general excitement I'd forgotten the soloist.

We worked like mad for the next two hours. Hilda and I and the minister's wife, from whom we borrowed the church key, and who also became infected by wedding-bug virus. We had quantities of flowers, great wet sweet chrysanthemums and pale colored roses and fragrant stalks of narcissi, to work with and their magic turned the ugly little place into fairyland.

When it was done at last Hilda was quite overcome. She cried quietly all the way home, but it wasn't until I'd stopped in front of her apartment house and she was actu-ally getting out of the car that she offered me the expla-nation for her emotional storm. She said, "You think I'm hopelessly silly, don't you, Mary? Well, I'm not. It's just that her story is—was—mine. The last war, you know. We didn't get married—we thought it was wiser to wait—and then he—he never came back."

She nodded abruptly and walked away.

I had exactly three quarters of an hour to get ready and it wasn't made any easier by the fact that Father was home and dressed and roaring like a Bashan bull with questions of where I'd been and why I always waited till the last minute. . . .

I didn't listen to him. I shut my bedroom door and let him rave.

My best velvet dress, my newest smartest hat, white gloves, best fur coat, Mrs. Horstill's super corsage, a last scramble for wedding marches et al, and I was ready. Father chose to drive which meant that the ten minutes I'd managed to save were completely wasted.

The church looked and smelled like heaven but I had no time for more than one quick glance at its interior. Hilda and the bride and the bridegroom were already there—I waved at them and hurried over to open the organ. Already there were several khaki backs visible in the pews.

The soloist arrived about the time I was nicely under way with the *Liebestraum*. I had no time to waste on him then, so I merely nodded when he laid his music on the bench beside me. I did manage one whisper, "Key's all right?" and he said "Quite!" in a firm English-y tone which startled me so that I unintentionally omitted an essential sharp.

The wedding was beautiful. From beginning to end. The organ console was so placed that I sat at right angles to, and facing, the aisle down which the procession came and the look on the little bride's face—happiness or Hilda or something had done things to her; she was beautiful if only for that one brief moment—was sufficient to repay me a thousand-fold for my efforts in her behalf. The soloist, too, turned out to be something pretty special—later on I learned he had sung small parts with the Metropolitan—so that for once the familiar wedding chestnuts turned out to be unexpectedly fresh and delightful. Father was as impressive as only he can be if he wants to, and the minister was adequate. As for the bridegroom—well, I doubt if white satin or music or chrysanthemums meant anything to him. He had eyes only for the bride.

The wedding supper, impromptu as it was, went off beautifully too. There were only a half a dozen wedding guests, fellow soldiers from the Army camp, and Hilda in a sudden excess of hospitality invited them, too, to come along down to the Sweet Shop. It's dangerous to mention food in the approximate vicinity of a soldier. They all accepted with pleasure. And came.

It was a gay friendly little supper. I sat between the minister and the Metropolitan baritone—he was a handsome brute—and just across from the bridal couple. The bride had gone back to Hilda's apartment and changed her white satin for something unexciting in the way of a tailored suit. But Mrs. Horstill's flowers did a quite satisfactory job of dressing up the plainness, and the girl's face did the same thing for her uninspired felt hat. She looked absolutely transfigured with glory.

The bridegroom looked dazed.

After dinner, we all waited around on the somewhat flimsy pretext of seeing them off—they weren't going anywhere; we knew that, only to the hotel—but we all pretended royally. The bride kissed Hilda and the groom did his best to wring our hands off.

Then it was over and we still lingered awkwardly, suddenly conscious now that our reason for merriment had passed, that we were all strangers one to the other.

It was Father who snapped this coil. He did it by glancing at his watch, deciding that he'd been away long enough from the USO and announcing his imminent departure. Everyone else took the hint and went first.

Hilda and I waited after the rest—to settle the bill—and it was while she was counting her change that I heard a laugh I knew, glanced through the door of the nearest private room and, by so doing, got the shock of my life. For Chris was there—Chris Latimer—seated at a table for two and the woman opposite him wasn't Faye. It was his ex-wife—Nola Powers.

3

It was none of my affair but, just the same, the sight of Chris with that woman spoiled the rest of my evening. I felt depressed and out of sorts. Worst of all, I kept thinking of Faye and the perfectly marvelous dinner with which she'd meant to surprise Chris. What had happened to that dinner and where was Faye? Crying her eyes out at home most likely.

I decided Chris was a fool—that Faye was a fool—and that I was a bigger fool than either of them. What difference did their affairs make to me? Six weeks ago I hadn't known either of them. I almost wished I didn't now.

Almost—but not quite. So what? Stop fussing for the love of Allah, I told myself. Chris is forty—Faye is twenty-four; they're both grown and responsible—it doesn't concern you. The smartest thing you can do is keep yourself out of trouble. . . .

I stopped right there, chilled.

It was the first time I'd actually come out and acknowledged to myself that I thought there might be trouble. Trouble of what sort I didn't know. Mercifully. But I've Scotch-Irish ancestry and I was "fey" that night.

I got my senses back over a Sunday rest. Monday was bright and sunny and the most exciting thing that happened—until night, I mean—was Alice Wilson's telephone

call. She was asking everyone, she announced brightly, to
come to her apartment after the tryouts. She knew we'd
have a lot to talk about.

"Everyone?" I asked doubtfully.

"Oh, not our prima donna, darling," she said with the
little giggle that I so detested. Imagine a Benda-mask
relaxing into a giggle! "But everyone else and that means
you, of course."

I said thanks. But I was still doubtful. Perhaps she
sensed it. Anyway she giggled again. "The author'll be
there though."

That woke me up. "Mr. Kearnes? Why, I didn't know
he'd come yet—"

"Oh, heavens, yes! He was ringing my bell at eight
o'clock this morning. No danger of him letting anyone
put on his precious play without the benefit of his nickel's
worth of advice. We're old friends, you know—Gordy and I."

I hadn't known but I wasn't surprised. Alice is the sort
of person who's old friends with anything that has a draft
classification. I said, "What's he like? I don't think I've
ever seen his picture. Is he good-looking?"

"We-ell," Alice said, "not really so good-looking but—
oh, there's something about him . . ."

There certainly was. I knew that as soon as I saw him.

The afternoon dragged. I spent it trying to decide
whether or not I meant to try for a part in this show—I
knew I meant to; whether or not I'd take it if I were offered one—I knew I would; I'd be afraid I'd miss something. I considered what I'd wear and shrank from the
Scylla of over-dressing on one side and the Charybdis of
under-dressing on the other. In the end I wore a tailored
suit and a beret.

As early as I thought I decently could, I went down
to the Y auditorium, where tryouts were always held, but
there were plenty of people before me, most of them I

suspected out of curiosity and a desire to see the cele-brated Nola Powers. A sprinkling of khaki revealed that some of the soldiers from the USO rooms had drifted over, probably for the same reason. Or perhaps in search of entertainment. If it was the last, they certainly got it.

Not that things didn't start out peacefully enough. It looked very much like an ordinary tryout night. Madeline Cummings, the dramatic teacher at the high school, was at the door with the yellow typewritten slips that Chris asks those wanting parts to fill out. She said anxiously. "You're going to try out, aren't you, Miss Thorpe? Oh, do. Hardly anyone is. I think they're afraid."

I said, "So am I." And it wasn't any lie. But it wasn't of trying out that I was afraid. It was that old "fey" feeling again.

I took a slip anyway and slid into one of the side-aisle seats close to the back. The stage lights were on and Chris was standing down by the footlights sorting scripts. There was a sort of expectant hush over the auditorium, the same sort of a hush that ensues just before an umpire pulls down his cap and says, "Play ball!" Everyone seemed to be waiting for something. I took a look around and de-cided that, as the great Miss Powers was not in evidence, they were probably waiting for her.

A huddle of gray squirrel in the front row on the right betokened Faye's presence and I thought jubilantly, "Good for her! I'll bet it took nerve to come out tonight! Hurrah for our side!"

I wasn't alone long. Almost at once Alice Wilson said, "Move over, will you?" And I moved, although grudgingly. I wasn't in the mood for company tonight.

Alice looked gorgeous. She's a beautiful woman at any time, with an ivory skin and a perfect profile which she dramatizes by drawing her dark mahogany hair straight back into a low knot on her neck. Her eyes are very dark and very blue and her mouth is as red as Max Factor can make it. She goes in for the decorative in dress, costume jewelry and plain dark crepes, although her sport things, when she does choose to wear them, cost money. Tonight she was all in black, even to stockings, which isn't usual in Nashiona.

There was a mystery about Alice—at least there was to me. Probably the rest knew all about her. Actually she's Mrs. Wilson but she was "Alice" to everyone. Where Mr. Wilson was, or if he ever existed, I didn't know.

Alice loosened her furs with that familiar breathless giggle. She said, "Well, I stole a march on this gang all right, all right. *Who* do you think brought me down here tonight? Gordon Kearnes himself! And, oh Mary, the play's simply wonderful and there's a part in it that he wants me to play—the name part—"

I said, "Oh-oh, what gives? What about Nola?"

Alice frowned. "Oh, she'll have the best part, of course, but— You see, the play's about two women. It's called *The Good Woman,* and there's a good woman who's bad essentially and a bad woman who's good—that'll be Nola. Now do you see?"

I said I didn't particularly, and she said, "Oh, bother! You'll just have to wait, I guess." Then in a different tone, "There's Gordy now—coming down the aisle."

I turned, curious to see the man who'd beaten Chris's time, so to speak. And then I didn't believe he had, for the playwright was a bird-like little man who'd scarcely come up to Nola Powers' ear. Sartorially he was correctness itself in dinner jacket and lapel flower, but he had a mane of black hair no brush nor comb could tame and little raisin-eyes behind thick-lensed glasses. His mouth looked mean.

I said honestly but not very wisely, "Well, I don't see why any woman would throw Chris Latimer over for a thing like that!"

"I don't know what you're talking about," Alice said coldly. "And anyway you've got the story all wrong. Gordon's a very brilliant man!"

I muttered something about he'd have to be to get over his other handicaps, and asked if she'd seen Miss Powers. Alice hadn't. She said, "Don't worry—Nola'll be the last one. She'll have to make her entrance."

She did, too. She arrived about ten minutes later, wearing a red dinner dress and escorted by the Junior Chamber of Commerce committee who were obviously having the time of their lives. It was a little like the arrival of royalty for Chris and Gordon Kearnes at once moved forward to greet them, and the whole group stood and talked for a moment. Then, with considerable manner, Nola Powers was established in a front seat and there was an entrancing little squabble among the members of the committee as to which one should have the privilege of sitting next to her.

Alice gave a little wiggle. "Oh, isn't this fun?"

But I couldn't see it. My eyes were on Faye Latimer. So far as I could tell, she hadn't even looked in Nola Powers' direction. I wished I was sitting beside her.

Nola's furs were adjusted to her satisfaction. All at once her voice rang out clearly. "But what are we waiting for? Do let's get on with it!"

They did. The farce of the tryouts began without further delay. I say "farce" because that's what they so obviously were. Chris was taking no risk with casting this play. These actors were hand-picked. One by one, they were called to the stage and read over the parts—Alice Wilson and Pete Dunbar, Mark Kerrigan and Johnny Forrester, myself and Rita Carstairs and Victor Jameson. Save for myself they were all tried regulars in the Little Theater plays. I knew. I hadn't studied the file of their old programs for nothing.

The sprinkling of outsiders—hopeless, most of them, but eternally hopeful—who had signed tryout slips were disposed of in short order. Most of them were high school or business college girls, ill-dressed, unfledged youngsters with neither voice nor presence to commend them. A couple of quick groupings did for them. Sorting out the half a dozen extra men whom Chris had inveigled into coming down, took longer. But gradually the cast began to be assembled.

The play had good parts for nine people, four women and five men. There were the two women, good and bad, foils for one another, the mother and young sister of the one labeled "good." The men included the husband of the "good" woman, the brother of the "bad," a lawyer, a gangster and the sister's fiancé. It was the part of the sister for which I was tried.

I had it too. From the very start, I knew the part was mine even though the consciousness of Nola Powers in the audience made me awkward and self-conscious. I would have known it was mine even if Chris hadn't grunted at me the first time I came off the stage to "stick around" awhile.

I did. Only I didn't go back to my original seat. Instead, defying the lightning, I went and sat by Faye. She didn't move nor speak but, after a second, she slipped a cold little hand into mine. I pressed it. That was all.

So far as I could tell the cast was lining up something like this: Alice Wilson for Annice, the "good" woman, name part of the play; Nola Powers for Roselle, the bad one; Mark Kerrigan for the gangster part; myself, Mary Thorpe, for Lisette, Annice's sister; Pete Dunbar for Lisette's fiancé; Rita Carstairs for Annice's mother; Victor Jameson for Roselle's brother; Johnny Forrester for the lawyer; and Ross Langdon, a stranger, newer in Nashiona than I was myself, for Annice's husband. The minor parts of maid, butler and gangster's henchmen were left untouched. They could be filled in later.

During all of this time, Nola Powers had been sitting in the front row attended by her three cavaliers and such other males as would approach within talking distance. She had laughed and smoked and chattered, keeping only a nominal eye upon the stage where Chris worked so patiently, grouping and reorganizing, shifting parts about, watching for discrepancies of weight and height and voice. Only when Alice Wilson moved or spoke as Annice did the font of Nola Powers' merriment dry up. Then she sat silent, smoking quickly, her eyes hard and cruel.

But if Nola Powers had chosen to divorce herself, in effect, from the actual casting, Gordon Kearnes certainly hadn't. I don't think he sat still for a minute. He kept bobbing up and down to whisper in Chris's ear. Sometimes he walked back and forth in the aisles, pausing now and then to scribble voluminously in a small black notebook. I'll admit I found his restlessness upsetting but I told myself it was all right, it was to be expected. After all, the play was *his*.

At last Chris seemed satisfied. He had been working mostly from short scenes that brought his cast on in two's and three's. Now he clapped his hands sharply and called for a reading at the end of the first act. This brought on the entire cast with the exception of Miss Powers and Chris read her part in a low uninflected voice.

It went pretty well. I thought that Chris need not feel too ashamed of us. Evidently he agreed, for after saying, "Curtain!" unemotionally, he added, "Hold it a moment, please . . ." and turned to look out into the house.

It was late—after eleven—and a large percentage of our audience had seeped away. Only a few scattered heads showed against the light that sifted through from the lobby beyond the swinging doors. In the front seats, only two of the members of the Chamber of Commerce committee remained and there was an empty seat between them. Miss Powers had disappeared.

Nor was the author in evidence. Chris said, "Well!" and lit a cigarette. His eyes were angry. "As we appear to have been temporarily abandoned—"

One of the representatives of the Chamber of Commerce spoke up then. If Latimer referred to Miss Powers, he said, clearing his throat, he believed that she and Mr. Kearnes had gone back stage a few minutes ago.

Chris said thanks and trampled on the cigarette. The rest of us stood uneasily for a moment and then Alice's giggle broke the momentary tension. "Well, I suppose we can sit down while we wait her ladyship's pleasure!"

I was closest to the door. Chris looked at me. "See if you can find them, Mary, there's a good girl."

It wasn't an assignment I cared for but I went.

"Back stage" in the Y auditorium doesn't mean much. The stage itself is small, and to give depth the canvas flats are usually set flush with the brick wall of the building so that no passageway exists between the wings. There are no real wings, either, only spaces, jump off's for entrances and most entrances have, of necessity, to be made from the left. If your entrance comes from the right, it means that you have to be there, costumed and in place, before the curtain rises. It isn't convenient and it demands considerable readjustment of stage directions, but Chris manages to put on good shows in spite of its handicap.

Switchboard and curtain controls are on the right. From the left a flight of four cement steps rises to a door that leads into what is euphemistically termed the "green room." It's a large bare room, unfurnished except for chairs and a few tables. This room is connected with the lobby by a long passageway lined with Y classrooms, and here the cast assembles. Here, too, when a play is actually being put on, Chris erects a temporary dressing room for the women out of unused flats. The men usually make their changes in the property room, a long narrow unfinished space that runs behind the classrooms.

"Back stage," then, really means the "green room," and it was there that I made my way. The fireproof door at the top of the little flight of steps stuck a little. I had to put pressure upon it to open it. It opened a crack. . . .

It was then that I heard the voices. I suppose I should have gone back to the others, or else gone ahead into the green room. I did neither. There was something in the tone of those voices that stopped me cold. I stood right where I was, holding that door open a little, and listening shamelessly.

The voices belonged, indisputably, to Nola Powers and Gordon Kearnes. I hadn't heard the playwright speak as yet but that made no difference. The voice was right for him—a soft voice, silky almost, but with a layer of something underlying it hard as steel.

He didn't even speak very loudly. It was Nola Powers who did. Her words had an edge to them as though hysteria was about to breakthrough.

"I won't be made a fool of, Gordon. I told you that before I came out here. I've no intention of playing second fiddle to any woman—least of all to her!"

"No one asked you to come here," Gordon Kearnes said placidly. "It was your own idea. As for the other—just what have you got against Alice?"

"Against Alice—Alice Wilson?" Scorn filled her voice like a brimming cup. "You ask me that! I hate her—isn't that enough?"

"They're none of them friends of yours, are they? Why Alice more than the rest? She's not such a bad little thing—you know, Nola—pretty, clever, amusing—"

I heard the rasp of her hard breathing.

"What do I care how amusing she is. She comes out of that cast, Gordon!"

"She does not!"

"Then let her play Roselle—I'll do Annice. I won't be humiliated in my own home town—"

"You'll do what I say and shut up! Alice stays. This is my show. If you don't like it, you know what you can do."

"What I can do," she repeated thoughtfully. I heard the papery rustle of her dress as she moved. "Why, yes, of course I do. Thanks for reminding me."

"Now, look here!" He was definitely conciliatory now. "I didn't mean anything by that and you know it. After all this is my show—haven't I the right to say who's to be in it or not?"

"I don't know," she said quietly. "Have you?"

He groaned. "Be decent, Nola. What difference can it possibly make to you if Alice is in or out?"

"None." Her tone was light and airy. "But the question doesn't arise. Alice is *out!*"

He groaned again. He said, "Before God, I don't understand you. There are times when I think it would be a positive pleasure to wring your neck—to get my hands about your lovely long throat and squeeze it—"

She cut him off then. "But you won't, will you? Cowards never kill. They're too afraid for their precious skins. You're a coward, aren't you, Gordon? Oh, not that I count on that alone—I've taken precautions. Coming here it was advisable."

"Precautions—what the hell do you mean?" The question snapped at her.

Her voice was lazily amused. "Wouldn't you like to know? But I'm not a fool, Gordon—I'm not going to tell you what they are. Only—I wouldn't advise you to start anything. You might find out. You and that darling Alice of yours—"

Kearnes said, "You devil!" and there was a sharp cracking sound. It might have been a slap. I couldn't tell, but just the same, I decided that this, whatever it was, had gone far enough. It was time and past for my entrance. I let the door slip back, imperceptibly, and turned to tiptoe back down the little flight of steps.

I was thankful for the iron rail that guarded the steps because my knees felt wobbly. All of a sudden they were wobblier, for I discovered that I was no longer alone. Ross Langdon, the newcomer in the cast, was standing just inside the door that opened from the stage. How long he'd stood there, I had no way of knowing. Probably long enough to have caught the whole picture. The hot tide of embarrassment flushed my face. I said, "Oh!" weakly.

He was kind. He acted as though it were the most ordinary thing in the world to walk out into the wings and catch someone eavesdropping. He gestured with his cigarette, cocked one eye at the door. "Trouble?" he asked laconically.

"They've been quarreling," I said desperately. "I—I didn't think it was the tactful thing to break in. I thought I'd wait until they'd cooled down a little."

He laughed. Softly. It was a nice laugh. He had nice white teeth, too, and twinkling blue eyes and smooth fair hair that broke at its edges into the hint of a wave. He said, "Oh, well, it does happen in the best of families. Anything I can do?"

"No, thanks," I said. "I'm going in now . . . making plenty of commotion so they'll be sure to hear."

"All right." He dropped the cigarette to the floor and stepped on it. "Latimer was getting impatient. I'll tell him you'll be right along, shall I?"

I went up the steps again, noisily this time, I banged on the door and then pushed it open. I might have saved myself the trouble. The room, save for the penetrating sweetness of Nola Powers' perfume, was quite empty.

Disgruntled I returned to the stage. Chris glanced at me. I said, "I'm sorry—I couldn't find them—they must have gone." Then I was silent. For Nola Powers, calm, poised, gracious and alone, was undulating slowly down the left aisle of the auditorium.

At once Chris transferred his glare to her. He said, "My God, where've you been? We're all set here—we've been waiting—"

"I'm so sorry, everybody." Her voice was clear and completely unruffled. You wouldn't have guessed from her manner that two minutes ago a man had implied that choking her would be a privilege and a pleasure. She stood quite close to the stage and her face in the light that bent down from the borders was composed, even a little amused. I thought again how lovely she was and how thoroughly every fiber of my body disliked her.

She had laid her hand on Chris's arm and he moved restively as he spoke. "I thought we'd give you a run through of the end of the first act—give you an idea—"

"Oh, why bother? It's late. Everyone must be tired and if you are satisfied, Chris—I'm sure it will be a pleasure to work together. There's just this one thing—Gordon asked me to speak to you about—it's a little difficult to tell you—"

As she spoke she was moving deliberately, backward along the aisle down which she'd come. It was evidently going to be a private conference. Chris scowled and followed her. But before he went, he said, "All right, people. Rehearsals start tomorrow at seven-thirty. Probably here. If there's any change, you'll be notified."

We straggled off the stage. The excitement was over and now we were very definitely in the throes of a let-down.

I found my coat and hat and scrambled into them. Beside me Alice Wilson was doing the same and repeating over and over, "Remember—you're all of you coming over to my place now. I don't care how late it is—it's not too late for a party. And anyway you promised. You're coming, aren't you, Mary?"

I muttered something—what I don't know. In spite of myself, I couldn't keep my eyes from that corner where Nola Powers and Chris were deep in conversation. I had an earnest desire to get out of that auditorium, and an equally earnest desire to stay for fear I'd miss something. For something was due to happen. I knew it in my bones. I even had a sort of a hunch as to what, precisely, it would be.

In the end I didn't miss anything. For almost at once Chris left Nola Powers and walked down to the stage. He stood there for a moment, fussing with the scripts that were piled before the footlights, before he spoke over his shoulder. His voice was grim, "Just a minute, Alice—"

I knew then, knew that in whatever game it was they were playing, Gordon Kearnes had lost and Nola Powers had won. I knew, too, that I couldn't stay to witness Alice's humiliation and defeat.

I turned and fled from the auditorium as though demons were after me.

4

I wasn't alone going out, only the leader of a general exodus. But once outside we had nothing to say. We stood huddled together under the hard light of the street lamp as though, having arrived thus far, we waited for some sort of leading as to what we should do next.

It came, prosaically enough, from Mark Kerrigan. He stifled a yawn. He said, "Well, it looks as though Alice gets it where the chicken got the ax. No party tonight. Oh, hell! I'm going down town and get drunk!" And followed, at least the primary action, to the word.

It was an effective breaker-up. I went home with the Dunbars. We tried to talk a little, desultorily, but it wasn't a success. Molly said she wasn't surprised, that it was an old feud: Nola'd always had it in for Alice.

"And not without reason," her husband muttered. "Still, it's awkward, dragging out old skeletons. For two cents I'd throw my part in—we all ought to. It'd serve the lady right."

"You'll do no such thing," Molly declared with spirit. "This thing's going over. Besides, you wouldn't be spiting Nola—it'd be Chris you'd hurt. And that's not fair."

Pete groaned and agreed.

I said, "But what happens next? Someone'll have to play Annice. And who is there?"

"Me," Molly suggested modestly, and Pete laughed and let the car shift sideways while he made a pass at her and rumpled her curls, "Not you, bird-brain. You're too little. Besides, you occasionally show a glimmer of genuine ability. No, you can bet your boots it'll be someone innocuous—someone Nola's not afraid of."

Chris called me, twenty minutes after I'd reached home, and offered me the part. I said, "Chris, you're joking!" and he assured me that he wasn't, that Miss Powers herself had suggested me.

There was food for thought in that remark. I said slowly, "So she's not afraid of me, then." When Chris asked me what I meant, I repeated Pete's conjecture.

Chris was silent for a moment. "No, you've got it wrong," he said at last. "Anyway, if you are right, you can give her a surprise, can't you? But I think she honestly likes you and it wouldn't be such a bad solution. Molly could do Lisette."

I said, "But, Chris, how could I? Alice—"

"Oh, so that's what's worrying you. Well, don't let it. I'll look out for Alice, give her a fat part later on. Annice wouldn't do much for her and she knows it—it was Kearnes talked her into it."

I protested that I still didn't see how I could do it, that I'd never feel right about it, and he told me roughly not to be a fool—to think it over and I could let him know in the morning.

I replaced the hand set and wondered what in the world I ought to do. I'd been perfectly honest with Chris—I really wouldn't feel right taking Alice's part from her—but just the same I wasn't sure enough of my footing with the Theater crowd to want to refuse. Besides, playing the name part in this particular show, with the whole city primed to make it a civic occasion, would undoubtedly provide an opportunity I'd be a fool not to take.

The telephone rang just then and I reached for it languidly. Father, I supposed. To say he'd be a little later than usual, coming home, and would I see there was coffee ready for him.

It wasn't Father. It was, of all people, Alice Wilson.

"You're a fine bunch of rats," she accused me gaily. "I said I was giving a party and I've enough sandwiches to feed an army and everything that goes with them and here I am—all alone—with nobody to feed but Gordy and Chris."

"Chris!" I said stupidly. Had he called from *there?*

"Why, of course. Oh, and Faye's here, too, but she's such a little mouse I overlooked her. Listen, we're holding a council of war and Chris says you've an idea I wouldn't want you to play that part just because I've been thrown out on my ear."

"Would you?" I practically gasped.

"Mind? Of course not. Don't be an idiot. Why should I care? I certainly don't yearn to walk in that woman's shadow."

"And you think I do?"

She laughed. "Listen, Mary, I think—we all think—you've got a fair chance of showing the lady up. If you can, you'll have our collective blessing. Don't worry about me. Chris won't let me down. He'll have a play for me in the spring and it'll be a honey. I'll come out with the Oscar for the best performance of the year—wait and see if I don't! In the meantime you buckle down and work. Call Chris in the morning and say you'll take that part and praise the Lord you've got the chance to do it!"

It was all very stimulating. I said, "Well—" uncertainly. "But you did get a dirty deal, Alice. We all thought so. Why'd Chris let her get away with it?"

"Because she's got him where the hairs are short. It's her system with men. It doesn't work so well with our sex.

And don't get it into your head my account with Nola Powers is closed. I'll make her rue the day she was born before this play's over. I'm the gal that can do it, too. You just watch my smoke!"

I had a sudden idea. I said, "Listen, are you saying all this in front of Chris and Mr. Kearnes! Because I don't think—"

"Heavens, no!" Alice said heartily. "I'm in the kitchen and the door's closed. Gordy and Chris are glooming in the library and Faye looks like the wrath of God—"

"Chris ought to have more sense," I interrupted indignantly. "Keeping her up, I mean. She ought to be home and in bed. Having a baby's no fun and when on top of it your husband's ex-wife enters center stage with a fanfare of trumpets—"

Alice stopped me. "What did you say?" Her voice was sharp with surprise and some other emotion I didn't understand. "What's that you said? About Faye?"

"Why, that she's going to have a baby," I said stiffly. "I don't suppose it's any secret. She told me herself. Last week."

"Oh, my God!" Alice said slowly. "Are you sure? Does Chris know?"

"I suppose so. Husbands generally do, don't they?"

Alice ignored that. "If he knows— Oh, Lord, what a mess! What a perfectly ghastly mess!"

She hung up abruptly then, leaving my questions sputtering into thin air. At once Central began her "Number please?" routine as a gentle reminder that the line was still open. I was reminded. I replaced the hand set.

And now what? I asked myself. My own private opinion was that everyone in the Nashiona Little Theater had gone out of his or her mind. They were like kettles of water into which dry ice has been introduced secretly so that the resultant boiling and bubbling come as a shock to those

who behold the phenomenon. It was all too much a conspiracy of silence. Of course I knew I was an outsider but
even so . . . Why on earth should Alice throw a fit over the
Latimers having a baby—scarcely an event that concerned
her—and still endure with nonchalance the passing of an
opportunity such as an appearance in Gordon Kearnes'
play would have given her?

I couldn't answer that. It baffled me. I went to bed.

Chris called me in the morning. So did Alice. So also
did Molly Dunbar. Chris wanted to know whether or not
I'd decided to change over to the Annice part. I said that
I had. He said, "Thank God!" as though he meant it and
hung up fast as if afraid I'd change my mind. Neither Alice
nor Molly wanted anything but a re-hash of the night-before's events. I obliged them.

I had one more telephone call before lunch and this
one, surprisingly, came from Nola Powers. She was all
graciousness, her voice bland as honey. She was begging
a favor from me, a tremendous favor. Probably I didn't
know—(I hadn't)—that Mr. Kearnes was very much dissatisfied with the Y theater? It was too small, and disap-
pointingly equipped, and most unfortunately not available
for all the rehearsals that would be necessary if the play
was to be ready in a little less than five weeks. He had
taken up the matter with the Chamber of Commerce and
arrangements had been made to lease the Olympia—did I
know where that was?

Of course I did. The Olympia was an eight hundred-seat
theater that, once in use almost exclusively for vaudeville
and stock, had, with their passing, degenerated into a
third-run movie house. Just recently it had been closed for
redecoration but no re-opening date had been announced.
I admitted I knew of the theater, from the outside at least.

Then would I come with her this afternoon on a tour
of inspection? Rehearsals would begin *there* tonight—oh,

didn't I know? How criminally careless of someone! Chris, she supposed, but the poor lamb was so busy that we must forgive him! It had probably slipped his mind. Oh, and while she was on the subject, she just must take time to tell me how enchanted she was to know that I would play Annice. It was a lovely, lovely part—she'd longed to do it herself—and it was delightful to feel it was in safe hands. (If that was a compliment for me, it was also a slap at Alice.) She was very happy about it.

I, being not so happy, thanked her as politely as possible and then asked bluntly why, if the first rehearsal were to be held at the Olympia that night, she couldn't wait till then to see the theater.

She sighed, audibly patient. I didn't understand, she said firmly. It was a little difficult to explain. Like all artists, she was exceedingly sensitive to places, and strange surroundings were apt to have a deleterious effect upon her art. That, of course, must not be allowed to happen. Not here—not now. "I," she announced throatily, "have come back to Nashiona possessed of a certain reputation which it is imperative that I uphold. I need a chance to acclimate myself in solitude, to throw my senses open to receive the innermost vibrations of the theater, to learn and understand its hidden secrets—"

There was a lot more of this sort of blah but eventually, for lack of breath or subject matter, she was silent and I, in that silence, found to my horror that I was agreeing meekly to her proposed tour of the Olympia.

I was furious with myself as soon as the thing was said, but there was nothing to do about it. Nola Powers was voluble with thanks and it was settled that we should meet that afternoon at the theater, I having declined, rather brusquely, her invitation to come down to the hotel for lunch.

The time of our meeting was set for three and it was nearly half past before I reached the Olympia. One of Father's unscheduled weddings had occurred to upset my plans and I hadn't been able to reach Miss Powers at the hotel in time to warn her.

I was breathless and apologetic when I hurried into the lobby of the theater, but I needn't have been. There was no one in sight but the janitor who was dabbing polish on the metal of the outer doors. He was an oldish man, surly and suspicious, and he gave truculent answers to my questions. Naw, he hadn't seen no one around—certainly not no lady. Yes, he'd been around all day—morning, too—in and out and he hadn't seen a blasted soul. Naw, he didn't stay in one spot polishing that blasted brass all day, but he'd been at it quite a spell now, save when he'd just stepped into the restaurant next door for a cuppa cawfee. Naw, he didn't think the telephone hadda rung; if it hadda, likely he'd answered it.

It was very peculiar but then so were most things connected with the Little Theater just now. Well, I could wait—for a while at least. I stepped boldly into the lobby, met the janitor's frown with my best smile. Did he mind? It was more comfortable inside.

Naw, he didn't mind. It was all one to him what I did. He had his own work to do and if I got in his way he'd tell me so.

With this gracious permission I retreated to where one of the radiators promised a little heat and stood there, my eyes on the glassed entrance doors through which Nola Powers might be expected to appear. I supposed it was the way of genius to be late for appointments. True I, too, had been late. . . .

I grew weary after a while. The janitor finished his brass and took himself off on other errands and I was alone. I moved down to stand beside the entrance doors but Nola wasn't visible and there was nothing else to see. The theater had been built at a time when it was anyone's guess in which direction Nashiona would grow and the Olympia's builders had guessed wrong. It now stood in a warehouse district. Cheap hotels and cheaper restaurants surrounded it and its audiences were drawn quite frankly from that class of people who scorned to pay the "forty cents and tax" price of the first-run theaters and were willing to wait for their pictures. One visit there, during my noviciate in town, had been enough for me. The place had been poorly lighted and smelly, the screen a flickering disgrace. The seat to which I'd been ushered had been broken and sagging; I was suspicious of the probability of mice, or their big brothers, rats; while high overhead the tireless dance of two creatures, which could have been none other than those anomalies of the animal kingdom, bats, had appalled me. My first visit had been my last.

Now, something, perhaps the influx of the soldiers, had moved the management of the theater to clean up and, on the face of it, they had done excellently. The lobby smelled of paint and soap suds. Brass shimmered softly, plate glass glittered. Even the heavy ropes, that looped through metal posts served to divide and control crowds, were new.

I became interested and forgot the recalcitrant Nola Powers. Back of the lobby, there had been, I remembered, a spacious foyer. Had that, too, been touched and renovated? I pushed through the glassed doors, opaque with new hangings.

It had. The foyer was wide and gracious. Dim lights, amber, bloomed above the exit doors and revealed the splendor of new carpets, mirrors, davenports and tables. Even the leather of the swinging doors, once shabby and tattered, had been replaced.

Not so bad, I thought. The Olympia, old as it was reported to be, had responded well to kindness. Now, if they'd just replaced those broken and disreputable seats—

To make certain of that, it was necessary to enter the body of the theater. The heavy swinging doors squawked protestingly as I pushed through them—a need for oil was certainly indicated there—but save for their squawk there was no other sound. The janitor had long since vanished.

I stood at the head of the main aisle waiting for my eyes to grow accustomed to seeing. Except for lights above the exits and, in the box ceilings, the theater was completely dark. A curtain of midnight velvet blotted out the stage opening and similar curtains formed the backgrounds for the double boxes that were placed at balcony level on either side. Before me the semi-circles of seats glimmered whitely in proud new dust covers.

It was the dust covers that really brought me into the theater. I was suspicious of them. I wondered if they covered new seats or only a multitude of old sins. Six, seven, eight—eight seats down and on the left—that surely had been the seat I'd occupied on that never to be forgotten visit. If it still were broken—I walked briskly down the aisle.

It wasn't. It was obviously new, the latest thing in theater seats, and comfortable enough so that, out of inertia, I stayed right where I was, sitting in it: there was no law I had to wait for Miss Powers on my feet. Besides I was tired.

Gradually my eyes grew accustomed to the darkness. I could see the polished top of the grand piano, the brass rail that guarded the orchestra pit. On the fronts of the box details of ornate carving showed. I tipped my head to gaze upward at the great central chandelier and the carved and painted ceiling. No bats today, thank heaven. Perhaps the cleaning process had done away with them too. Or perhaps they were merely sleeping, most probably in the huge central chandelier. Unlighted it ought to make a wonderful home for bats.

The thought was horrid. I shivered and sought hastily for distraction. I found it at once. The curtains that backed the box to my left were billowing outward in visible motion.

I don't know why that in itself should have shocked me so, but for some reason or other it did. Cold ran suddenly down my backbone like the tracing of an icy finger. I was conscious of my mouth's dryness, that I was clutching my purse with a death grip even while my good sensible brain protested that it was nothing, no more than a draft; the janitor was around somewhere. He must have opened a door and the resulting swoop of air . . .

My eyes hurt with their anxious staring. The curtains were still again but it was some moments before I found it possible to relax, even to draw a free breath.

I forced myself to look away. I told myself not to be a fool. There was a perfectly logical explanation for that movement of the curtains—there had to be. What was the sense of being afraid? There was nothing here of which to be afraid.

Or was there? The words and their conclusion were brave but just the same I felt unaccountably jumpy. The palms of my hands were wet. Why? I didn't know. Unless it was the general eeriness I of the place. If there was anything spookier in the world, I thought, than an empty theater in the daytime, it was an empty church at night. Both gave you a sense of space, of brooding vastness; of dark and secret places filled with the hideous possibilities of the unknown. Sounds in the tremendousness of their silences were apt to be magnified beyond proportion to their importance, that I knew. . . .

Was I hearing a sound?

Suddenly I was on my feet. This was ridiculous. Nola Powers or no Nola Powers, I wasn't going to stay here a minute longer and be frightened to death. Let someone else explore her old theaters with her—I was bowing out and that right now.

It was unfortunate though, that I thought it necessary to pause at the aisle head for one last glance at the source of my fear. For this time there could be no mistake about it. The curtains were moving again and between their darkness I caught the blurred pallor of what must most certainly be a face. . . .

It was too much. I turned and fled. Back in the lobby, the janitor had resumed his polishing. He vouchsafed only the briefest of glances to my going.

5

A quarter of a block's fast walking brought me back to my senses. It was half dusk now. Neon signs were stabbing the twilight with their shafts of clear color; on the corner of Meredith and Seventh, busses from the airport were unloading their night's cargo of soldiers, free of the post, on pass. One or two, recognizing me, spoke but I was in no mood for fortifying army morale. I said, "Hello!" and hurried on.

One thing of which I was determined was this: I was through doing favors for Nola Powers. Nashiona wasn't my town; its Little Theater was mine only in the sense of adoption. The bonds of courtesy and obligation could be stretched too thin. From now on let someone else be sensitive to them.

The house was dark and lonesome when I reached it. Father wouldn't be home for dinner; he never was. I went around flicking on lights—which I needed badly for moral stiffening—and reflected that short of a miracle we never saw one another any more. Father was so busy taking care of soldiers and seeing to their wants that his own daughter went neglected and unsuccored.

I'd worked myself up into a fine state of gloom by the time I'd heated soup and cut a grapefruit. I wasn't hungry, anyway, and what was the good of cooking an elaborate meal for one person? None that I could see.

I carried my tray into the living room, lighted a fire in the fireplace and pulled a big chair close enough so that I could put my feet on the fender—we had a fender, thank goodness; it was one of my reasons for taking the house.

The fire crackled and I sipped my soup and let myself go all out for melancholy and self pity. Perhaps I wouldn't even go to the rehearsal that evening. That would show them—what, I didn't know, but something. Here I was, slated for the name part of *The Good Woman,* and nobody's thought it important to notify me of the change of place for rehearsal. That I knew anyway was thanks to none of them. Very well, then—officially I didn't know and I wouldn't go. It would serve them right.

The Dunbars called at seven. Molly was as excited as a seven-year-old with Christmas in the immediate offing. Darling, where had I been all day? She'd tried and tried to call me. She and Pete would pick me up just before seven-thirty. Did I know that Chris wanted her for Lisette and that they'd changed the place of rehearsal? Of course I didn't—how could I? She was too silly. That was what she'd wanted to call me about.

She was still excited when they came to get me, thrilled almost past coherence with the prospect of playing Lisette. "I don't care if it's a big part or a little one," she said, her dark curls bobbing with earnestness. "I haven't any patience with these people who don't want anything but leads. Besides, I'd take anything—even the maid with two entrances—to be in this play. Pete's in it and you and everybody—I just couldn't bear being left out!"

There were plenty of parking places near the Olympia—not much of anything happens in that neighborhood after night. The theater itself showed only a single dim light in the ticket office. We had to try all the entrance doors before discovering that the one farthest to our left was open.

"Isn't this fun?" demanded Molly as she skipped into the lobby. "Just think—a hamburger joint next door and a bar on the corner if the boys think they have to have a drink once in a while!"

Fun, I thought drearily, following her, wasn't the word for it. The foyer was as I'd seen it in the afternoon—amber bulbs at the exit doors—but two of the table lamps also were lighted and they shed a reassuring glow over the emptiness. I felt better in spite of myself.

"Fun!" said Molly ecstatically and pushed open the leather swinging doors.

Here, in the innermost core of the theater, there was light—plenty of it. The dark stage curtain had been raised. The footlights were on and they illuminated a shabby interior set, relic, I suspected, of long ago vaudeville days, within whose triple walls a row of straight wooden chairs were stiffly aligned.

Such members of the cast as were present occupied front row seats. Chris Latimer, cigarette smoke curling whitely above his head, was leaning against the orchestra rail. On the stage, far to one side, Gordon Kearnes sat at a small table. His black hair was disheveled. He was writing busily.

Apparently we were the last to arrive. Automatically I checked over the list—Rita, Molly, myself, Pete, Mark Kerrigan, Johnny Forrester, Victor Jameson and Ross Langdon. All present and accounted for. Of course there was Nola Powers but you couldn't expect royalty to be on time, I thought grimly. We'd only to wait long enough and she'd make her proper entrance.

As though our coming was a signal, Gordon Kearnes shuffled his papers together and stood up, peering outward, trying to pierce the glare of the footlights.

"It's seven-thirty, Latimer," he said querulously. "What are you waiting for? Is everyone here?"

Chris didn't even turn his head. He contemplated his cigarette and there was an ugly set to his mouth, "All but Miss Powers," he said shortly.

I suppose having a play put on is a trying experience for the author. Certainly Gordon Kearnes seemed to find it so. He proceeded to give way to hysteria and not very prettily.

"Well, damn it, where is she?" he exploded. "That's your job, Latimer, notifying your people. You can't expect me to oversee every petty detail—I've got too much to do. You called her, didn't you?"

"I did not." Chris's voice sounded serene but his eyes were not. "The only communication I intend to hold with the lady will be when she's here on my stage taking my direction. The rest of it's up to you."

Kearnes sputtered. "But, damn it all, man—"

"Up to you," Chris repeated evenly. "You brought her here. I had nothing to do with it."

I think Gordon Kearnes was dangerously near to apoplexy at that. He opened his mouth, thought better of it, and then said in what was almost a squawk, "All right—all right. But you're wasting time. You can get started, can't you?—while I'm calling her!" and, distractedly yanking at his hair, scuttled off the stage and out of sight.

Chris stepped on his cigarette as though it had been a worm.

"All right," he said softly, "we *will* get started. We're going to read this whole play through first, checking for mistakes in the script. After that, if there's time, we'll run through the first act to note down positions and entrances. Here are your scripts."

Mine was the first handed out, but Chris stopped me as I moved to climb the narrow flight of steps that led from the right side of the orchestra pit to the stage. "Just a minute, Mary. I've something more to say and perhaps it's just as well if that chattering jackanapes doesn't hear it. It's about this play. It's going to be a rush job—you all know that. We're going to have to rehearse like hell to get it ready for the opening date—five weeks from today. If any of you doesn't realize that, he or she'd better turn in his or her part right now."

He waited a second. No one moved.

"All right—I'll take it for granted you all understand the situation and are agreeable. Now, there's something else. This is a new play and a pretty damn good one if my judgment means anything and I think it ought to. But it's a play that's in a state of flux. Nothing about it is set or settled yet. Moreover we've got the author here to complicate matters and he's paying the bills so he's more or less got the whiphand. You've all got to expect changes—lines cut out, new ones added, business changed at a moment's notice. You've got to be ready for whatever happens. Some of the changes you'll understand, some may not make sense to you. But that mustn't make any difference. Keep your mouths shut and do what you're told." He stopped then and for the first time smiled. "You see," he said confidentially, "you're my players—this is my Little Theater—and it's up to you to show a bunch of lousy professionals what you can do."

Mark Kerrigan said, "Ya-ay! That's the old pep talk, gang!" and Pete said, "Attaboy, Chris! We're with you!" But Chris wasn't listening. His smile had disappeared into a frown. "There's just one other thing," he said slowly. "About Nola—Nola Powers—"

What that one thing was, we never heard. Gordon Kearnes reappeared on the stage. He was mopping at his forehead with a handkerchief. He said fussily, "She's not at the hotel. I've called and called. Her key is at the desk. No one recalls seeing her—"

"She's probably on her way here," Chris said imperturbably. "That is, if she knew about it."

It was time for my nickel's worth. "Oh, she knew all right," I said and then almost bit my tongue silencing it. Why couldn't I keep still? Nola Powers was nothing to me.

Nobody seemed curious as to why I'd chosen to speak with such authority. Gordon Kearnes *did* give me a rather penetrating glance, but Chris only said, "Then in that case she'll probably be here. All right—on the stage, everyone! Have you all pens or pencils? Mary, you've got the opening speech."

The opening speech—from the thickness of the script handed me I rather thought I must have the closing one and all that went between as well. Hastily I subsided into a chair and fumbled the papers open. I said brilliantly, "Oh—ah—'Oh, Lisette, is that you, dear? Come in for a moment. There's something we must talk about. I've just heard a most distressing piece of news. Roselle's going to have a baby.'"

Gordon Kearnes jumped to his feet.

"Just a minute, Miss—oh, yes—Miss Thorpe. Now, that's a very important speech, you know. It sets the mood for the entire play—gives you the key to Annice's character. You must put into it the whole essence of the woman—the velvet smoothness of her voice that only serves to cloak the iron inflexibility of her will. Try it again, will you, dear?—And this time see if you can't get into the spirit of the woman herself—"

Chris cut him off.

"No spirits tonight, Kearnes. We're reading for mistakes. We'll save the spirits for Friday if it's all the same to you."

It wasn't all the same to Kearnes—that was evident—but he subsided, cowed for the moment. Something like a flash of triumph lit Chris's eyes as he turned back to us.

"All right, Molly."

Molly read Lisette's line—"Annice, who in the world told you that?"—all in one flustered breath like a child confronted with a new primer. Gordon Kearnes groaned aloud and Molly, jumping nervously, let her sides slip rustling to the floor. Chris's eyes flicked in my direction. I read the next speech with neither spirit nor intelligence.

Again Gordon Kearnes groaned dismally. Chris looked at him coldly. "Are you ill, Kearnes?" he asked dangerously. "Or is it merely hearing your own lines read for the first time? Because if it is I'm inclined to wonder at the effect they'll have upon our audiences—"

Beside me, Johnny Forrester was hugging himself and chortling, "Oh, frabjous day! Calloo, callay! I wouldn't have missed this, not for six hundred dollars!"

I would. Definitely. It went on like this for seven more pages, Gordon Kearnes articulate with agony and Chris grimly determined to keep control while the rest of us stumbled along as best we could. With the seventh page came Nola Powers' entrance. There was no Nola. Chris turned and surveyed the body of the theater, empty except for Alice Wilson. Chris said, "Miss Powers!" and his voice grated.

There was no answer.

Chris slapped down his script. "Miss Powers is not here," he said obviously. "Alice, do you mind reading for us until she comes?"

Gordon Kearnes was on his feet at once, his face a mask of pure horror. "No, no! My God, no! She'd never stand for that—never! You don't understand—"

Chris's voice was unfriendly.

"We've got to do something," he pointed out unnecessarily. "I can't keep this group sitting around waiting for her forever."

"I know—I know," Gordon Kearnes was mopping his brow again. "I don't understand it—she promised me

there'd be no tricks. Perhaps I'd better go and telephone
again—"

"Perhaps you had," Chris agreed coldly. "We'll wait for
you." He raised his voice a little. "Take a break, everybody.
Thanks just the same, Alice—I'll give you a raincheck on
that reading!"

It didn't mean much then, but later on, I was to remember those words of Chris's with a shudder.

Johnny Forrester was drawing me to my feet. "Come
on—have a smoke and a promenade. These damned kitch-
en chairs are harder than rock to sit on!"

Obediently I stood up. He lit a cigarette for me and we
moved back stage to stand by the wide double doors that
centered the set.

"How'd you like it, huh?" Johnny was asking. "If Gordon thinks he'll get away with that temperamental stuff
around Chris, he's nuts. Chris is about as malleable as
granite."

I said, "Uh-huh!" but I was only half listening. For
Gordon Kearnes was back and this time he'd dropped all
his affectations. He looked honestly worried. He said,
"Chris, I can't get her and I don't understand it. She's not
in her room."

"He ought to try someone else's room!" said Johnny in
my ear.

"No one's seen her since morning. I don't like it, I tell
you. I'm afraid something's happened to her."

I had an uneasy feeling that perhaps this was my cue.
After all, there'd been that rather inexplicable performance that afternoon. If, by any chance, Gordon Kearnes
was right and something *had* happened to her—

"Wait!" I said making up my mind. "There's something
I'd better tell you." Starting down toward the footlights,
I at once went into a sort of ballet dance of preposterous
attitudes from which Johnny rescued me.

"What the—?"

"I stepped on something," I said with what dignity remained to me. As if to confirm my words there was a rattle into the tin trough of the footlights.

"You dropped something!" Johnny said gleefully.

"I did not!" I retorted. "I tell you I stepped on something that rolled—"

"Here!" Chris reached into the footlights and thrust something into my hand. "Now, what were you going to say?"

Unfortunately, for the moment, I couldn't say a word. I just stood there and looked at the thing Chris had given me. It was round and golden, the cylindrical case for a lipstick, and on it, in tiny diamonds, were the initials "N.P."

"Well?" Chris sounded impatient. "What is it? Your make-up can wait."

"It's not my make-up!" Words returned to me in a rush. "Look! It's hers—Nola Powers'. It means she *was* here after all!"

"Nola's—good God! Let me see!" It was Gordon Kearnes shouldering in, bending over my outstretched hand. "Yes, it's hers right enough—one she always carried. I've seen it a hundred times."

He put out his hand to take it but Chris was ahead of him. Chris had it, was turning it over and over. "Well," he said at last, grudgingly, "if it's really hers, I suppose it does prove that she was here sometime. But when?"

"But that's what I'm trying to tell you!" I knew I was incoherent but I couldn't help it. Some vestige of the strange unreasoning panic that had touched me in the afternoon was upon me again. Once more I was afraid and once more I didn't know why. "She—Miss Powers—called me just before lunch. She wanted me to meet her here—at the theater—at three o'clock—she wanted to look around. I came and I waited and—and she never came!"

"What?" It was a concerted question, spoken as by one throat, for now they had all drawn near and were listening. The strength of it appalled me. "She never came," I repeated desperately. "But she was here." For evidence I pointed to the lipstick.

"Yes," Chris said quietly. "It looks as though she'd been here. The question is, where is she now?"

No one could tell him. No one knew.

We stood awkwardly, watching Chris manipulate the lipstick. Slowly he separated it into its two parts, looked at the stub of scarlet grease, as slowly replaced the cover. Gordon Kearnes' hand was eager, reaching for it, but Chris, eying him coldly, returned the cylinder to me. "We'll let Mary keep it," he said quietly. "She found it. But now I think the rest of us had better I have a look around."

There was a blank little silence. Then Mark Kerrigan spoke. "But, my God, Chris, what are you getting at? Finding that lipstick doesn't mean one single damn thing. How'd you know from that Nola was here this afternoon?"

"I don't," Chris said levelly. "That's what I think we'd better try to find out. See if you can rouse the janitor, will you, Johnny? Try the furnace room."

We were uneasy, waiting. We couldn't help it. We didn't talk. We lit cigarettes and crushed them out, and watched the lobby doors as though in hope that, even now, a belated Nola Powers would make an appearance.

She didn't.

Johnny came back and we turned to him with the relief that prospective action, in moments of stress, can bring. The janitor was with him and the janitor was plainly not pleased at having been forced to quit his comfortable fire. His little pig eyes were hostile as he replied to Chris's questions.

Naw, he hadn't seen nobody that afternoon. Oh, there'd been some woman come in— I stood forth. Yeah, her. She'd told some yarn about expecting to meet somebody there but so far'd he'd seen nobody but her come. Naw, he didn't know just how long she'd stuck around. Quite a while, he thought, for he'd plumb forgot all about her and then all of a sudden she'd gone shooting past him like a bat out of hell. Acted like she'd been scared outa her wits. She was the only one he'd seen.

"I was here about an hour," I interpolated. "And the reason he didn't see me was because I waited in here!"

The janitor ignored me completely. He had other weightier problems on his mind. Chris's proposal that he help them search the theater had no appeal. Pressed, he admitted grudgingly that he s'posed it was possible he might have missed seeing someone come in—always s'posing that anyone *had*. He'd been "in and out" and the theater was a big place.

"It don't make no sort of sense to me though," he whined. "Looking for someone you ain't sure ever was here. Where'd you figure on starting?"

"Anywhere," Chris said. "It doesn't matter. Perhaps you're right and I'm making a fool out of myself but I'm not taking any chances. I don't like the idea of finding her lipstick here. Turn on some lights, will you? All the lights you've got."

As the janitor moved reluctantly away, Molly Dunbar said a little breathlessly, "But every woman carries a lipstick, Chris. And there must be lots who have the same initials."

Chris only shrugged. "Could be," he said briefly. "You girls stay here. We'll make this as quick as possible."

I made up my mind to the inevitable. "Wait a minute, Chris," I said. "I've something else to tell you." And told it. The thing I hadn't told before. The reason why I'd been seen leaving the theater like a "bat outa hell." The incident of the swaying curtain and the pallid peering face. "It was from that box," I finished, pointing. "Perhaps you'd better start there."

My story was received in the sort of polite silence that chills. It was obvious that no one believed me. Chris said, "Well, yes—that's interesting. Thanks, Mary. We'll look around. Come on, fellows. We'll take the balcony first."

Disgruntled, I perched on the stage edge and watched them "take" the balcony. It wasn't what I called a search at all. The central chandelier was lighted now and it was possible to watch them walking up and down, glancing cursorily into the boxes and behind the rows of seats. Presently they disappeared through a door that led to back stage regions and we heard the clatter of their footsteps on the stairs. Then nothing but silence.

"Well!" said Alice Wilson in a long drawn breath of complete and utter scorn. "If this isn't the most idiotic performance I've ever heard of! What's got into Chris? It's your fault, too, Mary Thorpe! What in the world made you think you had to inspire this crusade—"

"I didn't," I protested. "I only found the lipstick—"

"You only found the lipstick!" Alice flung at me. Her eyes were cold with venom. "So you did—so what? So Nola Powers is temporarily out of circulation and isn't that too bad and what difference does that make to you? She'll be back—don't worry. No danger of her disappearing permanently. Faces in boxes and curtains that move—I never heard such rubbish!"

"It isn't rubbish," I said feebly. "It's true—every bit of it."

"I don't see why you should blame Mary," Rita Carstairs said reasonably. "She was frightened this afternoon and no wonder—a theater's a gloomy place when there's no one in it. And I don't quite see what else Chris could have done—once Nola's lipstick was found. It was a gesture he had to make."

"Fiddlesticks!" said Alice but more calmly. "There may be some excuse for Mary but there's none at all for Chris. He knows what Nola's like!"

I was grateful. I got up from my lowly seat on the steps and walked across the stage. "I suppose we are being silly," I admitted. "Wouldn't you think they'd be through down there pretty soon?"

"I've never been below stairs in a theater," Rita said placidly, "but I imagine there are lots of places to look—dressing rooms—cellars—"

"Do you remember the *Phantom of the Opera?*" Molly asked with a gurgle. "I saw it once—when I was quite small but I've never forgotten it. That theater had cellars under it, and caverns, and an underground lake or something, and that awful skeleton-y thing murdered people and then drowned them—"

"Oh, stop it, for heaven's sake!" Alice was off again. "Haven't you any better sense than to talk about skeletons now?"

The edge of hysteria was so patent in her voice that Molly sat open-mouthed. Alice saw it, tried to smile; it was a sad affair. "Sorry, Molly, but this ridiculous business has my teeth on edge."

"That's because there's nothing for us to do but wait," Rita said soothingly. "I hate to just sit myself—if it's only for a taxi. Why don't we look around a little ourselves? Then when the men come back, we'll be done with it and we can all go to work again."

It sounded sensible. Rita was the sort that did make sensible suggestions. Calm and reasonable and not easily ruffled. Molly had jumped to her feet. "Let's! What a splendid idea! Where'll we start?"

"There's the stage," I suggested but without enthusiasm. I had no stomach for this.

"There's nothing to look around here," Alice grumbled.

There wasn't. Behind the flimsy canvas walls of the set that had been erected for our convenience, the stage stretched vast and empty. The picture screen had been pulled high into the flies. Against the brick back-wall stood two huge papier mâché vases. There was a wooden platform and a pile of canvas to the right; two step ladders, some empty paint buckets, a couple of sawhorses and a square wooden box to the left.

"There's nothing here," Alice said again.

"I read a story once," Molly offered brightly. "They tied a body to a sandbag or a sandbag to a body and they pulled it 'way up high—

"You and your stories!" Alice snapped. She kicked viciously at one of the papier mâché vases and it wobbled. She straightened it. "This is absolutely the limit! I'm going to find Chris and the others and tell them exactly what I think of them."

"There's that box," Rita said speculatively. "Perhaps we ought to look there."

The box. With one movement we turned to stare at it. It was big and square, a packing box. Light boards covered its top. A roll of black paper leaned against it.

"My mother used to pack blankets away in a box like that," I said at last. There was no point in the remark. It only covered an awkward silence.

"Well, Nola's no blanket," Alice sniffed. "That box isn't big enough to hold her—I can tell that from here!"

There was another silence. Then Molly said, "Well, what are we waiting for? If she can't be in this, why don't we look and be done with it? *I'm* certainly not afraid!"

She wasn't. Or if she was, the fear was well hidden. There was bravado in the swing of her brief skirt. She lifted off one of the light boards.

The box was taller than we'd guessed. Molly was tiny but its top stood even with her breast. She lifted another board, bent her curly black head— Then suddenly, to our horror, began to scream. And kept on screaming. And screaming . . .

Nola Powers was found.

6

It was Alice who made certain. She ran to Molly, pushed her aside and then bent her own head for one swift glance into the depths of the box. When she turned away, her face was green.

"It's Nola all right. Call the men, somebody. She's dead. Her face—oh, my God, her face . . ."

But there was no need to call the others. They had heard the screams and now came storming up the stairs, Pete Dunbar in the lead. He caught his wife and held her, sobbing now, against his shoulder while he glared at us. "What the hell's going on up here? What have you been doing to her?"

Again it was Alice who answered. "Nothing," she said dully. "It's just that—that Nola's been found. Molly found her. In there." She gestured toward the box.

I'm not certain just what did take place then. My own legs gave way suddenly and I found myself reaching for a chair. Blackness surged from somewhere over my eyes and I shut them for a moment. I remember saying to my-self, "You mustn't faint—you mustn't faint. Hang on to yourself, you little fool. Nobody's got time to bother with you—not now—"

Blessedly it worked. When I opened my eyes again, it was to see with a clarity of vision that surprised me. My moment of weakness had gone unnoticed. The others were too preoccupied with their own. I glanced about me. Rita Carstairs, shocked for once out of placidity, was sitting upon one of the sawhorses, very stiffly and straightly; mechanically she tore her handkerchief into shreds; her eyes were wide and fixed as those of a sleepwalker. Molly still shivered against Pete's shoulder, while Alice Wilson, trying to light a cigarette, was having difficulty bringing match and tobacco together.

The men made a little huddle about the packing box, all except Pete who still scowled over Molly's head and Ross Langdon, more of a stranger even than I in this milieu, who leaned against the two-by-four that braced a canvas flat, jangling the coins in his pockets and whistling a soundless little tune between his teeth. It was Chris who turned from the box and its contents first. He looked white and sick. "She's been strangled, I think. You girls better get out of here—she's not a pretty sight. Mark, if you'll help me—"

"Just a minute." It was Ross Langdon. "Help you what? What are you going to do?"

It was the wrong note to take with Chris. Czar of his little kingdom, Chris brooks no interference. "Do?" he repeated haughtily. "Why, get her out of there, of course. What'd you think?"

Langdon eyed him levelly. "I think I wouldn't." His voice was lazy but steel underlay it.

Chris's eyebrows rose sharply. "What do you mean?"

Ross Langdon took a while answering. He lit a cigarette, drew in a lungful of smoke. Then, "Any of you ever mixed up in a murder before?" he asked quietly. "Never mind—it was a foolish question. All right—what I'm trying to call to your attention is that most police forces prefer the body of the corpse in *statu primus,* if you take my meaning."

Chris's anger sloughed away. "The police," he repeated vaguely. "Oh, yes. The police."

"The police?" This time it was Alice on a high-pitched note. She dropped the cigarette she'd just managed to light, crushed it beneath an impatient foot. "You mean that they'll come down here and ask questions—that we'll have to answer them—"

"Of course they will," Johnny Forrester said impatiently. "Good lord, Alice—use your head. This is no damned rehearsal. This is the real thing. The curtain's going up. This is the *show!*"

"We'd better be notifying them," Ross Langdon said quietly. "Latimer, will you—"

But Chris failed to answer. He just stood there, staring straight ahead of him. He looked dazed.

"I'll go," Johnny offered. "There's a telephone in the box office. Anybody else I ought to call? How about a lawyer? Why don't I get Ed Grimes down here too? He'd look after us—"

But Langdon shook his head. "Better not. See what they have to say first."

It was queer, I thought, how simply he was taking over, queer that we listened and obeyed. Still, he was the only one entirely detached in this business. Presumably all of the others had known Nola in those far-away days when she had lived in Nashiona, had known her well. Gordon Kearnes, too, then and later on in New York. Even I had had contact, passing though it had been. Only Ross Langdon stood apart. The janitor, too, of course, I thought with a sudden giggle, catching a glimpse of that glowering individual, hovering indecisively on the outskirts, one of us now, unwilling and by accident. Surely he couldn't have known Nola Powers—

Ross Langdon was speaking again, taking charge. "We don't have to stay here, you know. Why not move out to the foyer? There's nothing we can do now except wait for the police and we'll be more comfortable away from—from all this."

It *was* better in the foyer. We drew chairs and davenports together in a wide circle, lighted all the lamps. Tension lessened. By the time that Johnny appeared to report that the police would be right over, we were seated, all but the janitor who continued to prowl restlessly in the background.

It was Rita who asked the question we all wanted to. "The police—when they do come—what'll they do? Will they keep us here all night? Arrest us?"

Ross Langdon was reassuring. "Oh, I hardly think so. They'll ask questions—fingerprint you, perhaps. I don't know anything about your force here but I don't imagine they have a great deal of experience with murder. Nashiona isn't like Chicago or New York. One murder a year—would that be the average?"

"Just about," Mark Kerrigan said. "Two at the outside."

"Well, then," Langdon said and spread his hands. "I doubt if we'll have much to fear."

Comforting though the thought might be, it seemed to set Gordon Kearnes off. Up to now he had said nothing, following in the wake of the others, his brow blackened, his fingers twitching nervously. Now he went up like a skyrocket. "One murder a year—my God, think of it!—and that one had to be Nola! I told her not to come here but she wouldn't listen—oh, no, she had some game of her own on—she laughed at me. Well, she won't laugh any more and what's going to happen now?—that's what I want to know! Capper and Stein will shy off—wait and see. They've never been too keen on this play and without Nola—it's just my damnable luck this had to happen! If she'd listened to me—but no—what does she care if my play is ruined—"

"Oh, shut up, Kearnes!" Mark Kerrigan growled. "Forget your damn play! Nola's dead—I don't suppose she got herself murdered just to spite you!"

"What we ought to do," Molly piped up unexpectedly, "is try to find out who murdered her and why."

Help came from an unexpected angle. "I betcha I know!" It was the janitor, stilled for the moment from his prowling, his malignant little eyes fixed on me. "It was her! I told you she came shooting outa here this afternoon like a bat outa hell. She had plenty a time to kill t'other one 'tween the time she came and the time she left."

"Nonsense!" This was Chris, struggling up through the heavy fog of his own bewilderment to my defense. "Miss Thorpe barely knew the woman who was murdered. You told us over and over that Miss Powers hadn't been here—"

"Well, she was, wasn't she?" That was unanswerable. "She mighta sneaked in past me or something—"

"Listen!" said Rita Carstairs in a tense low voice. "Sirens!"

"Sure," said Johnny Forrester from the door where he'd gone to stand. "Sirens. They never travel without the blasted things. Three or four blocks to go and they roar along wide open. Remember the time the Dillinger gang held up the bank here and they roared up, sirens screaming, and got picked off and lined up by the lookout outside with the machine gun? The Nashiona police—bah! They're nothing to worry about!"

But I wasn't so sure, once I'd seen them. They appeared numberless as the sands of the shore when they came piling in through the lobby. Actually I believe there were only eight—a photographer, a fingerprint man, a man in an ordinary business suit who was addressed as Lieutenant Dreyer, two patrolmen who immediately took up unobtrusive posts at the doors, and a stout gray-haired man whom the others called "Chief." The coroner and a

short redheaded man hailed as "Doc" arrived a few seconds
later.

They didn't waste much time on us. Lieutenant Dreyer
in the lead said, "All right—where's the body? In there?
Someone come along and show us. You the janitor here?
You'll do—you ought to know your way around. Who's in
charge here? You—oh, Latimer—yeah, I remember. Come
along. The rest of you stay where you are. We'll get around
to you presently."

We stayed. Conversation, under the eyes of the stal-
warts guarding the door, failed to flourish. We smoked
in silence or stared at the carpet, at the walls or at the
lamps—anywhere rather than at the faces of our fellows.
Them, we couldn't bear to see.

I kept a wary eye on my wrist watch. It was nearly
eleven o'clock and Father never reached home until after
twelve. He was none too crazy about my interest in what
he called "play acting." What was he going to think if I
didn't get home from our first real rehearsal until two or
three in the morning? And what would he say when he
learned why I was detained?

The hands slipped over another five minutes. "I'll bet
that janitor's having a heyday," I thought glumly. "I'll be
lucky if I don't find myself charged with Nola's murder
on his say-so. He'll hand me over to them all wrapped up
in a neat little parcel without a pang of compunction. Of
course Chris is there too. Perhaps he can help."

He did. I found that out the minute the police started
to interrogate us.

I say "police" but it was actually Lieutenant Dreyer. As head of the homicide department it was his job.
Chief Hanover, who sat unobtrusively in the background,
was there merely as a spectator. Or so I thought. I was
wrong. The chief, in spite of the fact that he'd been a small

groceryman before he picked off the plumiest of Nashiona's appointive jobs, was no fool. I learned that later.

One of the patrolmen had deserted his door and was producing a stenographer's notebook and pencil. "Hold your caps, everybody," I thought and felt my fingernails dent my palm, "we're taking off!"

We were. Lieutenant Dreyer eyed us—he was as weazened and bloodless as his name implied—cleared his throat and began. "We'll take your names and stories in a minute. Before that—which one of you is Thorpe?" He consulted a paper. "Mary Thorpe?"

I indicated that I was, not too enthusiastically. Lieutenant Dreyer said, "Uh-huh." This, I was to learn, was his favorite remark. With it, he ran the entire emotional gamut. His "uh-huh" was sarcastic, disbelieving, congratulatory or derisive as the mood allowed. This time it was a mere grunt and lightly passed over, but his eyes on me were shrewd and cold. "We got a statement signed by Oscar Anderson, custodian of the Olympia building, in which he states you visited this theater this afternoon. What have you got to say about it?"

I'd been expecting it but just the same it was a shock. "Could I see the paper?" I asked out of a dry throat.

"Uh-huh." He gave it to me and I read it through. It was short and to the point. Not in Oscar's language however—I had appeared "agitated," I had left "hastily."

I returned it. "It's all true enough," I said. "I *was* here. And I think his times are correct. I was late—it must have been about half past three when I came in and it was between half past four and five when I left. It was beginning to be dusk—the street signs were lit. And I'll admit the 'agitated' too—if you call being scared to death 'agitated.'"

"Uh-huh." He let that pass. "How'd you happen to come down to the theater at that time, Miss Thorpe? Your director here says that the rehearsal time was set for seven-thirty."

"Miss Powers—Nola Powers—had asked me to. She wanted to look around the theater and she didn't want to be alone."

"You knew this Nola Powers well?"

"No. I'd met her once—at the train. I'd seen her at the play tryouts, that was all."

"Uh-huh. How'd she happen to make this appointment with you if you didn't know her?"

"I don't know," I said helplessly. "I can't explain it. She might not have felt free to ask the others— I'm sorry. It's the only thing I can suggest."

I got my first taste of Chief Hanover here. He leaned out of the shadows to ask, "What do you mean—she mightn't feel free to ask the others?"

I couldn't tell him. It wasn't my story. Besides, what I actually knew was so little. . . .

"Perhaps I put it clumsily," I said. "I only meant that I'd been the one who'd met her at the train when she came. She might have thought I'd be less likely to be engaged than the others."

I don't think it went over but he grunted and retired into the shadows again. Lieutenant Dreyer took over.

"How long have you lived in Nashiona, Miss Thorpe?"

I explained that. Also who my father was and why we were here. Lieutenant Dreyer said, "Uh-huh. Before you came here, you lived where?"

I told him.

"How far's that from New York City?"

I did a little lightning calculation. "About ninety miles, I think."

"Uh-huh. Run up to New York every once in a while, did you? Often? Uh-huh. Ever run into this Nola Powers there?"

This was too much—it was worse than too much. It was ridiculous.

"Certainly not!" I said indignantly. "Nola Powers was a well-known actress. Compared to her I was—I am nobody. My interest in the theater is purely academic. I had no contacts with Miss Powers. There was no way in which I could, conceivably, have known her."

"Sure of that?"

"Of course I'm sure." I was angry now, angry and frightened. "What are you trying to do? Do you mean that you think *I* killed her? Because I didn't!"

He accepted my statement. "Miss Thorpe, according to the coroner, the woman called Nola Powers had been dead some seven or eight hours. That'd fix the time of death between three and four this afternoon which would make it fit in pretty nicely with your own time of visiting the theater, wouldn't it?"

"But," I said, "but—oh, this is too silly! Why should I kill her? What reason would I have?"

"We don't know yet. Don't fly off the handle, Miss Thorpe. We're not saying you did it—not yet. But you were in on the ground floor, so to speak. You had the opportunity."

"Listen to me," I said and this time I wasn't frightened at all. Only angry. "I'm going to tell you exactly what *did* happen this afternoon!"

I began with Nola's telephone call. Relentlessly I traced the rest of the afternoon's activities—lunch, the trip to the bank, the unscheduled wedding that had made me late. I told of my entrance into the theater lobby, my questions to Oscar Anderson and his reply that he hadn't seen anyone come in. I told of standing in the lobby until I was tired, of venturing farther into the foyer, of entering the theater auditorium. I mentioned the seat in which I'd rested. If Lieutenant Dreyer was impressed, he failed to show it. He looked thoroughly bored and only evinced interest when I produced my tale of the moving curtains and the face that had appeared so briefly between them. "That's why I left the theater in such a hurry," I finished. "That's why Mr. Anderson thought I was 'agitated.'"

I don't know whether Lieutenant Dreyer believed in the face or not but at least he asked questions about it— questions that I either couldn't answer or answered unsatisfactorily. Which box was it? The left one? Was the face a man's or a woman's? Young or old? How would I describe it? A pallid blur—featureless? That wasn't much to go on, Miss Thorpe.

"I know it," I said wretchedly. "I'm sorry but that's all I saw—really. I'm shortsighted. I suppose that's the reason."

"Uh-huh," said Lieutenant Dreyer and passed to other things all equally unsatisfactory. I admitted going home— walking. I'd met a few soldiers, spoken to them—no, I was sorry but I didn't recall their names. I met so many. I'd had supper alone. I'd been alone until the Dunbars came by for me.

That seemed to finish it so far as he was concerned. It didn't for me. It was unthinkable that they could be suspecting me of Nola's murder and yet—unless the coroner was wrong, and I prayed that he had been—she'd been killed during the hour I'd spent in the theater this afternoon. My reason for being there was weak enough and the police had only my word that we hadn't been old acquaintances and enemies, but surely—surely they couldn't think that I'd killed her! There must be some way of convincing them—

I had an inspiration.

"Look!" I said and thrust out my hands, my slender, small, five-and-a-quarter-size-glove hands. "They said she—Nola—was strangled. How could I choke anyone with hands like these? They're useless! Why, I can't even unscrew a jar of fruit or open a bottle of olives—"

"Nola Powers," said Lieutenant Dreyer incisively, "was not strangled by hands. She was stunned first and then a thin scarf was tightened about her throat. Even hands like yours could have done it!"

"But scarcely tipped her into the packing box, do you think?" Ross Langdon said unexpectedly. "Miss Thorpe is rather small. Nola Powers must have been at least three or four inches taller."

Deliberately Lieutenant Dreyer shifted in his chair to stare at him. "And who asked for your opinion?"

"No one," Langdon admitted pleasantly. "I was merely pointing out a trifle that might have escaped your notice. And while we're on the subject—not that I wish to intrude!—I'm sure you realize that it's getting late and that we're all extremely anxious to get out of this place as soon as possible. Since Miss Thorpe obviously cannot be the murderer and since one of the rest of us may very well be—" there was a gasp from someone at that—"don't you think it would be wise to leave her for a while and push on into—er—greener pastures?"

Lieutenant Dreyer had turned a deep purple. He half rose. "Why, you—you— Who the hell do you think *you* are?"

"That's right—that's right," Ross Langdon, said soothingly. "Who the hell am I? Why not talk about me for a change? I'll be glad to tell you. Name known under—Langdon, Ross. Aged thirty-five. White. Male. Blonde hair, blue eyes. Height, six feet exactly. Weight, one hundred and seventy-five. Present occupation—none. Draft classification—"

"That's enough." The spate of words had curled if not cooled the lieutenant's anger. "Maybe you're right, Mr.

Ross Langdon," he said in a purr loaded with pure venom.
"Maybe we'd be smart to look at you for a while. Maybe
if Miss Thorpe here would look at you real good, she'd
recognize your face for the one she saw I between them
box curtains. You ain't too small to have handled Nola
Powers—"

"Here—whoa up!" Langdon interrupted. "I was merely
creating a diversion—not trying to bring the entire swarm
of bees down upon my own head. As a matter of fact it
wasn't I who frightened Miss Thorpe this afternoon, nor
did I kill Nola Powers. I have the best of alibis, one I
doubt whether you'll care to challenge. But, if you believe
Miss Thorpe—and I do—someone *did* frighten her this
afternoon—someone *did* peer out between those curtains—
someone *did* kill Nola Powers. It wasn't I, but," he swung
his arm widely, "it may very well be one of these others.
You're barking up the wrong tree, Lieutenant—two wrong
trees. Try again."

I really thought Lieutenant Dreyer was going to disin-
tegrate into little pieces at that. He jumped to his feet, his
hands working, and started for Langdon. What might have
happened next, however, remains problematical. He was
stopped. By his chief who chose this moment to emerge
from his retreat among the shadows.

"Now, wait a minute—wait a minute," he said in a
slow drawl that somehow managed to be both peaceable
and commanding. "Dreyer, you go sit down. I'm ashamed
of you—letting yourself get all het up over nothing. You
cool off while I talk to this young fellow myself. Ever
play poker, Dreyer? Seems to me like you're just sticking
out your neck with a measly little four flush in your fist
while somebody else holds a full house." He turned toward
Langdon. "That right, son? You keeping some pretty good
cards dark?"

"That's right," Langdon admitted, but he was frowning. His eyes were hard and bright.

"Figured so." The chief shifted his chair an inch or two forward and folded his hands across his comfortable stomach. "Some of your biography struck me as right curious too—those parts about your name and your occupation, for example. Want to explain that a mite, son?"

Langdon seemed to make up his mind to something. He nodded. "Yes. I think so. It'll have to come out sooner or later. I'm a private detective, here in Nashiona at Miss Powers' request. I was," his mouth twisted in a bitter little smile, "hired to protect her."

"Protect her?" Gordon Kearnes' voice rose horridly in a crescendo of surprise. "Protect her from whom for God's sake?"

Ross Langdon looked at him. "If I had been able to find out that, Mr. Kearnes," He said levelly, "I can assure you that Miss Powers would not be lying back there on the stage—murdered."

He turned back to Chief Hanover, proffered a sheaf of papers which he drew from his breast pocket. "My license, credentials, all the rest of it, are here, sir. You can check them over. You'll see that my name is Langdon, right enough, and that I'm a private detective—"

For the second time Gordon Kearnes intruded himself upon the attention of those present. "A private detective," he repeated in a queer thick voice. "That's what she meant then— You're the precautions— Oh, my God—"

With that he got to his feet, stood swaying for a moment, and then fell forward.

7

It's bad enough to have to witness a woman's collapse. A man's, being unthinkable, is so much worse. Not that we had a great deal of time to consider it.

Lieutenant Dreyer, for instance, thought that he'd committed suicide. With one spring, he was beside Kearnes, feeling frantically for pulse and heart. "Get the doc—get the doc!" he bellowed. "What'd he take? Quick—someone. You—" this was to Pete Dunbar—"you sat next to him—why the hell didn't you keep your eyes open."

"Poison!" Rita Carstairs breathed—she had occupied the chair on the other side of Gordon Kearnes. "He took poison. Then—why, that'd mean that he was the one who killed Nola!"

A little stir passed over us, a stir as of relief, almost too great to be borne. Because if Gordon Kearnes were the murderer . . .

Unfortunately it was dissipated almost at once. The doctor, summoned by one of the patrolmen, sniffed away all possibility of poison. Heart, he diagnosed matter-of-factly. Too much excitement probably—no, there was no immediate danger, rest and quiet were what he needed. Stranger in town, was he? Oh, the playwright. Staying at a hotel? Well, in that case he'd advise a hospital.

He busied off to put in a call for an ambulance. We subsided into our chairs again. The nightmare, after all, had *not* been ended.

In the general shifting, I found myself next to Molly. She said, "Oh, dear, it's awful but I can't help wishing that he *had* taken poison. Then it would be all over and we could go home. Nobody really likes him—nobody'd care . . ."

Nobody, I thought savagely, barring some far away theatergoers to whom a new Gordon Kearnes play was a milestone in a theatrical season.

"I suppose," Molly was continuing wistfully, "that he *could* have been the one to kill her. Heart attacks can be faked, can't they?"

"I doubt if that one was," I said grimly. "He wouldn't want her dead. It might upset his play. Don't you remember what he said about the producers wanting Nola in it?"

"No talking there!" Lieutenant Dreyer thundered. The ambulance had come and gone, taking Gordon Kearnes with it. The lieutenant was free to devote his time to those remaining. He eyed us sternly. We stopped talking with guilty haste.

I sneaked another look at my wrist watch and groaned. It was half past twelve. At this rate it would, be morning before they let us go. *If* we ever got to go at all.

Ross Langdon was standing beside Chief Hanover. The chief, who had taken only the most perfunctory part in the Kearnes excitement, was scowling over Langdon's papers or credentials or whatever he'd called them. Now he bundled them all together and returned them to their owner.

"Look all right, son," he said mildly. "Seems like you're now in the clear. 'Course I ain't saying we won't do some pretty thorough checking but if so's you can prove you're who you say you are—"

Revolt lifted its head. "And what the hell'd that prove?" Mark Kerrigan growled. "So he's a private dick—so what?

Nola could have been his client and he could have killed her just the same!"

"I didn't say he couldn't have," the chief observed mildly. "How about it, young fellow? Seems like you ought to have an answer for that."

"I have." Ross Langdon permitted himself a wintry smile. "I met Nola powers one week before she came to Nashiona—my secretary'll verify that if you care to get in touch with her. Private detectives can't afford private feuds, Mr. Kerrigan. They're too damned hard up—at least my kind are. My agreement with Miss Powers called for two thousand dollars—and expenses. I received one thousand dollars as a retainer. The other thousand was to be paid upon her return in safety to New York."

"Sounds reasonable," the chief said almost as though he were arguing the matter with himself. "'Tain't business to kill the goose before it lays the golden eggs—if after. All right, son—you've opened up some brand new highways. Want to go a little further and tell us just what Miss Powers was scared of and why she wanted a bodyguard to protect her?"

"I'll tell you what I know," Ross Langdon said somberly. "It's not very much. Perhaps it'll make sense to some of you—it doesn't to me." He drew a long breath. "I met Nola Powers for the first time on the 28th of October when she came to my office with a card of introduction from a former client of mine for whom I'd recovered some stolen jewelry. She told me of this proposed trip to Nashiona. She told me that she didn't want to go—that she was afraid for herself—but that she could see no way out of it. Kearnes was exerting considerable pressure—"

"But that's not what he said," I interrupted impetuously. "Just a little while ago. He said that he'd thought all along it was a mistake for her to come back to Nashiona but that she'd insisted. You heard him!"

"I heard him," Ross Langdon agreed, "for what it was worth. I can only say that it didn't agree with what she'd already told me. She wanted very much to do the play—she said it was the sort of part that made an actress. She said it would do for her what *Rain* had done for Jeanne Eagels. She said that returning to Nashiona and playing the part in its tryout there was Kearnes' condition for her playing it later in New York. She told me that she was afraid to come back."

"Afraid?" Pete Dunbar repeated. He sounded honestly bewildered. "Afraid—here in Nashiona? For God's sake, why?"

"She didn't tell me. She only hinted. She—she told me something of her life here that first day." He shot a guarded glance in Chris Latimer's direction. "But that was all. She gave me to understand that she had reason to believe that she would be in actual danger if she returned. She promised to tell me more later, hinted at blackmail or something of the sort. It wasn't the kind of interview I was accustomed to have with a prospective client. If I hadn't been temporarily at loose ends, and more or less broke, I'd have turned her out of the office in short order. But she'd made it plain that she was willing to pay well for protection and, as I said before, I could use the money." He shrugged and then went on in a different tone. "On top of that she was damned attractive. She had charm, a sort of glamor—she fascinated me. I suppose the truth is I lost my head a bit. She had that effect. She dazzled you—gave you the impression that she was promising all sorts of things—and it was only after she'd gone that her enchantment wore off and you realized that all she'd promised had gone unfulfilled."

"Yes," said Chris softly. "We know."

"It was that way with me. Oh, I cursed myself roundly after she'd gone. There I was with a thousand dollar retainer fee and an additional five hundred dollars for expenses

and I'd promised to leave the next day for Nashiona, and
I hadn't the slightest idea in the world what I was to do
when I got to Nashiona, or what sort of danger I was to
look out for. I considered myself reasonably clever and yet
I hadn't been able to pin the lady down to anything definite and, poor fool that I was, I'd only that moment realized it. I tried to reach her and succeeded after two hours'
telephoning. I told her the thing was impossible: that I
couldn't leave New York, that perfect trust was imperative
between investigator and client, that I was giving up the
commission and would return her money in the morning.
She laughed at me until she realized that I was in earnest,
and then she changed completely. She begged me to go and
to go at once. She promised that she'd explain everything
once we were both in Nashiona. Her spell recaptured me.
I agreed to go."

"Uh-huh!" This was Lieutenant Dreyer. "And after you
both came? Did she keep to her part of the bargain?"

"She did not!" There was a weary sort of indifference
in Langdon's voice. "There was a wire from her waiting
for me at the hotel. In it she said that I was to make no
attempt to contact her—that it would be better if when
we met we did so as strangers. When she wanted me, she
would contact me. Under no circumstances was I to meet
the train she'd come in on. She suggested that I try for a
part in the play. That was all. I was disgusted—sore—but
what could I do? I'd let myself in for it and she was the
boss. I played along with her. I kept out of sight. Monday
night at the tryouts I saw her for the first time. She pretended not to recognize me. I'm not accustomed to having
my hands tied nor to working in the dark. I went back to
my hotel and thought it out. I wrote a note asking her to
see me. I told her I was giving up the case—whatever it
was. I told her I was returning to New York. This morning
my answer came. She called me, asked me to meet her in

the lounge at two o'clock. I was there. She didn't come. I
waited until four o'clock. Then I took a taxi to the depot
and bought a ticket for New York on tomorrow's train.
Here it is." He tossed an envelope in Dreyer's direction.
"You can check on it all you like. There must have been a
dozen people who saw me."

The two heads—the chief's and Lieutenant Dreyer's—
bent over the contents of the envelope but it was the chief
who re-folded the long slip of paper and tucked it safely
away in his pocket.

"I'll just keep charge of this," he said amiably. "Don't
mind, do you, son? You won't be needing it for a spell."

"No." The knuckles of Langdon's hands, clasped so
casually about his knee, showed white for an instant. "No.
I'm not going away—I'm staying. That fee I had from
her—I haven't earned it. I couldn't save her from whatever
it was she feared—I don't think anyone in a like situation
could have done it. But there's one thing I can do—I can
help find her murderer. And that's what I am going to
do—stay until I learn which one of the people here it was
who killed her!" Like needles of ice his eyes moved from
face to face, stabbing at us.

There was uproar at that. Several of the men jumped to
their feet, protesting. I heard Molly sob aloud. In default
of Pete, whose voice was loud in denunciation, her hand
clutched mine, clutched until it hurt. Even Oscar Anderson joined in the row. Only I remained passive and for the
best of reasons. I hadn't killed Nola Powers. I knew it if
no one else did.

It was Chief Hanover himself, moving ponderously
into the center of the confusion, who eventually calmed
it. "Now—now—now," he said placidly, "we won't never
get nowhere carrying on like this. Everybody sit down and
keep quiet. We still got free speech in this country and
Langdon here's just exercising one of his constitutional

rights. You see, I ain't got any sure way of knowing whether he's right or wrong. Maybe all you folks sitting around
here's got the right to be insulted and make a fuss and then
again maybe you ain't. Not that you don't talk a bit reck-
less, son," he turned to say reprovingly to Ross Langdon,
"what with not knowing no more than you're claiming to
know. Just the same, I think we'll pass that for the time
being. There's a point or two in your own story could bear
a mite more clarifying. This man Kearnes seemed mighty
upset when you spoke your name tonight, didn't he? Acted almost, as if he might have heard it before, which don't
square away so good with what you said about Miss Powers
wanting who you was kept secret. Got any answer for that?"

"Only what she told me," Langdon said stubbornly.
"That no one knew who I was nor why I was here."

Once more the urge to speak out—to tell what I knew—
was sharp as the thrust of an elbow in my side. Equally
strong was the urge toward silence. After all, why should I
be so gratuitous with what I knew—or thought I knew? No
one had asked me to talk and still . . . Mentally I reviewed
the mystery stories I'd read in which beautiful-but-dumb
heroines concealed, until the last page of the book, vital
information. Well, I didn't know whether the information
I had was vital or not but I didn't propose to conceal it.

"I think Mr. Kearnes knew something," I said firmly.
"I overheard him talking to Miss Powers last night at the
theater. They were quarreling. She said she wasn't afraid of
him because she'd taken precautions. I thought he struck
her then—"

I had provided another sensation. Ross Langdon was
temporarily forgotten while Lieutenant Dreyer, keen as a
foxhound on a new scent, dragged from me the story of
the night-before's quarrel.

I told it badly. My words sounded lame and ill-chosen
and, even to myself, the mood they attempted to convey

seemed unconvincing. They gave the impression, I'm afraid, that I stood listening outside that door for hours, instead of the actual brief passage of time.

Ross Langdon, appealed to, confirmed some of my story. Yes, the director, Latimer, had sent him to see what had become of Miss Thorpe. He had found her outside the green room door, on the point of entering. Yes, she had spoken of a quarrel. . . .

"Uh-huh!" said Lieutenant Dreyer in what must have been, for him, high glee. "I think we got something that time. What'd you think, Chief? Kearnes and the lady quarrel—it gets pretty hot—he slams her down. Today he finishes the job." He spread his hands in a wide gesture. "Pretty neat, huh? That'd help explain that heart attack, too. Might have strained his heart when he dumped her into that packing box. Just general excitement's no reason for a man having a heart attack—"

"Not," I asked softly, "not if the man were her husband?"

There was a moment's stony silence. Then Alice Wilson spoke sharply: "Husband? What are you talking about?"

"But I thought," I stammered, "I supposed— I'm sorry, but— I thought of course they were married—"

"Well, they weren't!" Alice snapped. "I don't care what you thought or supposed. Nola Powers never married any-one—and certainly not Gordon Kearnes!"

"She never married anyone," Chris Latimer confirmed suddenly and drearily, "never anyone but me."

Lieutenant Dreyer's mouth dropped open. He gulped. "What the—" he began but the old chief moved to intercept him. "Now wait a minute—wait a minute! Everybody keep quiet—you, too, Dreyer. 'Tain't no use getting excited and glowering at me neither. For a while I'm going to have the floor. Put your pencil down, son—" This was to the grinning patrolman who had been acting as stenographer. "I'm feeling in the mood for philosophizing some and we'll just keep it off the record. This ain't no proper kind of investigation anyhow. Somewhere along the line it went clear off the rails. That's what comes of being an old fool and not having what you might call experience with murder. Take the kind we have 'round here mostly—a couple of fellows have a mite too much to drink, get into an argument and one whams the other over the head harder'n he means to and the one that's been whammed dies. Likely enough the whole thing took place before plenty witnesses. Now this here Nola Powers' murder's a horse of an entirely different color. Mr. Langdon over there thinks one of the people in this room done it. He's stood right up in meeting and said so. All right. You ain't the sort of people who go brawling around in taverns and engine rooms. That's evidence admitted as they say up in the court room. You're educated or leastways you think you are—none of you'd be caught dead saying 'ain't' and messing up grammar like I do. You'd call yourselves the 'intelligensia' of Nashiona, I reckon, and don't none of you go looking surprised neither at me using words like that. Maybe I'm smarter'n I look or maybe I just read a book once when I hadn't nothing else to do. But me knowing a big word or two's got nothing to do with it. The point is that, while maybe you're thinking I'm only a dumb old fogy who got the job of police chief in Nashiona by reason of being a good friend of the mayor's, you want to remember I've held onto that job mainly by getting results. And results are just what I aim to keep on getting. Even when I find myself up against a murder case like this one—"

He paused and for a moment looked sternly at us. In turn we looked back. We saw a short, stout, ordinary looking man in a wrinkled gray suit whose waistcoat was crossed by an old-fashioned watch chain. He had thinning gray hair, a somewhat straggly gray mustache and eyes that were shrewd and sensible behind gold-rimmed spectacles. Heaven only knew what those eyes saw in us although his next words furnished a possible clue.

"I don't know much about this lady that got herself murdered—only her name and what you folks have told me and what your director said while he was looking at the body. He said she used to live here, five years or so ago, and that she'd acted in some of his plays before and that she'd been his wife. . . . 'Tain't no use scowling at me like that, Dreyer, 'Twa'nt my fault if you were messing around and didn't hear. . . . As I said before I didn't know her, but that don't mean anything because I never was much for these shows put on by home folks—give me vaudeville or a good movie every time—but it stands to reason that if she used to live here under such circumstances that she wasn't no stranger to the rest of you. That being the case, I'm inclined to pay more attention to Mr. Langdon's notions. Maybe he knows what he's talking about and one of you did do it. Now—now, don't none of you go to getting excited. Probably I ain't insulting more than nine out of ten of you—I'm excepting Mr. Langdon, you notice—and maybe he's wrong and then I'm insulting the tenth one too. But whether I am or not don't make no difference now. What does make a difference is that this is different from the killings we're used to around here, and we can't go at it bullheaded like we do at them. The way I look at it's this: Here's a round dozen of you caught as you might say in the law's toils—eleven for I'm going to count Oscar Anderson out. I've known him a right smart number of years and how a dumb Swede like him'd get mixed into a highbrow murder I wouldn't know! All right—there's eleven of you—and here's something you can call significant or not according to how it strikes you—three of that eleven

—four, if you count it twelve with the murdered woman—four come from New York and its vicinity and the other eight from right here at home in Nashiona."

Again he paused for breath and I frowned, seeking to grasp something significant out of what were no more than obvious facts. I failed. It didn't matter. I understood it almost at once.

"Now, this not being a tavern killing, there ain't no half a hundred witnesses around all yelling their heads off for a chance to say how it was done, and so it appears to me as though the smartest thing Dreyer and I can do is concentrate on just why the lady was murdered. The motive, they call it in highbrow detection. And once you get talking about motive you run spang into that significant point I was telling you about. Either Miss Nola Powers was killed by one of the three who came from the same part of the world she's been inhabiting lately—and at the risk of finding myself out on a limb later, I'm going to say at the moment it sounds plumb unlikely to me!—or else she was killed by somebody who knew her before and who still lives right here in Nashiona, and that don't make good sense neither. Because it takes us right back to the motive aforesaid and what kind of a motive." For the first time his voice lost its intrinsic geniality and became grim, "I ask you, what kind of a motive's going to last over more'n five years and then form the basis for cold-blooded murder?"

He took a second or two for the full force of his words to penetrate. Then, his meaning becoming evident and horrible, fear in a feather-brushing of cold swept over us. No one spoke. We sat rigidly. Watching, as he moved backward into the shadows from which he'd so briefly emerged. From them his voice came to us slow and easy-going again, the faintest of chuckles underlying it.

"And now that I've done about everything I know how to confuse this investigation, I reckon I'll go home to bed.

I'm an old man and I like my sleep. Dreyer here'll be in charge. To his way of thinking, and mine maybe, too, he oughta been from the start. Dreyer don't like being interfered with and I don't know's I blame him but with me being an interfering fool in the first place and his boss in the second. . . ." He chuckled. "Don't go thinking I'll miss anything either. Jim here," he laid a fatherly hand on the young patrolman's shoulder, "Jim'll get it all down in black and white for me to read over tomorrow. Ever read a literal transcription—them's two more five dollar words for you!—of just exactly what you once said to somebody? It can make right queer reading. G'night, everybody."

With a queer little duck of the head, he turned and stumped away. The patrolman, saluting, swung open the door. Lieutenant Dreyer drew an audible breath, let it die away in a hissing between his teeth. So did we all. It was as though we knew a new era had begun.

8

I don't know what happened after that because, once Lieutenant Dreyer took charge, he decided to interrogate us separately. Evidently he thought I'd been drained dry of information for he only asked me a few questions and then told me I could go home. The patrolman at the door obligingly called a cab.

Our house was lighted brilliantly from attic to cellar for Father is one of those people who, once home, manage to investigate every room in the house and never think of turning out a light.

I paid the driver and looked at my watch. It was half past two. I thought, "Whoops! Now for the fireworks!" and opened the door.

Father was in the living room. The chandelier and all the lamps were lighted and a brisk fire rumbled in the fireplace. Apparently he'd been reading for there was a toppling pile of *Americana's* beside him. But when I came in he was sulking in a big chair, his feet on the fender. Smoke from his pipe curled bluely about his head.

I kicked off my goloshes and snapped out the top lights. "It's a good thing," I observed, "that the practice blackout's tomorrow instead of tonight. You'd have every air warden in Nashiona ringing your doorbell."

"This is tomorrow," Father said severely. "Tomorrow morning. Young woman, where have you been?"

I took an extra long breath and told him.

I knew he'd take it big but I hadn't known just how big. I'd expected he'd be furious, that I'd be forbidden to have anything more to do with that "crazy, stage-struck bunch of fools," that I'd be told a murder was no more than he'd expected from the very first time he'd heard the name, the Little Theater. He didn't take it that way at all. He wasn't furious; he was only excited. He demanded details—every detail I could think of—and then he got more excited. He walked up and down and waved his arms; he analyzed trivialities; he insisted upon the thumbnail sketches of each person who'd been present; he suggested possibilities that hadn't occurred to me and that probably never would to Lieutenant Dreyer. In fact, it was with great difficulty that I kept him from I going right down to offer his services to the police.

"Murder," he said largely, still wearing a path on our plain blue-green carpet where footsteps definitely show, "why, murder's drama, Mary! The purest form of drama. You talk about being a student of the theater—what can the theater offer you better than I this? The question of life and death—"

"Well, it was death all right for Nola," I said soberly, "and I suppose it'll be a question of life for somebody if they find out who did it. But for the rest of it . . ." I shivered slightly. "It wasn't so dramatic and wonderful down there at the theater, Father. It was horrible. Just think. Those people have known one another for years, they've been in and out of one another's houses, working together, playing together. I've only known them for a couple of months but I've liked them. We've been friends. Only—I don't know whether we'll ever be again. Not after this."

"Not after this? Nonsense!" But he stopped prowling around and came to sit on the davenport beside me. "Exactly what do you mean?"

"I mean that everything changed with Nola's death. We were different—all of us—and it was worse after the police came. It was as though we'd never seen one another before. It was dreadful. Looking at them—at Pete and Molly and Rita and Chris—and wondering if one of them killed her, and being afraid, and yet half-believing, and knowing that they were thinking about me, too, and wondering—"

"'Cry murder in the market place,'" Father quoted bitterly. "You don't need to tell me. I've seen it happen before. Once let suspicion raise its ugly head and reason and common sense fly out the window."

"It's not only reason going out," I said, bitter in my turn. "It's unreason coming in. It's hate, too, and fear and a kind of desperate hope. It's wondering which one of them did it and why. . . . Why, even now while I'm talking to you, I keep thinking about it, and dividing them, and saying it couldn't be Chris, and why would it be Alice, and all the time I've a sneaky horrid feeling that perhaps I'm wrong and it is one of them after all. I like them— I think they're swell—and yet just the same . . ."

"I know—I know," Father growled. "You'll have to cultivate detachment, Mary. Look on it as a problem to be solved. Forget you're concerned in it in any way— Think of yourself as of it but out of it. It may be difficult—"

"Not for me," I interspersed hastily. "Lieutenant Dreyer's the one who's finding it difficult."

"What?" Father seemed to swell slightly over his normal six-foot-two-inch height. "Do you mean to tell me that some little whippersnapper of a policeman dares to believe that my daughter—"

"He doesn't know I'm your daughter," I offered pacifically. "Not that I really think he'd care. He'd just say, 'Uh-huh,' and drive in harder than ever. And, of course, my being at the theater this afternoon did look suspicious."

"Dear God in heaven!" said Father. He sat down heavily and mopped his forehead. "You were at the theater this— What in time were you doing there?"

So I told him, and Father promptly pooh-poohed first the waving curtains and then the face. He pooh-poohed them separately and with vigor. He said they were no more than manifestations of nerves. He said if I'd stop drinking so much tea and coffee, and eat decently, and condescend to wear my glasses once in a while instead of going around half-blind . . . He said he'd a good notion to put on his coat and go and talk to that fool Lieutenant Whatever-his-name-was right now.

I stopped that. I said, "Oh, no, you don't. You wouldn't like Lieutenant Dreyer and what's more important he wouldn't like you. Now, the old chief's rather a darling but you can't see him. He went home to bed long ago!"

"And a very sensible man," said Father rising. "Suppose we emulate him."

But we didn't—not right away. First we went out to the kitchen for a pot of the coffee, of which I wasn't supposed to drink so much, and some rather Dagwood-ish sandwiches. It was after four o'clock when we finally went up the stairs.

Father's not fifty yet and he's forever announcing that he needs no more sleep than Thomas Edison, but this was one time he overslept. The sun was shining brightly on the west wall of my bedroom when I awoke to hear the doorbell ringing madly and Father grumbling on his way downstairs.

Still wrapped in a fog of sleep, I decided that it had nothing to do with me and shut my eyes only to have them shaken open again with Father's hand on my shoulder and his voice in my ear.

"Get up," he was ordering. "Your darling chief of police is downstairs and he wants to talk to you!"

I got up. All the time I was washing my face, zipping a housecoat over my pajamas and running a comb through my hair, I was aware of Father's mutterings as he dressed in the room next to mine. There was the customary complaint that he couldn't find his razor blades. There was the debate over the suit he'd worn yesterday—did it need pressing of could it go one more day? There were remarks concerning the laundry's ways with his clean shirts. Most tragic of all, his shoe lace broke as he hauled on it. I decided that this was definitely not going to be one of Father's best days.

Which was the reason I poked my head into the living room and spoke briefly to Chief Hanover. "Are you in a hurry to talk or can you wait until I put the coffee on? We've simply slept until all hours and Father's like a bear with a sore head until he gets his breakfast."

"Plenty of time—plenty of time," said the old chief comfortably. "Maybe I can help you. I scramble a mighty mean egg myself."

He was alone. Neither police car nor Lieutenant Dreyer lurked in the offing—I peeked, when I had a chance, to see. He followed me out to the kitchen and while I measured coffee, he investigated the ice box. I don't know about the scrambled eggs but he was a master hand with grapefruit.

Breakfast was ready when Father finally appeared, his brow still black over the traitorous shoe lace. I'd mixed waffles—they're about as quick as anything—and the iron was smoking-hot and, without being told, the chief had warmed the syrup.

I'd set the table for three and, without apology, Chief Hanover took his chair and, after polishing off his grapefruit, attacked, his first waffle with gusto.

"My wife don't believe much in hot breads," he remarked after his third. "You folks ever have any of them real old-fashioned buckwheat pancakes? Mr. Thorpe, sir, I wouldn't be surprised but you've just acquired yourself a boarder!"

But, once the mixing bowl was emptied of batter, he sobered quickly and came to the point of his visit. It was my trip to the theater in which he was interested and in the face I thought I'd seen between the curtains. Father started right in on his version of the affair but the chief shushed him with a peremptory finger. He questioned me carefully. The face—had it been a man's or a woman's? Would I say it belonged to someone tall or short? Was the coloring dark or fair? How long had the face remained between the curtains?

To all the questions I shook a regretful head. I didn't know. I hadn't been able to tell. In feeble extenuation I proffered the fact of my nearsightedness.

No shushing kept Father from getting his nickel's worth in then. "I pay out sixty or seventy dollars so she'll have glasses suitable for every occasion she can think up, and then she won't wear them because she thinks they're unbecoming."

"I do wear them," I said, stung to defense. "When I'm reading or at a show or around the house."

"You haven't even got them on now," Father derided.

He had the last word in that argument. I hadn't.

Chief Hanover, however, wanted to see the glasses and, after some rather hectic search under fire of Father's gibes, I managed to dig up one pair. The chief looked through their lenses and put them down with a sigh.

"Women," he told Father, "will be women so far's vanity goes and there ain't much mere man can do about it. But knowing what I do now, young lady, I'd advise you not to get into no car accidents without you've got them spectacle things clamped to your nose. And now, seeing's how I don't know no more'n I did when I come, I reckon I'll be going."

Father went, too, almost immediately, after remarking that he didn't like the idea of me staying alone today and why didn't I come down to the USO rooms where he could keep an eye on me.

I didn't want anyone keeping an eye on me, I said crossly. As soon as he'd gone, I meant to lock the doors and go back to bed.

I hadn't had half enough sleep. Besides, it was just possible Alice or Chris or someone'd call. If they did, I wanted to be here.

Father grunted and left after that, promising to telephone every once in a while.

He was the only one who did call. Although I did exactly as I'd said—locked the doors and went back to bed—I couldn't sleep.

I found myself lying wide awake and listening tensely for the telephone to ring. It didn't and after a while I gave up all pretense of sleeping.

I was in no mood for reading and I had no desire for meditation so I filled up the day by going in for beauty culture. I washed my hair and set it. I took a long luxurious bubble-bath. I manicured both fingers and toes. I dressed in my newest afternoon frock and stepped into my highest-heeled pumps. And then, dismally, I was dressed, and it was only three o'clock, and there were still hours to put in, and I couldn't read and I mustn't think. . . .

I was just at the point of calling Father and telling him that I'd changed my mind, and that I'd be down after all, when the doorbell rang.

It made me jump a little. I wasn't really afraid but just the same, after last night, a doorbell's ringing gave one to think.

The bell rang again, impatiently, and I braced myself.
"Oh, come on, Mary," I muttered—Father's not the only
one in our family who talks to himself. "Probably it's only
a bill collector . . ."

It wasn't. It was Ross Langdon.

I know that I gaped at him—if he wasn't the last person
I'd expected to see, he certainly was the next to the last
and my reactions were way behind schedule anyway.

He took off his hat very nicely. He said, "Oh, hello,
Miss Thorpe. Do you mind if I come in and talk for a
minute?"

Just as, wordless, I was about to swing the door open, I
became aware that, queerly enough, I did mind. For no particular reason, I didn't want him in the house—I didn't want
anyone. The house was sanctuary. Within it, its doors locked
and bolted, I was safe. Once its safety was invaded . . .

Moreover, what did I know of this man? I'd seen him
only twice before. Was I to take the assurance of his identity simply from his own assertion? Chief Hanover had,
apparently, but ought I? How was I to be certain he wasn't
Nola Powers' murderer—perhaps the owner of the blurred
face I'd glimpsed between the curtains? True he'd given a
convincing enough explanation for the times concerned,
but alibis had been faked before now. I was alone in the
house. Once I'd admitted him, it would be a simple matter, if he wished, to silence me forever.

But I couldn't stand there unanswering forever. Already
he was looking at me curiously. I made an effort and got
my voice under control. I said, "Oh, I'm sorry. You see, I
was just going out myself." I gestured toward my hat and
coat, visible on the hall settee—thank God, I'd brought
them downstairs.

He looked and quirked an eyebrow. He said, "Oh, too
bad. But since I've a car here, why not let me drive you?"

I hesitated but I couldn't think of any plausible reason why not.

I said, "Thank you—that will be nice. But I'll have to telephone Father first—let him know where I'm going. You see, yesterday I went to the theater and I didn't tell him. . . ."

He took no pity on me. He said, "Miss Thorpe, are you afraid of me?"

I said, "Of course not!" and he smiled.

"Not that I blame you if you are, or your father either. Go ahead and call him. We'll settle the other business on the way down."

I hope! I thought as I gave my number.

I got Father right away. I told him what I was going to do and who I was going with. He said, "Langdon—is he one of that theater gang?" When I admitted that he was, he said, "Okay, Mary. Be careful. I hope you know what you're doing."

I didn't. That was the trouble.

We said nothing for the first block or two. Ross Langdon was busy with the car which was a Dodge and definitely aged. It showed a tendency to balk and refuse gas so that its temporary sputterings and stallings kept him occupied. For my part, I was searching desperately for something to say.

I found it as we reached the edge of the park. I strove for lightness and gaiety and achieved only abruptness. "What happened last night, after they let me go?"

He shrugged and shifted hopefully into third. "How should I know? They chased me out right away. Dreyer doesn't like me, so now I'm trailing the chief. This is his car incidentally."

"Not really?" I was surprised. "Then does that mean that he—that you—I mean, that you're—er—working for him?"

"It means that so far as the chief's concerned, he's accepted me and my credentials. That's what you really wanted to ask, isn't it? Dreyer's another story. 'He don't like big city dicks' is the way he phrases it. For my part I don't care much for small city ones."

"Neither do I," I said soberly. "Not the chief—I really like him."

"So do I. As a matter of fact, he's the one who suggested I come around and talk to you. He's got an idea you know more about that curtain-peeper than you're telling. If you're shielding anyone—"

"I'm not." For the fourth or fifth time I explained that I was shortsighted and that, even if I hadn't been, the distance across the theater was too far and the light too dim for positive identification.

He nodded thoughtfully. "I know. We tried it out ourselves this morning but just the same I'd feel easier in my mind if everyone else concerned was equally convinced."

"You mean that whoever it was might think I knew and just wasn't telling? But that's silly! Everybody knows I can't see without glasses. . . ."

He said, "Um." There was silence while we traversed a half a block. "Look here," he resumed in a different tone. "There's something I'm going to tell you. I don't know whether I've any business to or not, but you don't belong in this mess any more than I do. I thought if we could talk it over a little, I might get some of it clearer in my head. I'm one of those fellows who likes to hear himself talk anyway, and when I'm around the chief I get precious little chance."

He stopped and after a minute I said slowly, "I don't have to talk. I won't tell anyone if that's what's worrying you."

"Good." He chewed his lip for a moment, staring straight ahead, "How well do you know Chris Latimer?"

"How well? Oh, I don't know. I've been at his house lots of times—I've worked with him at the theater. That's about all."

"Married again, isn't he?"

"Yes. His wife's name's Faye. She's a lot younger than he is. She's a darling."

He looked vaguely uncomfortable. "Yes. Well. Early this morning I went down to see Chief Hanover. I wanted him to get my status straightened out before Dreyer took a notion to stick me for impersonation or something. After some difficulty I persuaded him to ring up my friend Inspector Ingalls in New York and get an okay for me. As soon as he found out how easy it was to talk half across the continent, he ran up quite a bill for which the citizenry of Nashiona will have to pay. He'd found some names and addresses in Nola Powers' bag and he talked to a couple of them, and then he got the bright idea of chasing out to the hospital and seeing Gordon Kearnes. Kearnes supplied the name of Miss Powers' lawyer. We talked to him."

"Well?" I said impatiently when it appeared that he didn't mean to go on. I was conscious of a vague feeling of apprehension but I strove to shrug it off. "What did he tell you?"

"Several things. Among others that Nola Powers was surprisingly well-off for an actress—even for a successful one. Her estate will amount to something over seventy thousand dollars." He stopped again.

The feeling of apprehension was strengthening. In a very small voice, I said, "And who—who gets the money? That's what you're trying to tell me, isn't it?"

"The money," said Ross Langdon slowly, "is left unequivocally to her dearly beloved husband, Chris Latimer. Now what do you make of that?"

9

I couldn't answer him. I felt sick all over. "My dearly beloved husband"—that was Chris—Chris Latimer. But Chris hadn't been Nola's dearly beloved husband—he was Faye's, poor flower-like Faye who was going to have Chris's baby . . . Chris's baby! Abruptly I remembered Alice Wilson's telephone call after that ghastly Monday tryout and her surprise and shock at hearing the words. "Oh, my God! Are you sure? Does Chris know?" and my own flippant answer: "I suppose so. Husbands generally do, don't they?" Well, if he *had* known, and if his marriage to Nola, by some fantastic legerdemain, was still binding and he had known that, too, wouldn't that be a possible motive for murder? Chris loved Faye. But Chris was no murderer—of that I felt certain. And yet—there had been that dinner meeting at the Sweet Shop of which I'd been so accidental a witness. Chris hadn't wanted Nola to come to Nashiona. . . .

I was aware that Ross Langdon was studying me curiously.

"I'm sorry if it's a shock to you," he said tentatively. "I know you like Latimer."

"I like Faye," I said.

"Faye—oh, yes. His wife. I mean his present wife—oh, damn it! Well, you understand. But don't take it too seriously. If the Powers-Latimer marriage existed, it doesn't now. Latimer and his Faye can be married all over again."

"It's not that," I said slowly. "It's—well, you see, Faye's going to have a baby, and if Chris knew that and then found out that he and Nola Powers were still married . . ."

He whistled softly.

"Yes—quite. Look here—the more I learn about Miss Powers the less I like her. For one thing there's that money—seventy or eighty thousand dollars is a lot to acquire in five years on the stage. Suppose the lady had gone in for some healthy blackmail on the side. Has Latimer any money of his own?"

"I think so," I said reluctantly. "That is, I think he inherited some. They never go without things and his job can't amount to much."

"All right. Well, then, say she's been nibbling at it and now, with this baby crisis approaching, she sees a chance to make a killing. She comes out here. Latimer knows why she's come. Say she's bled him white before and he can't afford any more—"

"But," I objected, "that would make Chris the murderer."

"You don't think he is?"

"No."

"Hum. Well, neither do I! How about this Faye? Suppose *she* found out. The female of the species is more deadly—that sort of thing."

"You don't know Faye. Nola Powers was a peony; Faye is a—a bluebell."

He looked amused. "All right—wash out Faye. Where do we go from there?"

He had given up driving and pulled up against a convenient curb. I made no objection. If I'd doubted him before, I didn't now. Instead I found myself, illogically, liking him.

"To bigamy, I think," I said doubtfully. "How could a man not know whether his wife had obtained a divorce or not?"

"You make it sound complicated but I think it was actually very simple. We found out quite a bit from that lawyer as I told you. Nola Powers went to Reno the first summer after she left Nashiona. She began divorce proceedings all right. Latimer was no doubt notified then. He didn't contest the suit. Nola remained in Reno for part of the required time. Then, without notifying her lawyers, she left Nevada. The case went by default. Latimer probably thought it had gone through all right. No doubt he married again in good faith."

"But how could he? Wouldn't he be notified that it never took place?"

"Probably. But he might not have opened the letter. These artistic people—you know what they're apt to be over mail. If he received any letter from Reno, my guess is he'd most likely assume it contained the final papers and tuck them away somewhere. It may come out at the inquest."

"Inquest!" I repeated, startled. "I'd forgotten there'd have to be an inquest. Will I—I suppose I'll have to go?"

"You will. We'll all have to. It's the law."

"When will it be? "

"Tomorrow, Hanover said. But you'll be notified."

"And all of this—about Chris and Faye—will it have to come out?"

"I don't know," Langdon said soberly. "It depends upon how strong a case the state will think it can make against him. I don't mind telling you I think it will. Because the state's attorney's no fool—what I've seen of him—and this is the sort of case that can give him a big leg up the political ladder. On the other hand, *and* for the same reason, he may decide to play it safe for the time being, in which case we'll have the old 'person or persons unknown' verdict."

"What do you mean—'the sort of case?'"

He waved his hand impatiently. "Newspaper stuff—well-known actress slain—new play by well-known author—local scandals—the twice-married Mr. Latimer. . . . Lord, there's material enough there to keep the papers going a month at full speed, and when and if it gets to a trial . . . Well, you wait. All the big-paper boys will be here."

I shivered a little, not from cold.

"Do you know anything more?"

He shook his head. "Only one thing and it may not be important. I told you Dreyer can't stand me at any price and while the old chief's friendly enough he has his moments of wanting to be alone. No, I've made up my mind to this: whatever I find out will be without help from anyone, barring the crumbs I pick up here and there. If I'm in this thing, it'll be independently."

He was off the subject. "What do you know?" I insisted.

"Oh." For a moment, he studied me, thoughtfully, eyes narrowed. "Well, it may not amount to anything—I told you that. But have you noticed that your friend Mrs.—is it?—Wilson has extraordinarily long fingernails which she keeps painted brilliantly scarlet? I noticed them particularly at the tryouts Monday night. Her hands are beautiful, you know, and she takes pains that you see them. Well, last night I noticed them again. Two of the nails are broken off to the quick."

Once more my throat tightened uncontrollably. "But that mightn't mean anything," I managed to say. "I'm always breaking my fingernails. It's perfectly easy to do. Just making beds or opening cans—"

"I told you it probably wasn't important."

"Besides—how could a woman kill Nola Powers?"

"Rather easily, I'm sorry to say. She was knocked unconscious and then strangled. With a scarf—a woman's scarf."

"It might have been her own."

"Doubtful. Miss Powers wore black accented with touches of soft rose. The scarf was a peculiarly blatant shade of orange. Would you combine orange with rose?"

I shook my head. "But it wasn't Alice I saw between the curtains," I protested feebly.

"How do you know?"

I didn't. I said, "Oh, for goodness sake, let's stop talking about it. The only thing I know for certain is that *I* didn't kill her."

His grin flashed whitely.

"My situation exactly. It's nice we can eliminate two of the suspects, isn't it?"

Two of the suspects—he must mean the other was himself. For the first time I let myself believe. I nodded. "Nice," I agreed.

He drove me down to Father then. He did more. He came into Father's office and made himself so agreeable that he quite won Hilda's heart. Not Father's, although my parent did go so far as to say, after he'd gone, that Langdon seemed "a sensible young man with a good head on his shoulders" and that he (Father) should think he (Langdon) would feel out of place in a crowd of escaped lunatics like that theater crowd. I ignored that as it deserved.

Father is adamant about meals—he eats at six-thirty or knows the reason why—and there were still a couple of hours to kill before he'd be ready for dinner. Languidly I considered all possibilities for filling in that time, and then rejected them. I didn't want to walk down town, and there wasn't time for a show, and I certainly was in no mood for calling on people.

Eventually Hilda solved the problem by putting me to work. There's never any time to loaf around a USO and today was no exception. In no time at all, I found myself mending gloves and sewing on buttons for importunates. That done I helped a jilted lover compose a letter of congratulation to his erstwhile sweetheart, now someone else's bride, and still had time for a half dozen games of cribbage with a "dese, dose and dem" boy from Brooklyn.

The "dese, dose and dem" boy was both grateful and garrulous. He'd heard of the murder, as who hadn't, and he insisted upon talking about it between games.

"It was tough luck," he said. "J'ever see her in the movies or on the stage? I have, lotsa times. She was swell. The boys had been kinda hoping she'd come out to the camp and give us a show or something. Lotsa stars do it other places. Who'd you think killed her?"

I counted fifteen-six, pushed over the cards, and shook my head.

"Don't know, huh?" He looked indulgent. "Whatta yuh want to bet that Kearnes guy did it? You know, the writer guy. She coulda known him in New York, couldn't she? Well, then . . ."

She could and she had. I'd my own opinions about the Gordon Kearnes-Nola Powers tie-up and I devoutly hoped the police had, too, but I wasn't just broadcasting for the fun of it. I shrugged and shifted two white pegs forward and then back again.

"So you ain't talking, huh? Okay-okay. But suppose I told you I saw them two eating lunch together yesterday and fighting like wildcats all the time they ate. What'd you say to that, huh?"

My heart jumped a little but I tried to sound coolish and indifferent. "I'd want to know how come you happened to be off the post yesterday and again today?"

He grinned at that. "'Sa military secret, baby. No, honest, I ain't kidding. Them two were in Dalrymples yesterday about one o'clock and boy, were they taking it to the mat!"

One o'clock yesterday at Dalrymples! Gordon Kearnes certainly hadn't mentioned it! He'd even said that no one had seen Nola Powers since morning. Why?

I did my best to coax further details and failed. He said, "Aw, come on, let's play another game." He said yeah, he guessed lotsa people'd seen them and naw, he didn't know what they were quarreling about—he was too far off to hear. Plainly he had lost interest and I accepted the cards he dealt me in a fog of conjecture that scarcely let me observe the figures they displayed.

I did manage to get his name and squadron number before Father arrived looking for me. I had an idea they might be important. Father didn't agree. We argued it all the way down to the restaurant, Father's contention being that I didn't need to play detective, that that job belonged to the police, and that they certainly wouldn't overlook Gordon Kearnes. As for my Brooklyn discovery—was it my idea he'd been the only person in Dalrymples that noon or that the others present were dumb, deaf and blind?

I gave it up after a while—I was only succeeding in sounding silly and there's never much use in arguing with Father. He's outtalked too many football teams. Just the same, if I'd been certain of locating Ross Langdon, I'd an idea he'd be interested.

It was quite dark when we emerged from the restaurant and Father pushed me into a taxicab. "You go home and get some sleep," he ordered. "You're out on your feet right now. And stop worrying about the murder—we pay a police force to do that!"

Neither one of us remembered the impending blackout. If we had, I doubt if Father'd have waved me off with such equanimity. I doubt, too, although this is definitely second-guessing, that I would have gone.

Father still blames himself bitterly. "I might have known," he groans. "If I hadn't been a blithering fool—!" And then, in an obvious attempt at face-saving, "But you—what in time was the matter with you? You could have gone over to one of the neighbors. . . ."

I never answer that. What I could have done, and what I did, are two different things. Besides it never occurred to me that I had any reason to be afraid.

I got the news over the radio about the blackout. I'd come home, made a fresh pot of coffee—for, contrary to Father's injunction, I felt no need for sleep—and, the quiet of the house getting upon my nerves a bit, switched on the machine. It was tuned to a local station and the announcer was repeating blackout instructions. The sirens would go on at ten o'clock. We were to turn off all lights promptly. Keep the radio tuned but be certain that its back bled no light. We were not to use the telephone except for emergency. We were to stay off the streets. We were not to drive automobiles—air-raid wardens would be on the alert for infractions. The blackout would last exactly twenty minutes during which time army planes would patrol the sky. . . .

The information droned endlessly. I dragged myself out of my chair and went on a tour of investigation. Cellar and attic lights were off—good. The upstairs rooms showed darkly in order. Downstairs was all right too. The lamps in the living room could be cut off when the whistles sounded. That done, I wouldn't need to worry about drawing blinds or curtains. A fire in the fireplace would be out of the question, I was afraid—it would throw too much light.

Rather to my surprise, I began to find the proceedings interesting. I even had a practice blackout myself to determine just how much light the backless radio revealed. It was plenty, and after I'd struggled for a while with a coat and a rug that persisted in sliding off the top, I decided to do without the radio. Twenty minutes wasn't so long and I doubted if they'd have anything of pressing importance to impart in that length of time.

The rest of my preparations were simple. Cigarettes and matches and an ash tray on the table beside the big chair that was sideways to the window. As an afterthought, a flashlight and Father's revolver, loaded with blanks, for which I made a second trip upstairs. These, too, I placed on the table. Good—excellent! Now let the hurricanes roar. I was ready.

I suppose the whistles blew at ten o'clock but I didn't hear them. The wind was wrong or they weren't strong enough or something. However our clock gives a sort of warning whirr just before it strikes so I was ready. I switched off the radio and lamps and established myself beside the window.

It was fascinating to watch the lights die. One by one the windows of the neighboring houses darkened. Last of all the corner street lights blinked out.

The world as we knew it was lost and dead. The snow that still covered the ground turned the shadows to gray. The houses were only blobs of dark against it. There was no moon, no stars. The sky was dull and lifeless with the promise of more snow. A little wind moaned softly to stir the bare branches of the trees. The ordinarily busy street was car-less and deserted.

The silence was so intense as to hurt. I lit a cigarette, shielding the match's flame and holding the glowing end downwards when I remembered. I was clumsy about finding the ash tray. Finally I took it in my lap.

The rooms about me were opaque with blackness. Only the French windows at the far side of the room showed as light patches in the surrounding dark. The blackness seemed to swell and pulsate; it was as though, unseen, the very size and shape of the house was changing. I had the feeling that if I moved to touch a boundary wall, it would not be there, familiar to my hand's reaching.

It was a disquieting sensation, but only a sensation, I
told myself. Houses didn't alter themselves just because
they went temporarily lightless. Nevertheless it was queer
that the impression of endlessness and space persisted. It
bothered me. I just couldn't understand it or get it out of
my mind. Perhaps blindness is the true fourth dimension,
I thought idiotically, because it nullifies those other senses
upon which our sight depends.

There was movement outside. The slow clunk of footsteps in the snow. An air warden, I thought, making his
rounds or a stray pedestrian on his way home in defiance
of the regulations. I flattened my nose against the window
and watched the vague figure pass.

A car came crawling along the cross-street and carefully negotiated the corner. A single monstrous eye glowed
dimly where two should have been. A doctor, I surmised,
summoned hurriedly to some sick bed. Or a police car,
guardian of our safety, patrolling the lightless streets
on which, without its surveillance, mayhem and outrage
might have their way.

But not all took such a kindly view, I discovered. Whistles sounded shrilly and from three directions figures con-
verged upon the car. That scarce-seen figure *had* been an
air-raid warden, I decided, and he was now exercising the
prerogative of his office in stopping and questioning this
one-eyed car. The several whistles must come from brother
wardens responding to his call for assistance. It was very
interesting. I felt as though I were privileged to sit in on a
private little drama that was being enacted for my benefit.

And then, drama, air wardens and car fled abruptly from
my mind. For suddenly, surprisingly, I was hearing a sound,
a sound that should not have been audible in that quiet
and tenantless house—the creak of a complaining board.

It came from the kitchen. I knew that board. Ever since
we had taken the house, its protesting squeak had followed

my progress from pantry to stove. But it never squawked unless someone trod on it. . . .

Unless someone trod on it! I was bolt upright now, my eyes staring into the dark from which the sound had come. My heart accomplished a strange bit of levitation; I found its beat fluttering uncomfortably in my throat. My eager eyes began to blur with the blackness.

The creak came again. Clearer this time. Someone or something was making a cautious way into the house. But who and why? Had I—Oh, I knew I had!—failed to check door and window locks? But why should I have checked them? I'd never done it before. It was definitely Father's job. But Father wasn't here—in a wave of blackness it came over me: there was no one here—no one but me.

I was afraid then. Blood throbbed a quickening drumbeat in my ears. The creaking of the boards had ceased. Strain as I might to hear, I heard nothing.

Silence lapped about me yet I was tinglingly aware of a presence, too—the presence of an alien—an intruder. Somewhere—perhaps within this very room—he was now standing, safe-hid by the darkness, watching, orienting himself, biding his time, waiting for the opportune moment. . . .

For what moment? It was a question for which, sickeningly, I had no answer. Who stood there in the darkness—why he had come—these were mysteries for which there was no need of immediate solving. What did matter—and terribly—was that because of his presence an unknown danger threatened.

Sound broke into my consciousness then, the dear familiar sounds of normalcy. Gruff voices, the grinding of gears; the air wardens were giving clearance to the wandering car.

I had a spurt of courage then. Perhaps it was engendered by their nearness or it may have been the courage of despair. At any rate I leaned far forward, my eyes once more stabbing into the impenetrable dark and spoke.

"Who's there?" There was no courage in my voice—it croaked, unrecognizable, "Who's there?"

With the question came swift movement. Out of the blackness a blacker shadow disengaged itself. It hung for a moment, shapeless and menacing, limned against the clear gray panes of the French windows—and then began a slow and silent advance.

Instinct alone guided me. The thinking part of my brain gave over to pure terror. There were a dozen things I suppose I could have done—gotten to the front door perhaps, screamed for help—I did nothing. Sheer panic ruled me. I forgot all about my careless preparations, forgot the revolver and flashlight with which I'd provided myself. I forgot everything except that upon the street air wardens prowled, looking for forbidden lights, and that above my head there was a lamp with a hundred-watt bulb. If I lighted it, they must surely come. . . .

I raised my hand and jerked at the swinging chain.

10

Things happened then . . . and swiftly. Light came up in a blinding flood. I had an instant's glimpse of a black-clad figure that flung up arms and fled. There was a crash as a chair went over and then the slam of the back door. At the same time a cacophony of whistles rose upon the street, footsteps stormed the porch, the doorbell shrilled,

I ran to the door and dragged it open to face the dark and truculent thrust of an unknown jaw. "Turn them lights off, lady! What the hell—! Don't you know this is a black-out?"

In far-off mockery, sirens wailed.

The truculent jaw relaxed. "Okay—leave 'em on. Black-out's over!"

The blackout was over—that meant I could flood the house with light if I chose. But light or no light, I'd still be alone. How did I know the intruder had really gone? What if the slam of the door were only a blind and he were still inside? Once this man had gone—

My teeth began to chatter then. I reached out and snatched at the jacketed arm upon which the warden's armlet showed reassuringly. "Don't go," I said. "Please— you don't understand. Someone was in the house—that's why I turned on the light. I knew someone'd come. I was afraid—"

"Someone in the house, huh? You mean a burglar?" the owner of the jaw rubbed it, intrigued.

Over his shoulder, two new faces peered. "What's the trouble here, George?" The voice was familiar. It was Pete Dunbar's. He said, "Hello, Mary. Anything wrong?"

"Wrong!" I repeated, hysteria riding high. "Someone was in this house, I tell you. I was all alone—I turned on the lights—it was all I could think of—I—I . . ."

Pete took quick charge. His hand went to the wall switches, flicked them upward. More light bloomed. He put his arm around me. "Here—sit down. It's all right—everything's all right. You don't need to shake so. We'll look around—"

There was tangible evidence that someone had been in the house. I saw it myself for, in spite of Pete's adjuration, I tagged along. The back door was unlatched. Water blobs stood accusingly upon the kitchen floor. There were even faint traces of wet upon the living room's taupe carpeting. In the outer entrance way there lay the most damning evidence of all—a longish strip of bright chiffon.

Pete did his best to keep me from seeing. It wasn't good enough. I saw the scarlet strip's quick disappearance into his coat pocket. "What's that?"

His boyish face was troubled. "I didn't want you to see," he said reluctantly. He drew it forth. Silently we stared at it, the stranger air wardens forming a background of curiosity. I said slowly, "A chiffon scarf. Nola Powers was strangled with a scarf like that."

Pete said, "Yes," and wadded it into his pocket again.

"What are you going to do with it?"

"Give it to the police, I suppose."

"For fingerprints?"

"Maybe. This bird might have worn gloves—probably did. Anyway I don't think you can always take fingerprints

from cloth. They didn't get any from the scarf that strangled Nola."

Curiosity got the better of George of the truculent jaw.
He said, "Strangled—say, what *is* all this? Nola Powers—
she was the actress who got killed down town, wasn't she?"

Pete sighed. "Yes. Now it looks as though whoever
killed her was after Miss Thorpe too. I'd better call the
police, Mary."

I nodded. "Call Father too. Tell him to come home
right away. I can't stay alone—I don't ever want to be
alone again."

"You won't be," Pete said reassuringly. "I'll wait until
he comes. You fellows can go if you want to," he told the
other wardens. "There's not much danger our prowler'll
be back."

But George and company gave no sign of departing. I
doubt if you could have driven them away. They settled
themselves comfortably on the davenport and stared, owl-
eyed, as Pete made his telephone calls. I didn't care. To my
mind, the more present the merrier.

Pete put up the hand set. "They'll be right out," he said
unnecessarily.

"All right," I said and shivered. Reaction was setting
in. I felt as though I'd never be warm again. I was also
bewildered.

"I can't understand it," I broke out at last. "Why would
anyone want to kill me?"

Pete shrugged. "Perhaps you know too much."

"But I don't know anything!" I was ashamed of myself.
It was a wail.

Pete looked unconvinced.

"Evidently our murderer doesn't agree with you."

"If it *was* our murderer."

"Who else would it be?"

"Oh, for heaven's sake! How should I know?" Male logic has always infuriated me. "If it was he—or she—it's simply insane! I don't know anything, I tell you!"

"He or she—you mean to say you don't know whether your—your visitor was a man or a woman?" Pete asked curiously.

"Of course I don't!" I snapped. "The light blinded me. I just saw a figure and that only for a moment."

"Nearsighted again?" Pete asked softly.

I glared at him. "Don't you believe me?"

"That you're nearsighted? Oh, yes, *I* do. But perhaps the—the murderer doesn't."

My mouth opened. "You mean that he thinks that I'm not at all? That I was lying about seeing a face between those box curtains and not recognizing it?"

"Could be," said Pete. He jangled the coins in his pocket and eyed me unsmilingly.

"But," I said, "I didn't think anybody really believed me when I said I saw the face in the first place. They all acted as if I were mad."

"Yeah," Pete said. "But if there *was* a face and you saw it and it *was* the murderer, he'd know it, wouldn't he?"

It was unanswerable. I shivered some more.

"But how could he know that I'd be here—alone? I might not even have been home—I wasn't until late—"

"He could have been watching," Pete said gently. "You don't pull your shades down very well, do you? Anyone standing outside, under those French windows, for instance, would have a clear view of the room."

We all looked at the windows and agreed. George, clearing his throat noisily, opined that maybe, if he'd just take his flashlight and look around a little, he'd see something.

Taking our silence for agreement, he and the other man, who was now introduced to me as Dr. Summers, went off and Pete and I were alone. We didn't talk. I was experiencing too much let-down to have anything to say and Pete was restless, prowling the room. He paused by the table and studied my blackout cache, and his eyebrows quirked upward. "Revolver, huh? You must have been expecting trouble," he observed. He lifted the revolver, broke it open. "Blanks— Good God, Mary, you can't kill a man with blank cartridges!"

I didn't answer that—there *was* no answer—and he put it down again and roamed off toward the windows outside of which George and the doctor were presumably taking observation.

I think it was at that moment that I realized for the first time just what Nola's murder had done to me. Because, all of a sudden, I found that I was suspecting Pete! Wondering where he fitted into this and how he'd happened to be so providentially upon the spot when George's whistle shrilled. Of course I'd known he was a block warden—I'd heard Molly tell and retell the tale of the woman who'd called in great agitation to demand the "block-head"—but the Dunbars lived farther south. What then had Pete been doing in this neighborhood and how did I know that he hadn't been the unknown intruder? True, he'd been prompt to answer the warden's call for aid but even if he had been the prowler he could have accomplished that with ease. It would have only meant running around the house and joining George and company upon the porch. Who would have noticed or asked questions? And he *had* known Nola Powers when she lived in Nashiona—he was one of the eight to whom Chief Hanover had referred. How did I know that the story he'd spun so glibly about the murderer's problematical doubts of my nearsightedness was not the truth and so told to disarm? How did I know that he, Pete Dunbar, husband of Molly, wasn't himself the murderer?

I was glad when George thumped back to make his report. Yeah, there were footprints under the window all right but you couldn't tell much about them, the snow was so trampled down. Couldn't even tell where they'd come from—the walks were shoveled too clean. (I nodded—well I knew Father's passion for clean cement.) Still he reckoned you could say somebody's stood outside and looked in. Maybe when the police saw the tracks . . .

"Man's or woman's?" Pete asked and, for the second time, silver jangled in his pocket.

George didn't know. Man's, he'd say, though lots of women had big feet. His own wife wore nine's.

I didn't care about his wife. "Well," I said bitterly, "if he stood there and watched me, it's no wonder he knew just where to come. I suppose I made a pretty distinctive silhouette at the front window. Talk about making things easy . . ."

The police and Father arrived just then. Father was about two yards in the lead, so that, by the time the police were actually inside, he was entirely the angry householder and remarkably articulate and accusatory concerning the inadequacy of police protection and the rights of taxpayers and property owners.

Not that Lieutenant Dreyer was what you called calm himself. "What the hell do you mean," he demanded, "racing a police car down the street? I've a good mind to take you in for that. Impeding the police in pursuit of their duty . . ."

"Duty! God all mighty, man! She's my daughter! Do you think it's likely I'd let you keep me from getting to her?"

Lieutenant Dreyer was sulphurously silent.

However, if the events of this night did nothing more, it served its purpose. For the first time the police treated my story of "the face between the curtains" with the respect that I, at least, thought it deserved. Before, their interest had been cursory and semi-indulgent. Now they suddenly developed a passion for detail which I, to the Lieutenant's expressed disgust, was unable to gratify.

"But you must have seen something," he persisted, "or else why'd he try to kill you?"

"I told you what I saw," I protested wearily. "A face. Just a face. I don't know who owned it. And if that's the only reason for killing me, someone was wasting his time and energy!"

"His time and energy!" said Lieutenant Dreyer rather awfully. "Okay—have it your way. But if you should happen to remember that missing something, you'd better hot-foot it down to the station."

"Don't worry," I promised. "I won't even wait that long. I'll telephone you."

Beyond pestering me, the police did little that night. They stood around and looked at the now but-faintly-to-be-discerned markings on the floor. Ditto with the footprints under the window. They made a half-hearted test for fingerprints on the back door's lock and knob and found none. Not even the chiffon scarf which Pete surrendered, gave them pleasure. Presently, promising to return in the morning, they went away.

Pete, too, departed, after assuring us he was at our disposal day or night, and, the show over, George and Dr. Summers decided to go with him.

Father and I were left to stare at one another.

Not that such period of trance endured. Father, as usual, had convictions and voiced them. He had not been impressed by the sight of the Nashiona police in action and he wanted to tell me why. I listened until I wearied. I said at last, "Oh, for goodness sake—what good does it do to talk about what they should have done and didn't? Let's forget it for tonight. I'm going to bed."

"Oh, no, you're not!" Father snapped. "We're going to work this out somehow. An attack on your life—that's serious, Mary, whether you think so or not. You're in danger—"

"Are you telling me?" I asked. But I sat down obediently. "Well, what can I do—or we? I've already told you everything I know."

Father glared. "You've 'told me all you know!'" he parroted bitterly. "Well, it's not enough. God knows I've never demanded a high degree of intelligence from you but is it too much to expect a reasonable amount of common sense? If there's one sensible person involved in this incredible mumbo jumbo I'd like to get ahold of him for about five minutes. . . ." He stopped and snapped his fingers. "There is! That young fellow you brought into USO headquarters this afternoon. A private detective, wasn't he? Get him out here!"

"Now?" I objected. "But it's late! Look at the clock."

"Not as late as it was last night when you got home," Father said grimly. "Go on—call him. If you don't, I will."

I had no difficulty reaching Ross Langdon. He was at the hotel and his voice saying, "Yes?" seemed all of a sudden the sanest, safest thing in a tottering world.

I didn't waste any time on preliminaries. I said, "This is Mary Thorpe, Mr. Langdon. Someone tried to murder me—just now in the blackout—"

I heard the whistle of his quick-drawn breath. "Where are you? At home? Not alone? Good. I'll be right out."

He was there within five minutes. He gave me one quick considering glance—apparently to make certain I was still in one piece and operating under my own steam—and then addressed himself to Father.

"Sir, if I'd had any idea that anything like this could have happened—"

"Believe me," I interrupted, "if *I'd* had any idea—" and then my fool teeth began to chatter like castanets. Whatever conclusion I'd meant to draw went completely out of my mind. I said, "Oh, skip it!" and began to weep.

It brought their attention to me with a vengeance. Ross Langdon looked startled and Father horrified. He petted me. He said, "Baby—baby. You've been so brave—I've been so proud of you. Can't you hold up a little longer? We'll take care of you—nothing'll happen to you now. . . ."

"That's what they always say," I sobbed. I suppose it was hysteria—it certainly sounded like it. "Not tonight perhaps. But what about tomorrow and the day after that . . ."

"She's right," Ross Langdon said heavily. "It's all right to talk and make promises but we'll have to do more. We'll have to guarantee those promises. Just the fact that our killer has failed this time doesn't mean that he won't make another attempt."

"Our killer!" I repeated. The impersonality of the expression angered me. "What do you know about him? You haven't even heard my story yet!"

Their glances were indulgent. Ross Langdon knelt and took both my hands. "Look, Mary. I don't need to hear your story to know that something's happened to frighten you terribly. One look at you would tell me that . . ."

One look at me—I didn't like the sound of that. I pulled away from his hands and went out to the hall mirror. He was right.

I had the appearance of one to whom something had just escaped happening.

There was powder and lipstick in my purse. I used it. As an afterthought I put on my glasses.

I got back into the living room just in time to hear Father say, "Hilda. Hilda will know."

"Will know what?" I asked just to call attention to my existence in case they'd forgotten me.

"You can't stay here alone, Mary," Father told me. "Not any more. You're going to have someone with you—someone I can trust—every minute of the day. And night too." He added grimly.

"How lovely," I said. "But surely you're not planning to spare me Hilda? I thought that without her the USO'd fold up and go out of business. Still, I can think of worse people to have trailing me—people I'd dislike more, I mean."

"You can get it out of your head that I'm giving up Hilda," father said sternly. "No. But very likely she'll know someone we can get."

She might at that, I thought. Capable, brisk, clever, Hilda achieved the impossible. No doubt she'd take Father's problem in her stride and solve it with a minimum of time and effort.

"Don't you think," I asked Ross Langdon, "that it's about time you found out just what did happen here tonight?"

It was certain that he displayed far more interest than I'd been able to evince from the police. Some parts of my story he made me repeat—mainly the parts that dealt with my activities immediately preceding and during the blackout. The red scarf, to me the most sinister and disturbing thing in the category, he waved away. "Too obvious," he said. "What I want to know are the details that don't hit you in the eye. Anyone can guess what that scarf was for. What I don't understand—"

I didn't find out what it was he didn't understand just then for he took a sudden notion to dash into the kitchen and view the blobs of wet of which now only the faintest of chalky stains remained. He looked at the door knobs, dusty with fingerprint-powder. He borrowed a flashlight and went to stand for moments under the French windows while I, morbidly aware of his inquisitory eyes, sat on the davenport and shivered.

It was Father, however, who discovered the overshoes. He came wandering in from the kitchen, a frown drawn hard between his brows. "Look here, Mary," he said, "where'd the overshoes come from?"

I said, "What overshoes?" and he nodded over his shoulder.

"The ones in the kitchen. Under the table."

I had a queer sinking feeling. "Why, I supposed they were yours. I saw them—they were in the middle of the floor and Lieutenant Dreyer picked them up and put them out of the way. I never thought—"

"They're not mine," Father said bluntly. "Mine are still at the USO. Get Langdon in here, will you? I'm damned if I don't think we've got something to go on at last!"

Even Langdon thought so. He walked warily about the overshoes. "Well, well, well," he said cheerfully. "What goes on? On the largish side, aren't they? Wonder if that proves anything or not. Looks as though our friend found overshoes a trifle clumsy for gumshoeing and took them off—didn't have time to take them with him, he was in such a hurry to depart. Umm, I could bear to know two things at this point: First, what was Pete Dunbar doing to be so Johnny-on-the-spot, and second, did he go forth air-wardening in overshoes or not."

"He didn't have any on," I said. "I noticed—he had brown oxfords—those monk things that officers wear. But I—I honestly don't think he had anything to do with this."

"Why not? Just because he's a friend of yours—because you like his wife—doesn't write him a clean ticket."

"It's not that," I said slowly. "I thought all that myself—a little while ago. Oh, not about the overshoes—I didn't know about them. But that it could be Pete. Only—now I'm wondering if it was."

"Mary, for God's sake, stop burbling!" Father commanded. "If you've any real reason for exonerating the fellow, all right—let's hear it."

"I don't know whether you'll call it a reason or not," I said with dignity. "It's just that—well, the more I think of it—that figure I saw—I wonder if it was a man at all. I wonder if it could have been a woman!"

11

They gave no cheers. They avoided my eyes. Father even looked worried, as though he doubted my sanity. He said, "But they're men's overshoes, Mary."

"What of it?" I asked. "If it was a woman and she expected to stand under my window and she knew she'd leave tracks of some kind—for people *don't* shovel snow from underneath their windows—and she didn't want you to know she was a woman—"

"Could be," said Ross Langdon. "But wait a minute before you go on with any more of your involved reasoning. Mary, what makes you think all of a sudden, that it could have been a woman?"

"I don't know whether I can make you understand," I said slowly. "It was the way she or he covered its face. You see, I pulled on the light unexpectedly and whoever it was couldn't afford to be recognized. So his first instinct was to cover his face. Not that I would have recognized him probably if I had been able to see. You know how it is when you've been in the dark for a while—light blinds you just at first. I suppose he was blinded, too, but he didn't lose his head. He—well, a man would naturally throw up his arm to shield his face, wouldn't he? This one didn't. That's what I remember. He threw up his hands."

Father said, "Good Lord!" and sat down hastily. He looked at me with something—I don't think it was admiration—in his gaze. He said, "If that's all you've got to go on—"

"I'm a woman," I said smugly. "I ought to know something about it. It's the same principle as automatically trying to catch a ball in your skirts—whether you're wearing skirts or not."

"I suppose you think that sort of theory would hold up in court," Father snorted. "Gentlemen of the jury, we submit that, because our client hid her face in her hands instead of in the crook of her elbow—" His voice faltered, stopped; he glared at me. "What in the name of heaven was I trying to prove? Hang it, Mary, you've got me all muddled up!"

"You'd taken your case to the jury a little too soon," Ross Langdon said absently. "Crook of the elbow, eh? I wouldn't know about that being a typically masculine gesture but you make it sound reasonable. You didn't happen to notice anything a trifle more definite, did you, Mary? Longish hair or honest to goodness skirts or anything like that?"

I shook my head. "No. All I know it was someone in dark clothes. But it wouldn't have to be skirts, you know. Almost every woman nowadays has slacks and wears them."

"Too true," Ross said. "Well, as a theory, it's interesting. I can't even find very much wrong, with it. The point is, she wouldn't have to wear the overshoes—she could carry them until the moment came for making tracks in the snow. Taking them off for a trek through the house is reasonable too. What I can't see is why bring them in at all? Why not leave them outside?"

"So they wouldn't get lost," I said promptly. "If you left them outside and had to get out in a hurry, you mightn't remember where they were, but if they were inside, ready to your hand—"

"They *were* forgotten," Ross Langdon reminded me. "Which rather spoils that."

"Or if they were left outside, some other prowler might see them: and make off with them. There's always someone taking a short cut through our yard. You can see footprints in the snow."

Langdon made a gesture of despair. "Now you're killing your own theory. Why couldn't it have been that same short-cutter who made the tracks under your window?"

"It could have been, I suppose," I said, "but you've still got the overshoes to explain. They're here, and they're not Father's and they're certainly not mine. . . . Listen! If it was a woman, why couldn't she have borrowed the overshoes from someone—her husband, or . . . That way she'd have to get them back because if they were missed there'd be a lot of explaining to do."

"There you go again," Father said disgustedly. "How do you know she didn't buy the things? That way there'd be no explanation."

"They're not new," I said. That was irrefutable. Father subsided. "Would there be any way of checking on them— finding out who they do belong to? I mean, you could hardly advertise. . . ."

"Hardly," agreed Ross Langdon. "No, I'm inclined to think you're right—either your visitor was a man and the overshoes were his own, or a woman and the overshoes were obtained in some way—borrowed or stolen. But I suspect, if that's so, that the only way we'll learn it is through some innocent party's slip of the tongue. It might be a good thing if you'd listen a little when you're among your friends."

"I'm not sure I *have* any friends," I said bitterly. "It was bad enough after Nola Powers' murder but I did think there were one or two of them who might be innocent. Now, I don't trust anyone."

"It might be a good idea if you didn't," Ross Langdon said gravely.

Eventually we made a list of the people we could definitely connect in any way with Nola's death and the ones who might possibly be involved in the attempted attack on myself. There were only two qualifications—acquaintanceship with Nola or with me.

It wasn't a very long list because I didn't know many people in Nashiona. On the masculine side there was Pete Dunbar, Chris, Gordon Kearnes, Johnny Forrester, Mark Kerrigan and Victor Jameson. On the feminine, Faye Latimer, Molly Dunbar, Rita Carstairs and Alice Wilson. Kerrigan, Forrester and Victor Jameson were unmarried so there was no wife complication to consider.

After some thought and to Father's horror I added Hilda Adams' name to the list of women. "For all I know she could have been acquainted with Nola Powers and she certainly knows me," I said in answer to Father's protests. "She was in the car when I met Miss Powers and I introduced them, but that doesn't mean she couldn't have known her before. They were all queer and stiff, coming up from the station. Nobody talked or made any effort to be friendly."

"Hilda! Hilda Adams!" Father was angry. "I don't see why you don't put me on your list, too, and be done with it; or that other one—that girl who was going to be married!"

"That little mouse?" I laughed. "Why, she was the complete stranger in a strange land. *She* wouldn't have anything to do with it."

Which was all I knew.

The list made, we sat and looked at it for a while. "The point," I remarked, "is that I'm not apt to see any of these people now unless I go deliberately into their homes, and that's a little too much like sticking my head into the lion's cage to appeal to me at present. As for going around asking leading questions—well, none of them are dumb; they'd catch on right away."

"It's unfortunate this thing tonight had to be public property," Ross Langdon said slowly, "You'd have had a better chance if it could have been kept secret."

"Secret!" I said. "With Pete Dunbar in it? Anything Pete knows, Molly knows too. And Molly's the world's champion chatterbox. Besides there's George and Dr. Summers. And the police. Somebody's sure to talk."

"Yes," Ross Langdon said. "So far as seeing these people—" he tapped the list—"is concerned, I wouldn't worry. I've an idea you'll have plenty of opportunity."

"As how?" I inquired.

"Gordon Kearnes was released from the hospital today."

There was meaning in his words. I struggled for it. "Gordon Kearnes—do you mean—oh, you can't—that he wants to go on with the—the play?"

He shrugged. "The play's what he's interested in," he reminded me. "Genius is usually single-minded and whatever else you call him Kearnes is a bit of a genius. For the rest of it, there's little difficulty. The cast is intact except for Nola Powers, and Alice Wilson is ready and willing—"

"If you think I'm going on," I said, "you're crazy!"

"Oh, yes, you are!" Father said surprisingly.

And Ross Langdon snapped, "Don't be a fool! Why not? You want to get this thing settled once and for all, don't you? Here's your chance. You—we, if you like—can learn more in three nights of rehearsals than the police can hope to in ten years."

"Suppose one of them tries to murder me again," I objected.

"No one will," Ross Langdon said quietly. "I'll be there."

I might have reminded him that so he was to have protected Nola Powers. I didn't.

Not long after that he left.

Believe it or not, Father wakened me before eight
o'clock next morning and dragged me down to the USO
with him. I was furious when I got the sleep out of my
eyes, but it made no difference. He was adamant. "I'm not
leaving you here alone in this house," he told me. "From
now on until we get someone to stay with you you're going
to be under my eye!"

"A fat chance you've got of getting anyone to stay with
me!" I muttered inelegantly.

As usual, I was wrong. That peerless paragon, Hilda,
accomplished the impossible in about three telephone
calls. There was a woman—a Mrs. Ferguson—whose husband had died the preceding spring. She had little money
and no training but she'd been able to rent the cottage she
owned to a captain and his wife and had been now reduced
to life in a rented room, which she disliked heartily. She
would be delighted to accommodate Mr. Thorpe, and an
interview was speedily arranged.

I had no doubt of its outcome. "I don't like it," I told
Father gloomily. "She's a widow and you're a widower.
What'll happen is she'll marry you—you wait and see! I
bet she's little and timid and a good cook. What I want's
protection. There'd be more sense to it if you moved Ross
Langdon in!"

"And let him marry you?" Father asked neatly. "Think
again, baby—think again!"

I wasn't present at the interview with the lady. I had to
attend the inquest which was set for one o'clock, because
the coroner, who was also an undertaker, had sufficient
funerals to clog up his morning. I didn't go alone. Ross
Langdon came for me.

I suppose all inquests conform to a definite pattern
but this was the first I'd attended and the proceedings
awed and frightened me. It was a bit shattering to know

that from our halting testimony this jury of three—bank-
er, baker and merchant, as Ross classified them—were
expected to pass with authority upon the who and how of
Nola Powers' slaying.

I don't know whether inquests are customarily private
or not, but there were few present who weren't closely
connected in one way or another with the murder. Chief
Hanover was there and Lieutenant Dreyer. There was a
bald youngish man whom Ross Langdon said was the state's
attorney and a thin dark one who was the sheriff of War-
bega County. And, of course, there was the cast, director,
and author of *The Good Woman*.

Our seats were far to the back so that I got little
opportunity to study my fellow players save when they
occupied the witness chair. Chris's appearance, particularly, appalled me although, knowing what I did, I couldn't be
surprised. He looked pounds thinner; the modeling of his
cheek bones stood out sharply and the blue-gray eyes were
sunk in pits of shadow. In sharp contrast, Alice Wilson,
dressed in what I suspected you called "gay black," looked
as smug and triumphant as the cat who'd swallowed the
canary. Gordon Kearnes brought her and all through the
inquest, in disregard of Coroner Marston's sharp glances,
their heads were closely together, their tongues active.

I don't think anyone expected much from the inquest—
not even the police. If anyone did, he was disappointed.
The verdict, "death by strangulation at the hands of a person or persons unknown" dropped without a ripple into
the pool of expectancy. Ross Langdon touched my arm. It
was all over. We went out.

Not very far, for Gordon Kearnes was almost immediately upon our heels. We understood, didn't we, that
Nola Powers' death would neither postpone nor cancel the
production of the play? It was distressing, of course, but
he trusted that we were all sufficiently seasoned troupers

to concur in that old cliche that the show "must go on."
Dates had been set, local and national publicity released,
the whole machinery of production set in motion. Nothing, not even personal considerations, must be permitted
to stop the play. Latimer, who might be said to have more
reason for being averse to the idea than the rest of us, had
agreed to go on and Mrs.—uh—Wilson had been prevailed
upon to take over Miss Powers' role. So we could see . . .

We did indeed, we agreed gravely. Gravely, too, we
promised to meet at the Latimer house that evening to
finish checking the script of the play. After that, rehearsals would go back to the Olympia, but for this one night,
this first meeting, as it were, after the tragedy, we might
be more comfortable in less memorable surroundings.

Safely away from him, I exploded. "'Less memorable
surroundings,' indeed! As though the Latimer house won't
be saturated with memories! I detest that man. 'Prevailed'
upon Alice— What does he take us for? Of course she took
the part—her tongue was fairly hanging out after it all
along! I'd hate to bet she wasn't the one who killed Nola
Powers after all, killed her just to pay her back for being
kept out of the cast!"

"Easy—easy," Ross Langdon counseled. "If I were you,
I'd look around twice before coming out with remarks of
that sort. Kearnes or anyone might have heard you, for
all you cared, and even though he does show a slight bias
toward Mrs. Wilson—"

"I don't like him either," I said stubbornly. "If you
think I care what he thinks . . ."

Ross Langdon lost patience with me then. "I think
you're a little idiot," he said bluntly. "Come on—I can't
waste any more time over you today. I'll hand you over to
your father as I promised and then I'm off. Let him see if
he can make you see reason."

Reason about what? I walked the three blocks between the funeral home and the YMCA in a sulky silence, but at the door I relented a little.

"Are you coming for me tonight?" I asked meekly.

He couldn't help grinning—probably at the meekness.

"I am. And in the meantime endeavor to keep out of trouble, will you? Although probably your father'll see to that."

He did. He was dictating letters thirteen to the dozen when I came in, but he stopped long enough to tell me that I could call a taxi and go home anytime I wanted to. I'd be quite safe. Mrs. Ferguson was eminently satisfactory and she had—with Hilda's help—already moved in.

I was curious enough to do just that little thing. "Eminently satisfactory"—from whose point of view I kept wondering? Men were perfect idiots when it came to hiring people, my own father not excepted, and I was willing to bet my next month's allowance that Mrs. Ferguson'd prove to be a fluffy little simpleton with a hard luck story and no brains. Well, if she had any notion that living in a widower's house meant automatic marriage with the widower, she was due to find out differently. I had no intention of sharing Father with anyone.

It's a good thing that wasn't an actual bet for I'd have lost it hands down one minute after I inserted my key in our white Georgian door. She was tall and Amazonian with thinnish white hair and the face of a horse in silver-rimmed spectacles. And she was a good ten years older than Father. I breathed a sigh of relief.

There was no awkwardness of explanation needed for our meeting. She came into the hall, peering shortsightedly through those preposterous spectacles and wiping her hands on an apron she must have brought with her—that voluminous blue-check was none of mine. She said, "You

Mary Thorpe? I'm Sarah Ferguson but I guess you know all that. Your Paw said he don't come home nights for supper so's I figured I'd just fix up something light and tasty for you and me—omelet and salad and an apple pudding. Do you want tea or coffee to drink? Your Paw said you'd be going out this evening so maybe we better eat early so's you'll have plenty of time to fix up after. Or if you wanted, you could go and lie down now for a while—your Paw said you didn't get much sleep last night."

"Not much sleep last night"—that miracle of understatement finished me. I went off into whooping hysterics from which I emerged presently to weep upon her shoulder.

She was all comfort. She patted me. "There—there," she crooned. "Cry if you want to, lovey. You're just a little bit of a thing and according to what your Paw says you've had a mighty unsettling experience. Your Paw ought never to have left you alone."

The upshot of it all was that I went to bed for a two-hour rest and had my dinner on a tray.

I even slept for a while because I didn't hear the telephone. It was Mrs. Ferguson who told me of the call. She said she guessed someone wanted me pretty bad for they'd called three times. "But," she said virtuously, "I told her I wouldn't wake you—not for nobody. You need your rest."

I was in a hurry. Ross Langdon was downstairs and I wasn't dressed. So I passed it off.

"Her," I said. "Oh, well, it was probably Molly Dunbar or Alice Wilson. It doesn't matter. I'll see them both tonight."

Only part of that was true. It did matter and it wasn't Alice or Molly. Mrs. Ferguson didn't know, of course—how could she?—but I can't help wishing now that she'd wakened me when the calls came through. I think—and Ross does too—that, had she done so, the mystery of Nola Powers' death might have been solved that night.

But she hadn't called me.

12

Ross Langdon gave me some gratuitous advice on the Latimer doorstep. "Don't talk tonight," he said. "Listen. It's just possible there may be something worth hearing."

"What if they ask me about last night?" I wanted to know. "Someone's almost sure to. What'll I say?"

"Tell them what happened and leave speculation alone. Remember Dunbar can check on your story."

I shivered a little and it wasn't from the cold. I said, "Ross, haven't the police found out anything yet? I don't think I can stand it much longer."

"You can. By the way, the funeral's tomorrow. Kearnes has been holding things up until Nola's New York attorney gets here. It'll be private but we're expected to go."

"Will you go with me?"

"Yes." He gave my arm a little shake. "Buck up now. No good going in there like a frightened rabbit. It'll only add more thrill to the chase."

That was a nice thing to say, but it had its effect. Anger or pride or something stiffened my knees. I threw up my head.

"That's better," he approved. "Oh and one other thing— I'd forget the overshoes for tonight. We'll keep them as a sort of ace- in-the-hole."

It wasn't as bad, going to the Latimers', as I'd expected. It was very much like other evenings I'd spent there. The long bare room was brilliantly lighted. Faye was still playing Tchaikovsky, and Chris and Gordon Kearnes stood on the dais beside a small stage model that had been placed on the grand piano. They were talking colors. The others were seated around, some in chairs, others on the huge floor cushions that formed an integral part of the Latimer furnishings.

We were the last. We said, "Hello!" and "How are you?" and "Sorry to be late," and then Ross Langdon went back into the hallway to remove his overcoat while I piled my things on the heap the other women's made on the window seat. I'd barely got them off when Chris stepped from the dais.

He clapped his hands for attention. "All right," he said. "Everybody here? Then let's get going. We've the devil of a lot to do."

But, before we got going, Gordon Kearnes had to make a speech. It was, I imagine, a masterpiece of its kind. He spoke very sadly and sweetly about Nola. She had meant, he told us, a very great deal to him. She had been the only part of his old life that had carried over with him into the new. He trusted that her murderer would soon be apprehended and punished. As we knew, the police were active but he had no fear that they believed her slayer to be one of our own little coterie. He did not think that we believed it either. Nola had had enemies—who in public life had not?—but that one of us had hated her enough to choke out her life was unthinkable. No, the police must prepare to look farther. For the rest, he was convinced that he—and all of us—must smother our private griefs, put aside our own personal feelings, and go on with the play. Nola herself would have wished it. He himself . . .

"It is in your hands," he said gravely, and sat with lowered head.

I wanted to say, "Baloney!" I refrained.

There were quite a few glances exchanged, but Chris gave us no chance to do anything with that perilous "something" which we held in our hands. "I take it," he said grimly, "that your presence here tonight signifies your willingness to go ahead with the play. If anyone wishes to change his mind, now's the chance. Anyone? All right—let's get started. Mary, you have the first lines."

The best I can say about that reading is that it wasn't the nightmare it could have been had Nola Powers herself ever condescended to read her particular lines. There were no remembered cadences of her voice to trouble us and Alice Wilson took over superbly—there was no other word for it.

"I shall cut my hair," she told us afterward—the reading had gone through in record time—while Faye was making coffee. "Oh, yes, I shall. Gordon says such a girl would most certainly have short hair. Shoulder length, I think—and a mass of curls just here—" She touched her eyebrows.

It sounded to me like an authentic copy of Nola Powers' hair-do and I shuddered, remembering black curls above wide-set topaz eyes.

Alice saw the shudder and was acid about it.

"What's the matter, Mary? Goose walking over your grave?"

Molly Dunbar plunged valiantly to my rescue.

"Mary's nervous and no wonder. After what happened—or almost happened to her—last night. . . ."

Alice's eyes were bright and hard. Too bright, I thought.

"Oh, yes. Pete was telling us. Have they found out anything—the police?"

Wordlessly I shook my head, not so much in obedience to Ross Langdon's command as to the fact that, temporarily, I had lost the will to speech.

"Oh, well, you can't expect too much of them, I suppose," Alice yawned. "This isn't a city with a high-geared police force. Old Hanover is a joke. Mark my words, Mary, they'll write off your little experience as unsolved and probably Nola's murder along with it."

There was a moment of silence, shocked silence. Then Molly spoke uncertainly. "But—but what makes you say that, Alice? It sounds so queer. Linking the—the person last night with Nola's murder. What connection would they have?"

Alice chain-lit another cigarette.

"Don't be a dope," she said bluntly. "Why shouldn't they be connected? Somebody murders Nola—Mary sees the murderer—somebody tries to murder Mary. Q.E.D. It's simpler than geometry."

"I didn't see the murderer," I protested weakly. "That is, I mean, I only saw a face—I didn't even see it clearly. I don't know that it *was* the murderer."

"Stick to it, kid," Alice advised. "Maybe if you say it often and loudly enough you'll have us believing you."

It was a nasty thing to say. I saw Rita Carstairs frown. "As though we didn't believe her, Alice," she said gently. "Tell me, Mary—last night—did you—I don't suppose you recognized whoever it was?"

I didn't let her finish. My "No!" cut in quickly. Too quickly, I saw glances exchanged. It was as though I'd protested too much.

It wasn't only glances. It wasn't glances that sent that queer little flick of tension down my spine. I didn't know who it was. I have only two eyes and I was looking at Rita. But I heard it. Breath withheld that expelled itself in a long slow sigh.

There was no way of telling from whom it had emanated; Alice, Rita, Molly and I—we formed a tight little group but the men, together, backed us. Faye was moving quietly from table to electric plate. I decided reluctantly that it might have been any one of them. I wondered if Ross Langdon had heard and if he knew, but I was afraid to risk a glance.

Alice lit another cigarette and crushed out a good half of the current one. "Oh, well," she said lightly. "Write it off as one of life's little mysteries. Which makes me think—we had a mystery of our own last night. Not yours, Mary—at my place. A pair of overshoes vanished into thin air. What do you think of that? Not as intriguing as your little adventure but in these days of rubber shortages . . ." She leaned back and grinned at me.

I could feel the pounding increase of my heart's beat. My voice sounded choked and breathless. "Overshoes," I said. "Why, how queer! Whose were they?"

"They belonged," Alice stated, "to Mr. Christopher Latimer and, from the fuss he made over their disappearance, I think they must have been gold-buckled or diamond-studded or something. How any man could bring himself to wear such priceless articles and then abandon them in the hall outside my apartment door passes my comprehension. They should have been kept in a vault."

"They were new, Alice," Faye said gravely. She put a plate of sandwiches on the table behind us and paused for a moment, her hand on the back of Alice's chair. "Chris had only had them a week."

"He ought to know what a walk-up apartment is like," Alice grumbled. "Anyone could have come in and taken them. Heavens, the fuss he made! He had all of us running around like crazy."

"All of us?" My voice was still rusty. "Was it a party?"

"A party?" Alice's eyes were shuttered, her voice insolent. "Not exactly. Officially it was a meeting of the Theater Board. We had to decide—whether to go on with this thing or let it drop. Chris was there and Gordon,

Molly and Pete, Johnny Forrester, Mark, Rita—all the old guard."

"I don't think it was so very official," Molly objected. "We just barely got started talking and then Pete reminded us of the blackout and everybody rushed off."

"Chris didn't," Alice said. "He hung around until it was almost blackout time, hunting for his overshoes, ringing doorbells and making a general nuisance of himself. If I thought burglary insurance would cover, I'd certainly put in a claim and see if that would shut him up!"

"But nobody'd steal overshoes!" Molly said. "Would they? What for?"

The question went unanswered for Faye announced the coffee done just at that moment, and there was a concerted rush for plates and cups. Personally it was a question I didn't need answered. I knew.

The rest of the evening was rather dull—dull for that crowd, I mean. We ate our sandwiches and drank our coffee. Conversation was general and desultory. Nobody seemed to have the heart to play the Capehart. It was early—just eleven—when the first move toward home was made.

As usual going home took quite a while. We had to unscramble hats and coats and scarfs and purses, and that all took time. I had just assembled my possessions and was tying my scarf under my chin when Rita Carstairs spoke to me. She said, "Mary, how are you going home? Do you have your car?"

I said that I hadn't—that I'd come with Mr. Langdon— and she proceeded, "I wonder if he'd mind taking me too? It's not much out of the way and it's so hard to get a taxi since the army camp's been here. The soldiers seem to want them all."

I said of course she could, and she smiled gratefully. "I wouldn't ask only I don't think I should walk. You see,

I twisted my ankle rather badly last night." In evidence she held out a shapely foot whose ankle's taping showed through the sheer silk of her stocking.

My eyes must have been fairly popping out. I lowered them hastily so that she wouldn't see. I muttered something about telling Ross and made my escape.

Twisted her ankle, had she? How? Where? Could it have been in a sudden wild dash from an unfamiliar house—a house from which, her errand undone and her presence jeopardized, she had found it imperative to flee?

I went over to Ross. My voice was shaking as I told him. "Rita's coming with us. She—she hurt her ankle. Last night."

He gave me a quick look. He said softly, "All right—watch yourself." And then louder, "Why sure—sure. We'll be glad to take her."

We didn't talk on the way to the apartment. Rita said the customary things about how kind we were to give her a ride and that was all.

Rita's apartment was about five blocks from my place. I sat beside Ross, squeezing my hands together and figuring the distance. Five blocks—that wasn't so very far. It wouldn't take long to walk five blocks. And Rita had left Alice's in time to get home before the blackout—Alice had said so.

The car stopped with a little jerk that threw me back against the seat. To my surprise Ross shut off the engine and opened the front door. "Do you mind if we come up for a minute? I'd like to talk to you."

The apartment building was at a corner and a street light flickered across Rita's face. I thought she looked frightened but she only said quietly, "Why, no. Of course not. Do come up."

Rita's apartment is beautiful. It's serene and ordered and irreproachably in good taste, but a little bit too much of a director's dream to suit me. I like a place to look lived in. This one didn't. It was as impersonal as Rita herself.

Perhaps that's a funny thing to say, but it's true. Just as the apartment appeared to be no more than the semblance of a house, so Rita was the wraith of a person. She wasn't good-looking but she was always beautifully and expensively dressed, and her hair and nails were perfection. But that was all there was to it. You had the feeling that all that was an elaborate facade that hid an empty house. No one lived there. Or perhaps Hans Christian Andersen expressed it better in his tale of the elf king's daughters who were "all front and no back."

I don't know whether or not Ross had sensed that too. We sat side by side on a graceful Empire sofa and Rita sat opposite. After that first flicker of fear her face seemed to have settled into its usual placidity. She simply sat and waited, without visible curiosity, for us to speak.

And Ross spoke. He said, "Miss Carstairs, when did you hurt your ankle?"

Rita looked mildly puzzled. "My ankle? Why, yesterday morning. In the fruit cellar. I climbed up on a box and slipped. Luckily Dr. Blackwell was at home and he taped it right away. Why do you want to know? What difference can it make?"

"Someone attacked Mary at her home last night," Ross said quietly. "Whoever it was was forced to get out in a hurry. Now, do you understand?"

"Understand? No." There was honest bewilderment in Rita's voice. "Mary—why should I want to harm Mary?"

"Mary saw Nola Powers' murderer," Ross said quietly.

She stared at him. "Nola's murderer!—But I didn't kill Nola! Even though I hated her—even though I'm glad she's dead—I wouldn't have killed her. What makes you think that I would?"

"I don't," Ross said. "Not now. But I had to be sure."

"To be sure." She repeated it after him like a child. "Why?"

"Because I need help—somebody's help—if this thing is ever to be settled."

"Why should I help you?" she asked quickly.

He shrugged. "Why not?"

There was a silence broken only by the quickening of Rita's breath. Then she said, "Listen, Mr. Langdon. I hated Nola Powers!—you've made me admit it. Do you know why? Because six years ago I had a sister—a younger sister about as old as Mary there—whom I loved very much. She was going to be married—the engagement had been announced—people were giving parties for her. Then he—my sister's fiancé—met Nola. She was Chris Latimer's wife then but she was looking for amusement. She—bewitched him, that's the only word for it. He forgot Kathy, my sister. The engagement was broken. My sister didn't care to live. One night she took an overdose of sleeping medicine. The verdict was 'accidental death' but I knew better. It was murder. Nola Powers murdered her just as surely as now she herself has been slain. Help you find Nola's murderer? No, Mr. Langdon—no, a thousand times no! I don't want him found because at last the score between me and that woman has been evened. Hunt him down? Never! I'd be proud to help him to go unhindered. For the service he's done humanity and me!"

"And what about Mary?" Ross asked quietly. He didn't look at her.

"Mary?" Her lip was caught between her teeth.

"Someone tried to kill Mary last night," Ross repeated. "He—or she—failed. But there'll be another night. . . ."

"You can protect her!" She was breathing hard again.

"Can we?" Ross asked softly. "I wonder. We can try, of course. We will. But that attack last night proves something.

It proves that the murderer is afraid and once fear has entered in—" He spread his hands in a wide gesture.

"Why should he be afraid?" Rita asked proudly. "He has no need. There is not one of us who wouldn't thank him—thank him on our bended knees—"

"The police?" He was watching her now. "Do you think Hanover is grateful? Am I? Is Mary?"

"Will you leave me out of it?" I asked furiously. "It's bad enough to know that someone tried to kill me without listening to you talk about it all the time. 'Mary's in danger'—'We'll try to protect Mary'—'There's another night coming'— Do you think it's fun to listen to things like that? You can bet you'd better figure out some way to protect Mary—she has no intention of dying so that Nola Powers' murderer can go scot-free!"

They were both looking at me. "All right," Ross Langdon said softly and it wasn't to me. "There's your answer. How do you like it? She's about your sister's age, didn't you say? She's young—attractive—her whole life before her just as Kathy's was—"

"Stop!" Rita Carstairs said. She drew her hand across her eyes. "All right," she said dully. "I'll do it. I'll help you. What is it you want to know?"

"Everything," Ross Langdon said promptly. "Everything you can tell me. About Nola Powers and the interrelations between her and the—'the old guard,' as Alice Wilson called it, of the Little Theater group. I want the gossip, the scandal, real or suspected, the feuds, the friendships. In other words, I want the complete low-down. Do you think you can give it to me?"

"I can try,", she said slowly. "But not now—not tonight. You'll have to give me time— It's only since—since my sister's death that I've been active in the Little Theater. It was she who—I'll have to get my thoughts together, you

must see that. Now I'm—I'm all confused. I hadn't expected— Tomorrow if you'll come—"

"We-ell," Ross Langdon agreed but I could tell he was
disappointed. "Very well—tomorrow. Will you set a time?"

"Early," Rita Carstairs said. "Yes, early, please. As soon
as you can come. Otherwise I—I might lose my courage."
She smiled faintly.

At the door Ross paused for one more question. "This
man who was to have married your sister—who was he?"

She winced. "Does it matter?" and then, weakly, "All
right, I'll tell you. It was Johnny—Johnny Forrester. Now,
go, will you please? I—I can't stand any more."

We said good-night and left her. There was nothing
else to do. She stood in the lighted doorway and watched
us go. At the foot of the stairs I turned and waved at her.
I'm glad I did. I never saw her again. Not alive.

13

I would have liked to have talked during our four-block ride to the house, but Ross Langdon wasn't having it that way. He only grunted when I asked him if he thought he'd learned anything.

"Anything that will help, I mean," I explained unnecessarily.

He shrugged. "Perhaps. Not that there's much to go on—yet."

"There's Chris's overshoes," I pointed out. "And Johnny Forrester."

He said, "Huh! So far as that goes we've unearthed a passable motive for Rita Carstairs and still—" I heard his breath suck in a little. Suddenly he hammered hard with his hand upon the wheel. "I wish I hadn't been such a fool," he said softly and bitterly, "letting her put me off like that. I should have stayed with her—knocked it out of her if necessary. Tomorrow . . ." He fell silent.

"Tomorrow?"

"I don't know—it may be too late. The wind was blowing our way tonight. By tomorrow it may have changed direction."

Well, that was true enough. I'd hate to count the times I've changed my mind overnight. So I didn't argue it. I only asked meekly if he'd take me with him—tomorrow—

when he went to test the wind's direction. He shook his head. "No—I'll do better alone. Surely you know how an extra woman can curdle the broth sometimes."

"But you'll tell me?" I begged. "What she says? I think I've a right to know."

"I'll pick you up for the funeral," he agreed. "I'll tell you then."

"All of it?" I was greedy.

"As much as is good for you," he promised gravely.

I had to be satisfied with that.

We'd reached the house, by this time. Lights starred it from attic to cellar. Ross Langdon gestured toward them. "No blackout tonight. Do you want me to come in with you? Are you afraid?"

I said I wasn't. "Not with Cerberus guarding my doorstep. Mrs. Cerberus. Her husband was a policeman. I think she must have been a desk sergeant."

He laughed at that but he followed me from the car none the less.

I had to ring—I'd forgotten my key. Mrs. Ferguson opened the door promptly and with its opening we recoiled, our eardrums shattered by the combined sound of radio and piano that was pouring itself through the living room's arches. I said, "What in the world—?"

Mrs. Ferguson glanced over her shoulder. "It's the army," she said complacently. "Your Paw he sent them up from that U-sew office of his. Nice enough boys but they're kind of noisy. Maybe now that you've come . . ."

She didn't sound too hopeful about it and Ross Langdon's eyes twinkled. "Your father's a smart man, Mary. I think you'll be safe enough tonight. I'll call you tomorrow." And with that he raised his hat and left me.

I walked over to the archway. The piano-radio combination was deafening. I peered cautiously into the room. Mrs. Ferguson was undoubtedly right. This was the army and they seemed to have moved in. A khaki-clad form lolled in the big chair beside the radio; another, upon the piano bench, swayed to the boogie-woogie his own fingers evoked. A third youngster knelt upon the hearth shaking a corn popper in rhythmic accompaniment to the music.

I looked at Mrs. Ferguson. I said, "Do you honestly mean that Father—?"

Mrs. Ferguson nodded. "He phoned a while ago. He said he was sending some boys out—reinforcements he called 'em. He said they'd see nothing happened to you. He said he spent his days and nights doing things for the army and now it was the army's turn to do things for him. He says there'll be more every night. Them's not all," she mentioned placidly. "There's another out in the kitchen eating. He said he was hungry and he was going to see what he could find—in the ice box. He musta found a lot," she added doubtfully, "the length of time he's stayed. I don't know. Maybe your Paw knows what he's doing but what there's going to be left for his breakfast when that locust gets through I ain't in any position to judge."

I laughed. I said, "Well, that's Father's lookout. For my part I think they look very nice and safe and I don't care how much noise they make. I'm going up to bed and for once I think I'll sleep!"

I did, too—sleep. I didn't hear Father come home nor the hooting of the taxi that arrived to convey the army back to its base. I didn't hear anything until Mrs. Ferguson toiled up the stairs in mid-morning to shake me awake.

"I wouldn't have woke you," she explained apologetically while I lay bemusedly and blinked at her and at the bright sunlight that flickered across my dressing table mirror. "It's that Mr. Langdon and he says it didn't matter if you was asleep—I was to call you. He's on the phone and he says it's important."

It had better be, I thought as I reached for a robe. The first decent sleep I'd had for eternities and then to be yanked out of it. . . .

I picked up the hand set. I said, "Well?" and my voice was noticeably frigid. "I suppose it's all over and wound up and you just couldn't wait to tell me."

He cut me off. He was equally cold. "I haven't anything to tell you—not in the way you mean. I merely called to remind you that Nola Powers' funeral is at one-thirty and that I'll pick you up at one sharp."

"Oho!" I said. "So the wind wasn't in your direction after all. I hardly thought it would be."

"I don't know a damn thing about the wind," he said curtly. "I didn't see Miss Carstairs if that's what you mean."

"Oh!" I stopped being funny. "But I thought—why not?"

"It wasn't for want of trying," he said grimly. "I told you I had a hunch about it last night. I rang her bell for the first time at nine o'clock this morning. I've been ringing it at intervals ever since. So far, no response."

"Oh!" I said again. It wasn't very brilliant but it was all I could do. "Have you tried to call her?"

"Yes." The voice was still grim. "The telephone doesn't answer either."

There was a silence.

"Oh, well, she probably changed her mind," I offered at last.

"No doubt. Or had it changed for her."

"What do you mean by that?"

"That she may have had another visitor after we left. One who persuaded her of the wisdom of keeping still."

"Oh!" There was that "oh" again but I couldn't help it. It's a useful expression. "Who?"

"How do I know?" Irritation snapped in his voice. "If all you're going to do is ask idiotic questions—"

"I'm not. I won't. Well—would you like me to try and call her?"

"You can try. But unless you can figure out some way to differentiate between your telephone calls and mine, I don't see what you'll accomplish."

Neither did I. The polished floor was getting chilly to my bare feet. I stood first on one and then on the other while I tried to think. I wondered how long this "fuzzy-around-the-edges" feeling was going to persist. Perhaps after I'd had my coffee. . . .

"Do you think she's there?" I hazarded. "Hiding in her apartment, I mean?"

"I don't know. And short of breaking in I can't see how I'm going to find out."

"Then there's really nothing we can do, is there?" I asked brilliantly. "Oh, wait! I know! The funeral. She'll be at that, won't she? We can get hold of her afterwards—try again."

"We can try—yes. However I've an idea that golden moment has gone from us forever." He sounded tired, irritated, worried. "All right—don't think about it. My fault and I'm sorry as hell I muffed it. Anything new happened there?"

I said, "No," and he hung up. I went upstairs, got my slippers and came back down again. There was coffee, grapefruit and rolls on the breakfast-nook table. I pointed to them. I said, "So something did survive after all. What was the matter—doesn't the army go for grapefruit?"

She snorted. "Your Paw was shopping early this morning—that's where them rolls come from. He says there's some more of them soldiers coming tonight and all of them hungry as wolves, like as not. You eat that grapefruit while you got it's my advice!"

It sounded good. I acted on it.

It was while I was drinking my second cup of coffee that she told me about the telephone call. Some woman had called several times. The last time she left her name and a number. I was to call her. It was important.

"Wallace?" I said. "I don't know any Wallaces. Or wait—perhaps I do. It seems to me I met a Mrs. Wallace somewhere—it may have been at church. I suppose there's a dinner or a meeting or something. Let her call again when I'm here. She will if she I wants me bad enough."

She did want me—bad enough. She did call again and I didn't answer, and after that it was too late.

It wasn't until I'd bathed and dressed that it occurred to me to ask Mrs. Ferguson about the police. I did it casually. A good night's sleep had given me a new perspective on events in general. What had happened now seemed a long time in the past, no more than vague remembrances out of a dream. The police, I said, it was queer they hadn't been bothering around.

I got a shock. They had. That very morning. Moreover they'd walked off with that pair of men's overshoes that had been in the kitchen.

I said, "What? Now where'd they hear about them? What did they say?"

They hadn't said much. Mrs. Ferguson had gathered that somebody'd telephoned them about losing some overshoes and when they saw those . . .

"They asked me and I didn't know nothing about them," Mrs. Ferguson said, "so they called your Paw and talked to him for a while. Then they took the overshoes away."

I said, "Damn!" and meant it. There, for what it was worth, went Ross Langdon's ace-in-the-hole.

I called Father. He was feeling very righteous and I suspect slightly guilty. He said, "I can't help it if Langdon wanted to keep them for his private amusement. When the police ask me questions, I'm not going to lie to them."

I said his scruples were commendable but that I thought they might have asked *me*.

It wasn't necessary, Father told me stiffly. I was asleep and anyway he knew as much about the overshoes as I did.

"That's just the point," I told him smartly. "I don't think you do!" I hung up before he could say anything more. That, I told myself, will give him something to worry about!

The telephone rang at once but I didn't answer it. Mrs. Ferguson appeared from the kitchen but I waved her away. "Never mind," I said. "It's only Father and I don't want to talk to him."

Now, of course, I know that it wasn't Father—that it was Beth Wallace and that she was making a last desperate attempt to reach me.

Ross Langdon arrived promptly at one o'clock. He was both preoccupied and grumpy. Not even my account of the rape of the overshoes got a reaction. He said, "Oh, well, what the hell! Suppose they have got them—why worry? It's only one more thing gone wrong along with all the rest of this screwy case. Let Dreyer play with them—see where *he* gets!"

Which ended that conversation.

So far as I could see, Nola Powers' funeral differed from other funerals I'd attended in only one respect: the crowd was outside the mortuary chapel rather than in. Word that the services were to be strictly private had gone forth, but that fact, publicized as it had been, hadn't kept a crowd of the avidly curious from attempting to savor all there was to see and hear. A solid press of men and women, held in half-check by blue-coated policemen, eddied about the low stone steps of the Marston Funeral Chapel. We had to almost fight our way through to the glass entrance doors. Once, in the push, my hat tipped sideways but Ross Langdon gave me no time to readjust it. He simply tightened the grip, he had clamped on my elbow and hurried me on. His face was grim.

But once beyond the glassed entrance doors we stepped straight into the familiar atmosphere of hushed quiet that pervades funeral homes. Thick rugs deadened our footsteps. The breathless scent of flowers vied with the underlying odor of antiseptic. Behind close checkered grills a muted organ throbbed. Exuding professional sympathy, Mr. Dewey Marston, correct in tail coat, carnation and snowy gloves, preceded us with mournful tread into the chapel auditorium.

I suppose the room would have accommodated a hundred and fifty people. There were thirteen of us gathered there. I know. I counted them. The Latimers—Chris, stiffly erect, arms folded upon his breast; Faye huddled close to him but with her flower-face held proudly high. Alice Wilson, somberly spectacular in black. Gordon Kearnes, a band of crepe blatant upon his sleeve. Pete and Molly Dunbar—Molly, her tongue for once silenced; Pete, slumped into his chair, his eyes staring steadfastly at the floor. Johnny Forrester and Mark Kerrigan, together. Victor Jameson, alone. Police Chief Hanover and Lieutenant Dreyer. A small spare stranger whom we later learned was Nola Powers' New York lawyer. Ross Langdon and I. That was all. Thirteen of us—

Thirteen! But it shouldn't have been thirteen—thirteen was wrong. Because one of us wasn't there. Rita Carstairs was missing!

Just for a moment there, I felt queer all over. I told myself it was all right—it had to be. Nothing had happened to Rita—she'd simply decided not come. But why? She wasn't a fool. Surely, like the rest of us, she'd know this wasn't the sort of funeral from which you remained away by choice. Attendance here was obligatory—a gesture owed to ourselves if not to Nola.

But I couldn't make it seem all right—not in conjunction with that inexplicable absence from the apartment, the unanswered telephone and doorbells. Where could she be? Surely she wouldn't have gone away—

My hands were cold, chilled by an unknown fear. I looked at Ross to see if he, too, had noticed Rita's absence, and got no help from him. He had. I could tell by his face. I put out my hand to touch him and drew it back. A voice—a young voice—was speaking.

"Lord, make me know mine end and the measure of my days. . . ."

The service had begun.

It was of the simplest. There were no pallbearers, no music other than that provided by the hidden organist. The youngish minister prayed briefly. Then the heavy velvet curtains, looped before the alcove that contained the casket, fell straightly and swished together. The young minister went out. It was all over.

We stood up uncertainly. We could go now. There was nothing to wait for. There would be no committal rites at the cemetery. That night Nola's body would be shipped to a crematory. After that—well, the ultimate disposal of her ashes would doubtless be up to the New York lawyer.

Constraint was upon us. We smiled at one another in the aisles, in the lobby, stiff little smiles that did no more than acknowledge presence. As we had come, we drifted away, still without speech, in ones or twos.

All but me. The others—Chris and Faye, Alice, Gordon Kearnes, the Dunbars—had gone. But Ross Langdon wasn't leaving. He was with the police chief and Lieutenant Dreyer. He was talking to them and they were listening. I waited.

He came over to me presently. He said, "I'm going to have one last try at Rita Carstairs' apartment. Dreyer and Hanover are coming along."

That was all. He put me into the car and drove off. The police, car followed.

I haven't any idea what road we took to get there—whether we drove fast or slow. I wasn't in any state to remember. I was cold all over now—shaking. This was to be the end, the answer to all questions. What would we find in Rita's apartment? Would it be silent, quiet, abandoned? Or would there be someone—something—there?

The car stopped. I looked up at brick walls, rosy in the slanting sunlight. Ross was out of the car, walking toward the police car which had pulled up behind us. He spoke for a second, came back. He started up the steps. Alone.

I was out of the car, too. Running across the sidewalk, calling to him. "Ross—Ross! Wait for me!"

He waited. He said, "I should have taken you home, Mary; this is no place for you. Why don't you stay in the car like a good girl?"

"I can't," I said. "I have to know—you know that."

"Yes. I know," he answered.

There were six bells below six mail boxes in the tiny foyer. Beyond a glassed door, buzzer-controlled, we could see the stairway leading upwards into dimness. Rita's apartment was on the second floor. Ross put his finger on the bell below her name.

We waited. Nothing happened. He rang again. Again. Still nothing. Ross's mouth was grim. He changed to another bell, pressed it.

This time the buzzer sounded. He opened the glass door. I followed him inside. Halfway down the stairway a woman stood looking at us. She said, "Yes? What did you want?"

Ross told her. She listened attentively. Why, no, she said thoughtfully, she didn't believe she had seen Miss Carstairs today. That was queer too for it was her day for cleaning—Miss Carstair's too. They usually met on the back porch where they shook dust mops and such. But she'd been at home last night—the lights had been on and she'd heard talking. Not to know what was said, of course, but this was an old building and the walls were thin. What did we think she could do?

Would she mind, Ross asked, going out on that back porch and rapping at Miss Carstair's door—calling to her? It might be that she simply didn't want to see us—if that was so, it was all right. Only we'd like some assurance that she was not ill, that nothing had happened to her. . . .

The woman looked frightened. She turned and walked away quickly. We waited. In silence. The woman came back. She looked more frightened now. She said breathlessly, "She doesn't answer. I rapped and rapped. The door's locked—I tried it—but the light in the kitchen—the electric light's burning."

I had only time to gasp before Ross Langdon's hands were on my shoulders swinging me around. "Go downstairs, Mary. Tell the others to come. And you—wait in the car."

I went downstairs. There were three men in the car. Lieutenant Dreyer had the door open. He said, "Well?" and I said, "He wants you to come."

I followed them in. I couldn't stay outside. I had to know. Ross scowled at me but he was too busy answering questions to bother with me. I stood beside the woman whose name was Green—I saw it on the door card. We both waited.

It seemed to take a long time. The caretakers lived in the basement and Lieutenant Dreyer went to look for them. Presently he came back, a stout gray-haired woman in tow. She had a lot of keys. One of them worked. The door opened. The four of them went in.

I could feel Mrs. Green's shivering. She said, "What is it? What're they afraid of? Do they think that she—that she—"

I said crossly, "Oh, keep still! I don't know, I tell you—I don't know!"

But I did. I knew, even before Ross opened the door and came out. He was very pale and grim. He shut the door behind him. He looked at me.

I said, "Is she—is she—?"

He nodded. "Yes. Same way as the other. Mary, the police car's downstairs. Will you go and let him take you home? I'll come as soon as I can."

I turned and went down the stairs, my hand groping for the stair rail. Behind me, I could hear Mrs. Green's voice, high and hysterical, asking questions. I didn't wait for the answers. I didn't want to know them. Not then.

14

Ross didn't come until after six. When he did, I took one look at his face and then got up and—in spite of the fact that my own legs seemed made of rubber—retired kitchenwards. Mrs. Ferguson was both sympathetic and resourceful. In no time at all the smell of coffee was in the air and she appeared, rolling the tea wagon loaded down with a variety of sandwiches and—how she accomplished it in these days of sugar rationing I don't know!—a fudge-frosted chocolate cake.

Ross's eyes brightened; he drank the coffee as though he needed it.

"Do I look that hungry?" he asked.

I shrugged. "Anything left over," I mentioned, "will be capably handled by the army tonight."

Mrs. Ferguson snorted and started out. I stopped her. "Don't go. You're in this too. Sit down and we'll get the story."

Ross's eyebrows raised delicately.

"Well, she is," I told him. "She's my bodyguard, isn't she? Besides her husband was a policeman. She's probably kept lots of secrets in her time."

Mrs. Ferguson said that she had. She got her knitting—something blue for the navy—and sat down.

I looked at Ross, registering expectation.

"All right," he said sulkily. "Have it your way. Where do you want me to start?"

"At the beginning, stupid!" I said crossly. "I want to know what happened!"

"It wasn't nice, you know." He avoided my eyes. "She was strangled—like Nola—with another one of those damnable scarves. A blue one this time."

I felt a little sick again. "I should think they'd try and find out about those scarves," I said. "Someone must have a regular collection."

"They know where they come from," Ross said flatly. "Or rather—where they came from. Latimer told them. A couple of years ago Molly Dunbar took the part of a dancer in one of the Theater plays. The costume was a rainbow affair with a skirt made entirely from those scarves. The costume was kept in the property room at the Y. It's not there now."

"In the property room!" I sat up straight. "Listen! The property room was open the night of the tryouts—I know it was! And everyone was—oh, wandering in and out. Anyone could have gone in and taken it."

"So Latimer says. He also says it was the last time the room was open and that he has the only key."

I digested that. "Then that means it probably was taken that night and—oh, I don't like this at all! It sounds as though someone had planned to kill Nola even then!"

"Good God, Mary!" There was an edge to Ross's voice. "You don't think this was any spur of the moment thing, do you? Of course it was planned—planned down to the last detail and smartly done at that. Think of the means used. No awkward guns or knives—nothing to buy. Simply an old costume—to which any one of a dozen people might have had access."

"But," I said, "surely somebody must have seen someone going in or out."

Ross shrugged and lit a cigarette. "That's what Dreyer thought before Latimer took him down and showed him. He's not so sure now. Latimer convinced him that there was no one permanently stationed in the green room and that, so far as the crowd in the auditorium went, they were constantly on the move—up and down stairs—"

"I know," I said. "Cokes and candy bars and what have you from the counter upstairs. No, if you picked your time carefully, no one would notice but—wouldn't the costume be seen? I mean, you'd have to roll it up some way."

"Doubtful. Latimer said it was only a wisp of a thing. He said it could be stuffed in a pocket or a hand bag. Molly's not very big, you know."

"No." I knew. "How many scarves were there—do you know?"

"How many—how do I know? What difference does it make?"

"None," I admitted drearily. "I just thought I'd like to be sure. A rainbow has six colors and the red, blue and orange scarves have been—been used. But there'd be at least three more."

"Good Lord!" Ross sank back and stared at me. "Well, there's something in what you say but . . . Do you always have such lovely thoughts, my sweet?"

"They're not lovely," I said soberly. "They make me sick myself, just thinking, them. And I think we'd better get back to the original subject—Rita Carstairs." If he thought he was going to call me pet names at this stage of the game he was wrong. "Where was she when you found her?"

He gave me a considering look.

"There were two mulberry colored chairs—one on either side of the fireplace—remember? They'd been pulled together near a tea table. There were two coffee cups on the table, a percolator, one glass with the remains of a highball."

I was leaning forward. "Fingerprints?" I breathed.

"No. Wiped clean. There were traces where ashes had been spilled on the hearth, but the ash trays were empty. There were no signs of a struggle. Miss Carstairs was simply leaning back in her chair. Dreyer says it was the same method as the murderer'd used before—she was knocked out with some heavy article and then strangled while unconscious."

"And no cigarette stubs, and the cups wiped clean," I said slowly. "It could have been a woman then."

"Yes?" Ross was watching me closely.

"I'm thinking of lipstick," I explained. "The kind I use is guaranteed indelible, but just the same it comes off a little. On napkins and cup rims and cigarette stubs. But if they're all gone—done away with—it'd be hard to tell. A woman would think of that."

"There was that highball glass. Any woman you know who'd require that?"

"Anyone—afterwards, I should think," I said with a shiver. "Before—I don't know. Alice Wilson, perhaps. Not Molly nor Faye—Molly can't drink anything; she says it makes her sick. And I can't imagine Faye and whiskey— Oh, wait! Rita! She was all upset when we left. What if she took a drink herself to steady her nerves?"

"Could be, I suppose," Ross Langdon said, "but in that case why wipe the glasses? Rita's prints were left on the one cup. It was only the glass and the other cup that were clean. No, I think you're right in that she needed a pick-up of some kind but she chose coffee rather than liquor. And, just as the coffee was done, someone else came."

"You and I were there," I said thoughtfully. "I could have had the cup of coffee and you the highball. Why don't the police suspect us? Or do they?"

"No." He drew a long breath. "Thanks to the woman next door—Mrs. Green. She told them she heard us go—

Miss Carstairs came to the top of the stairs with us—remember? She said it was later—perhaps by half an hour—when Miss Carstairs' buzzer rang again. She heard the door released, footsteps on the stairs, and after that voices for a long time."

"One of them neighborhood snoops—that's all she is," Mrs. Ferguson commented darkly. "I've met 'em before. There's one in every apartment!"

"Well, if she was snooping, it's too bad she didn't carry it a little farther," I said. "If she'd only been curious enough to take a peek out—did she?"

"She says not," Ross said gravely but there was a twinkle in his eye. "However the walls between the two apartments are thin. She is quite definite about the voices—a man's and a woman's. She was still hearing them when she went to sleep, and that was late, approximately one o'clock."

"A man's voice," I said. "Oh, damn! I had it all worked out that it would be a woman's."

"*What* woman?" Ross Langdon asked. "You don't want it to be Molly Dunbar—you insist it can't be Faye Latimer. Can it be that you're trying to push it off on Alice Wilson?"

"Alice," I began and stopped. "Why, I don't know. She'd be the only other one, wouldn't she? I'll admit I don't like her very well—not as much as the others. She's lovely to look at, but her giggle gets on my nerves and she never seems—oh, real. You can't get at her, the real her. She dresses beautifully, of course, and she reads all the important books and listens to all the right music and says all the correct things about them, but I'm never sure whether it's what she really thinks or what she thinks she ought to think. She's too—too something," I finished, "and I don't know what it is. Besides, I think her hair's dyed—the color's not right for her eyes and skin—and I know she's man-crazy. Look at the way she carried on over Gordon Kearnes!"

"My stars!" Mrs. Ferguson put down her knitting. "You sure don't love her none!"

"What's this Kearnes angle?" Ross Langdon asked.

"I'm not sure it's anything," I said doubtfully. "Only— she's always talking about him and calling him 'Gordie,' and she says they're dear friends, and it's certain that the first place he went when he arrived in town was to her apartment. Then it's the way she acts about him—possessive. Of course he's an important person and she may just be parading her intimacy with the great man. Or it might be something else. Alice fancies herself as an actress. Perhaps she'd like a chance at New York too. Gordon Kearnes did things for Nola—or so they say. Now that, she's gone—"

I stopped then, cold at the expression on Ross's face.

"Yes," he said slowly. "Now that she's gone." He got up and walked over to the window.

I said, "No. I don't believe it. She couldn't have seen that far—she wouldn't have planned to—to kill another woman just to have a problematical chance at a part that might eventually take her to New York. I won't believe it—I can't!"

"Why not?" He hadn't turned back from the window. "How well do you know Alice Wilson anyway?"

"Why, I don't . . . What do you mean?"

"Oh, Lord, I don't know." He was facing me now. "Who is she—what is she—what sort of a person lurks behind that lovely facade, I mean. She calls herself 'Mrs.' Wilson but where's the husband? Is he dead or divorced? How long has she lived in Nashiona? Who are her friends?" He made a gesture with his hands. "That sort of thing. Can you tell me?"

I shook my head. "I don't know her that well. I don't know her at all, really. When you're a stranger, you have to be contented with scraps of knowledge. You just accept

what people tell you. At least I do. I suppose I've liked
her. She's been nice to me. But I don't really *know* anything. I haven't lived here long enough. Molly could tell
you better."

"No," Ross said bluntly. "I won't try that again. Have
you forgotten Rita Carstairs?"

Of course I hadn't but at his words a sudden chill moved
along my spine. Ross was right. What we had done was the
sort of thing you couldn't risk doing twice. Last night we
had persuaded Rita against her will and because of that
she was dead.

Hopelessly I asked, "But what can we do? What can
anybody do?"

"The obvious thing. Drop out. Leave it to the police."

I looked at his stubborn mouth. "But you don't mean
to."

"No. No, you're right. I won't. But you will."

"I won't," I said. He didn't answer and there was a
silence during which Mrs. Ferguson's needles clicked in
brisk staccato. She finished a row, smoothed out the knitting and looked at it, her mouth pursed. Almost inaudibly
she spoke. "It's *women* they've been killing, ain't it?"

I looked at her blankly. The words just didn't register
in my weary brain. Maybe Ross's wasn't so tired. At any
rate he straightened and looked at Mrs. Ferguson with
something like respect.

"She's right," he said. "She's damn right! What a fool
I've been!"

"Wait!" I said. "What's she right about? I don't see." I
got it then. I said, "Oh! You mean that you should have
asked Mike or Johnny or—or Chris instead of Rita? That
because they're men they'd have been able to protect themselves. Is that it?"

He scarcely noticed. He was rushing ahead. "I picked
a woman—the one I was certain was the weak link in the

chain—and then was idiot enough to expect she'd be able to protect herself. Of course I should have asked a man—I'd have gotten the same information—"

"How do you know?" I demanded, disgruntled. "And what makes you so certain a man can protect himself either? If the—the murderer were someone he trusted . . . Besides, what difference does information make now? What does it matter? What we want to know is who called on Rita last night after we'd gone!"

"That's the way the police brain works," Ross told me. "I don't see it quite that way. Sure—find out who it was if you can but, frankly, I don't see how it's going to be done. No fingerprints, no clues, nothing but an orange scarf to which anyone of us might have had access. Oh, I'll grant you it narrows the field but it was narrow enough before. The fact that Rita herself opened the door to her caller argues that he was someone she knew and trusted sufficiently to ask him in at that hour of night, into an apartment she occupied alone. For all we know she might have called him herself—to ask advice."

"Johnny Forrester!" I said, electrified.

He shrugged. "Could be. But I doubt it."

"Look here," I said, "why couldn't they try to find out where we all went after we left the Latimers'? Someone must have known we were going with Rita. He may even have followed us. Then, if one of them can't furnish an alibi—"

"Wait a minute," Ross said. "Suppose we skip the alibi angle for the time being. You've raised a more important point. Who knew we were taking Miss Carstairs home?"

"Who? Why, everyone, I suppose. I mean, Rita asked me while we were getting our coats, and we were standing there all together—Molly and Rita and Alice and I. And then I went over and asked you—don't you remember?—and the men were all near you. They must have heard."

"Yes. That washes that out, I'm afraid." But he looked disappointed. "All right, you see how it goes, Mary. Common sense indicates that our murderer is one of the people who were at Chris Latimer's last night. The difficulty comes in trying to sort out which."

"If you could find out which one had the opportunity," I said stubbornly.

"Opportunity has to go hand in hand with motive," Ross said quietly. "Dozens of people might have the opportunity but unless one of them has a reason you can't connect. That's why alibis aren't taken seriously unless they're backed up with proof of one kind or another. So far as last night goes—well, look at it. It was about half past eleven when we left Miss Carstairs. Not too late for other plans nor too early to go to bed. We'd had lunch at the Latimers' but there was still time for a drink down town. For the rest, Alice Wilson lives alone—who's to prove what time she came in or whether, once in, she stayed? Kearnes and I are at the hotel—the desk clerk might have a check on us—but Kerrigan and Forrester stay in rooming houses. Not much chance of their landladies sitting up until they come home. As for Jameson—"

"You can leave him out of it," I said firmly. "He's only twenty. Five years ago, when Nola Powers lived here, he'd be a child. *He'd* have no reason for killing her. He probably never even knew her."

"All right. That leaves the Dunbars and the Latimers and any alibi from those quarters isn't worth a damn. Husbands and wives have a way of sticking together. No, the alibis don't amount to much. The motive behind the murder does. Not the *who* so much as the *why*. Or, that's the way I see it."

"We think we know why Rita was killed," I reminded him. "Because she was going to talk. I can't see that that's much help."

"Rita's murder was a by-product of Nola Powers'. The smartest thing we can do is to ignore it and concentrate on Nola."

Ignore it—I shut my eyes. The cold-bloodedness of the words made me feel a little sick. Still, I supposed Ross couldn't really be blamed. He hadn't known Rita.

"To do that," he was continuing, "we've got to go back in time. A long way back. Five years. That's why I tackled Rita, and the fact that she was killed so that she couldn't talk to me, goes to prove I was on the right track. Rita Carstairs knew something which pointed directly to the murderer of Nola Powers. Therefore she had to be removed. What that something was is the thing we've got to find out."

"You're sure that what she knew was about Nola?" I asked doubtfully. "Couldn't it have been something else— the identity of the person who attacked me or the one who was in the theater that afternoon?"

"I don't think so. I had to use the fact that you were in danger to make her willing to talk, remember? If that were all she knew, she'd have talked last night."

My brain seemed to be whirling round and round. I stood up. I said, "There ought to be some way of finding out. After all Nola lived here. People must have known her. She'd have had friends. . . ."

But Ross stopped me. "That's just the point. She didn't. Oh, I know what you're thinking—neighbors and acquaintances, that sort of thing. But you haven't got it straight yet—what we're up against. The police have been all over that ground and drawn a blank. Neighbors, yes—Dreyer's talked to them and yes, they remember the first Mrs. Latimer—they used to see her going in and out of the house. No, they never talked to her, not more than 'How do you do?' or 'It's a nice day, isn't it?' They were never in her

home. The Latimers discouraged neighborhood intima-
cies. All they cared about was the Little Theater and their
friends were chosen from among that group. No one was
surprised when Mrs. Latimer went away and there were
rumors of a divorce. The Latimers weren't supposed to get
along very well. She was no housekeeper and the poor man
never got a decent meal. It was all eating out or bakery
stuff. Sympathy ran to Mr. Latimer." He spread his hands
in a wide gesture. "Now, do you see why Kearnes and Nola
dared to come back? There was no open scandal—no one
but the inner coterie of the Theater crowd knew that Nola
left town in Kearnes' company and they kept quiet. A little talk, perhaps—a few guesses—but it died out almost
immediately. Kearnes had gone to New York to try his fortune there and Nola had gone, ostensibly, to Reno. Chris's
re-marriage put an end to gossip once and for all."

"You wouldn't think so if you'd been at the Y the night
Chris read us Gordon Kearnes' letter," I said. "There was
hate enough there."

"All right. But strictly among themselves, wasn't it?
That's what makes it so damned hard. The whole story is
locked tight within the brains of a little group who were
the Latimer intimates in the days when Nola was married
to Chris, a group who still remain Chris's closest friends.
There've been darned few admitted to that charmed circle.
What's more they intend to keep their common secret,
whatever it is—the meeting the other night at Alice Wilson's proves that."

"It's more apt to be a lot of little secrets," I objected. "Like Rita Carstairs' sister. Their ganging up together
is probably a selfish interest—to protect themselves. You
keep still about me and I'll do the same for you."

"And somewhere in that mess of little secrets is the one
that will lead directly to Nola's murderer," Ross said grimly. "The thing to do now is to ferret it out."

"You sound very confident," I said. "Somehow I don't think they'll talk—or be allowed to. Think of Rita."

"I am," he said, and again his jaw was tight. "It's for that reason that I'm going to the person I should have gone to in the first place. The one who knows the most about this sorry mess. I'm going to Latimer himself."

15

So we did—for I went too. But not without protest on Ross's part and argument on mine.

"What about Faye?" I asked. "She lives there, too, you know. Do you expect to keep her on the sidelines listening to Chris talk about Nola—always supposing he's willing to talk? I can at least take her off your hands!"

Ross looked doubtful but he agreed.

It was wasted energy, however. For it was Chris who opened the door and as he led us into the studio room, he spoke casually over his shoulder to me: "Sorry, but Faye's gone to bed. All this has been hard on her, and Rita's death was the last straw. I've had the doctor in and he says she'll have to take it easy for a while."

He was facing us now, had shaken a cigarette loose from a crumpled pack. Over the match's slender flame, his eyes met and challenged ours.

"We drove to Elkton this morning." Elkton was the seat of a neighboring county. "We were married there." He gave a short laugh and blew out the match. "Remarried, rather."

I was awkwardly silent. Ross cleared his throat and said, "Naturally."

Chris said, "It's been tough on Faye."

"I've never really described Chris before and perhaps this is as good a place as any to do it. Personally, from the time I met him, he fascinated me. I think he did most women. He wasn't tall—five foot-nine at most—and stocky rather than slender. His hair was iron-gray and his skin a warm clear brown, like a heavy tan faintly faded. I'd heard his face described as beautiful, but saintly was a better word. His eyes were gray-blue, startling against the brown face, and when he raised them you thought of stained glass and cathedral windows. His smile, however, was something else again. There was deviltry in it.

He wasn't smiling tonight. He waved us toward chairs, sat himself.

"No good pretending this is a social call, is there? What's on your minds?"

"Rita Carstairs' death," Ross said promptly and then there was silence.

Chris broke it at last with a short ugly laugh. "I thought so! You're not the first, you know. Kearnes has been here— 'My God, had I heard the news?' and 'My God, what will we do now? The play . . .' I got rid of him in short order. Then the police—I couldn't kick them out so Faye and I answered their questions—dozens of them. Finally they gave up, took our fingerprints and left."

"But there weren't any fingerprints," I said, unthinking.

Ross scowled at me. "How do you know? Not the murderer's, perhaps. But yours and mine are there some place—they'd have to be. We weren't careful."

"Yours?" Chris's eyes were bright now, bright and watchful.

"Yes. We drove Miss Carstairs home. Last night. We went up with her—to her apartment."

"In the light of what happened later, that was indiscreet, wasn't it?"

"Say inconvenient, rather."

"And that, too, was not a—a social call?"

"No. We went there to talk about Nola Powers' death."

The thing was out, naked between them. I looked from one to the other. Ross was cool, expressionless, as he reached for a cigarette but in Chris anger was rising, plain to read as mercury in a thermometer tube.

He threw himself back in his chair. He said, "Am I supposed to be flattered? You call on Rita Carstairs for information—and by the fact that you're here I'm assuming you didn't get it—and someone puts her beyond the giving out of information forever. Now you've come to me. Do you think I want to get murdered too? What the hell do you think you're doing, Langdon? Killing off the suspects one by one so that by the process of elimination you'll arrive at the answer and the killer? And what makes you think I will talk to you? You're not the police—you have no authority to ask questions, to poke and pry. Let me tell you something—unless you keep your nose out of places it doesn't belong, you'll have only yourself to thank if you wind up with a battered head and a scarf choking your larynx!"

Ross stood up. "Okay. If that's the way you feel about it."

Chris said, "It is the way I feel about it—and be damned to you!"

"Okay," Ross said again. He walked toward the door. "Coming, Mary?"

I said, "No—no, wait, please. Please wait." I knew Chris better than Ross did—I'd seen for myself some of the swift and furious tides of his temper. There'd been the chair he'd smashed at rehearsal, the juvenile he'd slapped in the face. But I knew, too, that the course of his anger ran out quickly. It was dying even as I spoke and the knowledge gave me courage. I ignored Ross, concentrated on Chris. I said, "It's not what you think—curiosity. It's not even helping the police or trying to wipe their eye. It's

my fault, really. I asked Ross to help. You see, someone
tried to kill me the other night."

I paused and Chris nodded reluctantly. "I know. I heard
about that."

"And I—I don't want to die."

"Who does?"

It was said mockingly but it sounded like the old
familiar Chris. My heart gave a little jump as I struggled
on—struggled because, while what I meant to say was an
out-and-out lie, it also seemed the surest way to achieve
the end toward which we strove. And so I said, "And Ross
doesn't want me to die either—not now at any rate—" I
glanced at Ross and tried to look properly adoring.

"Oh-oh!" Chris said knowingly. "Like that, is it?"

Ross looked dazed but I nodded brightly. "Yes—only
please don't tell anyone—not yet. It doesn't seem right for
us to be happy when those others—those others . . . And
so Ross said we couldn't just sit still and leave it all to the
police—we'd better do something too. And we did—only
Rita wouldn't tell us last night and now she can't ever
because she's dead. So then I said why not talk to Chris
because he knows more about Nola than anyone else and
this whole thing started with her murder. Nobody ever
tried to kill me before . . ."

"I see," Chris said. He swung his cobalt gaze toward
Ross, still standing by the door, still with that dazed unbelieving expression on his face. "My profoundest apologies,
Langdon. Anything of course that I can tell you. . . . But,
first, suppose we have a drink!"

He moved, cat-footed, from the room and Ross Langdon, with two strides, had hold of my wrist.

"Great Caesar's ghost, what was that for? Do you have
to broadcast our love affairs? Now the whole damn town
will know."

"We haven't any love affairs and you know it," I said. "And furthermore, you hush up. It was the only thing I could think of—you weren't doing so good by yourself!—and besides that, it's worked, hasn't it?"

"I'll tell you that later," Ross said and moved nimbly past to lean on the grand piano just as Chris re-entered, laden with a tray of bottles and glasses. In the little ceremony of mixing drinks, all awkwardness died. Indeed, Ross was so far recovered at the promise his glass held that he was able to grin faintly and second it when Chris proposed a toast.

They drank to me—"To Mary—long life and good health to her"—and somehow their eyes, smiling at me above the glasses, made me choke all up. As a wish, as a hope, it was fine. But, as a promise, it lacked something.

After that Chris threw another log upon the blaze that flared fitfully in the grate, splashed just a hint more of soda into his drink, and then settled into his chair.

"All right," he said. "Let's get at it. What can I tell you?"

I didn't like that. Not "What do you want to know?" but "What can I tell you?" There's a difference.

I looked expectantly at Ross. He was staring into the depths of his glass, his lips sucked in as though in thought. As I watched, he put the glass down and jumped to his feet, his hands going boyishly to his trouser pockets.

"It's a little hard to figure just where to begin," he said, "but suppose we take it like this. So far as I was concerned, the old chief had the right idea when he divided us into two camps—the ones who might have been connected with Nola during the past five years in New York ana the ones who had been a part of her earlier life in Nashiona. To my mind you can wash out the New York contingent—Kearnes and Mary and myself—with the exception of Kearnes who also comes into the Nashiona picture, for I believe that somewhere in Nola Powers' life in Nashiona we'll find the reason for her murder."

"So you came to me." Chris had laid his head back against the cushion. He looked very tired.

"Because I think you know what the rest of the theater group have agreed not to tell—Nola's relations with them."

"You're taking on a big order, Langdon. What makes you think I know anything," he smiled wryly, "about Nola's extra-curricular relations with the Little Theater group? What makes you think I wasn't the customary cuckolded husband? Or—better still—that, even if I do know something, I'll tell?"

"Because of Mary," Ross said simply.

"Oh, yes, Mary. You rang that bell before." Eyes narrowed, he studied me.

"The police have checked and gotten nowhere," Ross went on. "They've banged their heads against a stone wall. Now, it's up to you."

"My own relations included?"

Ross shrugged. "As you like. I'm taking it for granted you've been reasonably open there."

"Reasonably," Chris agreed. "Nevertheless I think I'll sketch the background. Nola as I first knew her." He drew a long breath.

"She was twenty—seventeen years younger than I— when I first saw her, and fresh off the farm. Her name wasn't Powers—it was something Polish and unpronounceable. She'd taken the name after her parents' death in a flu epidemic and she'd come to Nashiona looking for work. She found it—in the sausage department of the packing plant. I met her when the plant put on their annual musical show and I was called in at the last minute to help doctor a few acts. Nola *was* the show. She stood out from among those other clods like a—a white horse on a dark night. If you've ever seen her—?"

The lift in his voice was a question. I shook my head. "We didn't get into New York very often and tickets to her plays were hard to get."

"I've seen her," Ross said briefly.

"Then you know," Chris said, "how she could dominate a stage. She could do it even then—don't ask me how!—and I—I fell in love. One month after I met her we were married."

A log dropped in the fire then, hissing softly into sparks. He replaced it, went on.

"I don't think she loved me—I never have—but she was ambitious and just as a job in Nashiona had presented wider horizons than the little farm community where she was born, so life as my wife held more interest than stuffing sausages. Then, too, there was the theater angle. I was knee-deep in that. The Little Theater as such didn't exist then but a group of us had gotten together and formed a sort of amateur stock company. We called ourselves the Nashiona Players. It was entirely a private enterprise at first. We financed it ourselves and if we needed extra talent, we invited it in for as long as necessary and then dropped it again. For the rest, Nola and Alice Wilson alternated at feminine leads. Pat—Alice's husband—played the male—"

"Alice's husband!" It fairly burst from me. "I didn't know she had one! I mean—nobody ever mentions him. Where is he now? Does he live here?"

"He's dead," Chris said quietly. "He was killed in a hunting accident five years ago. Now, wait!" He'd caught my goggling eyes. "Don't look like that! It was an accident. No question of it being anything else. We were out pheasant hunting—there was a crowd of us—and Pat went back to the car for something—his pipe, I think it was. He wasn't careful climbing through a fence and the gun went off. The charge hit him in the heart and he was dead when we found him. It hit us pretty hard. He was a nice fellow, Pat."

Deliberately he moved to open a drawer and to display snapshots of a tall dark young man with laughing eyes and a dashing little moustache. Silently we looked, handed them back.

"And Mrs. Wilson's never remarried?" Ross asked. It sounded like polite conversation but Chris's eyes narrowed.

"No. Oh, don't think it's because she's still carrying a torch for Pat—they weren't getting along very well, as a matter of fact, when he died. 'Incom*pat*ible' Alice called it. I'd have bet on divorce myself inside of three months."

"Umm," Ross said. "Your wife have anything to do with it?"

"Pat's death? Good Lord, no! She wasn't even with us! Oh, I see what you mean—the divorce. I don't think so—I always thought it was that Pat and Alice just couldn't get along. Pat was in and out of our place a lot, but then so were a half a dozen other men. There wasn't a question of Alice being jealous."

"Were you?"

"Jealous of Pat?" Chris gave a short laugh. "Hardly. There was no necessity. Nola was *my* wife."

"Yes—I see," Ross said doubtfully. "All right—before we got off on the Wilsons, you were telling us about your Nashiona Players. Who else was in the group?"

"Well, besides Nola and Pat and Alice, there were the Dunbars—they weren't married then—and Kerrigan, of course, and Johnny Forrester. Kathleen Carstairs—" He shot a side glance in our direction.

"We've heard of her," Ross said. "That all?"

"I thought you might have," Chris said ruefully. "Rita always blamed Nola for Kathy's death, without actual

CRY MURDER   215

reason. The girl was a neurotic little fool and when Johnny lost his head—temporarily—she lost hers. Why Nola should have gotten credit . . .”

“Why indeed?” Ross agreed politely. “That all on your list?”

“All? Oh, no. There were a couple of others—women— they’ve been gone from Nashiona for some time. That’s the lot, though. Of course you understand that if we needed additional talent we co-opted it for as long as we needed it!”

“What about Kearnes? Wasn’t he with you?”

“Gordon?” An unpleasant smile twisted Chris’s mouth. “When I first saw Gordon Kearnes, he was a shabby, ill-fed department store clerk. He sold Nola shoes. He told her he’d written a play, showed her part of it. Nola knew a good thing when she saw it and brought it home to me. The result was we put it on in the fall —it was the *Outer Door*. We put on a couple of others too—*Spangles* and *Dark Remember*. They were good plays, not even the New York production changed them much. But I wouldn’t say that Kearnes was ever one of us. He hovered on the outskirts. We didn’t like him. We accepted him because we had to.”

“Had to?”

“He was—I suppose you’d call him a genius,” Chris said thoughtfully, “Art cuts its own paths, you know. You have to take what goes along with it.”

“How about the women? Mrs. Wilson seems enthusiastic.”

Something like a sneer curled Chris’s lip. “Alice’s fondness for Kearnes dates from his New York successes. Don’t let her fool you. He’s the home-town boy who made good. She’s convinced herself—but no one else; not even Kearnes, I’m certain—that they were dear old pals in the long ago past. Alice is an opportunist.”

“What did your wife—Nola—think of him?”

"As a man, she insisted that she detested him. Actually, I think she had a sneaking fondness for him. You do, for something whose growth you help to foster."

"She went to New York with him?"

"Yes." Chris was grim. "But don't get the idea it was because she loved him. It was simply that he could do things for her. Capper and Stein were interested in his plays by that time and Nola saw a chance that they'd be interested in her too. I called Alice," Chris said, "an opportunist a minute ago but she wasn't in it with Nola. Nola was like a climbing vine—she reached out and grasped at whatever support offered itself. She'd gone as far as it was possible to go here in Nashiona. It was time to move on. Kearnes offered an opportunity. She took it."

Ross drew a long breath. "Look here, Latimer," he said. "I met your wife—Miss Powers, that is—for the first time a couple of weeks ago. She was the complete New York actress—successful, magnetic, charming. Now you've given me an entirely contradictory picture. A farm girl, a foreigner, a sausage-packer in a packing plant—"

"And the wife of an unsuccessful small town dabbler in amateur theatricals," Chris finished for him. "Sorry—I don't blame you for being muddled. It's all true but—well, put it like this. Nola was a farm girl but not of the farm. Her people were well-educated, cultured. They left Poland during one of the political upheavals and came over here to sink every cent they possessed in a farm upstate. Nola herself spoke several languages. When her parents died, she was penniless. The sausage department was a stop-gap. So was her marriage to me. It served until something better came along."

"She was ambitious?"

"She was ruthless," Chris said and for the first time some actual emotion moved behind the mask his face presented, "where she herself was concerned. She knew what she wanted and she took it and it didn't matter who got hurt in the process. The fact that I loved her, that she was my wife, didn't matter one red hot damn to her. She was the one who mattered and she had it in her head that, given the chance, she could give Hayes and Cornell some pretty hot competition."

"She wasn't so far wrong at that," Ross said soberly.

Chris sighed. "No, she rather proved her point, didn't she? Oh, well, it's all done with now. Old wounds heal eventually and I'm married again. I'm happy. Faye and I are going to have a child. . . ."

But the old wounds hadn't healed—he wasn't happy. It was written irrevocably upon the haggard darkness of his face that momently had lost its likeness to an archangel's. It was a lost and fallen angel's now, and all of a sudden I was bitterly sorry for Faye.

He was going on.

"It's all been so useless and unnecessary," he was saying. "They didn't need to come back. It was just a gesture. We'd all forgotten. It should have stayed that way. Nola, wouldn't have been murdered then—or—Rita . . ."

His voice trailed off into miserable silence. My throat ached with pity of it.

It was Chris himself who finally broke the silence. He looked at Ross. He said, "Is that all you want to know? Because I'm sorry— I can't answer any more questions—do you understand? Not any more—not tonight . . ." Abruptly hysteria shook him. "I can't, I tell you—I can't!"

"Just one more question." Ross's voice was soothing. "Nothing very important—nothing to bother about. It's only that I'm curious. When she—Miss Powers—went to New York . . . No one picks up and goes places entirely without funds. It can't be done. Not in New York. You've got to have money and you said Kearnes had none. Who financed her then? You?"

Chris said, "I wondered when you'd get there!" and
jumped to his feet. He walked over to the hearth and stood,
his back to us. When he spoke, his voice sounded muffled.
"What makes you think that it could have been me?"

"I didn't. It was a wild guess," Ross admitted. "However I wondered. There was that will—her will. All that
money to you—there had to be a reason for it. But, just
the same, letting her go—it makes the whole thing wrong,
all wrong. If you did let her go—paid her way—why? In
God's name, why?"

"It was inadvertent," Chris said dully. "I didn't know."
He'd swung around now and was facing us. A glisten of
moisture showed along his upper lip. "I don't know why
I should tell you this, Langdon. It's none of your affair.
You've no right to ask questions—you admit that yourself.
I told the police I don't know why she should have left me
that money but it was a lie. I knew why—I think I do."

He drew a long breath.

"I'm supposed to have money—you've heard that,
haven't you?—enough so that I'm independent of my job.
That's the story. It's not true. My father left something
like twenty thousand in bonds. I never touched them.
They were my umbrella against a rainy day. They were in a
deposit box at the bank—a joint deposit box because Nola
had a few things there, too. Odds and ends of jewelry that
had been her mother's. I didn't think of the bonds until a
couple of months after she left me. When I looked in the
box, it was empty. And I knew then where the money'd
come from that had taken her to New York."

"The bonds were negotiable?"

Chris shrugged. "Quite. They were bearer bonds. Anyone could have cashed them. Well, there you are—there's a
motive for you—a motive of sorts. Want me to strengthen
it a little? I can. What if I told you that business hasn't
been good with me the last while—that I'm broke, losing

my home—my wife's going to have a baby? Suppose I told you that Nola'd acknowledged her debt to me in writing, told me she was making a will in my favor? Suppose I secretly engineered her return to Nashiona in the hope I'd get the chance to kill her and collect under her will? Suppose—"

But Ross stopped him then.

"That's enough," he said crisply. "That's a game you could play all night and get no farther, and God knows you had motive enough for killing her before. It's not guesses I want anyway—it's facts. Look here, Latimer, you said it was two months before you discovered the loss of the bonds and knew what money had taken her to New York. Two months is a long time to wait. What had you thought before?"

"Why, I thought . . ." Chris stopped. Abruptly his face showed pale. "I'm damned if I know why I'm telling you this but . . . I thought she'd got it from Kerrigan. Mark Kerrigan. He was trying to raise money all over town. A lot of money. Five thousand dollars."

16

Ross whistled softly. "Five thousand dollars is money in any man's vocabulary," he commented. "Know if he got it?"

"He got part of it," Chris said grimly. "Pete Dunbar told me that he'd written off the five hundred he contributed as a bad debt on his income tax. Funny thing, though—I'd have sworn . . ."

The telephone cut across whatever it was he'd meant to say. Funny thing about telephones. Sometimes their rings seem to carry within themselves a portentousness of danger. This one was without cessation, short sharp rings as though the operator herself was aware of panic.

It couldn't be, of course, I thought—it was all imagination—and waited for Chris to lift the handset.

He said, "Hello!" and at once a far away voice crackled. You could hear it but not understand it. Chris frowned, listening. He said, "Where? Now? All right—right away!" and hung up. And faced us, his eyes unbelieving.

"That was Dreyer," he said slowly. "He wants me to come to the hospital. Kearnes has been hurt—knocked on the head. I—I don't understand it. I told you he'd been here, didn't I? Just before you came. A police patrol car found him in Exeter Park. He was slumped over the wheel. Somebody's smashed him on the back of the head. They're afraid of concussion." He looked vaguely around. "I'd better go. . . ."

"Mind if I go along?" Ross asked.

Chris shook his head. "No—no. Come along. I—I can't tell them anything. Only that he was here." He moved toward the door, came back. "What about Mary?"

"Mary'll come too," Ross said.

"Oh, no, she won't!" I said. "Don't be idiotic. I'm allergic to hospitals. Besides, they wouldn't let me come with you. I'd be shut off in a waiting room or something. No, thank you. I'll stay right here."

Ross said, "We-ell . . ." but Chris spoke eagerly. "Will you? Do you mind? Because Faye's here and I hate to leave her alone. She's feeling so rotten."

"If you go out quietly enough," I said with meaning, "she'll never know you've gone. If she's sleeping . . . And you needn't look like that!" This was to Ross. "I won't go anywhere. I'll just sit here and read. I'll be perfectly safe."

"Yes," Ross said slowly. "I think you will."

Chris didn't seem so sure. As they went out of the room, I heard him say, "But how do you know? If some lunatic's around bashing people on the head . . ."

I didn't hear Ross's reply. Presently the front door closed.

I considered locking that door behind them and then changed my mind. There's something reassuring about knowing that exits are not completely closed.

The house was quiet, too quiet. I looked longingly at the big Capehart machine—Faye had lots of records I'd enjoy hearing—but I decided better not. She might be asleep and I could always read.

To that end, I crossed to the book shelves that lined the end of the room. Plenty to read here—Chris went in for books in a big way—but some of it, I thought, studying the titles, was decidedly queer stuff. Plays, but you'd expect that. Books on drama and staging, of course. But there were others that were far less understandable. Apparently Chris—for not in my wildest dreams could I conceive that it could be Faye—went in for horror and fantasy at its most horrible and fantastic. There were shelves of it—omnibus collections and anthologies; Poe in complete set; Dunsany, Blackwood and M. R. James; Collins and Stoker and de la Mare; Machen and Bierce and Wells. And there were others less widely known—Lovecraft and Hodgson; Smith and Merritt; Hearne, Metcalfe and Shiel.

The very titles intrigued me: *The Face in the Abyss. They Return at Night. Out of Space and Time. A Thin Ghost.* Not recommended reading for a person alone in a house, certainly not for one lately concerned in murder.

I moved away from the shelves, scanned other titles, returned, drawn by the same fearful fascination that I suppose originally impelled Chris to buy them. Very well, then, if I must, but one of the more innocuous ones . . .

Remembering the Orson Welles Martian furor, I selected the book that had been its inspiration and settled down to read.

I can't say that it was a comfortable reading. Remembrance of that reasonless panic of which this volume had been the source tinged my appreciation. Of course I didn't really believe in inter-planetary visitations but just the same—just suppose. . . . It must have been that supposition that made my hands cold, that kept the silence tightening until it rang like bells against my ears.

It was also the reason why, when a white figure appeared suddenly in the hall doorway, that I screamed. The white figure was Faye, wrapped in chenille. Her hair was loose on her shoulders, and she blinked a little as though the light hurt her eyes.

She said, "What are you yelling about?" and she sounded cross. "Where's Chris? I didn't know you were here."

I ignored the Chris part. I said, "Darling, I meant to run up and see you before I left."

"It wouldn't have done any good," she said flatly. "I wouldn't have let you in. My door's locked."

I digested that in silence. There wasn't anything to say.

"I'm afraid, you know." She shivered a little. "Afraid, all the time. Did you know that Rita's dead?"

I nodded. I was beginning to be afraid myself. Something was wrong here—oh, so very wrong.

"Rita's dead and Nola's dead," Faye went on dully. "I don't care about Nola. I hated her. But Rita—Rita was different. She was nice and kind and good. I liked her."

I said, "I know." I did. I felt exactly the same way myself.

Faye had taken a cigarette, lit it, but she wasn't smoking. She only stared at the glowing tip. "Do you know who's going to die next?" she asked casually.

I shook my head. I had my own ideas of a candidate but just the same . . .

The whole trend of the conversation was oddly disquieting. It had a horrible nightmare quality that went beyond believing. Surely this couldn't be Faye who was talking.

But it was.

"It'll be me," she was saying. "It's queer but I don't care. I don't think I want to live any longer. Once I did but not any more."

The breath that I'd been holding unconsciously released in a long sigh. I could understand this; it was normal and reasonable. I could even combat it. Gladly I spoke.

"You mustn't talk like that, darling. You'll be all right. Having a baby isn't so terrible any more. Chris will take care of you."

"I don't think there'll be a baby after all," Faye said without interest. "I don't care about that either. I don't care about anything now."

I got up then and went over to her. I put my arms about her and her body burned me through the robe. I touched her hand and it was icy. I laid my hand on her forehead. It was like fire. I said, "Darling, you're sick—that's what's the matter with you. You've got a fever. I'm going to put you back to bed and then I'll call Chris and the doctor."

Faye drew away from me. Now—blind that I had been—I saw the flush on her cheeks, the fever in her eyes.

"Not Chris," she said. "No. I don't want Chris. I don't want anyone. You can stay with me."

"I'll stay," I promised. "Only first we'll go upstairs and you can lie down. Have you a thermometer? I want to take your temperature."

It was useless. She moved away. She said, "It's not going to help. I'm not going upstairs. I don't want to go upstairs. You couldn't want me to either. Because then I'd be in my bedroom. When I'm in my bedroom, I lock the door. No one can come in then, no one. Not even Chris."

"You'd let *me* come in," I coaxed, "Wouldn't you? I'm Mary. You're not afraid of *me!*"

She examined me from those fever-blurred eyes.

"No," she conceded. "I'm not afraid of you. Do you know why? Because you're good. You're kind. You saw me and you didn't tell. You didn't tell anyone."

I was beside her again. I had my arm across her shoulders. Imperceptibly I was leading her toward the door and she hadn't noticed. Perhaps, if I could keep her talking . . .

"What didn't I tell?" I asked without particular interest.

"You know. Down at the theater. That day. You saw me. Between the curtains. You pretended you didn't know. But I knew."

"What theater?" I had dropped her arm. "What day? What do you mean?"

"You know." She sounded patient. "The theater. Where Nola was. She was dead."

I forgot that she was ill. I forgot everything except
the incredible thing she was saying. I'm afraid I shook
her. I said, "Faye! Listen to me! What do you mean? Are
you telling the truth? Were you at the Olympia that—that
afternoon?"

She pulled away again. Definitely this time. "Didn't
you know?" she asked querulously. "I thought you did. I
thought you saw me."

"I saw you," I said grimly. "But I didn't know who you
were. You were just a face. I never dreamed. . . . Why did
you go?"

"She telephoned me. She asked me to come down and
talk to her. I didn't want to talk to her but I went. She
said to be careful and not let anyone see me. I was careful.
Nobody saw me. But we couldn't talk. She was dead."

I took a long careful breath. "When was this? What time?"

"She said to come at four. I didn't know what we had to
talk about but I went. I went in from the alley—the stage
door was open. I went up on the stage. It was dark but the
interior set was up to make a room and there was a light
inside. She was lying on the floor. She wasn't moving or
breathing and I knew that she was dead. So then I knew
that I mustn't stay because someone might think I'd killed
her. And I hadn't, I'd only wanted to." She looked at me
anxiously. "You don't think I killed her, do you?"

"No," I said slowly. "No, I don't. But someone did."

"I was only there a minute," Faye said. "And I didn't
tell anyone. About seeing her. I wouldn't have told you
only you were there too. And I'd thought you saw me.
When I looked out through the curtains."

"But, good heavens!" I said. "Why did you go into that
box? You said you knew you had to get away—why didn't
you just go?"

"There was the janitor," Faye said simply. "I could hear
him walking around—moving things. And I didn't want

him to see me. So I thought I'd just peek out into the auditorium and see where he was. Only he wasn't in the auditorium. *You* were."

"I know," I said hastily. "Go on. What did you do then?"

"My head hurts," Faye said slowly. "Then? Oh, then I knew that if he wasn't in the auditorium he must be back stage some place and I was afraid he'd find Nola's body and—and me—so I went away as quietly as I could. When I came out of the alley I went east across the bridge and I kept going. I just walked and walked. I wanted to think. There was a place over there somewhere—I had coffee—and then I came back. Only across the viaduct this time. And then I went home. That was all. Only I was sick. I couldn't get Chris's supper. He had to get it himself and then he went to the rehearsal. He wanted me to go but I couldn't. Because I knew there wasn't going to be any rehearsal. There couldn't be. Because Nola was dead."

She swayed a little then but I caught her and held her upright. My brain was racing. Of course I knew she was ill—that I ought not to keep hammering at her—but I couldn't help it. This was the first thing I'd gotten my hands on—the first promising lead. . . .

I caught her hands and held them hard. "Listen, Faye—listen now. Think—try to remember. The janitor—those sounds you heard—what were they like?"

"You're hurting me," she said. "What difference does it make? They were just sounds. Somebody walking around, moving things. I heard something scrape along the floor."

My eyes must have told her for she stopped suddenly, her mouth half-open.

"It—it wasn't the janitor," she said softly.

"It couldn't have been," I told her. "He—he never left the lobby. I'm sure he didn't. He was there when I went into the auditorium. He was there when I came out again."

"Then who?" It was her hands that clutched at me now, her voice, taut and trembling, that demanded, "Who was it? Mary, tell me who it was!"

I couldn't. She didn't give me time. Her hands relaxed their clutching. She said on a long sigh, "Why, of course—I know. It was the murderer!" and slumped forward in a faint.

I caught her as best I could. I eased her down to the floor. I raced to the kitchen, crushed ice cubes in a towel, brought water. The tray of glasses and bottles was still on the coffee table. I moistened her lips with whiskey, pressed the icy towel to her forehead, rubbed frantically at her wrists. After what seemed to be hours, she opened her eyes.

There was no sanity left in them. They were dulled, expressionless. She moved her head and the towel slipped sideways. She tried to sit up. I helped her. She said, "What am I doing here? I ought to be in bed."

I said, "Darling, I know you ought. I'm going to take you there and then I'll call Chris."

She said, "Oh, no—Chris is busy. Don't call him. Don't call anyone. Promise you won't. I'll be all right—truly I will."

But she wouldn't. I knew that and so I made the promises—not to call the doctor, not to call Chris. The promises were lies. I meant them to be.

I was so afraid that my own teeth were chattering. I don't know how I managed it, getting her upstairs. She was like a dead weight in my arms. She only spoke twice. Once, halfway up the stairs, when she said, "It's like a merry-go-round, isn't it? Watching things go round." And then again, after I'd laid her on her bed, she said, "I remember now—oh, I remember!" and began to weep.

I covered her with blankets. Remembering what she'd said about locking her door, I took the precaution to remove the key. Before I went downstairs, I swept the bathroom cabinet free of medicines. I even took nail files and scissors from the bureau top, and Chris's razors and blades. I told myself there was no need, that I was just being careful.

Luckily I knew the doctor's name. I called him. He promised to come right over. I tried to reach Chris. I called the three hospitals and he wasn't at any of them. I called the police station. Nobody knew where Lieutenant Dreyer was. I called Ross's hotel. No luck.

The doctor came. I took him upstairs and then sat on the landing. He wasn't long. He came out, dragging at his upper lip. He said, "Where's her husband?"

I said I didn't know, that I'd tried to find him. I could try again. . . .

He negatived that. "No time. I'm calling an ambulance. I've got to get her to the hospital."

I trailed down after him. There was a lump in my throat but when he was done telephoning, I managed to get my voice over it. "Is she—?"

He looked at me gravely.

"She's a very sick young woman. Not only physically—there seems to have been some mental shock. I don't understand it. . . ."

He hesitated, turned and re-climbed the stairs.

The ambulance came. I packed a bag for Faye, went with her, crouched on a camp stool as I held her hand and listened to the banshee wail of the siren marking our passing.

At the hospital I was shunted aside. Faye disappeared into realms of whiteness and hard bright light. An intern touched my shoulder. "Dr. Blanchard wants you to try and find Mr. Latimer. There's a telephone over here. . . ."

I began the dreary round of calls again. No result, although I called every place and everyone I could think of.

I even tried Chris's own house number although I knew there was no sense in that—I'd left a note on the hall table. Presently inspiration came. I called the local radio station, authorized an emergency broadcast. Within twenty minutes Chris had called the hospital. Fifteen minutes later, he and Ross were there.

Chris was white and tired. He had only time to catch my hands and press them hard before the hovering intern guided him toward the whiteness into which Faye had vanished.

Now, at last, I could relax. I looked at Ross. He said, "What do we do now? Wait?" I shook my head. All I wanted was to get away. If I didn't, I'd an idea I'd be the next patient.

"What's the good?" I asked. "They don't want us. We can always telephone."

We didn't talk much, driving home. I did rouse enough to ask about Gordon Kearnes. "Out like a light," Ross told me. "Someone hit him an awful wallop. God knows when he'll be able to talk. It's been a swell night—first Kearnes and now Faye."

"Faye wasn't hit over the head," I reminded, him. "Except perhaps mentally. I think that something hit her there."

Ross was intrigued. "What the devil do you mean?" he demanded. But I wouldn't tell him. Not tonight.

He didn't offer to come in when we got to the house and I was glad. The house was quiet—my guardians for the evening were playing bridge. I called "Good-night!" to Mrs. Ferguson and wavered to the stairs up which she presently followed with hot milk and—after she'd glimpsed my hollow-eyed weariness—an offer of aspirin or sleeping tablets.

I didn't take them. I didn't want to sleep. I wanted to think. I had to think. That which I'd kept pushed resolutely to the back of my head ever since I'd talked to Faye was upon me now. Against the quiet and dark of my room, it seemed etched in letters of fire. There was nothing for it but to give myself over to its contemplation.

Which I did. Boiled down to the fewest possible words, it came to this: If Faye had been the person I'd dimly seen through the theater box curtains—and I had no reason for disbelieving her—then the blackout attack on me had not come because of the murderer's fear that I would recognize him or her as the person who had peered between those curtains. Faye wasn't the murderer—I was certain of that; there were a dozen reasons why she couldn't be. Therefore the blackout attack had had its origin in some other cause. And, if it had—what was it that I knew and didn't know that I knew? What knowledge did I have that could possibly endanger a murderer?

17

I suppose, eventually, that I slept for all at once it was
bright morning and Mrs. Ferguson was tapping on my
door with an assortment of messages. Breakfast was ready
"when I was" and she hoped I didn't mind being waked but
she'd cleaned all the rooms upstairs but mine and she'd
like a "go" at that before noon. Some Mr. Latimer had
telephoned and that nice Mr. Langdon was in the living
room waiting for me right now. My Paw'd like if I'd telephone him some time this morning so he'd know I was
still alive. And it was eleven o'clock so if I didn't mind
hurrying . . .

I minded but I hurried. I showered hastily, found slacks
and a clean shirt.

I thought that Ross looked tired. He shook his head at
my first question. "Breakfast now—we can talk later." I
shook my own head. Breakfast could wait. I had something
more important to do.

So I went to the telephone and tried to call Chris. He
wasn't at his office. I gave the house number although I
didn't expect anything from that. I was right. I tried the
hospital and Mr. Latimer wasn't there. I asked about Faye
and they were cagey. Mrs. Latimer was doing as well as
could be expected. I hung up and led the way to the kitch-
en dinette.

Ross and I were lingering over final cups of coffee when Chris himself rang our bell. We both answered it, Ross having convincing objections to my answering doors. We brought him out into the kitchen but he shook his head when we suggested coffee, cigarettes, breakfast. He looked tired beyond a man's endurance.

I poured the coffee anyway. I said, "How is she, Chris?"

He didn't answer for a minute. He sat slumped in his chair, eyes closed, and I had the notion that, for a second, he'd escaped into some other world of consciousness where nothing could hurt him. But, as I set the coffee before him, he opened his eyes and seemed to shake himself awake. Faye was better, he thought. She'd had the hell of a night—they all had—and there wouldn't be any Latimer baby now. But it wasn't only that. The doctor was afraid of something else, he wouldn't say what. Pneumonia, perhaps, or brain fever. She was queer . . .

"She won't see me," he said dully. "She screams when they even mention my name. They won't let me in her room. They've kept me outside, in some damnable waiting room where all I could do was walk up and down and smoke cigarettes. They won't tell me why!" Sweat was breaking out on his forehead; for a moment his eyes looked wild. "They won't tell me anything. They say, 'The doctor thinks it's best not to disturb Mrs. Latimer.' They say she's got to be kept quiet. But I wouldn't disturb her. I'd be quiet. I'd tiptoe in—I wouldn't even talk. If they'd only let me look at her— just make sure that she's alive . . ."

I couldn't stand any more of it. His voice was dreadful, hoarse, broken. I said, "Chris, don't. Listen to me. I was with Faye for a while—before the doctor came. I know what's the matter with her. It's not pneumonia—you can't get pneumonia from fear. *That's* what's wrong with Faye— she's afraid. She's afraid of everything and everyone—even of you, Chris. She's sick with fear."

"But," Chris began. He looked bewildered. "Why should she be afraid of me? I wouldn't hurt her—she knows that."

"She had her bedroom door locked," I said slowly. "She didn't want me to call you."

"Not *me!*" Chris said. He still sounded unbelieving. "She was frightened—yes. I can understand that. Nola's death, Rita's . . . But not of me. I'm her husband—I'd take care of her—I wouldn't hurt her—she ought to know that—"

Suddenly he broke off with a groan. His face was ghastly.

"I know," he said. "I *do* know—why she was afraid. I think I do. Poor baby! Afraid even of me! God knows I wouldn't harm her—how could I? When I love her?"

It was terrible to listen. I wanted to cover my ears so I wouldn't hear. I wanted to run screaming from the room.

Thank God, Ross stopped him. He said, "Wait a minute, Latimer—let's get this straight. You say you think you know why Faye's afraid of you. All right. Do you want to tell us about it?"

"Yes." Once more it was almost a groan. "I might as well. Perhaps I'm a fool—I'm in enough of a jam without handing you this but . . ." He took a long breath and when he spoke again some measure of sense and coherence had returned to his speech. "Kearnes came to see me last night. You know that. He was drunk and he said some things I couldn't take. He—we fought. We were in the studio, near the fireplace. His foot slipped on the tile. He went down and his head cracked against the andirons."

"You think Faye heard?" This was Ross, cool as a cucumber though my own nerves were fluttering.

"I suppose so. How could she help it? We weren't being quiet. There were loud voices—scuffling—I don't know what. She was upstairs . . ." Again his voice died away.

"And then?"

"I got panicky, I suppose. I should have called someone—a doctor, the police. I was afraid. The way things stood I couldn't afford to have him found in my house. If he were dead . . . Then my brain seemed to clear. I thought if I could get him out of the house, leave him where he'd be found later on, I'd be out of it. It would just be another of the mysteries the police were up against. So I—he isn't heavy—I carried him out, and put him in his own car, and drove it into the park. Then I came back. It's a lot of driving, but if you walk there's a short cut you can take—across lots. I was back in the house within twenty minutes."

"Faye heard you fighting," I said slowly. "She must have. Probably she listened at the top of the stairs, watched you carry him out. She must have thought he was dead, that you'd killed him. No wonder she locked her door—no wonder she was afraid."

"No wonder at all," he agreed humbly. "I thought she might have heard something. When I came back I went upstairs and tapped on her door. She didn't answer. I hoped she was asleep. So I went back downstairs. Then you came."

I had an instant's sickening vision of Faye, lying flat on her bed, or pressed into the farthest corner of the room, listening to the drag of the ascending footsteps, the cautious tap on the door, the slow descent. It made me brutal. I said, "She didn't come down until after you'd gone. She could have watched, made sure of that. She talked about Nola—about Rita. She said she'd be the next to die."

I'd hurt him. He stood up, violently, as though feeling the need for motion. He said, "Maybe if I could see her—explain. If she knew that Kearnes wasn't dead . . ."

"There's still Nola and Rita," I said tonelessly. "And me."

"Nola and Rita—! But, good God, I didn't kill them! I didn't attack you that night—I was home. Faye'll tell you . . ." He stopped, swallowed hard. "Maybe she wouldn't—can't. She was asleep—she'd gone to bed before the blackout. I was downstairs in the studio. But, even so—what if my overshoes were found here? They were stolen from Alice's. You know that. She told you. We hunted for them. Anyone could have taken them that night—anyone there. Good God! Say something, can't you? You can't think *I'm* your murderer!"

"You could be," Ross said briefly. "You've reason enough. Nola Powers was your wife. She'd left you, stolen property from you. Now, wait a minute! She'd lied to you. You'd believed that she had obtained a divorce from you— she hadn't. In that belief you'd remarried, were about to have a child. That non-divorce made you a bigamist, your child illegitimate—"

"Go on!" Chris said. "So I killed her in order that the whole mess would come out—become public property— give my friends a holiday at my expense. That makes sense, doesn't it? Don't you think I'd realize that murdering her was the surest way of making the whole affair public? Do you think I wanted that to happen?"

"I don't know," Ross said imperturbably. "You hated her. You made no secret of it."

"Why should I? Everyone knew it. She'd nearly wrecked my life once. Now it looks as though she'd managed a second time. But I didn't kill her. You can't prove that I did!"

"No?" Ross said softly. "But I can have a damn good try at it just the same!"

They were glaring at one another. I said, "Oh, for heaven's sake, stop it! You'll never get anywhere by quarreling. Chris, don't be a fool! Ross was only making out a hypothetical case against you. He's trying to help—"

"I'm trying to find a murderer," said Ross at his most uncompromising.

"It's the same thing," I insisted. "Chris says he didn't kill Nola. All right, then—he isn't the one you want to find! Why don't you work together instead of pulling in opposite directions?"

Chris was the first to give in. He sat down again. He said reasonably, "She's right, Langdon. Sorry I went off half-cocked but these last few days have been straight hell! All right. Go on with your case about me. Skip Nola—I know all you can say about that. What about Rita? And Mary?"

"You were in a position to know about Rita's movements—you knew that I was taking her home that night— you might have guessed that I'd try to question her. You could have followed us. She might have called you, asked your advice—"

"She didn't!"

"So you say," Ross said. "What's the alternative? Another uncorroborated alibi? Your wife asleep upstairs— you working alone in the studio."

Chris was silent.

"So far as the attack on Mary goes, you're equally vulnerable. Mrs. Wilson's apartment's not far from this house. You could have driven over here."

"But the motive, man—the motive!" Chris burst forth. "I'd have had to have a motive!"

"You could have had one," Ross told him. "If you thought Mary'd been in the theater the afternoon Nola Powers was killed and saw you between the curtains of the box."

I gasped at that. I'd forgotten that Ross didn't know that dream was dead. There hadn't been time to tell him nor did this appear to be the precise moment for enlightening him. I was afraid my information would prove too enticing a red herring and we'd all be off hot-foot on a new trail. No, better to wait, to tell him later.

Chris was speaking. He said stiffly, "I was in my office that afternoon. I didn't leave it."

"Except for a half-hour between three and four when you went out, ostensibly for a cup of coffee. The Olympia's only half a block from the Sheltham building."

He didn't point it further. He didn't need to. Even to me it sounded grim. Chris was sitting rigidly erect. Between his fingers a forgotten cigarette burned almost to its corked tip. His eyes were hard. "You checked on me!" His voice was deadly soft.

Ross shrugged. "What'd you expect? You were the number one suspect."

"But, damn it! I didn't kill her, I tell you!"

"No? Can you prove it?"

Chris slumped again. "How the hell *can* I prove it?" he asked dully. Meticulously he drowned the cigarette in his coffee cup. When he looked up, his eyes were expressionless. "All right," he said. "So it's like that. What'll I do now? Go to the police with that cock-and-bull story about Kearnes? You only halfway believe me. Do you think they will?"

"I doubt it." Ross was smoking evenly. "What about Kearnes?" he asked suddenly. "He'll come out of this eventually, you know."

Chris laughed shortly. "He won't talk. He's got his reputation, his public, to consider. Do you think it'll help him to admit he conked himself by a foot slip? Not likely. Not when there's a better story ready to his hand. Wait and see."

Chris was right. Gordon Kearnes never did admit the details of their quarrel, the abortive fight. When he did emerge from his blackness, it was to take refuge in a complete loss of memory. All incidents of the previous day, he insisted, were vague and uncertain. He remembered calling on Latimer—here his eyes had gone briefly to Chris, who with Ross and Lieutenant Dreyer had been summoned to his resurrection. He thought he remembered walking to his car but beyond that—he'd waved a hand—nothing.

"The blasted idiot!" Ross had grunted to me later. "But what could I do? Even if I could have nerved Latimer up to it, you can't just tell a dying man he lies!"

"He's not dying!" I'd said, shocked.

"I can't call the doctor a liar, can I?" He'd drawn fever-ishly on his cigarette. "Not that he's dying, by a long shot. But the doctor talks about inflammation. It was a pretty hefty knock he got and the doctor says there's danger in exciting him. I suppose he knows what he's doing."

"Well, there's one thing," I said after a moment, "if anything more happens while Gordon Kearnes is in the hospital, he'll be out of it. You won't be able to blame it on him!"

"Oh, there's a process of elimination going on," Ross had agreed gloomily. "Two dead—two in the hospital—you missed by a hair's breadth. I don't like it, Mary. It's too lively for me!"

Ross and Chris left me almost at once, Chris to go back to his office and Ross on the rather vague pretext of "looking around and seeing what he could see." Not being invited to accompany him, I announced that I'd go down later and see what Father was up to.

Ross seemed relieved. He said, "All right, baby. Be careful. I'll probably drop in on your father sometime this afternoon. We might have dinner together, h'mn?"

I said I'd think about it.

I was glad when they were gone. I had a lot of things to think about. Mrs. Ferguson was still making noises up-stairs so I poured a final cup of coffee and settled down in the living room to do a little serious thinking.

Not that it amounted to much. Try as I might, I invari-ably bypassed any reasonable train of thought in favor of something more alluring, which belonged in the realms of the purely conjecturable. I gave it up at last, said, "The heck with it!" and called Father.

He was in an irascible mood. He wanted to know what I meant by sleeping until noon and why I hadn't called him as soon as I was up? Here it was after one o'clock—he'd waited for me—and he hadn't had any lunch.

I said, "Darling, be calm. You shall have your lunch—not that I want any!—but I'll come and watch you eat. That is, if you want me to."

He said stiffly that he did want me to, so I dressed as quickly as I could, got my car and dashed for town. Half-way there, I remembered Chief Hanover's warning about my glasses and moderated my speed.

After lunch—which, in spite of his protests, conformed to the pattern I'd set—we parted. I'd meant to see a movie but Father raised such a howl about my going unattended that I gave up the idea and went Christmas shopping.

Which was how I happened to run into Alice Wilson.

We met in the roundabout door of Nashiona's biggest department store. I was on my way out—my shopping had been halfhearted—and I was trying to decide whether or not to give it up for the afternoon and go home. Alice had been buying things too. Her arms were piled high with packages. When she saw me, she stopped dead and waited until the door brought me around to her.

If she hadn't, I doubt if I'd have looked closely enough to recognize her. She was an entirely different Alice from the one I'd known. Her hair was cut for one thing and it cascaded to the shoulders of her loosely-belted polo coat. A childish felt hat was jammed on the back of her head and she wore little girl oxfords. It was a new metamorphosis—a determinedly younger-than-she-was one—and I didn't like it.

In other aspects, however, she was herself. She said, "Oh, hello, Mary. I thought it was you. I've just had my hair cut. How do you like it?" Blessedly she didn't wait for an answer but rippled on. "I'm nearly dead. My appointment was for ten o'clock and of course I've been shopping

lever since. I haven't had any lunch and I'm starved. Come
up to the tea room and I'll buy you a sandwich." I hesitated, trying to decide just how far going with her would
abrogate my promises to Father and Ross Langdon. Surely
nothing very desperate could happen to me across a table
in a crowded restaurant.

I said, "Well. As a matter of fact I haven't had any
lunch either. I was just going home."

She pounced on that. "Oh, do you have your car? Then,
I'll tell you—let's go out to my place. We can talk better
and I've eggs and cheese and a chocolate cake."

This time I really did hesitate. I was so long answering
that she caught on. Her eyes hardened. She said, "Oh, do
as you please! But I'm really not your killer, you know.
For that matter I'm taking as much of a chance as you are.
More, perhaps, for you're bigger than I am. If you're afraid
you can sit in a corner so that I can't possibly get behind
you to wham you on the head!"

That really wasn't to be borne.

I said, "Don't be silly, Alice. Of course I'm not afraid
of you and of course I'll come." The first part of that was
a lie. The rest wasn't. I went.

I've never been greatly surprised—as others have pro-
fessed to be—that men flocked to Alice Wilson's apartment. Men like to be comfortable and they're uneasy in
an atmosphere which gets its effect from pastel-colored
chairs and creamy carpets and crystal bric-a-brac. Though
Alice went in for the ultra modern in clothes, she boasted
that her apartment, save for walls and ceilings, hadn't been
altered in a half a dozen years and I'd say the results justified her. The chairs were big and dark and comfortable.
There were plenty of ash trays. The radio was expensive;
it neither blatted at you nor whispered irritatingly. There
were good lights where they were needed and they didn't
glare into your eyes. It was always possible to find last

night's paper, complete and neatly folded. A wide rack held stacks of late magazines.

Alice touched a lamp switch and then led the way to her bedroom.

"Come along," she invited. "I'll show you what I bought. Dresses—my dear, nothing I had will do with my hair now—but nothing! The whole thing's been sinfully expensive but Gordon would have it. So . . ." She shrugged as she stripped string from one of the larger bundles.

I was aghast. "But surely he's not going on with the play now!" I blurted.

"The play? Oh, no, I don't think so. I don't see how he can, with Rita dead and all."

I wondered if "and all" embraced the fact that he himself was now hors de combat, but I didn't have time to ask. She'd reached the lowest layer of tissue paper. "Look," she said, "at this!"

"This" was an ice-blue wool creation eminently suitable for some high school girl's Sunday afternoon dress. I said, "Very nice," and hoped it sounded as though I meant it. If it didn't, she didn't notice. She was rattling more papers.

"Now, this one," she said happily, "is velvet—black. Look at the wide cuffs and the collar—isn't it a darling? There's a little skull cap that goes with it. I got suede shoes—flat ones. That's really all I got today except my suit."

I'd already contemplated the suit—a violently checked affair—and once more I mumbled something.

"It's been such fun," Alice was saying. "Changing your personality is so good for you. I was getting in an awful rut—but completely. Of course, I'm going to have to be terribly careful of my weight—I won't dare put on an ounce—you can't wear these straight little things if you have *curves*. Not that I'll mind. I feel so deliciously *free* without those awful three-inch heels and that wad of hair simply skewered to the back of my head with hairpins."

She shook her mahogany locks at me. "I will admit that I
was scared stiff to do it. When Charles started to snip this
morning, I simply closed my eyes. But now it's done, I can
see that Gordon was wise."

"Gordon," I said grumpily. "What's he got to do with it?"

"Oh!" She looked at me, quickly cast her eyes down
again to where her fingers fumbled with layers of tissue
paper. "I forgot you didn't know. I'm going to marry Gordon."

I was speechless. I wanted to say, "if he lives—if he
lives," and I couldn't get it out. Was it possible she didn't
know where Gordon was or what had happened to him?

"I—I hope you'll be very happy," I managed at last.

Alice nodded briskly.

"Oh, we will. It's been hanging fire a long time now.
We'd have been married ages ago if it hadn't been for Nola
but, of course, now that she can't interfere any more. . . .
That sounds terribly callous, doesn't it? But it's true. She
did all she could to keep Gordon away from me. Out of
my way, darling. I'll just slip these dresses on hangers and
then I'll make our tea. . . . Why, what in the world's the
matter?"

I suppose I'd made some sort of a sound. I couldn't
help it. It must have been an appalling one for Alice had
stopped abruptly, one hand still holding open the closet
door, and was staring at me with exasperated curiosity . . .

"What's wrong?" she repeated. "Mary, if you could see
your face!"

I didn't care about my face. Neither could I answer her.
I could only point to where, just within the shallow closet,
a cascade of bright chiffon eddied in the sudden draft.
I'd never seen it before but I knew only too surely what it
was. Molly Dunbar's rainbow ballet dress.

18

"What on earth—?"

It was still Alice and she was getting mad. I didn't care about that. My voice returned to me, to some extent manageable. I said, "Where did you get that dress?"

Her eyes were big and round. "*What* dress? That old thing! Why, from the prop room at the Y. But I don't see . . ."

"How long have you had it?"

"Why—why, I don't know. Yes, I do, too. It was the night of the tryouts—remember? I slipped in and got it. A club I belong to is going to have a masquerade party. I only borrowed it. I don't see what you're making such a fuss about. It's none of your affair."

"Isn't it?" I asked grimly. Conquering an instinctive revulsion, I slipped the dress from its hanger. There was a wisp of a bodice—lavenderish blue—and to it was gathered a full skirt made of the six primary colors. About the waist were the scarves—there must have been at least twenty-four of them—caught by a single corner beneath a wide silver belt. "Look!" I said and pointed. Among the swirl of soft chiffon, jagged ends showed where a knife had cut. Three scarves were gone. Red, blue and orange. "Now," I said, "do you understand? It was an orange scarf that killed Nola."

"But—but . . ." The velvet dress, unnoticed, had fallen from her suddenly flaccid hands. Her eyes were wide and strained. "No, I don't understand! How could it have come from—from here? The dress was all right when I took it. I looked to see if it needed cleaning and it didn't. Surely I'd have seen . . ."

All at once she shrank backwards, away from me, from that mutely accusing dress.

"You don't think—Mary, you can't!—that—that it was I who killed her!"

I said crossly, "No, of course I don't!" and then began to laugh. It was mad laughter and, after a minute, I tossed the conglomeration of raped chiffon aside and gave myself up to it. I wasn't laughing at Alice. I laughed at myself, at the glib way in which I'd exonerated her. Was I mad, I wondered. Was everyone mad? Just so Chris had protested his innocence and just so I'd agreed with him. Chris couldn't have done it, Alice couldn't have done it, none of the Little Theater crowd could have done it and yet someone had. Someone had strangled Nola, had killed Rita, had launched that abortive attack on me. It couldn't just not be anyone, no matter what their protestations. . . . Tears streamed down my cheeks. "It's so funny!" I gasped. "It's so awfully funny! Don't you see—?"

Alice didn't. My laughter did something to her, pulled her together. She took me by the arm and shook me. She said, "Mary, you're hysterical! Stop it!" She pushed me down on the bed. "Stay here—lie down—I'll get you a drink!"

So I lay there obediently while tears rolled down my cheeks and that gargantuan laughter shook my teeth to chattering. It was funny—it was *funny* . . .

Alice was back with a glass brimming with sherry. She offered it to me; that, too, was amusing. I said, "P-p-poisoned?" and shook again at my own humor.

Alice didn't find it funny. "Certainly not!" she snapped. She snatched the glass from me, took a quick gulp. "There! You can see there's no cyanide in it! Now, for heaven's sake, drink it and snap out of it!"

So I did. The wine helped. I sipped it and gradually the tears stopped and my teeth ceased chattering. Presently I sat on the edge of the bed and wiped my eyes. I strove for normalcy. I said, "You'd better hang up that velvet dress— It'll get all lint."

"Let it," Alice said, but she picked it up and tossed it to the bed. She was still snappish. "If you think you can navigate, come into the other room. I want to think."

Thinking, with Alice, took the form of walking back and forth, smoking. I sat stupidly and watched her. That was the essential difference between Alice and me, I remember telling myself. In times of stress she wanted to think. I wanted someone to think for me.

About that time, Alice did too. She crushed out her cigarette and moved decisively upon the telephone. "I know what I'll do," she said calmly. "I'll call Gordon."

That brought me upright. "But you can't!"

She eyed me stonily. "Why not?"

"He can't come. Don't you know—?"

She didn't so I gave her a brief resume of the night's happenings. She listened, frowning. The frown gave an odd aspect of maturity to her face, incongruously youthful amid its flowing hair.

When I was done, she shook her head. "Gordon always was a fool," she said quietly. "Well, he's out. I suppose there's no chance of my seeing him?"

I said I didn't know, I doubted it.

"What next, then? Shall I call the police?"

But there was little enthusiasm in her voice, none in my soul.

I thought of Lieutenant Dreyer and shuddered. I said, "Don't you think we ought to—well, talk it over first?"

Alice looked at me curiously. "Get our story set, you mean?"

"I didn't mean that," I said. "The police will ask questions. Lots of them. If you don't have the answers . . ."

"Well, I don't! At least, I don't think I do. But I suppose we can see. Go ahead—you ask questions and I'll try to answer them."

That wasn't what I wanted. "It needs a third party," I said vaguely. "Maybe we're too close to the whole thing—we can't see . . . I'll tell you!" I said with forced brightness. "There's Ross Langdon. Why don't we call him?"

"That's the New York detective you've been running around with?" Alice asked indifferently. "All right—I don't mind. Go ahead and get him."

There was no trouble "getting him." He was at the USO, waiting word of me, and none too patiently either. Meekly I gave my whereabouts. He agreed to come. I heard the slam of the receiver.

We were just sitting down to our scrambled eggs and toast when he came. Alice had insisted upon eating. "Murder investigation or no murder investigation, I'm hungry!" she said roundly. "My head's always clearer when my stomach's full!"

Maliciously I mentioned "curves" but she only shook her head. "I can't be bothered with curves today. Besides, maybe I wasn't so smart after all, cutting my hair. Maybe tomorrow I'll want to kick myself. I don't like any of this, you know. It makes me feel queer —afraid. I almost wish Gordon and Nola hadn't come. It all seemed so wonderful then but now—I don't know. . . ."

There were plenty of eggs for Ross. "I seem to eat at the damnedest times," he said in mild objection but he accepted the plate.

We didn't waste much time eating. It seemed only a second or two before we had pushed coffee cups away and Alice was leading the way to the bedroom.

"There it is," Alice said. She came no farther than the doorway. "Mary nearly had a fit when she saw it. I—I can't believe it myself."

Ross whistled softly. "Where'd this come from?"

"I had it," Alice said bitterly. "All the time. The trouble is, I didn't know what I had."

"Not a crime in itself." Ross had the costume in his hands and was scrutinizing those stubby, telltale ends. "Red, blue and orange gone. Well, that's all right. No more needed, we'll hope. Or," he was suddenly thoughtful, "perhaps our murderer counted on the costume's accessibility."

"And just what do you mean by that?" Alice asked sharply.

"Just what I said. How long have you had this, by the way? And where'd you get it? And why, in the name of all the gods, haven't you put two and two together before now?"

Stiffly Alice repeated her story. About the club party and going to the property room. "It was just before I came in to the auditorium. It was in my muff all the time I sat by Mary. I went as soon as I came in because I was afraid I'd forget—I was planning a party that night, remember?" She smiled faintly. "The property room was unlocked and the dress was hanging on the rack just inside the door. Nobody saw me but they wouldn't have thought anything of it if they had. I didn't look at it very well—only to see if it were clean—but I'm almost sure it was whole and complete then. I haven't touched it since. Not until now."

"That's clear enough," Ross said. He tossed the dress aside. "Let's go out to the other room and figure this out, shall we? If you're right and the costume was complete when you took it, then those scarves have been hacked off since it's been in this house. I take it for granted that it wasn't you."

"It wasn't!"

"Then it must have been someone who was present in this house. The thing to concentrate on is who it might have been."

"I don't know," Alice said. She sounded troubled. "I don't like to think . . ."

"Nola Powers was murdered the day after the tryouts," Ross said. "That leaves only a short period of time to account for. Think. Who was here between—oh, say eleven o'clock Monday night and three or four the next day?"

"I'll try," Alice said. "I'm afraid. I won't be much good—going backwards isn't my line. There was my party—I'd invited the whole crowd to that—only it flopped. They were all afraid to come after Nola ran me out of the cast. Only Chris and Gordon showed up. Oh, and Faye."

Faye! I felt as though somebody'd punched me in the stomach. Faye had been there. She could have taken the scarves. What if it were Faye herself who was the murderer, and her whole story no more than a lie told to disarm suspicion? Faye had no alibi for the murder times any more than Chris. She'd "gone to bed early"— she was "asleep." The whole theater episode could have been fabrication. She had heard "things" but saw no one—no one but Nola. And me. And there was Rita—if Faye had come knocking at her door, Rita would have let her in, no matter how late. She wouldn't have been afraid, not of Faye. No one would. And who better than she would know Chris's overshoes the night of the blackout— But wait a minute! Had Faye been at Alice's that night? I didn't think so. Hadn't Chris said he'd gone home early because Faye was alone? Of course she needn't have stayed at home—she could have come to Alice's for the overshoes, taken them while everyone was still inside, but that indicated a cold-bloodedness of intent and a carefulness of planning that surely was foreign to Faye's nature, Faye was as simple and open as the flowers in spring.

Or was she? Was that simplicity, that openness, no more than skillful dissembling? Were there depths to Faye none of us—least of all me—suspected? I didn't really think so but just the same . . .

And then it came to me. Of course—Gordon. Gordon proved it. Faye hadn't smashed Gordon over the head. . . . But wait again! I was getting mixed. According to Chris, no one had smashed Gordon over the head—he'd fallen. But what if someone had—what if Faye had? What if Chris's story were a lie to protect *her?* If he'd come in and found Gordon on the floor and Faye standing over him with—say, the poker—in her hand . . .

No, it was too ridiculous! I wasn't going to think it. Not about Faye. Resolutely I forced myself to listen to Ross.

"The Latimers and Kearnes," Ross was repeating. "Anyone else?"

Alice appeared to think. "Well, Mark—Mark Kerrigan—came after the others were gone. He was very drunk. I didn't let him stay."

"No one else?"

"Not that night," Alice said firmly. "Mark was the absolute limit. I chased him out and then turned out my lights and went to bed."

"And next day?"

"You'll have to give me time to think. In the morning Pete and Molly Dunbar were in—they didn't want anything special, just to talk the whole thing over—curiosity, I guess. How was I taking it—Nola's snub—things like that. Chris ran in on his way to work—he'd left some scripts here and he wanted them. He only stayed a minute. Then Gordon came—about eleven."

"Stay to lunch?"

I held my breath. Because he hadn't. He'd had lunch with Nola at Dalrymples.

Alice's smile was wintry. "No. He told me he was lunching with my hated rival. She'd insisted on it."

"That all?"

"All who came? Yes. I was out myself in the afternoon."

"No chance of anyone having a key—getting in on the quiet."

"I don't give out keys," Alice said superbly. "Not even to my friends."

"All right—that's the list. The Latimers, Kearnes, Kerrigan, the Dunbars—and yourself."

Alice blinked at that but she nodded.

"Where was the dress all this time?"

"In my muff while I was at the Y auditorium. I told you that. When I got home, I shook, it out and hung it on the back of the closet door. Where Mary saw it."

"Anyone see you hang it up?"

"No. I went home alone—Gordon and Chris still had things to talk about. Faye waited for them. I wanted to have the apartment open when the party got here. Only it didn't come. I rushed in, put away my coat and the dress and forgot about it. Until now."

"Any of them in your bedroom that night?"

"Oh, I don't know. They all could have been and I probably wouldn't have noticed. I was in the kitchen part of the time and I did some telephoning."

She had. She'd called me.

"Gordon and Chris and Faye were in here. I think Faye left her coat on my bed. The men might have too—I don't remember. There's no entrance hall and it's more convenient. Then the bath opens off my bedroom—it's strictly a woman's apartment, Mr. Langdon. I seem to remember

Chris going after the ash tray on my dresser once but he couldn't have been more than a second."

"How about the others? Next morning?"

"Pete and Molly, you mean? I suppose they might have been in—I don't remember. Pete was wandering around the way he does—he's usually pretty restless. I was at the telephone for a minute. I wasn't watching."

"No, of course not. And Kerrigan?"

"Oh, Mark!" Something happened to Alice's mouth then. It went thin and hard. "I told you he was drunk. He wasn't only drunk—he was sick. I was disgusted. He wobbled into the bath and I slammed the bedroom door on him. When he came out, I gave him some whiskey and called a taxi. I don't know what he did in there—beyond being sick all over my tiles!"

"The drunkenness couldn't have been faked?"

Alice glared at him. "Certainly not!"

"Sorry—merely checking up. After all, Kerrigan is supposed to be an actor. Let's go back a bit, shall we? Know any motive these seven—yourself included—would have for killing Nola Powers?"

Alice shrugged. "What do you call a motive? We were none of us mad about her. I suppose my own motive's as good as any. Nola and I were natural antagonists. Rivals, too—since we both played leads. I thought she treated Chris like the devil and I said so. The result was we fought every time we met. But only with words. I didn't kill her."

"And the others?"

"My dear Mr. Langdon, are you trying to get me murdered by any chance? If you think I've forgotten that Rita Carstairs knew or suspected something and was on the point of telling it . . ."

"She put off the telling. You needn't. Carry on."

Surprisingly Alice laughed. "All right, but I don't know anything—truly. Chris—I imagine you've got a pretty clear idea of what his motive could be without me. Faye, too. So far as the Dunbars go, Nola did make a play for Pete—they weren't married five years ago—but Molly was made of stronger stuff than Kathy Carstairs. She stuck and got her man. As for Mark—well, I always thought he was completely gone on Nola. He was as lost as Chris after she went away."

Now, I thought, was the time to ask about that five thousand dollars Chris said Mark had borrowed, but Ross didn't. He said, "And Kearnes?"

"Gordon?" Alice hesitated a moment. "He was dazzled for a while. Like the rest. He got over it."

There was a consciousness of pride in her voice, a smugness. Making a choice between the two, Gordon Kearnes had chosen Alice! But—when had he made his choice? After Nola was dead?

I wanted to ask and didn't dare.

"Avarice, hatred, jealousy, fear," Ross said softly. "Those are the common motives. If we could find one—one of them . . ." His voice died away.

"Fear'd be the strongest, wouldn't it?" Alice asked. "Fear for yourself, I mean. And if that's so, aren't you beginning at the wrong end? Someone's afraid of Mary, aren't they? That attack on her proves it. Well, then, if you could find out what she knows—whom she saw in the theater—"

"Wait!" I interrupted. "I *do* know who it was—I found out last night—and it doesn't help a bit. It was Faye."

"Faye! Faye Latimer!" Ross demanded. "Good God, are you sure?"

"She told me. I should have told you last night only—"

"Never mind the apologies," Ross said grimly. "You can tell me now. Get on with it."

I did my best. "I don't know whether you can get much sense out of Faye," I finished. "About times, I mean. But I think she must have arrived just after Nola was killed and while her murderer was still hunting for a place to hide the body. That packing box was back against the brick wall behind the interior set, if you remember. If he'd been back there, Faye could have heard him and if she was quiet enough he wouldn't have seen her. She was only there a minute . . ."

"Faye was lucky," Ross said grimly. "However I can't see that it lets you out. I don't suppose you've the ghost of an idea what it is you know?"

I shook my head and Ross grunted, transferring his gaze to the floor. "There were thirteen of us originally," he remarked. "A bad number. Two of that thirteen are dead— two in the hospital—while, as for you, only the grace of God has kept you out of either category. I'd like to feed you a dose of scopolamine!"

Scopolamine—the truth drug. "But that's dangerous," I objected.

"So is carrying dynamite," Ross snapped. "Well, if that's it, it's all too much for me," he said and stood up. "I think this is the moment we call in the police. Not that I hope for a lot from them. They were supposed to be tracing this dress and a long way they got with it! If I may use your telephone . . ."

We didn't have to wait long. It was Chief Hanover himself who puffed up the stairs and sank, beaming, into a big overstuffed chair.

"Nice place you got here, ma'am," he said approvingly. "Comfortable—a man could rest himself here. Wood matches, too, by golly! If you don't mind, I reckon I'll have me a pipe."

Alice indicated that she didn't mind and he occupied himself with the task of getting his old briar alight. It took a while and all the time, although his hands were occupied, his eyes were studying us. Presently he gave a grunt of satisfaction.

"All set," he informed us, "Seems like I listen better if I got my old pipe going and I reckon that's what you brought me here to do—listen. What's on your minds?"

We let Ross tell him. He did it concisely. Chris's story. Faye's story. He exhibited the dress, summarized what Alice had told us.

The chief listened in silence. He asked no questions. Only, occasionally, a stronger draw on his pipestem produced a thick whistling noise. When Ross was done, he took the pipe from his mouth and knocked its ashes into a convenient bowl.

"Well, well," he said mildly. "That's quite a story and a mite worrying in places. Don't know what I think about it—yet. Don't know's Dreyer's going to care much for it neither. Can't quite see, on the face of it, just where it's going to fit into his program. You see, Dreyer's kind of got the notion the case is closed. Don't know's I agree with him wholly. Still and all . . ."

"Closed!" It was Alice. I don't think I could have said a word if my life had depended on it and as for Ross—Ross had turned away and was lighting a cigarette.

"Yes, ma'am. That's what Dreyer pretty near thinks and darned if he hasn't talked our state's attorney into agreeing with him. Not me yet, he ain't, but maybe after a while he'll get me, too, where I'll be seeing the light."

"But who?" Alice said. "Who is it?"

"Who is it?" Chief Hanover sat back and beamed benignly at us. "Well, now, nothing's proved yet, mind, but one of your actor friends up and slipped out of town last night and from information laid, as you might say, in our lap, Dreyer and me got reason to think he might have known considerable about Miss Powers' killing—might even, due to pressure from the past, have done it himself. Yes, sir, Dreyer's pretty sure Mark Kerrigan done it!"

"Mark Kerrigan!" Alice repeated. She sounded as stunned as I felt. "But how—why—I don't see . . ."

"No, ma'am, I don't suppose you do. But maybe you'll change your mind a mite before I'm through here. Funny thing," he had picked up his old pipe and for a second time was packing it with tobacco, "funny thing, when your call came through, I was just about getting ready to hist myself out of my chair and come out here to have a talk with Mrs. Wilson. Not about this murder or Kerrigan, but about something that has sort of points of similarity as you might say."

He stopped then to strike another of the "wood matches" over which he'd rejoiced previously. As its flame died, he looked directly at Alice.

"Kind of wondering what it could be, huh? All right—I ain't aiming to keep you in suspense. What I came to talk to you about—" He paused for a long, luxurious draw on his pipe. "What I came here to talk to you about specific was another murder. 'Twan't never proved as a murder but just the same . . . Happened about five years ago. Five years ago this fall. During hunting season. Know what I'm talking about now, Mrs. Wilson? I'm talking about the accidental shooting-murder of your husband—Pat Wilson!"

19

"Pat? Pat murdered?" Alice's hand was at her throat. "I don't believe it!"

"Which is certainly your privilege, ma'am, at this stage." The chief was like a bland and smiling Buddha. "I don't mind telling you I find it a right perplexing notion myself."

"It's ridiculous!" Alice had recovered herself. "It's—oh, I don't even want to think about it! It's completely insane!"

"The question never came up before, I take it?"

"Certainly not! Why, there was an inquest—a coroner's jury. The insurance company sent out an investigator."

"Insurance—umm. Got a right smart bit of insurance, didn't you, ma'am?"

"Why, yes. Does that matter? It was fifty thousand. Pat always carried heavy insurance and this paid double. That's why the insurance company man came. He tried to prove it was suicide. He couldn't."

"Suicide clause?"

"Yes." Alice looked at him defiantly. "Don't they all? Some of Pat's was within the two-year period. That's why they tried to make it suicide. But it wasn't. It was an accident. It couldn't have been anything else. Pat wouldn't have shot himself—never in this world. He loved being alive."

"How about somebody shooting him?" The question came quietly but for the first time the chief was completely alert. He was leaning forward, narrowed eyes on Alice's face. His cherished pipe had gone out.

Alice's laugh sounded angry. "Shoot Pat? Don't be absurd! Why? There'd have to be a reason, wouldn't there? Everybody liked him—why, Pat didn't have an enemy in the world!"

"Ma'am, there ain't nobody stands in that enviable position. There's always someone who hates his guts."

"I don't care!" Alice was breathing quickly now. "It's true. You didn't know Pat. Why, I—I was married to him and I liked him in spite of it!"

Laughter shook the chief. "Danged if you don't sound like a woman in one of them modern books. Married to him and liked him in spite of it, eh? Well—well. Still and all, you were having your own bit of trouble, weren't you?"

"Not trouble. I—we were going to get a divorce. Not because of trouble. We simply saw things different ways, that was all. Pat wasn't especially ambitious; I was. We thought we'd get farther—be happier—apart."

"Ambition ain't a crime," Chief Hanover observed thoughtfully. "Howsomever—you'll forgive me, ma'am— but Wilson's been dead these past five years and so far's I've been able to learn you haven't altered your way of living. Stayed on in the same place—went on just as if he was still alive. Looks to me as though the roots of your ambition had kind of wasted away."

"Perhaps." Suddenly it was as though shades had been lowered before Alice's eyes. "Perhaps I cared more about Pat than I'd thought. And then, my plans—well, something happened to them. It just was simpler, staying on here."

"Thinking of making a change now, aren't you?"

Alice's chin was high. "I'm going to marry Mr. Kearnes—if that's what you mean. But I fail to see what that has to do with something that took place more than five years ago!"

The chief sighed. He dug two fingers into his vest pocket and produced a much creased and folded paper. "If you'll just have a look at this, ma'am."

Alice looked and then crumpled the paper and flung it to the floor. She was breathing quickly, "It's ridiculous!" she said for the second time. "Anonymous letter! If you're going to believe that sort of thing—"

Ross recovered the paper and smoothed it out. I was close enough to peer over his shoulder. Together we read in rough block capitals: "Ask Kerrigan who killed Pat Wilson. Then you'll know who murdered Nola Powers and why. Ask Kerrigan."

The chief was droning on like an enormous bumblebee. "Now—now. There ain't no use getting excited. 'Course I ain't meaning to say we pay attention to all the letters we get—the ones that complain about the neighbor's dog in the garden or the beer party held next door. But this is a mite different. This relates to murder and maybe to a murder—by golly!—that nobody's knew was committed. 'Tain't reasonable to pass that over, now is it?"

"Pat wasn't murdered," Alice said stiffly. "I told you that before. It was an accident. Lots of men are killed—hunting."

The chief sighed. "I know—I know. Howsomever—just the same—Dreyer and me figured we'd better do a little investigating. So we put on our hats and went to see this Mark Kerrigan fellow."

"And he wasn't there!" Alice said. "He's a salesman—he might have been away on a trip. But of course that wouldn't matter. He killed Pat. His absence proved it. Q.E.D."

"No, ma'am, it wasn't exactly like that. Kerrigan was there all right and he asked us to come in pretty and polite as you please. Dreyer tells him what we want to see him about and he says sure, he'll be glad to tell us what he knows, which ain't much, if we'll just excuse him till he washes his hands on account of having been changing a typewriter ribbon and gotten ink all over his fingers. And that's where us two dumb fools made a mistake. It being a boarding house, the bathroom's down the hall a piece, and Kerrigan goes out saying he'll be back right away. He leaves the door open and we sit down. Only he ain't back in a minute and pretty soon Dreyer gets suspicious and he goes over to the window and looks out and kind of opines maybe that dark blue car with the packing-house insignia that was out in front when we came in belonged to Kerrigan. The car's gone and Dreyer goes tearing down the hall and the bathroom door's locked. So he pounds on it and some old girl inside bawls him out hearty. It's a nice thing, she says, when she's accommodating enough to take her bath in the afternoon so's everybody else can have theirs mornings and nights, that she can't have half an hour's privacy and she don't care if it is the police wants to get in they'll have to wait! So Dreyer apologizes and sorta slinks away with his tail between his legs and we take counsel. We talk to the cook in the kitchen and she says Mr. Kerrigan came down the back stairs and said he had to go away sudden and if any mail came for him to please hold it. Then he goes off around the side of the house and that's all she knows. So we thanks her and come away."

Alice's eyes were very bright. "You just came away!" she repeated scornfully. "That makes sense, doesn't it? Leaving the house unguarded—"

I saw Ross smile a tiny little smile but the old chief merely blinked. "No, ma'am," he said mildly. "We didn't do exactly that. We left a man at the front and another at the back. Wasn't no good worrying about the sides for the man in back could watch the back and one side if he got himself located right and the man in front likewise. But I reckon it's all wasted energy. To my notion, Mr. Mark Kerrigan ain't coming back—not right away."

Some of Alice's bravado was gone. Her mouth looked pinched. She said, "But you don't really think Mark murdered anybody, do you? Running away—that's not conclusive. Anyone could be afraid."

Chief Hanover shifted comfortably in his chair. "Ain't that a pretty incriminating question?" he wanted to know. "Supposing I say 'yes' and he ain't, or 'no' and then it proves he is. No, ma'am, I don't think he did it. That's where Dreyer and me disagrees. Dreyer's real busy right now warning the state patrols and radioing descriptions and such, but me, I've somehow got the idea that when he does get hold of Kerrigan he ain't going to have so much. To my notion, Kerrigan just don't want to talk so he takes the quick way out. Maybe he knows something and maybe, he don't. Maybe he just suspicions that he knows something or maybe he thinks he's protecting someone. Whichever way it is, if he ain't here he can't talk. Which is why," the chief paused and beamed at us, "I come over to see you, Mrs. Wilson, you being, as you might say, the interested party. 'Course I sent up to Walton County for a transcript of the inquest testimony but it may be a day or so before it gets here. In the meantime," he hitched his chair forward a little, "what's wrong with you telling me about it—informal-like—so's I don't get any wrong ideas to start off with?"

Alice was completely cowed. She hesitated, glanced at Ross. She said, "Well, I suppose—I don't see why—I mean, I can't tell you so very much but of course—" She stopped for a minute and then started over. "It was so very simple, Chief Hanover. Pat owned a cottage at Lake

Metaka. You know the sort of place—just a shack—but the men used it for hunting. They all hunted—all our crowd. That week-end, we wives went too. None of us cared to hunt but we were useful when it came to driving cars and cooking meals, and we could always play cards. Nola and I and Molly and Rita—" She caught her breath at that and I guessed that she was remembering that, of the foursome that had gone forth so gaily that autumn to drive cars and cook pheasant and tally bridge scores, only two remained.

"And the men, ma'am?" The chief looked sleepy but I was willing to bet sleep was far from his thoughts.

"The men?" Alice said vaguely. "Oh, you want to know who went? Well, Chris and Pat, of course, and Gordon and Pete Dunbar—he and Molly weren't married until that December—and Mark Kerrigan."

"Forrester?" It was the first time Ross had spoken in quite a long time. I saw the chief's eyes slew around toward him and then away again.

"No." Alice was definite. "Pat asked him but he wouldn't come. You see, Kathy Carstairs hadn't been dead so very long and Rita was coming with us and I don't think he wanted to meet her or us. Johnny avoided us, rather, that fall. No, that was all—five men and four women. We really should have had another girl—for Gordon—but there was no one he wanted us to ask." She made a vague gesture.

Mentally I lined them up. Pat and Alice, Nola and Chris, Peter and Molly, Gordon alone, Mark Kerrigan and Rita Carstairs— It hit me then. Mark and Rita! I looked to see whether Ross or the chief had noticed but, if they had, they weren't showing it.

Alice was going on. "It was a Saturday that Pat was killed. It was a beautiful day. Friday it had rained and we'd played bridge all day, but Saturday the sun was shining and we were sick of cards. We decided to go with the men. We all did, except Molly. She had a headache. I was with

Pat and Chris. Mark was with Pete. Rita and Gordon were together. Nola didn't come into the field. She stayed in the car—Chris's car. Pat had ours. When we got to the field we were going to work, Pat pulled the car into the ditch and Nola followed him. We coaxed her to come with us but she wouldn't. She said she had cigarettes and a book and she didn't like walking through cornstalks anyway and besides she had low shoes on. So we left her."

Again she briefly paused.

"You know what pheasant hunting's like. It's hot and its dusty and mostly you just keep pushing your way through cornstalks and waiting for the birds to rise. We didn't have any dogs with us. The field was a big one and we lost sight of the others almost at once. Once in a while we'd hear a shot but that was all.

"It was heavy walking and I was tired, but Pat and Chris got several birds. It was about four o'clock when Pat said he was going back to the car for some shells. I didn't want him to go—I said he could use Chris's shells—but he laughed at me and said he wouldn't be long. And then he went and Chris and I sat down on the ground and waited. We didn't talk—we both knew Nola was at the cars and I supposed Chris was blind-jealous. He always was where Nola was concerned. I wasn't jealous but I was mad. I had an idea that cigarettes and books weren't the only things Nola had in that car, and I thought Pat was drinking too much. So we just sat there.

"I think we heard some shots but I couldn't swear to it. I couldn't at the inquest. Out hunting you get so you don't notice guns popping off and there were a lot of people out that day. Pretty soon Chris said he was wasting time and if I didn't mind he'd go on without Pat. I didn't mind. I said go ahead.

"I heard some more shots after he left but I didn't pay any attention. I didn't wait there very long either. I was

too mad. If Pat thought he could leave me with the bugs
and cornstalks, while he had a private party with Nola, he
was crazy. So I started back to the cars. Halfway there I
met Mark. He was coming to find me. He told me they'd
just found Pat. Apparently he'd been climbing through
the barbed wire and the trigger caught. The safety catch
was off the gun. The shot had torn through his heart and
lungs. He had died immediately."

For just a second, she sat perfectly still.

"I couldn't believe it," she went on slowly. "I still can't.
Pat knew all about guns. He wasn't careless. It didn't seem
possible that he could have left the safety catch off. . . ."
Her eyes were wide and unseeing.

Chief Hanover moved abruptly. "The best of us make
mistakes, ma'am. And then?"

"Then? Oh, well, Mark took me to the cars. He wouldn't
let me go to Pat even though where he'd climbed through
the fence was close enough so I could see—I could see . . ."

"I was all alone. Nola wasn't in the car. No one was.
I just sat there and tried to think. I couldn't. I couldn't
realize that Pat was dead.

"Mark kept asking me if I'd be all right while he went
and got the others. I said I would. I don't know how he
called them all in but he did. Some of them had gone over
into other fields but pretty soon they were all there. Nola
and Rita came over to me, but the men just stood around
and talked. Chris said the sheriff'd have to be called and
that he and Pete would stay with the—with Pat. So Mark
put the rest of us in the car and we drove to Metaka.
He took us to the hotel—Gordon, too, because his nerves
were all shot; he was shaking like a leaf—and then he went
on to find the sheriff. It was night before they let me see
Pat and then it was just for a minute at the Funeral Parlors
in Metaka. That's when they told me there'd have to be an
inquest." Her voice died away.

"Umhum," Chief Hanover said ponderously. "I compliment you, ma'am, on telling the story. You made it like a picture. The inquest was held the next day?"

"Yes. It was 'death by misadventure'—isn't that what they call it? It only lasted a little while—the inquest. The whole thing was so—so plain. Pat's gun was right beside him. It was loaded and one shot had been fired. The shell was beside him on the ground."

"What sort of a gun was it, do you know, ma'am?"

"It was a Remington automatic twelve gauge using shells with number six chilled shot." Alice's voice sounded as though she'd said the words so many times they'd become meaningless.

"Uh-huh. The usual." Chief Hanover was grim. "Shell found beside him, eh? Know if they had the shell tested to make sure your husband's gun fired it?"

"Why, I don't know. I suppose they did. Could they tell?"

"Murder with shotgun or rifle's a curious business, ma'am. Not easy to prove. Take a revolver now. Fire a shot at a man and maybe the slug stops in the wound and you got something plain to read as a book. Ever hear of ballistics, ma'am? Well, maybe not. But a shotgun's sort of different. Nothing to go on but a lot of ball shot, unless'n you got the shell with the hammer mark clear and even then there's a lot of peculiar possibilities—"

He cut that off with a snap and I wondered what those peculiar possibilities could be. He didn't say.

"Are you still trying to make this a murder?" Alice demanded. Her assurance was coming back. "Because how could it be? It was an accident—not even the insurance man could make it anything else and goodness knows he tried hard enough! What do you think you can do—now?"

"Me? Why, nothing, maybe, ma'am." The chief was unperturbed. "As you say, five years is considerable in the past but even you'll admit that, taken along with what's happening now, it's right peculiar. Maybe it means something and maybe it don't but I kind of feel I ought to *know* about it, being as it's the same people and all. I don't suppose you'd know, from the inquest and all, ma'am, just where those same people were supposed to be located at the time your husband died?"

"Oh, I know," Alice said wearily. "At least I know what they said. I don't think I've forgotten any of it—I don't think I ever will. Pete and Gordon came back together—they'd gone into another field. I think they were the last to come in. Chris—I told you about Chris. He stayed with me for a while and then went on alone."

"How long'd he stay with you?"

"How long? How do I know? Time's relative, isn't it? It might seem longer or shorter sitting in a cornfield. Besides he didn't go toward the fence."

"Could have doubled back, couldn't he?"

"Perhaps. But it wouldn't have taken Pat long to get to the fence. It wasn't far. He must have died while we— Chris and I—were still together." She shivered slightly.

"Got a point there," the chief conceded. "Kind of like an alibi for him—you, too, ma'am, of course. And the others?"

"Well, Molly hadn't come with us—I told you she'd had a headache. Gordon and Rita hadn't stayed together either. It was a poor combination anyway. Rita was keen on hunting and she didn't like Gordon. She said he was a rotten shot and that all he ever did was miss and scare the birds. So, by mutual agreement, they decided to split up. Rita said she didn't have any luck at first but that about four she got a couple of birds. She knew she wasn't far from the car so she decided to take them back to save carrying them. That's when she found Pat. She was still beside the body when Mark came up. And then Gordon."

"Wait a minute," Ross interrupted. "You just told us that Dunbar and Gordon came back together."

"Did I?" Alice asked indifferently. "I must have made a mistake then. It must have been Chris with Mark and Rita."

"And what did Kearnes have to say?"

"Gordon? Let me think." She wrinkled her nose in pretty concentration. "Well, he said he'd only tried one shot—and missed it—so he just wandered around. Until he met Pete. He didn't really like hunting—what he wanted to do was absorb local color. You see, this was before Capper and Stein got interested in his plays and he was talking about writing a novel."

"Uh-huh." The chief was noncommittal. "Well, I reckon that accounts for everybody pretty definite, all excepting this lady you call Nola Powers. Where was she?"

Once more Alice concentrated. "Well, she was at the car—I told you that. She said she'd read and smoked and waited until she was bored stiff, so she thought she'd see if she couldn't find some of us. She said she saw Pat in the distance and called to him but he shouted something about being right back and for her to wait. She waited for a while and then, when he didn't come, she went on. She said she thought she heard a couple of shots in the direction he'd gone but she didn't think anything of it. She couldn't find any of the crowd so she came back to the car. That was when she heard about Pat."

"A couple of shots, huh?" The chief pounced on that. "Now we're getting somewhere. Seeing that your husband's gun had only one shot fired, I could be curious as to who fired the other one."

Alice looked scornful. "There mightn't have been two. Nola could have been wrong. And any way it's hard to tell where a shot's fired when you're out of doors. You ought to know that. Besides, the doctors said it was Pat's gun that did it. It was fired close—close to his body. It—it tore him to pieces. It was terrible." Suddenly her hands came fluttering out. "Go away—please go away. Don't ask me any more questions. I can't answer them, I tell you—I can't! Go away, all of you—let me alone! Let me alone!"

There was nothing to do but go. We went.

Outside Ross shut me into his car and went back to confer with Chief Hanover. They talked earnestly for a few minutes. The chief looked comic with that rainbow dancing dress thrown over his arm but there was nothing funny about his face. Nor about Ross's when presently he came to me.

I let him start the car before I asked questions.

"What did he say?"

"That I was to watch you as though you were worth your weight in gold."

"Why?" I said before I thought, and then, "Oh, fiddle! I don't know anything—I told you both that." Ross grunted so I went on. "Do you think he was murdered?"

"Pat Wilson? Probably."

"But—"

Ross didn't let me finish. "Look here," he said, "you heard what the chief said about shot guns and murders. It was true. It's damn easy and almost untraceable. Shoot him with your gun and make sure that his is shot off too. Pick up your shell case and leave his there. . . ."

His voice trailed off meditatively.

"But," I said, "who—?"

Ross shrugged. "Take your choice. You've a wide one. Leave Molly and Rita and Pete out of it. You've still got Latimer and Kearnes and Kerrigan, Alice and Nola—"

"Nola's dead," I said flatly.

"All right—Nola's dead. But she could have seen something—known something. It could be the motive for her own murder."

"Then why wasn't she murdered before? It was September when Pat was killed. Nola didn't leave Nashiona until late October. I know. I asked Molly."

"Don't ask me for reasons. But there probably is one."

We were silent the rest of the way. It was on my doorstep that I had a last brilliant idea. I said, "Well, there's one thing. Now that Mark's gone—run away—we will be able to check on him. If nothing more happens . . ."

But I was wrong. It didn't work out like that. For even while we were talking, Mark—poor blundering Mark—was being picked up by a state patrol and brought back to Nashiona.

20

I was all set for a quiet evening. I didn't get it. Ross wanted me to come down and have dinner with him but I said I was tired and that was true. I said I wanted to relax and forget murderers and that wasn't. The honest to goodness truth was that I wanted a little peace and a chance to exercise my own brain without being forced to consider the opinions of others.

As I said before it was wishful thinking. Not that it didn't start off according to schedule except for the fact that Mrs. Ferguson was obviously startled to see me. She said, "You going to be here for supper? And me without a thing cooked except for an apple pie which would have been a lot better if I could have got Jonathan apples instead of them Winesaps the store's so fond of stocking!"

I said I didn't care, with a vague remembrance of scrambled eggs and what-not in the offing. "Tea and toast will do me," I said. "I'm so tired I'm numb. I'm going to get into something comfortable and then just sit. Let's have our supper on the tea wagon in front of the fire."

Which was one part of the program that was carried out. I found the velvet hostess pajamas that Father had discovered somewhere or other and given me for my birthday. I combed my hair out of its waves and tied it back with a ribbon. I even unearthed a pair of glasses and put them on. It was going to be that kind of an evening.

It wasn't. Promptly at seven, while we were still lingering before the fire, the army arrived. They were young, slightly abashed but cheerful. They murmured their names hastily with hopeful eyes on the remainder of the apple pie. There were four pieces. I distributed them while Mrs. Ferguson hurried to plug in the percolator and measure coffee.

It was the first time I'd been in residence, so to speak, and forced to cope with the entertainment problem. The pie and coffee interlude was brief. While Mrs. Ferguson collected plates and silver, I sought desperately for some form of amusement.

As it happened I needn't have bothered. One youngster, who gave his address as Long Island, pounced gleefully upon Father's New York papers which follow us wherever we go and proceeded to catch up on home news. Another, a hawk-faced youth from Texas, complete with gentle drawl, said that if it was all right with me he'd like to write some letters. He was 'way behind on his correspondence and his girls were sure enough burning up the wires. I agreed that such a situation was serious and established him at the far end of living room where there were good lights, a table desk and Father's cherished typewriter upon which he fell with cries of joy. His buddy, another lanky Texan, now cast wistful eyes upon the chesterfield that lurked in a darkish corner and muttered something about, "Gee, it would be swell to have a nap!" He was on the graveyard shift, he elaborated, and this was his night off. Kind of foolish to spend it sleeping but so far he hadn't got the trick of restin' in the day time.

I told him to go ahead provided he didn't snore. He took me at my word.

This wasn't so bad. Three down and only one to go. I was cheerful as I came back to the fire and my remaining guest.

He was a rather small man, dark and inconspicuous, but disturbingly familiar. Since he'd entered the house, he'd spoken only when speech was necessary—"Thanks" for the pie and "Cream but no sugar" in reference to the coffee. However, each time I'd glanced his way, he'd smiled at me eagerly and toothily. There was something reminiscent about that smile. It hinted of more than merely the courtesy owed a chance hostess. It was as though it meant something special to him and would mean the same to me once I obtained the proper perspective.

With some such vague idea in mind, I established myself opposite him. I said, "And now what can I do for you? Have you any particular heart's desire?" He surprised my complacency then. He grinned once more, widely. He hitched himself a bit farther forward on his chair and said, "You haven't forgotten me, have you, Miss Thorpe?"

So I'd been right. I *was* supposed to know him. But why—what—where? I cast about me wildly. I said, "We-ell . . ."

He didn't seem to notice. He was driving straight ahead. He said, "I've been hoping I'd see you some place around before they shipped me out—at the USO or somewhere. I talked to your friend but I wanted to see you, too, and thank you for the swell wedding you gave me and Beth."

So that was it and that was why his face and smile had been so familiar. That scrambled-together wedding the night of Nola Powers' arrival—Hilda and the flowers and the impromptu dinner at the Sweet Shop. And the pallid thin-faced bride must have been "Beth."

I drew a breath of relief. I said, "Of course, I remember. The wedding was fun. Only—I'm sorry—I'm afraid I've forgotten your name."

"I didn't hardly expect you'd remember," he told me. His smile was still cheerful. "Meeting fellows as you do—hundreds of them, maybe. It's Wallace—Dave Wallace."

Wallace! I found myself sitting a little straighter. Wallace—there was something about that, too—something I ought to remember. Hadn't it been a Mrs. Wallace who'd telephoned several times?

Of course. I relaxed. "Your wife tried to call me," I told him. "Several times. But I was always out. I'm sorry. I would have liked to talk to her."

He said, "Yeah. She wanted to talk to you, too. Oh, not about the wedding," he went on in quick disclaimer as I started to speak. "I mean, she'd have thanked you for that, too, of course. Only this was something else she wanted to tell you. Something special. About the murder you got mixed up in."

"About the murder you got mixed up in. . . ." My hands were gripping the chair arms now but I kept my voice casual. "Nola Powers' murder?"

He nodded. "Yeah. Something she overheard. She didn't know if it was important or not—she thought maybe you'd know. She was awful interested—never having had anything to do with murders before and that Miss Powers being an actress and her coming up from the depot in the same car with Beth and all . . ."

He would have been content to drone on forever. Flesh and blood could stand no more. I said, "What did she hear?"

He blinked at me. "Well, I don't know's I can tell you exactly. It wasn't me heard it anyway—it was her."

"You can try, can't you?" Then, as he still blinked, "What I mean is she probably told you too. You could give me an idea."

He remained obdurate. "I don't know's I rightly could. I might get it wrong and then where'd I be? Besides Beth's going to write you about it. She said she was."

I didn't find that particularly consoling. I said, "Listen, Mr. Wallace. What your wife heard may be important. Very important. Lots of things have happened since Nola Powers was killed. A second murder for one thing. For another there's me. You know about what happened to me. It's the reason you're here tonight. I don't need to tell you that. What I am trying to tell you is that this thing isn't ended. Other things may happen. Someone tried to kill me. He might try again. Or he might kill someone else. You see, we don't know. We haven't any idea who the murderer is or what's in his mind. Now if your wife knows something that would help . . ." I paused invitingly.

No good. His face was a study in frowning concentration, but his head waggled negatively. "I'd be scared to try. It wasn't much anyway—just two people she heard talking in an eating place. One of them was that Nola Powers—Beth recognized *her* all right but she never seen the other. Didn't know for sure if it was a man or woman. She was waiting for me, see?—setting in one of them booths at the hotel coffee shop and this Nola Powers came in and sat in the booth behind. She was waiting for someone, too, and after a while whoever it was came. Beth didn't see him or her, and she never heard anything he said but she heard Miss Powers. I guess an actress' voice carries good, and anyway them booths are nothing but shells and they were sitting back to back. Beth didn't think the other guy stayed very long because when I come Beth says for me to look in the booth behind when I took off my coat because there's a famous New York actress sitting there with someone and she wondered who it was. So I looked and the lady was there but she was alone, and I said she didn't look like no actress to me—she had one of them tan coats like everyone wears and her head all tied up in a turban and dark glasses—but Beth said she was and I didn't know what I was talking about. She said Miss Powers was probably

trying to be in—incog-something but she'd know her voice
and walk anywhere." He brooded darkly for a moment. "I
guess it's hard to fool women."

"What day was this—do you remember?"

"Well, now, let's see. We were married Friday because
Saturday was my day off and it wasn't Sunday because Beth
was out to the camp so it must have been Monday. Yeah,
that's when it was—Monday. I got leave and came in as
quick as I could but it was after five-thirty—must have
been darn close to six, I'd think."

Five-thirty—six. Well, that was all right. It had been
Tuesday noon that Nola Powers and Gordon Kearnes had
quarreled so conspicuously in Dalrymples. I said, "And
your wife thought that what she heard was important?"

He shrugged. "Not at first. You know how you sit and
listen to people when you're killing time and what you hear
sort of goes in one ear and out the other. But after this
Nola Powers got herself kicked off she began to remember.
She wondered if maybe she ought to tell somebody about
what she heard only she didn't know who to tell. She was
afraid if she went to the police they'd just laugh at her,
and then she thought of you being concerned in it, and she
decided she'd talk to you and see what you said. Only she
never could get you when she called, and then she had to
go and of course it was too late."

"Go?" I repeated. "You mean your wife's gone? She's
not here?"

"Now, she's back in Paynesburg. She had to get back
to her job. At the mill." He sounded surprised that such a
logical conclusion hadn't occurred to me.

"And you don't feel that you can tell me more?"

He became very earnest about it. "Look, Miss Thorpe.
If it'd been me in that coffee shop instead of Beth, I'd
tell you all I could. Only it wasn't, and I'm in the army,
and the army's got all sorts of queer rules about things

you wouldn't think was important. I'm all the time bumping into some of them and I don't rightly know just what they'd think of me horning into a murder where I had no more'n a secondhand right to be. No, sir, Miss Thorpe. As I see it the best thing you can do, since you didn't get to talk to Beth, is wait till her letter gets here and maybe then you'll know. She's going to write you."

There was no good in further urging. I stood up. I said, "Well, maybe. But if you don't mind, I'll get a second opinion. This is too much for me."

So, much for my avowed intent toward self reliance.

I got Ross right away and he wasn't too pleased. He said, "Look. I thought we were taking the evening off."

I said, "I was. But not now. Something's happened. You'd better come. I need you."

I should have been more careful of my language. He was at the door in record time, quite pale for him, and, after he'd taken in the absolute normalcy of the living room—typewriter clicking spasmodically, papers rattling, the more or less gentle sound of sleep—the Texan *did* snore!—he pretended to collapse against the stair balustrade.

"What's the idea?" he scolded. "You said something'd happened. I rushed out here prepared to do battle and what do I find? A social evening at home, by gum!"

I picked him up. "Prepared to do battle—what on earth are you talking about? I only said I needed you. And I do."

"Unfortunately you didn't make yourself clear. Considering that all our chief suspects are on the loose again—"

"They're not!"

"Oh, aren't they? Kearnes came out of the hospital this afternoon, very picturesque with a bandage around his head. You can't keep that guy down! And the state police hauled in Kerrigan and deposited him at the station a while ago, but not even Dreyer could hold on to him. I saw

him—Kerrigan, I mean—a few minutes ago going into the
Academy Bar. He had a lawyer with him and they were
both mad. Kerrigan said if he ever found out who was responsible for stirring up the Wilson story there would be
a murder, and Dreyer wouldn't have any trouble hanging
it on him! As for suspect number three, he's presumably
holding his wife's hand at the hospital, but I've no sure
way of knowing. I didn't take time to check."

I disregarded some of this as foolishness. I said, "Chris
or Mark or Gordon Kearnes. Does it have to be one of
them?"

Ross gave me a quick look. "Oh, no," he said gently.
"There's always Mrs. Wilson or the Dunbars."

I sighed. We always seemed to go round in a circle and
here we were at the starting point again. I said, "That's
why I called you. There's a chance—a very slight one—of
narrowing it down a little. This is Private Wallace, by the
way—Ross Langdon. Now, Ross, it's this way. Mr. Wallace's wife . . ."

I skipped through the story myself, appealing only to
Wallace for confirmation at critical points. Ross smoked
and listened and, when I was done, raised a speculative
eyebrow. "Well, I don't know. According to your story,
she didn't actually see anyone. And a one-sided conversation—"

It was my discovery, my story. I was jealous of it. "It's
worth a try," I pleaded. "It might mean something to us.
There could be names . . ."

"Maybe. But a casual conversation to which no particular importance is attached at the time and over a period
of days . . ."

I said nothing. There was nothing to say.

Ross scrutinized the end of his cigarette. "Oh, well,"
he said at last. "I'm a sucker for a long shot. I always was.
Where is your wife at the moment, Mr. Wallace?"

"Beth? She's at home. In Paynesburg."

"Paynesburg what? Does she have a telephone?"

"Paynesburg, Vermont. Sure she's got a phone." Abruptly the implications of that last penetrated. "Say! You don't mean you're going to phone her, do you? Good gosh! It's later there than it is here. She'll be scared to death!"

"No, she won't," Ross said. "We'll let you talk to her." He looked at me. "What about it? Any chance of a little privacy?"

"There's an extension upstairs in Father's room," I told him. Then, doubtfully, "You don't think you ought to tell Chief Hanover?"

"Not at this stage of the game." He took the telephone and balanced it in his hand. "All right, Mr. Wallace—you know chapter and verse. Want to put the call in?"

It would take some time to complete the call, Central via Private Wallace informed us. Would we hang up? She'd call us.

Minutes dragged by. Private Wallace sat and glowered. It was plain he disapproved of the whole thing. The Texans finished writing and sleeping, respectively, and lounged in our direction looking for entertainment. There were introductions. The supply of New York papers ran out. Mrs. Ferguson appeared with a bowl filled with popcorn. We ate enormously. Ross smoked calmly but I was as jittery as a kid faced with his first bicycle.

When the telephone finally did ring, Ross motioned to Wallace. "You take it," he ordered. "We'll give you a couple of minutes for stage-setting before we come in." Halfway up the stairs, he said, "Who talks? You or I?"

"It'd better be you," I said. "Much better. I wouldn't even know what questions to ask."

So it was that I sat and watched while Ross said, "Yes . . . No . . . Are you sure of that?" and made spidery marks on the back of an old envelope of Father's.

I did my best to try and hear what she was saying but her voice came to me as no more than a thin quacking. Nor did Ross's face tell anything. The envelope was nearly filled with ink tracks before he said, "All right. Thank you very much, Mrs. Wallace. You may have helped a great deal. I can't tell yet. If there's anything more we'll get in touch with you. And now I'm going to turn you back to your husband."

Private Wallace came in as Ross replaced the hand set. He did it absently, his eyes on the spider tracks. He whistled softly.

I'd been on the outside looking in too long. "What is it?" I demanded jealously. "What did she say? Did you learn anything?"

Ross pushed the envelope in my direction and, when I burst out, "If you think I can read that—!" he said, "Hold everything. I'll translate. See what you think."

Roughly it went something like this:

Beth Wallace had entered the coffee shop about five-thirty that Monday evening. She had come in through the street door and taken a seat in a booth about halfway along the side, her back to the entrance. She had only been there a few minutes when Nola Powers came through the hotel door. Mrs. Wallace recognized her—

"Even though she was all wrapped up like a mummy, Mrs. Wallace knew her and how—by all that's holy!—do you think? By her walk and her perfume. Women!" said Ross.

"Entirely reasonable," I said. "Don't stop to argue. Go on!"

Well, Nola had taken the next booth and ordered tomato juice. Mrs. Wallace didn't think she was alone very long because almost at once she heard Nola's voice, low and controlled and beautifully clear.

"And that's all she ever did hear," Ross said regretfully. "Just one-sided like a telephone conversation. Whoever

was with her must have been almost whispering. When I
think what might have been averted if that fool woman
had given in to her natural curiosity and made an excuse
to stand up or leave the booth—anything so she'd have
had a chance to see who besides Nola Powers was in that
booth."

"If she had, she probably wouldn't have heard all that
Nola said," I remarked sensibly. "And by the way, are you
going to keep breaking up this with your own comments
or are you going on?"

He went on.

The first thing Mrs. Wallace had heard Nola Powers
say was, "So you *did* get here?" And the next was, "You
know what I want. There's only one thing I'll ever want
from you and you know what it is—you ought to know—"
There was a blank space then as though the second person
had talked long and earnestly, and then Nola had laughed,
an ugly taunting laugh. "Don't hand me that. You can get
money—you always have. And you'd better. Unless you
want to be the central figure in a murder case—"

"Murder!" I said. "What murder? Did she mean Pat
Wilson? Could she have? Oh, Ross, do you think—"

"I'm not thinking," Ross said briefly. "And, incidentally, who's making comments now?"

It was unanswerable. I subsided.

After that Nola had said, "Don't worry—I've got it. I
always have it. That little piece of paper's my most precious possession. And if you think I won't use it, just try
me! There's nothing I'd like better than to hand you over
to the police."

There'd only been one other speech. A long one. A
brusque, all-right-now-that-we've-got-that-settled, making-
arrangements one. "Tomorrow then—I want it tomorrow.
And in bills—no checks. I'll meet you at the theater—we've
excuse enough for that. About three. And I won't be alone

so don't try any tricks. I'll bring that baby-faced Thorpe kid with me—" And then, "Don't be silly. Of course you can." And then, menacingly, "You'd better."

That was all. Whoever it was she'd addressed must have gone then, for Private Wallace, a few minutes later, on the instigation of his wife, reported the booth, save for the actress, unoccupied.

I looked at Ross. "Wh-where are we? Does it make sense to you?"

Ross said, "Well, we've a motive. Problematical, but the meaning of that precious piece of paper is only too clear."

"A confession?" I said slowly. "Murder—she said murder, didn't she? But whose? Pat Wilson's?"

"Unless there's another in the offing of which we know nothing," Ross said moodily. He folded the envelope, carefully put it in his pocket.

I watched him dully. "I was 'the baby-faced Thorpe kid,'" I said after a while. "She wanted me for protection and I failed her." He didn't answer and presently I said, "What do we do now?"

"A lot of thinking. On the face of it, it's plain enough—blackmail and the poor devil bled to the limit. We've got to find out who could pay and did—who has the money or had—which leaves us about where we came in. Latimer or Kerrigan or Kearnes."

"Or Alice Wilson," I said. "She got a lot of money—insurance money—when Pat died. And you heard what Chief Hanover said—she hadn't changed her way of living. . . . This could be why."

"Yes," Ross said. He rose heavily. "Come on downstairs—we can't do anything more tonight. Tomorrow . . ." His voice trailed off.

At the stair's foot, he spoke again. "It's a mess," he said. "An ugly damnable mess and I wish it was over."

So did I. Oh, so did I.

21

The next day being Sunday, we took a rest. We needed it. Nothing happened. Father wasn't home—Sunday is one of the big days at the USO—but Ross and I sat around all day and talked. Not about murder.

The Sunday calm was only an interlude. On Monday we were back in the midst of things again. It was my idea to question the waitress at the coffee shop so when Ross handed the idea right back to me I had nothing to kick about. Nor, when the deed was done, anything to cheer about.

I was lucky, too. Nashiona restaurants all carry window signs "Waitress wanted" but I found the right girl simply by walking into the coffee shop and taking what I thought was the booth Nola Powers had occupied. The girl was short and stocky, black of hair and eye. She put her hands akimbo on her blue cotton hips and eyed me with suspicion. Yeah, she'd been here quite a while—two weeks. Yeah, she'd had this rank of booths from the beginning? What was it *to* me?

I was nice about it. I took a five dollar bill from my purse and displayed it. I said, "I want you to tell me something. I want you to remember back to a week ago Monday about five-thirty o'clock. There was a woman in one of these booths—a woman dressed in a tan polo coat and a turban and dark glasses . . ."

285

She spat at me then. She said, "Sa-ay, just what *is* this? How'd you think I'm going to remember that far back? Listen, lady, you know how many soldiers out at that camp? Thirty thousand, some say. All you got to do is double that and you get about the right number of wives and sweethearts and sisters that have come swarming into town to visit them. These booths is full all day long. If you think I can remember one lady a week back . . ."

"I see," I said. "I'm sorry. It was rather important. It's that murder case—you know? The New York actress who was strangled? She was staying in the hotel and she sat just about here that Monday night. I hoped you'd remember the clothes."

She sniffed at that. "Polo coats and turbans ain't nothing here. Dark glasses, neither. If she'd been stark naked now . . . Say, who are you anyway? The police?"

I said I wasn't the police. I said it very definitely. I wanted it understood. There was something about a penalty for impersonating an officer. . . . I said I was helping—I thought I might go that far in safety. Once more I delicately lifted the five dollar bill. I said. "Possibly if you'd try . . ."

She regarded it sourly. "Put that away," she ordered. "I can take tips but anything that big's a bribe and I don't take bribes."

It was a cause lost in the grand manner. "You misunderstand," I said. "It *is* a tip. Now if you'll bring me a malted milk . . ."

She must have understood after all. She never brought any change.

Ross laughed when I told him about it. I forgave him, however, since I had the pleasure of personally puncturing his own bright dream of what might have been and wasn't.

"Look, Mary," he'd said. "We know now that Nola's atmosphere-seeking trip to the theater was only a blind for an actual meeting with someone. We know that she wanted you along as a bodyguard. Now let's do a little guessing. I think you can stop worrying about failing the lady. I think the truth of the matter is that she failed you. Let's take it that way and see where we come out. Let's assume that something happened to—well, dissipate Nola Powers' fear of this individual. Let's assume that she was persuaded to go to the theater in his company."

"Very nice. But how'd they get in? The janitor swears he saw no one but me. Unless he was lying," I finished hopefully.

"If you can give me one good reason for his lying," Ross began and stopped. "Unless he was bribed—"

"Not bribed—tipped," I said smugly. "They don't take bribes in Nashiona. I know."

Ross scowled at me. "I don't know—I think that's out. If he'd been killed instead of Rita Carstairs . . ."

"We're getting a long way off." I was getting bored. "If you remember, the question was how'd they get in without being seen?"

"I wonder if they did," Ross mused. "The 'how' is easy—the stage door was open. Faye Latimer got in that way. But as for being seen . . . It seems to me there was a lot of traffic through that stage door and it stands to reason it all couldn't have gone unnoticed. The theater is halfway down the block. What'd be the matter with doing a little quiet checking among the employees of the buildings that back it? Some one of them might have noticed something."

"Lovely," I said, "but, darling, it's just not sensible. Do you know what's back of that theater? The river. And in the curve between it and the theater is part of the municipal parking space. Parking's free and there's apt to be hundreds of cars parked there at a time and people coming and going. If I saw anyone along there—I mean any of the

Little Theater crowd—I'd assume they'd just left their car
and let it go at that."

For the first time Ross looked distinctly deflated. I
became sorry for him. "Of course," I said, "that could
explain how they got to the theater. In a car, I mean. But
that's no help either. They all have cars—Chris and Mark
and the Dunbars—and me—"

"Kearnes?"

"Yes," I said reluctantly. "That is, he's had Alice Wilson's since he's been here."

Ross said, "Damn!" but there was no heart in it.

"Of course," I said thoughtfully, "I don't suppose knowing that the stage door was open or not is the sort of thing
you'd leave to chance if you were planning a murder. You'd
want to know definitely about it, wouldn't you? Perhaps
if you could find out whether or not anyone visited the
theater that morning . . ."

"Maybe you've got something," Ross admitted. "I'll call
Hanover and find out."

We didn't have anything. Ross was grim as he turned
from the telephone. "All right," he said, "you've guessed
it. There was a delegation there in the morning. To look
at the stage and make scenery plans. And *who* do you
think made up the delegation? Latimer and Kearnes and
Mark Kerrigan—who it appears is an important member of
Latimer's stage gang—and Alice Wilson. All right, you've
got it. They were all there, the whole damn crew!"

I sat down and held my head. I said, "Oh, dear!" It was
inadequate but all I could think of at the moment.

That was the day of the inquest into Rita Carstairs'
death. Once more we gathered, those who were left of
us. Lieutenant Dreyer was there and Chief Hanover and a
nondescript group of Rita's woman neighbors. It was much
the same as the other inquest save that the state's attorney

was a lot more interested and asked more questions. Even the verdict was the same. "Death by strangulation at the hands of person or persons unknown." To this, however, the jury had attached a rider. "We think by the same who strangled Nola Powers."

Whether or not that was allowed to stay I do not know. Certainly the jury were not the only ones to hold such a conviction. Scarcely without conscious volition the Theater crowd drew together. Mark Kerrigan, scowling still as he had scowled all that bitter afternoon. Gordon Kearnes, white bandage rakish about his head. Alice Wilson on his arm—Alice subdued and oddly unfamiliar in her new haircut and her juvenile style of dress. Chris, already giving word of Faye—"Better, much better, the doctor thinks. Well, flowers perhaps. She can't see anyone, you know. Not even me." Victor Jameson, his boyish face pink, his eyes frightened, edging away from us, disappearing around the corner at last to our mutual relief. Johnny Forrester, the nerves of his ravaged face twitching. Molly and Pete—Molly voluble, as ever; Pete, silent, as though beyond the help of speech. Ross and I. But we weren't important. Only by accident of God were we there. We were strangers, bystanders, interested, yes, but bystanders none the less. We didn't count.

It was Molly who suggested that we go to her house, talk it over. "We ought to," she told us. "This thing's getting serious."

"Serious!" Mark Kerrigan uttered a bark of something that might have been laughter but wasn't. "I'll say it's serious! When the police can back up five years to trump up a murder charge . . ."

"That's what's so silly," Molly said firmly. "If they're going to do things like that, we've a right to protect ourselves. Everybody knows that Pat's death was an accident."

Something, perhaps the lack of verbal agreement, stopped her. She looked around our circle. Her eyes were enormous. "Wasn't it?" she asked waveringly. "Wasn't it?—an accident, I mean?"

No one answered her. No one could.

But we went with her.

The Dunbar house was old. The rooms were large, the ceilings unfashionably high, but Pete and Molly had scraped and painted and redecorated until the general effect was of spaciousness and charm.

Molly bustled in ahead of us, adjusting the Venetian blinds to let the sunlight flood over the flower-splashed carpet. "Sit down, everybody. Pete'll bring drinks in just a moment."

We sat lumpishly. The clink of ice cubes came from the kitchen. One or two lit cigarettes. Mark crossed to the radio, flicked the switch. A voice swelled. Local news. "The inquest on the body of Rita Carstairs, prominent member of the Nashiona Little Theater, found strangled in her apartment Tuesday afternoon, has just been concluded. The coroner's jury brought in a verdict of—"

Mark's hand moved swiftly. The voice stopped. Mark turned on us, his eyes wild, his face distorted.

"God, what a ghoul's feast they're having! Wherever you go, whoever you talk to—not even the air's free of it. Nola—Rita—Pat . . ." Abruptly his voice ended on what was almost a sob. "They might have left Pat out of it. I didn't kill him—why should I? He was almost my best friend. It was an accident, I tell you—it was an accident."

Somebody thrust a glass into his hand. Neat brandy. He gulped it, subsided shivering. There was a long silence.

"It could have been murder," Alice Wilson said at last dully. "Chief Hanover said so. That's the awful part of it. But how are we going to know? How are we ever going to know?"

I wanted to speak, to tell them the reason Nola Powers had died, to suggest the existence of a paper that might prove Pat Wilson's death no accident but murder, but Ross shook his head at me so sternly that I kept silence.

"We're not going to know." Chris got up and plunked his glass down on the tea wagon. "Five years—that's a long time. The thing'll stymie itself—wait and see. The police can't prove anything and—damn it!—neither can we. As I remember those inquest proceedings, we'd all broken up. If one of us had killed Pat, it could have been anyone. We were all on our own. Any one of us could have followed Pat to the fence and shot him—"

There was a chorus of disagreement.

"Come off it! I was in bed"—this was Molly.

"Don't be a fool—most of us weren't even in that field!"

Over all the clamor, one voice, stentorian, Mark's. "But the gun, man—the gun! It would have had to be the same make—the same gauge—"

"Why?" Chris's voice was cold. "Any gun that used number six chilled shot would have done. There was one shot fired from Pat's gun and the shell was on the ground beside him. But it needn't have been that shell that killed him. All the killer would have had to do was pick up his own shell and put it in his pocket. He could have been the one to fire Pat's gun—"

Once more expostulation rose high. A second time Chris cut them short.

"All right," he said, "I've told you. If you don't believe, it's not my fault. Now, I'm going home. It was a mistake to come here—to think we could talk this out. It can't be done."

His was the signal for a general going. By ones and twos they remembered engagements, made excuses, departed. Presently only Ross and I were left. And Molly. Even Pete had pleaded his office and had gone.

There were tears in Molly's eyes as she looked at the discarded glasses, many of them scarcely touched. "I thought it would be such a good idea," she said, lip quivering, "to have them here. And it wasn't—they were hateful—"

"They were afraid," Ross said quietly. "Afraid of what they know—of what they instinctively feel. Don't let it bother you, Mrs. Dunbar. It wasn't your fault. You did your best."

We would have gone then, too, but Molly clung to us. Please stay—please, please. Smoke a cigarette—have another drink—she'd make coffee—anything. Only please don't go.

The end of it was we stayed. It wasn't so long—perhaps half an hour—and before it was over she had another guest. Gordon Kearnes came blinking into the warmth of the living room to join us.

He'd come back, he told us, on the chance that we hadn't all gone. He'd been at a loose end, hadn't known what to do with himself. He said frankly that his nerves were gone, and he had no office to which he could repair in time of turmoil. He'd meant to stay at Alice's but she'd kicked him out. All this talk of Pat had upset her. He'd be glad when the thing was over and he could take her away. For himself, he'd go like a shot only the police preferred that he stay. . . . He shrugged. Ridiculous, of course, but you couldn't argue with the law. Now that the play was definitely off there was no reason for his staying. "I don't kid myself, you know," he said peering owlishly through his thick glasses. "This crowd never had any use for me and they haven't now. If they could pin these murders on me . . . Or, better still," he smiled faintly, "if I could be murdered . . . Look here, Langdon, you're a detective of sorts. Get this—it may be worth remembering—if I'm found dead before this mess is untangled, it won't be suicide, no matter what the circumstances seem to say. I'm going on record before the three of you right now— I've no intention of killing myself! I find life too damn interesting!"

Not what you'd call a soothing note. My glance at Ross must have been revealing, for we left almost at once. To Molly's protests I pleaded that I simply had to get down town before the stores closed. She wasn't happy about it but she let us go.

It was almost five o'clock and the early winter dusk was upon the city. It was chilly and I snuggled deep into my furs as we lingered momentarily before the house, the men lighting cigarettes with a common match. Then Ross and I went to one car, Gordon Kearnes to the other.

I did my shopping and then walked the short distance to the YMCA building and the USO. But Father wasn't there so it didn't do me much good. I considered calling Ross and staying down to dinner, and then changed my mind. Not tonight, thank you. I was seeing entirely too much of that young man. A rest would do us both good. I decided to call a taxi and Mrs. Ferguson, and to go home.

I called the taxi first and then gave my own number. Central took her time ringing it, and when she did finally get down to it there was no answer. I hung on for quite a while but Hilda began waving at me that my cab had arrived so I gave it up. I remember thinking as I grabbed for bag and gloves, "Oh, bother! She's gone to the store!" and that was all I *did* think.

Until I'd paid off my driver and turned to look toward the house. I got a shock then. The house was dark. There wasn't a light in the place.

Ross says that what I should have done then was to ask the taxi driver to come in with me. "One more example of foolhardiness," he says and shakes his head. "You were lucky that time. Another . . ."

I'll admit I was a trifle uneasy going up the steps, but the fact that the door was locked reassured me. "She probably went down town," I told myself as I took out my key. "I just happened to get home before she did."

Even as I pushed the door open I touched the switches that controlled hall and living room lights. Everything looked normal and I sighed with relief as I dumped my hat and coat on a convenient chair and went to the stair foot to call, "Mrs. Ferguson! Mrs. Ferguson! Are you there?"

It was then that I heard the muffled pounding.

It came from the kitchen and it wasn't the sort of sound you heard in well regulated homes. "Mary! Is that you, Mary? Help! Help!"

I think I broke all records getting out to that kitchen. For the voice was recognizably that of Mrs. Ferguson and the pounding came from the pantry door which was locked from the kitchen side. I pushed back the catch and opened the door. I said, "For heaven's sake, what's happened and what are you doing in there?" She marched past me, her nose high, "Ain't your eyes working?" she demanded irritably. "What makes you think I'd choose a pantry to sit in when I might have had a parlor? What do you s'pose's happened? Someone locked me in, that's what?"

I said, "Nonsense! How could they? The catch probably slipped."

She eyed me haughtily. "It slipped all right but there was somebody's finger on it. Don't look at me like that, Mary Thorpe—it's the gospel truth I'm telling you. I been shut in that place for forty minutes and it was done deliberate. Over on the table's the I makings of a sponge cake I was starting when I had to go into the pantry for some baking powder, leaving the door open as I always do. Quick as a wink someone came up behind me and slammed the door and locked it before I could say Jack Robinson!"

I crossed over to the outside kitchen door and shook it. "That's impossible!" I said. "How could anyone get in? The front door was locked. So's this one."

Some of the hauteur went out of her. Guilt took its place. "Maybe it was and maybe it wasn't—the front door, I mean. I unlocked it to get the mail and I can't say as I recollect locking it again. Whoever 'twas most likely locked it when he went out."

"I can't believe it!" I said and I couldn't. "Who would it be and what in the world did he want?"

Mrs. Ferguson shrugged. "Search me! He was messing around in here a while and then he went upstairs by the sound of things. If it was burglars I'd advise we look up there."

"Upstairs!" I remembered my meager horde of jewelry, the emergency money that Father always kept in the bottom of his collar box. "Come on!"

But at the foot of the stairs my enthusiasm left me. I said, "I don't know. Perhaps we ought to call someone— the police. How I do we know whoever it was isn't still here?"

But on that point Mrs. Ferguson was definite. "He's gone all right—maybe five, ten minutes before you come. I heard the front door shut and then nothing more till you come in and started hollering. There wasn't nothing I could do but sit. Couldn't even get out of the window, your Paw's got the storm sash on so tight. Only way I could have got out was smash the glass, and I don't hold with breaking good windows."

I skipped the rest of it. I took what she said about the intruder's departure for truth and hoped she knew what she was talking about.

The hall upstairs was serene and undisturbed. So, apparently, was Father's room. His money was all there—

hastily I counted it— so whatever our visitor's motive had
been it wasn't burglary.

"Nothing of mine's gone," Mrs. Ferguson volunteered
as she bustled back into the hall. "Have you looked at your
room yet?"

"Right now," I said. "But I honestly think you were
dreaming—"

I stopped there because I'd opened my door and I didn't
think she was. Not any more. My room was a shambles. It
had been very thoroughly taken apart and the person who'd
done it hadn't bothered to put the pieces together again.
The bed had been stripped of its coverings and sheets and
blankets tossed untidily to the middle of the room. The
mattress stood on end. The rug had been partially turned
back. The pillows from my chaise longue had been thrown
into one corner. Shoes and slippers lay among the wreck-
age, oddly mismated as though they'd been inspected and
then tossed aside. The open closet door revealed further
desolation. Dresses and suits were awry on their hangers.
My best dinner dress was a crumpled mass on the floor.

Mrs. Ferguson looked over my shoulder and said,
"My—my!" in shocked disapproval. "So that's what he was
doing—the scamp! Anything gone?"

"I don't know yet," I said crossly, "I haven't looked.
And do you think 'scamp's' just the word? No one can tell
me it only took thirty minutes to accomplish this! I'll be
a week putting it back!" I made the gesture of looking but
I knew I didn't need to, that nothing of mine would be
gone. Whatever the searcher had wanted, I was convinced
it hadn't been my poor possessions.

Nor had it been. Everything was there, even my jewelry which had been dumped from its box to the dressing
table top. With one finger I inventoried it. Seed pearls,
platinum and diamond dinner ring, watch, diamond and
sapphire bracelet, a miscellany of clips and pins and ear-

rings. Well, that was all right, I thought with a sigh. Now for the rest of it . . .

I won't bother you with a description of the rest of it save to state that my beautifully kept chest and dressing table drawers had been stirred as though their contents were to be the ingredients of some new salad. A nail file had been used to probe my box of face powder, none too carefully as the spilled powder attested. My various hand bags lay empty upon the dressing table bench while their assortments of lipsticks, cigarette cases, compacts and little piles of change were on the chest top. Not even hats and hat boxes had been spared.

"Well, if this ain't a sight to behold!" said Mrs. Ferguson at last when her eyes had savored the destruction. She followed close as I went over to the closet. "Maybe, if we worked real hard, we could put it all back before dinner. Want me to help? All you got to do is say so. . . ."

I didn't say so. I told her to go downstairs; I told her that I was too angry to do any straightening now. I said I had to think.

That much was true. I did have to think, hard and quickly and I didn't want any distraction. She went, reluctantly, and, as soon as she had gone, I replaced the cushions on the chaise longue and threw myself down and began the thinking in real earnest.

This ransacking of my room had upset all my ideas. Heretofore I'd taken it for granted that the danger I held for the murderer was something intangible, knowledge that I had gained through sight or hearing. Now this ruthless searching of my possessions made it evident how wrong I'd been. The thing that had been sought had body, form and substance—that much was certain. The question now resolved itself into what that thing could be. Almost at once, I waved the question away. I didn't need to ask it. I knew. There'd been only the one thing in my possession

since the beginning of this affair to which I'd held neither
title nor right—Nola Powers' lipstick—the one I'd stepped
on on the stage, the one Chris had scrutinized and then
handed over to me.

Nola Powers' lipstick! I sat up then and stopped lounging. Was that the key to the whole affair? Could it be?
More impossibly still, had it been the repository for
Nola's "precious paper," the paper Ross and I had termed
the confession?

I was definitely excited by this time. Desperately I
tried to visualize the lipstick. It had been a nice thing in
itself—carved gold, initialed in diamonds—the sort of toy
a woman might cherish and keep with her. It had been unusually long, too—hadn't I sensed that without conscious
thinking? Suppose the lipstick part of it were only a blind
and that beneath it . . .

I caught my breath then. Why, of course, that was it.
And Nola's murderer, who most surely must have guessed
the significance of that extra length, had somehow failed
to find the lipstick. Perhaps it had fallen from her purse.
Or, even if he'd heard it fall, there mightn't have been time
to search it out. Nola had been dead. . . .

I had been riding high. Now I dropped swiftly as common sense pricked the bubble of my illusion. "What of
it?" I found myself asking myself. "What difference does it
make if you did have it once? It's gone now, isn't it? Well,
then. . . ."

Presumably it was—gone—and the knowledge made me
sick. I was the fool of the world, I told myself bitterly. To
hold it in my hand and let it go—

I pulled myself up sharply at that. Wait a minute! How
did I know I'd held it? How did I know that was the thing
wanted?

I was only guessing. So far as I knew, the lipstick might
be entirely innocent.

There was one way of proving or disproving that, I thought grimly. If I could find it—if the searcher had obviously seen it and left it behind . . .

I tried to think. What had I worn that night at the Olympia? My fur coat and the Glen plaid suit and a beret and I'd carried the black woolen bag with the plasticene frame. . . .

The contents of the bag were on the chest of drawers. There was no gold lipstick there. My fur coat had no pockets. That left only the suit, then—the suit of Glen Urquhart plaid.

It wasn't there. The pocket linings, pulled out, flapped at me.

I tucked them back, noting as I did, an infinitesimal rip in a side seam. I'd have to mend that, I remember thinking even as I turned away, sick with disappointment.

Had I proved anything? I didn't know. Perhaps Ross would when I told him. If I told him . . . At once I was asserting, "Tell him—of course I'll tell him! It's only fair!" . . . Only to be thundered down by some inner voice of whose existence I'd never dreamed. "You're a fool if you do. He doesn't know anything about gold lipsticks. He's never mentioned it—never thought of it probably. What good will it do if you bring it up now?"

I didn't try to answer that second voice. I didn't know how. It held too much of truth. For good or evil the lipstick was gone and there was nothing I, or Ross, could do about it now. Nevertheless, the refrain of my thoughts was with me as I went downstairs in answer to Mrs. Ferguson's summoning. "Tell Ross—don't tell Ross—you're a fool if you do—a fool if you don't—"

It was intolerable. I made a dead stand beside the telephone. Before I could change my mind, I gave the hotel number. Mr. Langdon hadn't come in yet, the clerk informed me. That was all right—I left a message. Then, and only then, did I go to my waiting supper.

22

He didn't call me until about nine o'clock. He said, "What now?" and when I had given him a brief outline he was quiet for a minute. "All right," he said at last. "Leave everything as it is. I'll be right out."

"I can't," I said. "We've put it back."

Again he was silent. "Quite the little housewife, aren't you?" he said nastily, finally, and hung up.

I didn't care. If he thought I was going to let him root about through my things . . .

But he was over his nastiness by the time he arrived. He listened without comment to our combined story.

"Oh, well," he said when we were done, "it was a lucky break, that's all. He took a chance and it was good. Finding the front door unlocked mightn't happen again in a dozen years."

"It won't," Mrs. Ferguson assured him.

"I can see how he got in," he said slowly. "What I can't understand is what he did with himself up to the time he shut Mrs. Ferguson into the pantry. *That* was the lucky part if you ask me. Suppose she'd been sitting here in the living room or coming down the stairs . . ."

"I'd have yelled," Mrs. Ferguson interpolated.

"It would probably have been your last yell then," Ross told her quietly. "Our—er—friend takes precautions not to be seen."

"Speak for yourself—he's no friend of mine," I began hastily but Ross cut me off.

"As for the rest of it—hiding—that wouldn't be hard. It's dark by five o'clock and there were no lights in the front part of the house. There'd be plenty of shadowy corners in which to stand, to say nothing of odd doors and heavy drapery that could be used for concealment. He probably counted on the nearness to dinner time to find Mrs. Ferguson in the kitchen. After that it was simply a matter of waiting until she'd stepped out of the kitchen—to pantry or cellar. Then all he had to do was move in quickly and slam the door. The door opens back toward the dining room. Mrs. Ferguson couldn't possibly have seen him. After that time was his own."

"What about me?" I wanted to know. "Suppose I'd come home sooner than I did?"

"You can thank your lucky stars that you didn't," Ross said bluntly. "However, you haven't spent much time at the house the last while and everyone knows it. Probably he felt safe enough there."

"And I had announced to all and sundry that I was going down town," I said thoughtfully. "It was almost five o'clock when we left Molly's and shopping takes time. . . . But, good heavens! I didn't say it to all and sundry! I only said it to you and Gordon Kearnes! It wasn't you. . . . Could it have been Gordon Kearnes?"

Ross looked troubled. "I don't know, Mary. On that point it looks bad for him. But, countering it . . . You see, sometime between six o'clock and eight someone went through his room at the hotel—literally cut it to pieces— pillows, mattress, even his Russian leather bags. It was so bad that of their own accord the hotel management moved him to other quarters."

"Gordon Kearnes' room," I repeated slowly. "But that doesn't make sense—unless . . ." I stopped then because I wasn't just sure what it was that didn't make sense. "You saw it?"

"I did. I seem to get in on the ground floor at all these little disturbances. I got back to the hotel about eight-thirty and the desk clerk had just given me your message when Kearnes came in. Nothing would do but that I'd go into the bar with him for a quick one. After that we went upstairs together—our rooms are on the same floor. Kearnes said he was tired and meant to go straight to bed, which suited me for I wanted to put in that call to you and I thought there'd be less chance of listeners in if I did it from my room. However I hadn't even found your number before he was banging on my door. He'd called the police and the hotel clerk, but for some reason he wanted me to see the mess too."

"You're a detective," I said absently. "Oh, dear, all this is crazy. How does he know it was done between six and eight-thirty?"

Again there was that thread of a frown between Ross's brows. "He was in the room himself until a few minutes past six. He says everything was all right then. After that he went to Alice Wilson's for dinner. He was just coming back when we met in the lobby."

"Between six and eight," I repeated. I was groping toward something that persisted in eluding me. "I still think it's crazy—oh, no, I don't!" Comprehension came. "It's wonderful! It's perfect! Don't you see what it means?"

"I see that it's too much for your feeble intellect," Ross observed. "If you'd seen that room all over feathers and mattress stuffing you'd have called it something besides wonderful."

"I don't care," I said. "It is. Because—don't you see?— if Gordon Kearnes' room was searched *after* mine, it means that what our—oh, our burglar—wanted wasn't found here. It means that he didn't get the gold lipstick after all!"

"Always providing that the gold lipstick was the object of the search," Ross said, but I thought he looked impressed.

"Oh, but it was," I said. "It would have to be. And of course if it wasn't found here, Gordon Kearnes was the most logical person after me to have it. I mean, that he might have wanted it as a keepsake—a souvenir—"

"Now, wait a minute," Ross interrupted. "You're attaching a lot of importance to that lipstick. Perhaps it's justified, perhaps it isn't. We can't know that until it's found. Which brings me to the point: Where's the lipstick now? Have *you* got it?"

"Why, no," I said, considerably dashed. "That is, I don't think so. I can't find it. But I *did* have it. Chris gave it to me—at the theater that night Nola was found. Ross! Couldn't that prove that it wasn't Chris? I mean that if *he'd* been the one who wanted the lipstick he could have kept it then. Because, on the face of it, the lipstick wasn't important. It was only evidence that Nola'd been there—in the theater. After she was found, it didn't matter any more. We just forgot it. I don't think the police ever heard of it. I certainly didn't tell them—I never thought about it. And I don't believe anyone else did either."

Ross was visibly thinking. "Maybe you're right. Now that I think of it, I don't recall hearing it mentioned. As you say, Nola was found and the lipstick didn't count—"

"But don't you see?" I interrupted eagerly. "That's exactly why it couldn't be Chris. No one would have thought it funny if he'd just put the lipstick into his own pocket instead of handing it to me."

"Could be," Ross said. "On the other hand, if he gave it to you, he might think it safe until he had the opportunity to pick it up again."

I said, "Well, that would go for any of them—they all saw Chris give it to me, they'd all know where it was. And one of them would know why it might be important. Because, of course, the murderer'd go through Nola's things after he killed her. The lipstick must have rolled out of her purse or something—perhaps he didn't notice it or perhaps he looked for it and couldn't find it. It was just an accident that I stepped on it that night."

"I wish to God you'd accidentally find it again," Ross said. "You're sure you haven't got it?"

I shook my head. "I've looked and looked. That's all I've done since I put in that call for you. It's not in any of my pockets and it isn't in the purse I carried that night. If you think I'm not plenty sick about it . . ."

"How could anyone guess the damned thing would be important?" Ross demanded savagely. "*If* it was. It doesn't seem possible. A lipstick! How could you get a paper into one, tell me that!"

"I'll be delighted," I said. "But, first, I think I'd better tell you about lipsticks in general and this one in particular. Because this wasn't just the ordinary kind, that you buy in a drug or department store and pay a dollar or two for. I think Nola's was real gold and it had her initials on it. That means the case was expensive and when she'd used up the original lipstick she wouldn't throw it away like you do the dollar kind. She'd get a refill and that would probably be expensive, too, because I don't think there was any propelling device in the case. I don't see how there could have been. It was capped with gold at either end of the tube and I think the refill was small and you just stuck it in. When what you could see was gone you bought a new one."

"All right—all right," Ross said impatiently. "I'll grant you all of that but it still—"

"Don't be in such a hurry," I said. "I told you I'd explain and I will. How you could put a piece of folded paper in it, I mean. You see, this lipstick of Nola's was different in another way, too. It was longer than the ordinary one.

It must have measured nearly four inches and I told you it was capped at either end. When I saw it first, I just automatically thought it was a double lipstick—that is, that it held two shades, one for daytime and one for evening wear. But now I'm wondering if one of those ends wasn't empty, if the holder you slide the refill into hadn't been taken out. A paper, folded small, would have gone in easily—there'd have been lots of room."

But Ross was shaking his head. "I agree with you it's a swell explanation but I'm not so sure it's the one we're looking for. If you remember, we all stood around and watched Chris open that lipstick—and it *was* lipstick. I saw it. All right, that part of it is swell but there's an element of luck to your reasoning I don't care for. He got the right end but suppose he hadn't? If that lipstick contained what you think it did, would Nola Powers have risked hiding a piece of property she considered valuable in a place where any curious person, given the opportunity, might have discovered it? The answer is 'No!'" he added kindly, "in case you want to know."

"Oh, no, it isn't," I said triumphantly. "Because both ends could have been the same—both held lipstick, I mean. The refills, without a propelling mechanism, would have had to be shallow. All she'd have had to do was pry one out, put the paper in, and then replace it. No one could possibly guess it was more than just what it seemed to be."

Ross stood up with a sigh. "All right, have it your own way," he said with resignation. "As I said before it's a swell idea. Unfortunately, without the lipstick I'm afraid it's unprovable."

I was afraid it was, too, but only for a moment. Then I had an idea. A big one. "Why can't we try and prove it?" I asked. "If I pretended I still had the lipstick and let them know it—I mean, asked different ones what I ought to do with it now that Nola's dead."

He came over and kissed me then. It was the first time. "You dear little fool!" he said. "You'd love to get yourself murdered to end this case, wouldn't you? Well, you're not going to, understand? I won't have it. You forget you ever saw that bit of dynamite—do you hear?"

I heard. I was very meek about it. But I didn't make any promises about it. I couldn't.

Ross stayed until Father came home. Of course the "army" was there, too, but we had a bunch of bridge fiends that night: and they spent their time around the card table. Which was nice, for Mrs. Ferguson, with a tact I wouldn't have suspected, left us alone. We had a number of things to talk about. We didn't say anything about murder.

As I'd expected, Father raged when he heard the story. This was the end, he announced. Police or no police, I was getting out of Nashiona. Tomorrow. I could go to Aunt Harriet. She'd be glad to have me and I'd find no nonsense about murders there. I could pack tonight—Mrs. Ferguson would help me—or by the Lord Harry, he'd help me himself! Anything to get me out of here.

To which I countered that I certainly wasn't going anywhere. Nothing had happened to me yet—nothing would. I'd be careful, doubly careful now. I had a good reason for wanting to stay alive. Of course, I said flatly, that if he insisted on putting me out of the house, I'd marry Ross right now and let *him* protect me.

It worked. Father gulped and subsided. Ross, was it? All right—good. He had only pity for the young man. If I thought he (Father) was sorry to relinquish guardianship over a headstrong daughter, I was mistaken. Let Ross take on the job—he'd find his hands full.

The argument continued for some time but it ended amicably enough. Ross went back to the hotel and we— Father, Mrs. Ferguson and I—went to bed.

But not to sleep. Father tossed and groaned most of the night and twice he came tiptoeing clumsily through my door to make certain that I slept. On both occasions I pretended well. I shut my eyes and breathed evenly. Satisfied he went away.

I had an early caller next morning. At nine o'clock. It was Molly Dunbar. She came bursting into the kitchen where I was having my morning coffee. She said, *"Will* you tell this woman that I'm all right and that I don't mean to kill you? What's the idea anyway? I could drive all around the army post easier than I can get in here!" She was furious, her black eyes snapping.

I looked beyond her to Mrs. Ferguson who indeed had the appearance of a bouncer-out. I laughed and kicked a chair. I said, "Sit down, Molly, and cool off. It's all right, Mrs. Ferguson—this is Mrs. Dunbar—and so far as I know she's never killed anyone yet. Want some coffee, Molly?"

Over the coffee, Molly became calmer. She said, "I don't care whether you like it or not but I've come to spend the day. I can't stay alone—I won't. There are too many things happening. Pete thinks I'm crazy but I'm not. I'm just scared."

I pushed the marmalade in her direction. I said soothingly, "Of course you can stay—I'll be glad to have you. And you don't need to be afraid here. We have lots of protection."

She sent the marmalade right back at me. "I can't eat," she said. "It's funny, you know, but when you read books and newspapers you think murders are—oh, sort of exciting and interesting. They're not—they're horrible. When it's people you know—people like Rita and Pat . . . The police were over last night. They asked all sorts of questions. Not that we could tell them much. Of course Pete was alone that day but they seemed to think that he might have seen something just the same."

"But Pete wasn't alone," I objected. "Don't you remember?— He was with Mark first—and then with Gordon."

"He was not!" Molly said scornfully. "I guess I ought to know! Who told you that anyway? Alice? Well, I'd like to know what she knew about it! She was too busy being the broken-hearted widow even though we all knew it was just an act. Why, everybody knew she and Pat were through, had been for months! But she wore black and wept on Mark's shoulder—it was disgusting!"

I still wasn't convinced. I said, "But I know she said it was Pete and Mark who went off together—"

"Well, she was wrong!" Molly said flatly.

"Molly's right, you know, baby." It was a new voice— Ross's. He came into the kitchen with Mrs. Ferguson beaming behind him. He rumpled my hair and reached for a cup of coffee. "I saw the transcript of the inquest evidence this morning. Hanover showed it to me. Dunbar and Kerrigan decided to go it alone that day."

She may have been right but I wasn't convinced. I said, "Well, but why would Alice lie about it? I mean, that if it was in the evidence it would be sure to come out."

"Let's, be charitable and say that she'd forgotten," Ross suggested.

"Or catty and say it was to protect Mark," Molly said brightly.

"Mark!" I said feebly. "But I thought—I mean—I thought it was Gordon Kearnes—"

"Oh, no!" Molly's voice was scornful still. "Five years ago it was Mark. You ask Pete. We all thought that as soon as the divorce was over Alice would marry Mark."

"Death's as good as divorce," Ross said cheerfully. "You might make a note of that, darling." I scowled at him and he went on. "Since the wedding never took place I gather, however, that something slipped. Know what it was?"

"Oh, well, afterwards Alice had Pat's insurance money," Molly said thoughtfully. "I suppose that was it. Mark just had his salary and he was always in debt. There never was any particular break—only they stopped lovey-doveying in corners. And then Gordon Kearnes started hanging around Alice—He was always at the apartment. I thought that was the money," Molly said soberly, "What I mean is, Alice was comparatively rich and Nola had nothing, and Gordon was crazy to get to New York. I've always wondered who was the most surprised—Chris or Alice—when he and Nola finally went away together."

"Ever wonder where they got the money?" Ross asked casually. He was lighting a cigarette but he kept his eyes on her face.

Molly shrugged. "Oh, there was talk. Mark had gone over to Nola on the rebound from Alice, we supposed, and he'd been borrowing heavily. The story was that he financed the trip. All I ever knew for sure was that Pete let him have the money we'd been saving for something special in the way of trips, and was I furious? Not that it did any good." She made a small gesture. "Pete said old Mark was in a jam and he had to help him out. Well, he did. And we've never seen a cent of that money from that day to this. Don't let's talk about it any more. It makes me mad just to think about it."

So we didn't. Talk about it any more, I mean. I think we all felt the need for a respite, temporary though it might be, and we took it gratefully. Even Ross gave himself over to play with an abandon of which I hadn't guessed him capable although there were moments, unguarded perhaps, when I caught him studying Molly with a concentration that disquieted me.

It snowed that day, thick plushy snow that overlaid the world with a veneer of white. Inside we had an open fire and luncheon on trays beside it. Ash trays filled to

overflowing and in the background the radio murmured
discreetly. If there was war news we shut our ears or we
reached out and moved, by tacit agreement, to another
station. We didn't know what was going on in the world.
This was our seventh day. This was peace.

The mood lasted until late afternoon—at least for Ross
and Molly. Then, feeling the urge for movement of some
sort, they went down to the basement game room and
played table tennis. I trailed along but I didn't play. I still
felt lethargic, tranced. It was good to let go, to rest.

Even now I don't know just how it started—Molly doing imitations, I mean. Of course I knew she could—I'd
heard her dozens of times. It was to Ross that it came as
a surprise, a new facet to a particularly dazzling diamond
which he was studying with interest.

Molly was in high spirits by this time. We had called
Pete and told him to come over for dinner. Waiting, they
played tennis. I watched them for a while until the separate little ringlets on Molly's head merged into a blur that
dimmed with distance.

I suppose I slept for the next thing I heard for certain
was Ross's laughter. It was open-throated laughter, loud
in the confines of that low-ceilinged room. I blinked the
sand out of my eyes and sat up.

Ross was lounging on one side of the table. He was
looking at Molly who was playing an imaginary game of
tennis. Not her usual game, someone else's. It was a game
of studied grace, of coquettish shoulder movements, of
tripping steps, of little meaningless laughter. It was Alice
Wilson's game and perfectly done. In spite of myself I
giggled.

Molly's gamin features had taken on a recognizable
semblance to Alice's sculptured ones too. Her controlled
sways and glidings were Alice's. The thing went beyond
art, it was caricature and if it was done with tongue in

cheek, at least the effect was definite. She even held the paddle as you might a tea cup—with little finger crooked.

She ended it at last, breathless, but under her own identity and Ross stood up. He said, "Good Lord, do you do that often?"

Molly shrugged. "Well, Alice always furnishes good material."

Ross's eyes had narrowed. "Anyone else?"

"All of us," I said, putting in my nickel's worth. "She's at it all the time. I've seen her do Mark and Pete and Alice and Faye—oh, do Faye, Molly! Please. It's so perfect."

Ross was still looking at her. "How about voice?"

"Why, Mister Lang—don," Molly cooed in Alice's very tones, "you surely didn't think this was just an imitation, did you? Because it isn't at all. Naturally I'm not sure that—"

Ross cut her off. "That's enough. How about the others? Can you do Nola Powers?"

Molly sat back and stared at him. It was plain she wasn't pleased. "Sure I can do Nola," she said. "She's easy. Mostly voice. Say, what is this? What're you up to?"

It was what I wanted to know, too, but I didn't find out. Because just at that moment Ross became aware of me again. He crossed over and half-lifted me from the couch on which I'd been sitting. He stood me on my feet and turned me toward the stairs. Very gravely he spoke. "Darling, this is a time for secrets: go on upstairs, will you, like a good girl? I want to talk to Mrs. Dunbar. It's—it'll be a sort of surprise for you—I'll tell you later—"

Perhaps, because I still hovered in that halfway land between sleep and waking, I went without argument. My feet dragged a little, that was all. Because I trusted Ross, as much probably as I'd ever trust anyone in the world. But I didn't like surprises. Or secrets. I don't think I ever will again.

23

I was giving a party. I didn't want to give one but that didn't make any difference. I was giving it just the same.

It was Ross's idea, born, I was certain, of that secret conference between Molly and himself. Not that he admitted it. He simply said, "Call them up—will you, darling?—and ask them over tomorrow night. Don't bother about Molly or Pete. They'll be here."

I said, "Why?" and he shrugged.

"Do we have to have a reason?"

I said, "Perhaps I can get along without one but what about the others? They're going to wonder."

"Don't worry about them," he told me. "They'll come. If anyone shows signs of balking, I'll talk to him."

I said, "Who do you want?" but I didn't need to. I knew. Sure enough. The answer came pat. "All of them— the Little Theater crowd. The ones who were at the Olympia the night we found Nola Powers."

So I called them. It wasn't a long list now. Nola was dead and Rita, and Faye couldn't come. There was only Mark and Alice, Gordon Kearnes, Johnny Forrester, Victor Jameson—I hesitated over his name but Ross's nod was imperative. And Chris.

Chris was the only one who refused to come. He didn't think he should. No, Faye was much better. No, she still wouldn't see him but the doctors thought that no more than a temporary condition. That was why he wanted to stay at the hospital. If she suddenly asked for him . . .

I handed the telephone to Ross.

I don't know what he said or what arguments he used. I had closed my ears. I only knew that presently Ross replaced the hand set with a satisfied grin. "He'll come," he said.

"Everybody will," I told him. "What are you going to do with them when they get here?"

His glance was thoughtful. "Well, we can always announce our engagement," he said lightly. But the lightness didn't last. Almost at once he was beside me, his arms about my shoulders. "Darling, trust me. It's only a chance but I've got to take it. There's no other way that I know of. You see, I know who killed Nola Powers and Rita Carstairs and Pat Wilson. The trouble is, I can't prove it. You can't always, you know. Deductive reasoning and hunches aren't evidence. You need something more concrete and I haven't got it. I don't think I ever will. This killer's clever, you know. So there's only the one thing to do—trick him into giving me the proof. That's what I'm going to try and do tomorrow night. With Mrs. Dunbar's help."

I suppose I was jealous. I said, "Why not mine?"

His arms tightened. He gave me a little shake. "You're not going to be that way, are you?" he asked reprovingly. "What's wrong? Jealous? Don't be—there's no need."

My voice shook in spite of my efforts to control it. I said, "If I hadn't lost that lipstick, you wouldn't need Molly."

He let me go with a sigh of exasperation. "My dear girl, we've discussed that lipstick before. If you had it and it contained what you think it does, it would help. But we don't know for certain that it was any more than it appeared to be—a lipstick—and in any case you don't have it. So there's nothing to do but get along without it."

It wasn't all jealousy. Part of it was hurt. I said dully, "I can look for it again. . . ."

He didn't see or understand. He patted my arm. "Of course you can, baby," he said. "Of course you can."

I went upstairs right after that. I said I was sleepy and that was true. But Ross didn't go. I heard Father come home and the army depart, yet a long time after I heard the murmur of voices. For the second time I felt the prick of tears against my eyelids. Now he was telling Father about it. He had told Molly. Why couldn't he tell me?

I didn't sleep much that night but somewhere, between night and morning, pride came to my rescue. Ross didn't want me to know—all right, so I wouldn't. I'd play along with him. I wouldn't even ask a question. I'd be good.

Imbued with such high resolves, I arose in the gray and cheerless morning and went down to a kitchen already fragrant with Mrs. Ferguson's cooking. Apparently the menu for the evening was going forward without my help. Chickens were baking in the oven. There was a chocolate cake, shiny with icing, under the cupboard shelves. I saw jars of black ripe olives, boxes of salted nuts, crusty hard-baked rolls that were still warm from the oven. I remained true to my decision. I complimented her and drank my coffee and played with my grapefruit. After that, I went into the front part of the house.

I stayed there. I did all the little things you always do before a party. Flowers came and I arranged them. I got out my best lace cloth for the table. I saw that there was plenty of wood for the fires and that the cigarette boxes were filled. After that I simply sat with folded hands and thought.

They weren't pleasant thoughts either. How could they be? Tonight—if all went well—our mystery would be ended. I had Ross's promise for that. But what if it didn't go well? What happened then?

I was up, walking the floor, by this time. Oh, this was impossible—it couldn't go on. I wouldn't let it. This was trickery—treason. These people were coming here in good faith. They trusted me. Ought I—could I betray them?

Cold reason took over then. The whole trouble with you, I told myself sternly, is that you don't know what Ross means to do. It can't be anything so terrible. And even if it were, wouldn't they live through it? By Ross's reasoning, one of these people was a murderer. He'd killed, not once, but three times. Once, perhaps, in passion but after that in cold-blooded calculation. Should the fact that he would be my guest tonight absolve him from punishment? More important still, should the fact that he was a murderer release me from the conventions of hospitality?

Oh, it was a horrible muddle! If there were only some way in which it could be ended, brought to a head, before tonight—

There was a way. I dragged myself upstairs and made a last desperate search for the gold lipstick. I didn't find it.

Time dragged on. Out of doors the day remained gray and chill. Within, the house rooms were dim with shadow. Nothing happened. Not even the ring of the telephone broke the stillness.

Ross came after lunch. We met and talked polite nothings. We spoke of the weather, the probability of a storm. He said how well the rooms looked and I thanked him for the flowers. After these lines of conversation fizzled out, he took a small velvet box from his pocket and tossed it to me.

"Wear it tonight," he said. "It'll give them something to talk about."

I pressed the spring. There was a ring inside. A diamond eye winked at me. I admired the ring, put it on. I let him kiss me. I was two people, there on the davenport with his arm about me. One of them exulted in the beauty of the ring, in the closeness with which he held me; the other was naked to fear, raw and quivering with apprehension.

I broke my vow then. I asked a question. I let my head rest on his shoulder—it was such a tired head. I said, "Will it be so terrible, Ross?"

He took a moment to answer. "I was afraid of that," he said quietly. "No, it won't be—terrible, as you call it. I told you it was only a chance—it may not work. If it doesn't, no harm's done except that I've made a fool of myself. If it does, there'll be no more murder in the Little Theater. Worth taking a chance for, don't you think?"

I wasn't sure. I looked at him soberly. I said, "You won't tell me who, I know that. But—how long have you known?"

His answer came promptly. "Since a quarter of nine last night."

He left me then—to make what I liked of it—for a light delivery truck, bearing a bulky something shrouded in canvas, was grating up the driveway. Whatever the bulky object was—it resembled a piano—it was carried into the play room below. I heard Ross's voice raised in direction but I didn't go. Let them scrape paint off the doorways, knock plaster off the walls. I was being good again.

I remained good even when, fifteen minutes later, Molly Dunbar, accompanied by three unknown young women, arrived at the door and demanded Ross. The names of the young women meant nothing to me although one's face was vaguely familiar. I took their wraps and directed them to the play room. Thereafter I sat on the davenport. Part of the time I looked at my ring. The rest I did nothing.

By four o'clock, they were still downstairs and I was weary of the distant sound of their voices. I went upstairs and lay on my bed for an hour. After that I took a long

hot bath. Later, as I brushed my hair, my face between the
dressing table lights looked wan, drained of color. My eyes
were enormous, black and blank. I thought, "I'll have to do
something about that" and so I found a dinner dress of flame
and gold and sandals of golden kid. I touched my cheeks
with rouge, I used my brightest lipstick. The result was
only halfway satisfying. I could do nothing about my eyes.

It was after six when I came downstairs and Mrs. Ferguson was rocking placidly in the living room. Mrs. Dunbar
and Mr. Langdon and them others had gone, she informed
me. Everything was ready and did I want a regular dinner
or what?

Even the thought of food made me shudder. Nothing, I
told her firmly, not even "what," and proceeded on to the
kitchen which was lighted and from which came the sound
of voices.

The kitchen was in beautiful order but Chief Hanover
was perched on a high stool before a plate of rolls and
salad, and two policemen were running wires above the
frame of the door that led down to the game room.

I forgot my intention to ask no questions. I said, "What
in the world—?"

The chief took another sip of coffee. Over the cup his
eyes twinkled at me. "Well—well. It's the little lady herself and looking mighty pretty too. Good cooks you are
here, Miss Thorpe. Don't know's I ever tasted better coffee
less'n it was what my old grandmother used to make back
in Vermont state. Bet you an egg went into this—you can
always tell egg coffee."

Maybe you could but I didn't want to talk about coffee.
Not now. I looked at the wires those others were laying so
carefully. I said, "But what are they doing? What is it?"

"That?" The chief broke another roll. "Just a little
something young Langdon asked for. You've heard of
microphones and recording devices and such?"

Microphones! All of a sudden my preconceived ideas of that evening were shattered. It wasn't going to be just a game or an abstract possibility. It was going to be real and inescapable. Ross was taking it seriously. He'd meant it when he said, "If it doesn't work, no harm's done except that I've made a fool of myself. . . . Worth taking a chance for, don't you think?"

The brittle tension that held my nerves relaxed. I said quietly, "What does Ross intend to do, do you know?"

Chief Hanover shook his head. "Nope. Don't know's I want to. Might be something illegal and then I'd have to crack down. This way saves both our faces."

The police made their last adjustments, went away. It was completely dark outside now. We lit the grate fire. There were candles on the mantel and upon the triangle of piano. I lit them. The room grew warm and the scent of the hothouse flowers swelled. My head began to ache.

A little after eight the doorbell rang. At once they were all there, standing on my doorstep, laughing in my hall. The men wore tuxedos; the women, glad of the chance, were in formal dress. Molly wore pale gold; Alice, as befitted a reminded widow, was in filmy black, a youthful black to match her now unsophisticated personality.

There weren't women enough; we were outnumbered two to one. The room was full of masculine black and white. Bottles and ice appeared from somewhere. Ross was making highballs. Someone held a glass toward me and I took it. The ice within was no colder than my heart.

Molly saw my ring and squealed excitement. There were exclamations, kisses, congratulations. Someone who was not me accepted them, smiled, said the proper things.

There was laughter in the room but no gaiety. We used words but they meant nothing. Smoke drifted across our eyes, veiling their secrets. We sat on the edges of our

chairs, wary without knowing why, waiting for we knew
not what.

Ross was watching the clock. So was I but without conscious reason. The hands crawled slowly. Time stood still
at half past eight, at a quarter to nine.

When the hour struck, Ross was on his feet. His voice
cut clearly across the bell-tones of the clock's chime. "We
have a little entertainment for you. In the game room. A—
well, shall we call it a dramatic sketch? If you'll take your
glasses and follow me . . ."

There was more laughter, questions, a general dousing
of cigarettes. As we straggled toward the kitchen, I saw
that Alice and I comprised the feminine contingent. Molly
had vanished.

In the kitchen, Mrs. Ferguson knitted beside the white
enamel table. On a shelf above the table, there were gera-
niums. I remember how red they were against the white.

I was the last to go down. No one had noticed the wires
that curled snake-like along the stair's baseboard. But I saw
them and, as mechanically I traced their hidden course, it
seemed to me that, behind me, the front door had opened
and that careful footsteps were tiptoeing across the hall.
I dared a glance over my shoulder, glimpsed Lieutenant
Dreyer's acid countenance, the chief's shadowy bulk. I
waited to see no more. I fled.

I was cold. In the game room, I knew, flames were leaping in the great brick fireplace but I knew, too, that they
would give no warmth to me. There was an old smoking
jacket of Father's hanging on a hook at the foot of the
stairs. It was double flannel, lined and warm. It smelled
faintly of tobacco as I slid my arms into it. I snuggled
deeply into its comfort. It was as though Father's arms
were about me, as though he himself afforded protection.

The game room looked oddly new. The table for tennis
had been moved back against the walk. Beyond it a row

of chairs sprawled in a comfortable half-circle to face an improvised stage, complete with the portable footlights of which Chris was so proud. There was nothing on the stage but the canvas-shrouded bulk I'd seen brought in that afternoon.

Ross stood beside the light switches. He didn't look like Ross. He looked as implacable as Justice, remote as God. When he spoke, his voice was strange, too, strained and metallic.

"Everybody sit down, please," he said. "By this time it's probably beginning to dawn upon you that this isn't a proper party at all. It isn't. But don't blame Mary for that. It isn't her fault. She's simply taken my orders."

With the unexpectedness of this, the small threads of conversation that had received new impetus with the move downstairs gave out completely. We scuttled for chairs. Mine was at the end of the row next to the wall.

Johnny Forrester was on the other side of me. His sharp newspaper nose was twitching with curiosity. He looked at me. He said, "Say, what the hell is this? What gives?"

I shrugged, pantomiming that I didn't know. It was true. I was only in the process of finding out.

Ross was speaking again. "You all know why I came to Nashiona. You know how lamentably I failed. I don't intend to fail tonight. And that being so I will tell you this. I know now who killed Nola Powers and Rita Carstairs and who, five years ago, killed Pat Wilson. I am sorry to say that it is one of you here in this room. Who it is I propose to prove to you tonight."

He paused then, of necessity, to let the little gasps, the quick drawn breaths, subside. He waited, watching us, his face unsmiling, cold and still. "What I am going to show you," he resumed at last, "is a scene taken from life. To six of you it will be new. The seventh will participate as a spectator where once he played a leading role."

There were no gaspings now. The room had frozen to silence. There was no breath. Only an intensity of waiting.

Ross's hand was on a light switch. He touched it. One half of the room darkened. At the same time the footlights rose to brightness. They picked out the dim far corners of the room, revealed dull stains upon the canvas swathings of the object that centered the improvised stage.

What was that object? I was leaning far forward now—so were the others. Beside me Johnny Forrester's hands were clenching, unclenching. He was muttering to himself, a ceaseless stream of incoherencies. "What the hell—what the hell—what the hell—"

It was inevitable that I wonder if the seventh man was Johnny. I shrank from him, pressing tightly to the far side of my chair.

Ross was stepping across the light barrier now, pulling at the canvas. It fell away to reveal a tall, wood-painted-to-look-like-mahogany settle, a matching table before it. It was plain what it was, one half of a booth, the kind that offers semi-privacy in restaurants or sweet shops.

Ross had stepped back across the footlights again. His voice came quietly. "I must beg your indulgence for the limitations of my stage. There is no curtain so the play will simply begin. You must use your imaginations. The scene is laid in the Coffee Shop of the Metropolitan Hotel. A soldier's wife, a stranger in Nashiona, is waiting for her husband to come from the air base." His voice lifted. "All right, Mrs. Wallace—we're ready now."

Mrs. Wallace! Even though I didn't believe it, I could feel my heart choking upward to my throat. Because the girl who stepped from behind the screen at the right of the stage was slim and pale and cheaply dressed. She might very well have been Beth Wallace. But she wasn't.

She stood for a moment, perfectly still, pausing as one might at the entrance to a coffee shop to survey its seating possibilities. Then, in a quick little rush, she was beside the booth, had slid into its shelter.

Instantly, from behind a second screen on the opposite side of the stage, another girl appeared. This one was blue-clad, gum-chewing, stolid. She carried a menu card and small tray with a glass of water. She slapped down the water, dabbed perfunctorily at the table, and presented the menu. The first girl pushed it aside. She spoke earnestly but too low for us to hear. The blue-clad waitress nodded and went away. The first girl fumbled in her purse, found a cigarette and lighted it. She glanced at her watch and then sat back, smoking idly.

There was the staccato tap of heels behind me. Others had heard—all about me was the white blur of turning faces. A wave of perfume brushed me, a familiar perfume, and then a third girl was walking toward the footlights. She was tall; she wore a tan polo coat, dark glasses that hid her eyes. A fawn-colored turban shrouded her hair.

Once more there was a harsh-drawn audibility of breaths. Someone said "My God!" in a stifled whisper. I didn't know who it was but I knew why they said it. Ross and Molly had done their work well. The girl that walked before us with that feline swaying walk wasn't Nola Powers. But by outward semblance she could have been.

She crossed the footlight barrier and approached the booth in which the pseudo-Mrs. Wallace sat. It was then that we were treated to a superb example of the "double-take" for the girl who played Mrs. Wallace glanced at the passerby casually and then, before our eyes, woke to a realization of the identity of the one who had passed. It was fine acting and in any other circumstances would have won her a round of applause. (Later I was to learn that she really was a soldier's wife and had been a player of "bit parts" on Broadway. Ross had met her in the Metropolitan lobby and persuaded her to help him.)

EDITH HOWIE

The girl who was Nola Powers had disappeared into the booth directly behind that of the fake Mrs. Wallace. At once the third girl, the waitress, came forth with tray and glass. And then for the first time, words were spoken upon the stage. That it was Molly Dunbar who spoke I had no doubt, but the words, the voice and inflection, were Nola Powers' own.

That voice, beautiful and unmistakable, belled out, filled the room.

"Tomato juice only. I will order later. I am waiting for a friend."

The waitress shrugged and walked away. The footlights dimmed. The lamps in our half of the room came up.

The alternation of the lighting gave us excuse to blink, to shield our eyes if we wished. No one spoke. I think we were too shaken. To hear that voice again, to recognize it and to know that never again would we hear it in reality . . .

It was a relief when Ross spoke. "You have just seen the prologue to our play. The footlights were dimmed to indicate the passing of a few seconds during which Miss Powers' expected friend arrived. We have chosen no one to play the part of that person whom we shall designate as X. When the lights go on again," he pressed the switches, "will you remember that X is now seated opposite Miss Powers in the booth? You will neither see nor hear him. The only voice you will hear from now on is that of Nola Powers, the only words those which, in like circumstances, she actually spoke." He half swung from us. "Are you ready on the stage? Then go ahead."

At the command, a quick chill ran down my spine. I don't know why. I still don't. Surely, of those present, with one exception, I had the best opportunity for knowing the thing for the mummery it was. That I didn't grasp that opportunity, Ross says, is a tribute to the actors. Perhaps. I doubt it.

The point is, I was cold. Sheer nerves or not, I was shivering uncontrollably. I thrust my chin deep into the collar of Father's coat. I pushed my hands down into the pockets with such force that one finger of the left broke a way between the threads at the bottom of the pocket. Automatically I jerked back and my ring, Ross's ring, caught against the opening. The ring was slightly large. When I pulled my hand free, the ring remained—between the outside of the coat and its lining.

At least the episode had sufficiently diverted my attention so that the shivering stopped. I thought, "Oh, bother!" and then, "Well, it's safe enough. I can get it out—" and then, abruptly, I forgot about it. My mouth dropped open. There had been a slit in the lining of the pocket of the suit I'd worn that night at the Olympia! Was that where Nola Powers' lipstick had gone?

I forgot everything—where I was, the voice from the stage—everything except the necessity of finding out. I pushed back my chair and rose. Suppose—oh, just suppose . . .

It was dark on the stairs. I groped upwards, opened the kitchen door. At once hands closed upon my arms, a torch flashed in my face. Someone said, "Aw, it's the Thorpe girl—let her go!" The police.

I didn't wait to see if there was any argument. I asked no questions. I only twisted free and fled. Through the living room—up the stairs. Hurry—hurry—for God's sake, hurry! My own room—lights—the closet door. Now the suit—the Glen plaid suit. The coat—the left-hand pocket—the one with the slit. Feel along the bottom—

I sat down abruptly. It was there. Something was there—something long and rounded and thicker than a pencil.

I committed mayhem upon that coat. I took scissors and slashed at it—never mind the lining. It could be relined. Cloth parted. It was there in my hand. Nola's gold lipstick.

I didn't try to open it, to pry out its secret, if secret it held. My only thought was to get it to Ross. Clutching it, I turned and ran down the stairs.

The police were still in the dark shadows on either side of the darker doorway. I passed them, scarcely seeing.

Down in the game room, the footlights still flared. The semicircle of chairs still held, but on the stage all action had been halted. Ross was speaking again. Panting, I leaned against the door frame and listened.

"—the last of our scene. You have now heard the words that the murderer heard. You know the reason why Nola Powers was killed. I am going to show you now the thing that the murderer does not know, the thing that has betrayed him. Molly—will you go back a couple of speeches?"

I almost believed it then myself. Had Ross been deceiving me all along? Was this it? Could it be that this was not trickery but actual knowledge? He was either very bold or very certain of his facts to risk the stroke that stripped his miming of illusion. Did he know? I couldn't tell.

There was tension in the room—you could feel it—but there was no sound. A vacuum of stillness rang in my head, unbearable as the brassy sound of gongs.

Molly was speaking now, still in that throaty compelling voice. "Don't worry—I've got it. I'll always have it—"

I don't know what had gone on before. I hadn't been there. But this time there was action. The girl who played Mrs. Wallace was sliding along the booth seat to its end; she was turning, getting carefully to her knees; she was going to look over—behind her—

I don't know now what it was that made me look away. A whisper of sound, perhaps. In the row of chairs before me, one had moved slightly backwards. I couldn't tell whose it was—the back was too high—and I hadn't known the order in which we sat. But I could see a chair arm and a wrist supported on a hand and a hand that held a blue and steely something—a blue and steely something that was trained upon the unconscious back of the girl upon the stage—

I did the only thing I could think of—I screamed. It was more of a screech really and it was followed by a tremendous clatter for in my attempt to rush forward, I fell over an unexpected footstool. Footstool and I went sliding across the floor.

There was confusion. Someone else screamed and chairs scraped and there was a rush of people to haul me to my feet. The lights came on and, as I stared dazedly about, I was conscious of a number of things: first, that the gun I'd seen, if gun it had been, had vanished; second, that the play as a play had ended, the actors were all on their feet, looking at me; third, that Ross still stood beside the light switches and on his face, plain to be read, was written the death sentence of his hopes.

I couldn't see him look like that. I pushed through the others as though they were not there. I ran to him. I said, "Ross—don't look like that. Please don't look like that! It's all right—I've got it. I just found it—Nola's lipstick!"

Hope replaced hopelessness. He snatched it incredulously. He wrenched the cap from one end, tossed it aside. With a slender knife blade, he pried viciously at the case. There was red on his fingers, red on the knife blade. The lipstick holder came free; it fell to the floor. He dug into the case, impatiently now, and the thin edge of a paper rose above the gold. He shook the case and there was a tiny roll of paper in his hand. It was then that his eyes met mine. "It *was* there," he said softly. "It was there—all the time!"

I didn't answer him. I couldn't. Something else was bothering I me. I counted and made certain. It was true.

There had been seven people occupying that semi-circle of chairs—six beside myself. Of that six only five remained. Gordon Kearnes had vanished.

24

I wasn't the only one who had counted. Mark said, "Kearnes, by God!" and in the resulting silence Alice sobbed once and then was still.

Chris's face was dark, his hands clenched to fists. "He's getting away!" he flung over his shoulder. "What the hell are we waiting for? Come on!"

I said, "Let him go—he's got a gun!" but my cry went unheeded in the rush of feet toward the stairway. Only Ross hadn't moved. He still held the narrow slip of paper for which two women had died. He said, "Wait!" and they heard him and stood. "He won't get away. The police are up there. Listen!"

He crossed the room and flipped over a switch upon an inconspicuous wooden box. At once voices crackled in the room. Gordon Kearnes' high and furious—"Let me go, damn you! Take your hands off me, you fools!"

Then came Lieutenant Dreyer's crisp and authoritative—"Gordon Kearnes, I arrest you for the murders of Nola Powers and of Rita Carstairs and of Patrick Wilson—"

Ross cut the switch and the voices were gone. He spread his hands. "You see?"

Alice Wilson said on a long wail, "But I don't believe it—I don't believe it!"

Chris spoke for the rest of us. "No, I'm damned if I do. God knows I want to believe it's over but where's your evidence? Nothing that was shown here tonight gives definite proof."

I said, "He had a gun. He was going to shoot Mrs. Wallace—" for want of another name I gave her that— "when she looked over the booth. I saw him. That's why I screamed."

The pseudo-Mrs. Wallace, suddenly pale, sat. I scowled at Ross. I said, "What if he had shot her?"

But Ross wouldn't admit such a possibility. "He was a notoriously poor shot," he murmured. Mrs. Wallace didn't seem reassured. She had the appearance of one who gazes with awe into the vistas of what might have been and didn't like what she was seeing.

Chris was staring at Ross. "You've more than that," he said. "Come clean. What's in that paper?"

For answer Ross moved a step closer to the wooden box. He said, "Hanover! I'm going to read a paper taken from a lipstick belonging to Nola Powers. It's a statement signed by your prisoner. Are you ready?"

He touched the switch and the chief's voice boomed. "Now, son, you hold your horses. You bring that paper up here where it belongs and stop your play-acting! You hear?"

But Ross was reading. "There's a date. September 24, 1938. Pat Wilson died on September 22—that's correct, isn't it? All right, here we go. The thing's in Kearnes' handwriting, if that's any satisfaction to you." He paused for a second and then went on, slowly, distinctly. "'I killed Patrick Wilson when he ordered me to stay away from his wife. He threatened to divorce her for cause and name me as correspondent. I am on the verge of a great career and I cannot afford a scandal. Besides I love Alice. When he referred to her in opprobrious terms, I saw red and shot him. He died laughing at me. At once I moved to protect myself. I slipped the safety catch of his gun and fired it. The shell fell beside him and I left it there. I put the shell from my own gun in my pocket and went back to the field. I thought no one had seen me, but I was wrong. Nola Latimer had. I am writing this under her compulsion but it is the truth.' And it's signed," Ross said with a quiver of triumph in his voice, "with his whole name—Gordon John Kearnes."

"Gimme that!" said Lieutenant Dreyer. We hadn't heard him come in but he was there, his hand outstretched. He snatched the paper, ran his eye over it. Shaken out of character, he said jubilantly, "We got it, Chief—we got it!" and then ran for the stairs. At their foot, he paused to say, "You folks stick around. The chief'll maybe have some questions he'll want answered."

We watched him go. Alice Wilson said bewilderedly, "But that paper means he killed them—Gordon. Why did you give it to him—oh, why did you give it to him?"

"Listen!" Ross said again. Once more he did something to the switches on the box. We heard Chief Hanover's voice, admonishing, and then, abruptly, Gordon Kearnes'. A dull voice now, without expression, all passion burned away. "All right—you've got me, damn you! I did it. I killed them. Nola and Rita—"

Ross cut it off then. Mercifully, I think. It was best that we didn't hear.

He was avoiding our eyes—Ross. He lit a cigarette, puffed at it. He said, "That's all, folks. The show's over, the curtain's down. You can relax."

But we couldn't. Alice was staring at him, staring out of blank bright eyes. She said slowly, and her voice was flat and dead: "You did it. Why couldn't you have left him alone? He wasn't harming you. He'd have gone away. Now—now they've got him and they'll hang him—hang him, do you understand? And it's your fault—it's all your fault! I hate you—oh, God, how I hate you! I loved him—Gordon—and now—" Suddenly she had started up and her eyes were wild. "Where is he? Where have they taken him? Not away—they couldn't have—not yet! I'm going with him—he's not going to be alone! I'm going, I tell you—You can't stop me—"

But they did. It was Chris, kind and firm, who said, "No, Alice," and caught her and put her down into a chair where she broke into tearing sobs.

Ross stood in front of her. He said uncomfortably, "I'm terribly sorry, Mrs. Wilson. Please believe me. It's true."

Alice didn't answer. She only wept on.

"Let her alone," Chris advised. "She's had a shock. Let her cry it out. It's the best way."

Perhaps it was but it was a terrible one. We stood around awkwardly, not knowing what to do nor how to do it. We might have been there yet if it hadn't been for Molly. She went to Alice and held her close and glared at us. She said, "What's the matter with you anyway? Can't you do something? We don't have to stay here, do we? She's all in pieces and she needs to lie down some place and be alone and get herself back to normal. The police have gone, haven't they? Well, why don't we go upstairs?"

So we did. It took some doing but presently Alice was resting in my bedroom with Mrs. Ferguson in attendance and the rest of us were back where we'd been when the party began—in the living room, a living room still bright with hearth fire and quivering with candle flame and sweet with roses.

Only it wasn't a party now. We sat about, frozen and shocked and silent. We smoked uneasily. And waited.

The unnatural silence piled up on me until I couldn't stand it any longer. I stood up uncertainly. I said, "I know this isn't the time to talk about food but just the same there's a buffet supper in the dining room. Perhaps if we'd have some coffee . . ."

The food helped. It unloosened tongues, calmed ragged nerves. There was talk again, mutterings of questions. "When's that damned policeman going to get here?" There were even invitational glances at Ross who'd retired into some private solitude and was pensively stirring his coffee, his forehead dark with thought.

It was Mark Kerrigan who brought him out of it. He planted himself squarely in front of Ross. He said, "Look here, Langdon, you put this thing over and I guess we owe you a vote of thanks or something. Technically I suppose we ought to sit around and wait for Hanover to give us the official lowdown, but in the meantime can't you tie up a few unofficial loose ends? After all it was you who uncovered Kearnes!"

"I know," Ross said. "I've been sitting here thinking about it, thinking how little I really knew and that if Mary hadn't produced that lipstick at the critical moment, and if that lipstick hadn't happened to contain the paper that was the motivating cause of the murder—"

"But you said you knew," I protested. "Yesterday you said you'd known since Monday night."

"I had," Ross said turning to me. "That is, I was pretty sure. The trouble was that I couldn't prove it without admitting to some illegal activities of my own to which Hanover might have taken exception were they called to his attention. You see, I'd caught Kearnes in a deliberate lie. Remember my telling you about the hullabaloo he raised over his room being torn to pieces? Well, that was all right—his room had been searched. The difficulty came in the fact that, immediately after Kearnes left the hotel to go to Alice Wilson's, I took a passkey I'd bribed a bellboy to get me and went to his room. I wanted to look through it for—well, for reasons of my own. I got the look all right. At five minutes past six, directly after Kearnes shut the door, the room was in exactly the same condition as it was when I was called to view it nearly three hours later. No one had gone in—I was positive of that because I'd been watching. Therefore the probability was that Kearnes himself had done the wrecking. Or else—why make a fuss at eight forty-five and not at five fifty when he'd originally checked in? Then Mary reported that her room had been searched around five o'clock. When I told her about Kearnes, she at once jumped to the conclusion that because his room had been searched after hers—remember Kearnes reported the destruction as occurring between six five and eight forty-five—it proved that what was sought had not been found in her house. Automatically she was classifying Kearnes with herself as a victim, exonerating him whether she knew it or not. I wasn't. Of course I had a little inside information that Mary didn't but just the same, so far as I was concerned, the whole set-up smelled to high heaven. Why should Kearnes go to all the trouble to stage an elaborate piece of trickery such as the ransacking of his room unless, by so doing, he hoped to achieve that very thing—to place himself beyond suspicion and in the position of a victim?

"Which was where," Ross said soberly, "Gordon Kearnes had been a bit too clever. That, by the way, was his main fault as a murderer. He saw events through the eyes of a writer of fiction. As in the case of most of those who create, the border line between reality and unreality, between truth and fantasy, had worn thin. Embrace truth by all means but not a truth unadorned. To be successful truth must be highlighted to convince. Kearnes approached murder as he approached the writing of a play. Given a detail, he picked it up a little, heightened its dramatic value. Take the matter of Latimer's overshoes for one thing."

"He was one of the first to leave Alice's," Chris growled. "I remember that. Yelling about the blackout and having to get back to the hotel."

"The overshoes weren't important in themselves," Ross went on. "They didn't even furnish a decent clue. No one in his right senses would abandon a pair of overshoes in a house where he meant to commit murder."

I said, "Don't. It makes me sick to think about it. And anyway how do we know we're not wrong? Perhaps we read too much into it—perhaps he never meant to kill—"

"He came prepared," Ross said sternly. "Oh, I'll grant you that he may not have wanted anything more than the lipstick. The point is he was willing to kill to get it."

I shivered.

"Some of Kearnes' other activities were peculiar," Ross resumed. "There was the fight with Latimer that put him in the hospital with a broken head. I'll admit that Latimer gave him the clue for that but the way he accepted the Latimer premise and built it up was nothing short of brilliant. Having heard both versions, I asked myself why. Why not tell the truth—why attempt to befuddle the police? Not for friendship's sake—there was no love lost between himself and Latimer. 'Fear of adverse publicity' Kearnes intimated, but the more obvious explanation was that he preferred not to court police attention. Again I asked myself why? Was it possible that there was something in Kearnes' past or present that couldn't stand daylight? I wondered.

"Frankly, at the risk of being accused of second-guessing, I am going to tell you that Kearnes was my choice for suspect from the moment Nola Powers' death was discovered. It didn't make sense any other way. The old chief was right—it would have to be a pretty powerful motive that would carry over five years of separation. Not that there weren't plenty of motives stirring around. Apparently all

of you had had reason to hate Nola Powers. There was Forrester—" Johnny winced and Ross spared him. We all knew
the story. "There was Rita Carstairs whose younger sister
had died at her own hand because of Nola. Chris, whose
personal fortune had been stolen, whose personal honor
was threatened. Faye Latimer who, by reason of Nola's
failure to complete a divorce, faced the birth of an illegitimate child. Kerrigan, Alice Wilson, the Dunbars—against
each of you a plausible case might have been raised. But—
there was still the hiatus of that five years. And there was,
too, one person in the picture who had bridged that five
year gap, one person who had never ceased to be a part of
Nola Powers' life. When the casual testimony of a soldier's
wife put us on the trail of blackmail—"

"Well, if you knew all that—figured it out," Molly
broke in, "I can't see why you didn't do something before
this! Couldn't you have checked alibis or something?"

Ross shook his head. "Alibis don't amount to much
at best. What's more, in present day Nashiona, I doubt
if they exist. There are too many strangers in town and
Kearnes was just one among many. Clerks and waitresses
and counter girls find better jobs and move on overnight.
They're overworked. They're too tired to remember faces
even if they had the time to note them. Perhaps if someone
unusually striking—"

"But Gordon Kearnes and Nola were recognized in Dalrymples Tuesday noon," I objected. "I told you that."

"Sheer happenstance," Ross insisted. "It mightn't occur
again in a dozen years. Besides I seem to remember that
you came on that bit of information quite by accident."

"That was before she was murdered," I said slowly.
"He must have made a last try to get her to let him off.
When she wouldn't, he took her to the theater or met her
there and killed her. Then he searched her purse for that

confession she'd made him sign. It must have been he—Gordon Kearnes—that Faye heard."

"Undoubtedly," Ross agreed. He looked at Chris. "You realize, I hope, that your wife was an exceedingly fortunate young woman to have gotten out of that theater alive."

Chris groaned that he did indeed realize it and I said, "But what about me? I was there too!"

But Ross shook his head. "It's not the same. You came into it only when Kearnes saw Latimer return the lipstick to you. I think Kearnes knew the secret of that lipstick and he knew, too, that until the contents of that lipstick were destroyed he remained in danger. Therefore the attack on you during the blackout, the later search of your room."

I said, "Oh, well, I suppose it's all right. You say it could have only been Kearnes and you probably know what you're talking about. But just the same it wasn't like that with Pat Wilson. Any one of that hunting party could have killed him."

"Pat Wilson's death was unprovable," Ross admitted, "except in the one way—by the murderer's actual confession. The hunting party was split up into individual segments. One shot more or less meant nothing in the general confusion. Short of someone who actually saw the shooting, there was no proof and, as it happened, Nola Powers was the only witness. For purposes of her own—whether because she had faith in Kearnes' ability to carve out the 'great career' he mentioned—and hoped to climb with him, or whether she merely hoped to serve out her old rival, we can't know. She chose, rather than to hand her knowledge over to the authorities, to hold it as a whip above Kearnes' head. It was an ever present menace. Once he disobeyed her ever-increasing demands, it would fall and he knew it. Living under a threat of that sort must have been unendurable. It wasn't much wonder," Ross said, "that eventually there came a day when he couldn't take any more and he killed her. Miss Powers, I'm afraid," he added apologetically, "wasn't a very nice person to know."

"You're telling us!" Pete Dunbar said. "Okay. So far I'm right with you. I'm willing to believe that Kearnes killed Nola because she was blackmailing him, and that he killed Pat because Pat was more than a little drunk and spoiling for a fight. I knew Pat and I liked him but he had the devil's own temper and a tongue like a rapier. And it was perfectly true that Alice had been having an affair with Kearnes. Platonic, maybe—I wouldn't know. Maybe she honestly liked him. At any rate that's all straight—I can swallow it. But what about Rita? I'm damned if I understand Rita. Why kill her?"

Ross frowned. "She knew something—something probably in regard to Pat Wilson's murder. And she was about to tell what she knew. She was the one who discovered Wilson's body so the probability is she saw something that day that she didn't understand. It was her sense of fairness, her reluctance to implicate anyone without reason, that was the cause of her death. I believe that she called Kearnes that night after we'd gone, called him to ask for an explanation of whatever it was she'd seen five years ago in that hunting field. He came, was admitted and killed her. For a second time he played in luck. No one saw him leave the apartment. He was safe."

"Tell us this," Johnny Forrester said. "Do you think Nola's death—like Pat's—was the impulse of a moment or do you think Kearnes brought her to Nashiona with the deliberate intent of killing her?"

Ross shrugged. "It's hard to tell. Nola had evidently been bleeding him for years. The more than seventy thousand dollars she'd amassed is evidence of that. Both she and Kearnes made money and spent it. I suspect that Kearnes, for all his success, was pretty hard up. That may have been at the back of his decision to kill Nola. If that is true, he may very well have engineered the tryout of his play here where feuds had already been established and old hates flourished. In that case, we have deliberate planning. Or it may have been that Nola's—persecution, shall we say?—of Alice Wilson touched off the spark. He may have been honest when he said he loved Alice. Certainly the first person to whom he went when he returned to Nashiona was Alice Wilson. My own opinion is that Nola's refusal to permit Alice to appear in the play signed her death warrant."

"And not a bad opinion neither," a new voice boomed. We whirled about. Chief Hanover was beaming at us from the doorway. "Now—now, take it easy, boys and girls. This ain't no official visit—this's by way of being a social call, our business having ended as you might say. Now, Miss Thorpe, don't you go bunging them big eyes at me—I'll just have me a chair and chat a spell, and then we'll all go home to bed. And when I say chat, I mean that any questions asked I'm going to ask them. I ain't rightly got all the facts in this case yet myself, and maybe I won't for another day or so, but the thing that concerns us all is we've got a murderer cold to rights. Thanks to Langdon and Miss Thorpe, Kearnes is safe in jail spilling out his soul to Dreyer, and once he's done I reckon he'll be glad to settle down quiet and rest a spell, he having put in a right lively ten days.

"Now, before I go on to the questions, I want to say I've been standing here quiet listening to Langdon expound for quite a while, and so far's I could tell he got most of his expounding correct. Kearnes killed Pat Wilson and Nola Powers and while we don't know all the details yet that much is clear and proven. As for Rita Carstairs, she was the one to find Wilson's body and seems she hove up in the middle distance about the time Kearnes was making his last arrangements and scuttling off into the cornstalks. I reckon you can put down Nola Powers as being responsible, for it's a sure thing that if she saw Kearnes kill Wilson she saw Rita seeing him. Why Miss Carstairs waited for five years to ask Kearnes to explain his actions is something none of us are going to know but when she did get around to asking she got the answer quick and convincing. Which maybe's a pretty plain object lesson in what happens when you hide things from them that rightfully ought to know them. And how, having pointed my moral, I aim to pass on for the moment to the subject of anonymous letters, one of which came to the police and opened up the subject of Pat Wilson's death. Kearnes claims he didn't write it. What I want to know's who did."

"Well—" Surprisingly it was Mark Kerrigan who squirmed in his chair. "Well, I did, as a matter of fact. You see, I'd been seeing a lot of Rita lately—she was a swell girl—and when she got killed I got sort of panicky. I thought that, if she'd known something important, maybe whoever killed her would think I knew it too. So I figured that if I cast a little suspicion my way and pretended to make a break out of town the police would keep an eye on me after that and I'd be safe. I knew damn well they couldn't prove anything. Call it cowardice if you want to—I don't mind. I hadn't killed anybody and I didn't want to be killed either. I picked on Pat's death because I'd always thought there was something fishy about it. I wasn't afraid they'd suspect me either. The only thing anybody'd have on me was the five thousand dollars I'd scraped together for Kearnes when he left town—"

"Kearnes!" Pete Dunbar exploded. "I thought it was for Nola."

"So did I, but I guess Kearnes got it. He gave me a song and dance about Nola needing money and not wanting

Chris to know and—well, I was plenty sweet on Nola just then, so I mortgaged my soul to get it. Then, later on, when I wrote her and asked her for some of it back, she said she'd never heard of it and that Kearnes had played me for a sucker. I guess he did."

"Perhaps I'd better say something here." Chris was on his feet. "You all know that Nola left her money to me. Well, I'm not taking it, barring the twenty thousand she stole from me when she left Nashiona. I think I'm entitled to that. But I think it's only fair that Mark get his five thousand back. For the rest of it, I don't give a damn. The state or the government or Gordon Kearnes or anyone else who wants it can have it for all me!"

The chief beamed approval. "Well, now," he said, "seeing that that's settled, I reckon I can go home to bed and rest peaceable in the knowledge that tomorrow morning, the mayor and the newspapers ain't going to be routing me out early wanting to know why the police don't give them some action on this here Nola Powers murder. They got their action now and I feel right Christian, particularly to them that did the work. Good-night, all. You can read anything else you want to know in the special edition the papers is likely printing right now."

He ducked his head once and departed and that was the last we saw of officialdom that night. But, although we had his permission to seek our own beds, we didn't. It was all very well to talk of sleep but we were wide awake. We sat and drank more coffee and talked it all over and roundabout until, suddenly, Father was home and we had it all to do again. Presently Alice was coming down the stairs, red-eyed but quite composed, and there was a little uncomfortable silence before Chris moved to take her home.

It was the signal for a general break-up. One by one our guests trickled away. Victor Jameson went first and then

Johnny Forrester and Mark. The Dunbars, too, began to make excuses, moved to find their wraps.

But I couldn't let them go without asking one question. It was fairly on the doorstep that I asked it and thereby tied the last knot. I said, "Pete, I've been meaning to ask you—I know you're an air-raid warden and all that but— how'd it happen you were in our block the night of the blackout?"

Pete's face was ludicrous. "Good God, Mary!" he exploded. "Do you mean you were suspecting me? The regular warden for the next block was sick, that's all. He happens to be a friend of mine so I took his place. Molly carried on for me on my own beat."

As simple as that.

They were gone at last and there was only Ross and I among the roses and the candles and the leaping hearth flames. Father long since had vanished into the kitchen, probably in search of bigger and better rations.

Ross was very close to me. He said, "Tired, darling?"

I didn't answer. I was busy, working my ring free of the lining of Father's coat and replacing it on my finger. That done, I looked at it for a long time and then I looked at Ross, at his nice, open, ingenuous face. I thought of what the ring stood for and I thought, too, that perhaps all the horror and uncertainty of the past days had not been too dear a price to pay in exchange for the things those days had brought.

I shook my head. I moved into the circle of his arms. "Not tired," I said. "No. Only happy. And very safe."

Additional classic detective fiction, suspense thrillers, and police procedurals can be found at:

CoachwhipBooks.com
(print)

Coachwhip.com
(epub)

NO FACE TO
MURDER
EDITH HOWIE

THE BAND PLAYED
MURDER

EDITH HOWIE

LOUIS F. BOOTH

THE BANK VAULT MYSTERY
BROKERS' END

BLOOD ON HER SHOE

MEDORA FIELD

THE SERGEANT HARTY MYSTERIES
JOEL Y. DANE
MURDER CUM LAUDE
1
THE CABANA MURDERS

www.ingramcontent.com/pod-product-compliance
Lightning Source LLC
Chambersburg PA
CBHW031103030726
47496CB00002BA/359